Tell Me Not To Kiss You

ELEE ROSE

Contents

Content Warnings   vii
Playlist   ix
Dedication   xi

CHAPTER 1   1
Fallon

CHAPTER 2   10
Mackenzie

CHAPTER 3   14
Fallon

CHAPTER 4   27
Mackenzie

CHAPTER 5   32
Fallon

CHAPTER 6   37
Mackenzie

CHAPTER 7   42
Fallon

CHAPTER 8   52
Mackenzie

CHAPTER 9   61
Fallon

CHAPTER 10   69
Mackenzie

CHAPTER 11   81
Fallon

CHAPTER 12   91
Mackenzie

CHAPTER 13   106
Fallon

CHAPTER 14   111
Fallon

CHAPTER 15
Fallon
120

CHAPTER 16
Mackenzie
128

CHAPTER 17
Mackenzie
134

CHAPTER 18
Mackenzie
140

CHAPTER 19
Mackenzie
148

CHAPTER 20
Mackenzie
154

CHAPTER 21
Fallon
162

CHAPTER 22
Mackenzie
167

CHAPTER 23
Fallon
175

CHAPTER 24
Mackenzie
183

CHAPTER 25
Mackenzie
188

CHAPTER 26
Mackenzie
198

CHAPTER 27
Fallon
206

CHAPTER 28
Mackenzie
213

CHAPTER 29
Fallon
218

CHAPTER 30
Fallon
226

CHAPTER 31
Mackenzie
235

CHAPTER 32
Mackenzie
239

CHAPTER 33
Fallon 250

CHAPTER 34
Mackenzie 257

CHAPTER 35
Mackenzie 261

CHAPTER 36
Fallon 266

CHAPTER 37
Mackenzie 275

CHAPTER 38
Fallon 279

CHAPTER 39
Mackenzie 284

CHAPTER 40
Fallon 291

CHAPTER 41
Fallon 295

CHAPTER 42
Mackenzie 300

CHAPTER 43
Mackenzie 306

CHAPTER 44
Fallon 311

CHAPTER 45
Mackenzie 316

CHAPTER 46
Mackenzie 324

CHAPTER 47
Fallon 332

CHAPTER 48
Mackenzie 338

CHAPTER 49
Fallon 343

Epilogue 353

Bonus Content 357
Acknowledgments 359
About the Author 361

Content Warnings

This book contains mentions of child abuse and mentions of homophobia. This book also contains sexual content and strong language. Reader discretion is advised.

Playlist

blowin' smoke teddy swims
body say demi lovato
i won't give up alex g
someone you loved teddy swims
can't help falling in love haley reinhart
control zoe wees
you say lauren daigle
only love can hurt like this (teddy swims) paloma faith
best part (daniel caesar) H.E.R.
ocean eyes billie eilish

Dedication

To the lovers who found each other in the most unexpected places.
This one's for you.

Chapter One

FALLON

"Why is it so big?!" In the center of my living room, I watched Drea struggle to set up the inflatable photo booth.

"That's what she said!" Drea shouted over her shoulder, laughing and slapping her knee as if she had told the funniest joke.

"Oh my God, nobody says that anymore." Rolling my eyes at my best friend, I threw myself onto the couch. "Maybe this isn't a good idea."

My other best friend, Penelope, took the spot next to me, placing a comforting arm on my shoulder. "Fallon, sweetie, this party is a great idea. This is your first chance at freedom since Bec—"

"Yes, I know," I replied sharply. "I don't need a reminder, thank you." The last person I wanted to think about was my ex-girlfriend.

For the past two years, I'd lived in Portland with my mom, stepdad, Brandon, and my five-year-old brother, Caleb, but ever since I could remember, I had dreamed of living in Seattle. A few months ago, I finally took the big step and left Portland.

Before everything fell apart, my ex convinced me that we should move in together. At that point, we had been dating for two years and the timing felt right. She traveled a lot for work and constantly had to fly to Seattle, and sometimes I would fly out to meet her. When she

"

suggested moving, there were no hesitations. I thought I was in love and I wanted to spend every possible minute together.

Clearly, it didn't work out and I was forced to move back home. I felt like such a failure, but after two years of healing, I was ready to get back out there and do my own thing.

Penelope smiled sympathetically, as if she read my thoughts. "Stop being so hard on yourself. You deserve this party. You deserve to get drunk and have a good time."

I chuckled. "You just want an excuse to party."

"True, but you know I'm right." She giggled as she playfully punched my arm.

"Ouch, Pen! I'm going to tell Drea you're hurting me!" I joked.

"Oh, please. I know you liked it. Enough stalling, let's go!" She patted my leg and stood, extending her hand to help me up. "Come on, let's finish before people start showing up."

I groaned on my way back over to Drea, who looked like she was about to curl into the fetal position in a corner.

Eventually, we got the damn photo booth set up. We had to move some things around to make it fit, but everything worked out. I had to admit, I thought the place looked fantastic.

I moved in only a few weeks ago, so there wasn't much furniture, but that meant fewer things getting broken during the party, right?

When we finished setting up, I checked the time. "Shit. It's already six?"

The party wouldn't start for another few hours, but I needed to finish getting ready and I still had no clue what to wear.

The shower water rained down on me as I wondered whether having the party was a good idea. I doubted it would get out of hand, but I didn't want to cause issues with my neighbors. The party would be good for me, though. That much was true. I deserved a night to celebrate my new independence, and I sure as shit deserved a fresh start.

"Oh, shit." As I was leaving the bathroom, I'd forgotten about the tornado that barreled through my room earlier that night, and when I saw it again, I wanted to cry.

Before my friends called for my help, I was failing miserably at choosing an outfit, and as I stood there again, preparing for the same battle, I seriously contemplated canceling the whole thing.

I searched the clothes I had scattered across my room. They were thrown on almost every surface, but nothing was catching my eye. Then I walked to my closet, where the remaining outfits resided, and took a deep breath. "Okay, relax."

After another thirty minutes of picking up the same clothes a dozen times, I finally landed on one and if I did say so myself, I think I looked pretty damn good.

I slipped into a green, off-the-shoulder, long-sleeved dress. It was short, stopping at the center of my thighs. It was also *extremely* low cut, but it fit like a second skin. It was probably over-the-top for a house party, but you never knew what could happen.

I heard a knock on the front door as I finished my makeup. Music was already filling the room, and a few people had started to arrive by the time I made my way down the hall.

I looked around the living room and grinned at Drea and Penelope, who were chatting with their dates. Penelope had been helping with set-up all afternoon, and her husband, Gregory, just showed up.

Drea brought her... well, I didn't exactly know what to call them. Drea brought Skylar, her long-time on-again, off-again partner.

Skylar was tall, tanned, and too sweet. Her hair was a rich, deep, sleek black bob, and her eyes were a sparkling emerald green.

Drea was gorgeous, and she had the sexiest English accent. Her skin was a beautiful shade of caramel, and she had stunning brown eyes. She was originally from Brighton, England, but moved to Portland when she was ten years old, and we had been best friends ever since.

Drea turned from the DJ station over by the bay window. "Damn, you look hot!"

The "DJ station" was technically a table with a large speaker and a tablet, but it still counted to me.

"What? This old thing?" I spun around and laughed. "Thanks." I had only worn the dress once at a birthday party three years ago.

"I agree," Penelope chimed in. She was pouring herself and Gregory a drink.

I looked around, taking everything in, and not only at the party set up, which was wild!

An inflatable photo booth in a one-bedroom apartment? What was I thinking? I had to admit, it was different, and that's what I wanted.

The kitchen counters were covered with various bags of chips, finger foods, and different types of alcohol, while the rest of the apartment was decorated with black and gold balloons.

The apartment was perfect for me. It was cozy and decently priced, but I picked up a part-time job to hold me over until I started working at the hospital. I was transferring as a nurse from the Emergency Department at a hospital in Portland, and I wasn't scheduled to start for another few weeks.

Drea and Penelope had been my best friends for over ten years. They used to live in Portland until a few years ago, when they both moved to Seattle for work. Drea was only a year older than me, and Penelope was five years older. She worked as an underwriter for a major insurance company outside of Seattle, and Drea owned a queer bookstore in town. When I first moved here, she offered me a spot at the store for as long as I wanted it.

Over the next hour or so, more people filled my apartment until it became too small, and I desperately needed a drink. After a few shots of Fireball, the worries from earlier seemed to have disappeared.

I'd been dancing alone for an hour when Drea's friend, Cara, walked in. They met when she was opening the bookstore three years ago. She was a publisher who worked with some of the authors Drea hosted for book signings.

After about twenty more minutes of dancing, I was heading for the kitchen when Cara approached me. I'd seen her at the bookstore a few times, and occasionally when I was out with Drea, but we've never said more than a few words to each other.

"Mind if I join you?" She handed me a drink and smiled. "Drea said you might need a refill. Don't worry, she poured it and watched me bring it over here, so it's been safe with me the entire time."

I wasn't concerned, but her comment made me a little cautious. Or it could have been the alcohol. Either way, I stared skeptically at the drink before I took the cup, returning her smile. "Thanks, Cara."

I sent Drea a threatening glare, who lifted her drink with a playful wink and a nod in response.

I loved my best friend, but she always tried to pair me off with someone. She thought *everyone* should have a person to share their bed with.

Cara was gorgeous with her blonde hair and blue eyes. She wore white skinny jeans and a red crop top that made her boobs look incredible. Her hair was in a high ponytail, and she was a few inches taller than me. The problem? I didn't know her that well, and I wasn't the type of person to jump into bed with someone I didn't know.

"How are you enjoying your party?" She took a sip and licked the remaining drops off her lips.

I raised my glass and grinned. "It's been pretty good so far. No one has gotten arrested or hurt yet."

She laughed. "Well, that's a good sign, I think. I see Drea and Skylar are getting along—for now."

I glanced over and saw Skylar straddling Drea while they were making out. I chuckled at my insatiable best friend. "Yeah, for now."

"So, how do you like Seattle so far? I know you just moved here." She shifted on her feet and leaned back against the counter.

Something in my chest warmed at the mention of the move, and I couldn't hide the sparkle in my eyes. "I love it. It has its similarities to Portland, but it's nice to breathe fresh air, you know? I needed a change."

"I agree, and I hope you find whatever you're looking for." She gently placed her hand on my arm.

I gave her a soft smile and leaned into the contact. "Thanks, me too."

I didn't know what I was searching for, but I knew I needed something *else*—something I couldn't find in Portland, not when I saw my ex and our life together around every corner. The trust and love we shared disappeared within minutes.

"So, can I get you another drink?" Cara asked, shaking me from my thoughts.

My cup of the *juice* Penelope and Skylar made was almost empty. They were always making new drinks, turning it into a competition to see who could make the strongest one. It was a wonder they hadn't thought of every possible combination yet.

"I would love one, thank you." I finished my drink and held it out to her.

More alcohol wasn't my best idea, honestly. I was starting to feel like

I was on a carousel at an amusement park and would most likely have to be carried to bed, but I told myself to stop overthinking for one night and just have a good time.

She took my cup and walked it over to the punch bowl. I looked over to where Skylar and Drea had come up for air. They were going out to the patio, but on the way there, they turned back and winked at me in unison.

"Weirdos," I muttered, but I couldn't hide my smile.

"Here you go," Cara said when she returned with a refilled cup.

I accepted it with a playful grin. "Thank you."

We stood in the kitchen, drinking and talking for a little longer. We didn't talk about anything of substance, which was nice. It felt good to have a relaxing conversation and not have to think too much about anything.

I was almost finished with my drink when a new song started to play. Cara beamed at me over the rim of her cup. "Would you like to dance?"

Warmth spread through me at her offer, and I nodded. "I would love to."

She slipped her hand into mine and led me to the living room.

Between the sensually slow song and the alcohol, I was feeling maybe a little too good. By the time the song was halfway done, we were both sweaty. We were facing each other, staring into one another's eyes as our bodies ground together. It looked like we were fucking with our clothes on in the middle of the living room. It was kind of hot, to be honest.

When the song was done, I was a little more than tipsy and a little horny, which was not a winning combination.

Cara put her hand on my arm and whispered in my ear, "Do you want to go somewhere a little more private and talk?"

Heat rushed to my face as I replied, "Lead the way."

With our hands intertwined together, she led me down the quiet hallway toward my bedroom.

We stopped next to the door, and I propped my leg against the wall with my head tilted back.

"This is better. It's not as loud back here, and I can hear myself think." I chuckled. It was rare for me to have any sort of party, and the loud music mixed in with the various conversations was making my head hurt. Okay, so maybe the alcohol was contributing to that headache as well.

"I agree, it's more... intimate. Every time we see each other, it's usually out with a group. We don't get the chance to talk alone very often." She leaned against the wall with one hand over her head. "I'm glad Drea invited me. It's a great party."

"Thanks." I gave her a soft smile as I played with a loose strand of my hair. "I'm glad you could make it."

"I don't know if anyone has told you tonight, but you look incredible." She grinned and took a sip of her drink.

I blushed and cleared my throat. "Thanks, Cara. So do you."

She pushed off against the wall and placed one hand above my head, essentially boxing me in. The alcohol, mixed with her close proximity, was making my body temperature rise.

"I was thinking... maybe we could go somewhere sometime? You know, just the two of us."

I couldn't hide my playful grin. "Is that your way of asking me out?"

Cara let out a soft chuckle. "Yes, Fallon, I would really like to take you out sometime." She brushed her knuckles against my arm and I barely suppressed a shiver.

Heat pressed against my face, and goosebumps formed where her knuckles traced along my skin. "Well..."

It was nice to be approached by someone, even if she was drunk. It had been a while. I wasn't sure she'd follow through with her offer, but I agreed anyway. It couldn't hurt.

"I think we can arrange that," I said.

She smiled and inched closer. "Great."

I was never one to make the first move, so it had to have been the alcohol that controlled my next actions, because I leaned up and kissed her.

She took her hand and placed it on my waist. Our tongues danced together, and our hands went from being tangled in hair, to wrapping around hips.

After several intoxicating minutes, she released us. "I've been wondering what that would be like."

I smiled at her, using the pad of my thumb to fix the lipstick that was undoubtedly smeared all over my lips. "Yeah, and what's the verdict?"

She grinned as she fixed her own lipstick. "It didn't disappoint. I would recommend you to a friend." She winked.

"Well, I'm glad I have your letter of recommendation, should I ever need it," I teased, adjusting my dress and kissing her cheek.

As I walked back to the living room, I looked over my shoulder and smiled. "Enjoy the rest of the party, Cara."

She was right, the kiss didn't disappoint, but I wasn't interested in anything else, at least not tonight.

"Well, welcome back little miss *hoe-stess*," Drea mused when she saw me returning from the hall. She was standing in the kitchen with Skylar nuzzled up behind her.

Penelope and Gregory were out on the patio talking with a group of people. She caught my eye, lifting her drink in a silent greeting.

I did the same before I turned to Drea and frowned. "I needed a refill? What was that?"

She put her hands up in surrender. "Hey, she offered. I just happened to mention that you looked lonely dancing all by yourself."

"Drea, please stop trying to sell me off," I pleaded.

She laughed. "I'm not trying to sell you off! I only want you to enjoy yourself, love. Which it looks like you have. Is there a particular reason why you look all hot and bothered, coming out of a dark hallway?"

I rolled my eyes. "I didn't hook up with her if that's what you're getting at."

"No, but *something* happened. I can see it all over your face, and I saw the way you two were fuck-dancing in the living room. Honestly, I'm surprised you're not pregnant already." She grinned stupidly on the other side of her cup.

I couldn't help but laugh. "First, you're drunk. I'm pretty sure that's not how it works, and *fuck-dancing* is not a thing. Second, I don't kiss and tell, sorry." I turned to join Penelope outside on the patio.

"Well, you should!" she yelled. "I'm your best friend. Where is your loyalty?!" I chuckled and flipped her off.

. . .

The hours sped by in a blur of dancing and laughing. After our hallway conversation, Cara met up with a group of people and started chatting with them before they all left.

I regrouped with Drea and Penelope, who were cozied up with their partners on the couch. Aside from feeling left out from being the fifth wheel, I was enjoying myself for the first time in a long time.

Chapter Two

MACKENZIE

What a fucking day! Time was not on my side when my alarm decided to give me the silent treatment, causing me to be late for work.

Work was a disaster, of course. Everything that could have gone wrong, did. Not to mention, my period had been kicking my ass all day. To make the day even worse, I stepped in a puddle on the way home!

Before I got off work, I planned on going to the bar to relieve some stress with a nice blonde or brunette. By the time I actually finished up at work, I was too tired to even entertain the idea, so I swung by the store for some wine and headed home instead.

When I finally got home, I dropped my keys on the table next to the door and kicked my shoes off.

It was well after ten, and I was exhausted. I stayed late at work to finish up a few things, but I fully regretted that decision. It was about a twenty-five-minute drive from my apartment, but every soul in Seattle was out. I hated traffic!

I grabbed a glass from my cabinet and settled down on the bench at my window.

Aside from my strong attachment to roofs and indoor plumbing, I rented this apartment because of the reading nook at the bay window overlooking the city.

It was as breathtaking at night as it was in the morning, which is why I sat there every day. I had lived in Seattle my whole life, and I didn't think I would ever get tired of looking at it.

I'd been hearing music all night, and it hadn't bothered me, but as I was coming back from the bathroom, a loud thud made me jump.

"What the fuck?" I said, grabbing my heart to make sure it was still there. Since I moved in, things had been pretty quiet until tonight.

I listened for another minute. The music was a little louder, and I heard another loud noise. I couldn't make out the song itself, but it sounded like a song you would dance to at a bar or a party. I shrugged it off and went back to my book. It wasn't any of my business.

I was hoping it would go away eventually, but it didn't. It was now almost one in the morning, and the sounds continued.

I walked closer to the door to see if I could hear anything else. All I heard was laughing, and the music grew louder.

"What the hell?" I muttered. I knew it was a Friday, but some people worked on the weekends, and it was the middle of the night. I tried to ignore the raging party across the hall, but I couldn't take it anymore.

I walked out of my apartment and listened to the sounds like a detective, trying to pinpoint where it was coming from, but it was obvious. As soon as I stepped outside, it was like the music was seeping through the walls.

The music came from inside my new neighbor's apartment across the hall, who I hadn't met yet. When they'd gone inside a few times, I only caught the door closing behind them, and a welcome mat showed up a few days ago. I didn't know who this person was, but I already didn't like them. They were probably some inconsiderate and immature frat boy. My last neighbor was an elderly, quiet man. *I miss Charles.*

I let out a huff and marched the whole seven feet to the door. I started with a knock, but stopped halfway through, realizing there was no way in hell they could hear it. Instead, I curled my hands into fists, and pounded on the door, alternating hands until someone answered.

They probably thought I was the police or the SWAT team, but I didn't give a shit. I just wanted to come home and relax in peace, which I could see wasn't going to happen.

I also polished off half the red wine that was sitting on my coffee table, so I wasn't in a raging party type of mood to begin with.

Usually, I wouldn't be this upset. It was only music, but after the day I had, and the alcohol, a pen drop would've sent me into a fit of rage.

In hindsight, I shouldn't have been confronting a stranger while drinking and on my period, but there I was anyway, banging on their door in the middle of the night. I hoped they weren't an ex-con or mafia type, because that would've sucked.

I pounded on the door for another few seconds until it flew open.

"Oh my God, I'm coming! Can I help—" The woman on the other side of the door cut herself off as she swung it open, her eyes meeting mine as my breath caught in my throat.

She was not a frat boy.

She continued after a few seconds of me staring at her. *Blink, you dumbass!*

"Uhh... Hi. Can I help you?" Her words slurred a bit, and I realized I had made a major mistake.

I cleared my throat and scowled at her, remembering why I was there to begin with. "Yeah, I hope so. Do you think you could turn the music down? Some of us are trying to sleep."

She looked at me, narrowing her brows as her tongue popped out to wet her bottom lip. Holy fuck! This was not the best idea.

I looked her up and down and suppressed a groan. She was painfully gorgeous, with her long, curly red hair which caressed her sexy collar-bones. I mean, seriously, who knew collarbones could be so hot?

She had a natural makeup look with light eyeshadow and a cupid's bow above her crimson, fucking red lips. Her skin was fair, and her eyes were a captivating shade of gray. And those freckles... my God, they were like a masquerade mask, forever embedded into her skin.

She wore the most maddening green dress, which showed off her shoulders and stopped halfway up her thigh. It was perfectly low-cut, leaving little to the imagination.

My mouth parted slightly on its own but I closed it, hopefully before she noticed. I tossed my thoughts away and cleared my throat.

She raised her eyebrows. "Excuse me?"

"Oh, I'm sorry. Are you so drunk that you can't hear me? Turn. Down. The music."

She scoffed, placing her hands on her hips. "No, I heard you just fine. What's your problem, and who exactly are you?"

My eyes traveled to where her hands now rested, and back up to meet her scowling expression. "I live across the hall, and my *problem* is that *some* of us adults are trying to sleep. See, we have these things called jobs, and they require us to get this thing called sleep."

That came out harsher than I would've liked. Maybe coming over here wasn't the best idea, especially because it seemed we both had been drinking.

"Well, excuse the fuck out of me, grandma. Lighten up."

I rolled my eyes and scoffed at her drunken attempt at an insult. "Grandma? I'm sure I'm not much older than you. What are you, twenty-one?"

"I'm twenty-four, actually, but thanks for the compliment. And how old are you? You look like you could pass for thirty-five." She smirked.

I narrowed my eyes. "It wasn't a compliment. And no, I'm not thirty-five, thank you very much. I'm twenty-seven, not that it's any of your business. Can you just try to turn it down if you're capable? Because looking at you, it seems like that might be a bit of a challenge."

She rolled her eyes. "Whatever."

I didn't bother to respond as I turned and walked away. Before I got to my door, I could have sworn I heard a whispered, "Bitch." I chuckled softly when she slammed the door behind her.

It seemed she may have been capable of at least one thing because I didn't hear a peep for the rest of the night.

I tried to go back to reading, but I was too pissed off, so I settled on taking a shower and went to bed.

By the time I got into bed, my adrenaline was still high. I was usually more laid-back and didn't typically get confrontational like that. But I was already on edge, and the wine certainly didn't help.

I mean, sure, attractive didn't even begin to describe her, but she was clearly intoxicated and inconsiderate.

I rolled my eyes and turned over on my side. I was glad the day was over, and I hoped I would never have to deal with her again.

Chapter Three

FALLON

"What a total bitch!" I turned toward Drea, who was now on the couch, cozying up to Skylar.

When I opened the door, I was stunned. The woman stood there wearing nothing but an oversized Guns N' Roses tee and black ankle socks.

I was fully prepared to give the party crasher a piece of my mind, expecting some middle-aged Karen type or a grumpy old man. What I wasn't expecting was to open the door and find a drop-dead gorgeous woman glaring at me.

Drea sat up on the couch and looked at me. "What happened? Who was that?"

I groaned. "That was my neighbor from across the hall."

"Were they hot?" Drea asked, which prompted a glare from Skylar.

I rolled my eyes. "She was so rude, and not to mention, she insulted me!"

I couldn't lie, she *was* hot, although I would never tell Drea that.

She had brown hair and the most gorgeous ocean-blue eyes. Jesus, those eyes! Her hair was wavy, falling just past her chest, and she had a small golden tribal-style septum ring.

I walked over to turn the music down. By the time I came back inside from my lovely chat, the place was almost cleared out. Only about a dozen people were left sitting in corners of the house—talking, kissing, or... groping? "Okay then."

Shaking my head, I lazily sat down on the couch, laying my head back, and resting my feet on the coffee table.

"What a night," I muttered, thankful it was now over. I always cherished spending time with my friends, but the party had taken a lot out of me, and I was ready for bed.

Drea rested her head on my shoulder, and I closed my eyes—mainly so the room would stop spinning. At this point, Drea and Skylar had gotten into another argument, and Skylar stormed off.

"I hope you enjoyed the party, Fal. Aside from grumpy gills, everyone had a really good time."

I took a deep breath. "It was a good party, huh? Thanks, Drea. I think I'm going to go to bed."

"Okay, love." She kissed my forehead and got up—to go find Skylar, I imagined.

I stood up a little too fast, which was a mistake because I was somehow forced to play a game of *Ring Around the Rosie* by myself.

"I think I have to make a pit stop first," I said, holding my hand over my mouth as I took off toward the bathroom.

Yup, big mistake...

The next day came, and I could have sworn I died and was reborn into a bright lightbulb. Every sound was amplified, and the sliver of light coming from my curtains was enough to make me relive my heart-to-heart with the toilet from last night.

Speaking of...

"Oh fuck!" I yelled as I jumped out of bed and ran straight into the bathroom.

This lovely back-and-forth dance went on for another thirty minutes before I went on the search for some water and much-needed pain medication.

"Why did I drink so much?" I complained as the never-ending headache continued. I wanted to be back in my warm bed.

It seemed like we were all going to be in the same boat tomorrow.

Drea was passed out on the couch—one foot resting on the back, one hand dangling toward the floor—while Penelope was on the floor, her long brown hair covering half of her face in a tangled mess. When I saw it was about two in the afternoon, I doubted they had plans to wake up anytime soon.

I went back to my room and buried myself under the covers, deciding it wasn't going to be my day either.

The hours slipped by, and at around nine o'clock at night, I finally woke up and managed to drag myself to the kitchen for something to eat.

When I got there, Drea was sitting in a chair with a trash can at her feet, curled up with a blanket.

"Holy shit, she lives," she said.

"Do you?" I laughed when she grumbled. She looked as if she had seen better days, but I was sure I didn't look any better.

"Who cleaned up in here?" All the empty bottles were gone, and the photo booth was packed away and by the door, ready to be returned tomorrow.

"Don't look at me, Penelope is the only one of us alive," Drea answered with a groan. I looked over at Penelope and grinned.

"You can thank me in the form of green paper rectangles with three digits on them—please and thank you." She smirked, holding out her hand.

I walked over to her and slapped my hand to hers. "Thank you very much, Pen."

She rolled her eyes and went to the couch.

"That was some party," Drea muttered as she took a sip of water.

"Tell me about it," Penelope replied. "I can't believe Jacob and Ariana hooked up. I thought he was gay!"

I laughed. "I'm pretty sure he's pan."

"Well, I can't believe you got into an argument with your neighbor. What was that all about?" Drea couldn't seem to let it go, while I was trying to forget about the whole night.

I sighed. "Please don't remind me. It was just a bitchy brunette coming to ruin a good time." The truth was that I couldn't stop thinking about it.

Maybe we were being too loud, but people played music all the time, and no one else complained. She didn't have to be so rude about it, and she didn't have to insult me. Couldn't she tell I was drunk and not in a clear headspace?

"She was a total bitch, Dre. I called her one when she walked away. It was more of a whisper under my breath, but I'm pretty sure she heard me because she laughed before I slammed the door. I'm going to have to avoid her for a long time."

Drea chuckled. "Yeah, good luck with that. She lives right across the hall. What are you going to do, make a run for it before she sees you? Be serious, you can't avoid her forever."

"That's exactly what I plan to do." At least I could try.

"Okay, but on a more serious note. Was she hot?" Drea sat up in her chair, soon realizing her mistake, and sat back again.

I couldn't help but roll my eyes. "I don't know, but it doesn't matter." I was tired of talking about her, and I was tired of thinking about her even more.

It wasn't like I hadn't seen an attractive woman before. There was just something about her I couldn't get out of my head.

Drea smirked. "Of course, it matters. You're single, and you could use some stress relief, love. Just go over there and apologize—over and over again."

I scoffed. "First of all, you're still drunk if you think that will ever happen." Ignoring her eye roll, I continued. "Second, I don't even know her name. And, Drea, I *cannot* stress this enough—I don't want to! Sure, she was easy on the eyes, but her shit personality is not my type. You know I don't hook up with random women. That's not my thing."

With a sigh, Penelope added, "Well, maybe it should be your thing. That party was supposed to be the start of a new life. A different life from Portland, your parents, and your ex. Live a little, babe."

"Listen, can we just move on from my love life please?" They both mouthed "okay," and that was that.

After a few hours, they decided to go back to bed, but I couldn't sleep. All I could do was lie there and think of a certain dark-haired woman.

I shook my thoughts away. Drea was wrong. It didn't matter how sexy she was in only a T-shirt and socks. It didn't matter how much I wanted to lift her shirt to see what was underneath.

I think I was a little drunk. My skin suddenly felt forty degrees hotter, and I could feel a tingle from my chest, down to my aching—

"Hell. No," I said out loud. There was no way I would touch myself, *especially* not while thinking about her.

"I need to go to sleep." I groaned and rolled over.

It was about 9:30 in the morning when I woke up. I still had a blistering headache, but I wasn't vomiting, so I'd call that a win.

By the time I went to get breakfast, everyone had left for work.

I was meeting Drea at the bookstore later, and then we were going to meet Penelope for dinner. I didn't have to meet her until six, but I wanted to get there before then to work a shift.

She said she didn't need me, but I begged. She really could use the help, and I desperately wanted to get out of the house. Plus, I loved the bookstore. It had become my safe space when I needed it the most.

Drea had been working hard running the store, and an author signing was coming up in a few weeks. Her regular cashier, Kaia, was out sick, so I offered to help out.

I had about thirty minutes before I needed to get ready, so I made some scrambled eggs and bacon and settled on the couch.

I was about to aimlessly scroll through social media when my phone rang. "Hi, Mom," I answered with a smile.

My mom tried to call once a week or so, just to catch up and make sure I was still breathing. One time when she called, I picked up, and all I heard on the other end was, "Good, you're alive," before she hung up.

"Hi, sweetie, how are you? Are you eating enough?" She always called to ask the same questions, but I knew how lucky I was to have her.

I sighed. "Yes, Mom, I'm fine."

"Good, good. How's work? How's Drea? I miss you girls."

"I miss you too, Mom." I cleared the crack in my voice. I always got homesick when I talked to my mom on the phone. She was so supportive when I left, and that made it harder to say goodbye. I was counting down the days until I could go back home. "I haven't started yet, but I've been working at the bookstore, and Drea is good. The store is doing really well."

"I'm so proud of her. Tell her that for me, won't you, sweetie?"

"Of course, Mom. How are you?" I replied.

"Oh, I'm wonderful, honey! Brandon and your brother are a full-time job, but you know how boys can be." She laughed. "Are you adjusting to the move okay? Have you made any new friends? Are the people treating you okay—"

"Mom, I'm fine!"

"I'm sorry, honey, I'm just worried about you."

"I know, but I'm doing okay. The people are great." Except for one woman in particular, but that wasn't important.

"Any pretty ladies in Seattle?"

"Mom!" I covered my face. I was not about to have this conversation with my mom.

"I'm sorry. I just want to make sure you're having fun."

I winced. "I gotta go, Mom. I'm covering at the bookstore. I love you. I'll call you later, okay?"

"Okay, sweetie. I love you. Give my love to Drea, and tell her to stay out of trouble," she replied.

I laughed at the thought. "I will, Mom. I love you, too." I cleaned up from breakfast and jumped in the shower.

I grabbed a pair of casual jeans and a black KISS sweater from my closet. We were having dinner at *Pepperjack*, which was a casual burger place a few blocks away.

Looking through my peephole to make sure the coast was clear, I took a deep breath and quickly ran out the door, locking it as fast as possible. I practically ran down the hall and took the stairs so I didn't risk seeing my new neighbor while waiting for the elevator. I could already tell it would get old, but I hated confrontations.

When I got outside, I looked up and froze. Across the street, staring at me, was a beautiful blue-eyed brunette.

We stared at each other for a moment until she crossed. I got out my phone, pretending to be on an interesting phone call, and booked it down the street. She didn't yell after me, and for that, I was grateful. Once I turned the corner, I stopped to catch my breath.

I wondered if she was going to call after me or follow me. She opened her mouth as if she wanted to say something, but when I took my phone out, she closed it.

I took a chance and slowly crept around the corner, but thankfully, she wasn't there. I pulled myself together and kept walking toward the bookstore.

I guess Drea wasn't lying when she said she didn't need my help. The store was dead all afternoon, aside from a few customers here and there. I spent my spare time cleaning around and talking to Drea.

The bookstore had been my safe space since it opened—an escape from my problems.

As soon as you walked in, there was a red neon sign that read, "Be who you are," to the right, hanging above the sapphic fantasy books section. A gold-plated sign reading "Open Book" rested on the wall behind the counter.

Toward the back, there were peach-colored loveseats that sat back to back. Random chairs sat in varying corners of the store with round wooden side tables.

Down the wall, toward the middle of the bookstore, there was a vintage cash register that was more than a hundred years old. It had those classic keys that went 'ka-ching' when you pressed them, and a big drawer that popped open to reveal compartments for bills and coins.

I made my way back to the front of the store, where Drea was cleaning up the display windows. The theme of the display often changed depending on any events going on or holidays coming up.

I came up and stood next to her as she took a step back to look at the display. "It looks good, right?" I asked nervously. I wanted her to be happy with how the store was coming along for the book signing.

We were still several weeks away, but I knew how she got beforehand. Things were always hectic in the store, so I was trying my best to make everything as simple as possible for her.

She smiled at me and bumped our shoulders together. "It looks great. You did an amazing job, love."

I had convinced her to put a book with some dahlias on a table next to the window. Given the book's name, it fit perfectly. They were also my favorite type of flower.

"Thanks, I thought so, too." My face lit up at the compliment. "Since Francesca is coming, I thought it would work well with the theme." Francesca Sibcy, a local romance author, was coming in for a signing of her new release, *Passionate Petals*.

"Please don't remind me. I still have so much to do before the signing." She groaned. She always got so stressed about these events, but they usually worked out flawlessly.

"Don't worry. You know you'll have plenty of help."

She let out a puff of air. "I know. It's just all the back-end stuff—making sure everyone gets paid, making sure everyone knows what to do and is happy, on top of setting everything up, and—"

"Drea, this is Francesca we're talking about. She's been nothing but friendly and open to all of your suggestions since you started working with her. Relax, okay? She's not Blair."

Drea was always warm and welcoming to her authors. Blair, though, was not a fan of hers, and the feelings were very much mutual. Nothing was ever good enough for her, and she always left Drea feeling on edge—more than a normal signing did.

She tensed up at the mention of her least favorite person on the planet, but it vanished when she cleared her throat. "I am well aware of that."

I rested my hand on her arm. "It'll all work out, Dre. I promise."

She nodded. "I know, I know. I can't tell you how truly grateful I am to have you."

I chuckled. "You've got plenty of time to show your gratitude. I'll give you the chance until my last day on earth—when my body rots and turns into fertilizer."

"Is she freaking out again?" Skylar came up and wrapped her arms around Drea, pressing a kiss to her shoulder.

I laughed. "Would it be Drea if she wasn't?"

Drea rolled her eyes. "I am not freaking out, okay? I am being a conscious business owner and planning to ensure a smooth corporate event."

We both looked at her and laughed. "What the hell did she just say?" I asked Skylar. "She's losing it, isn't she?"

"I had to convince her to relax last night because she was spiraling just a tad. But the level of convincing I had to do may be considered highly inappropriate in public."

I chuckled as Drea swatted her arm. "Alright, alright. You won't be convincing anyone to do anything tonight if you don't let us get back to work."

Skylar and I gave each other a knowing grin that said we both knew that threat wouldn't hold up, and got back to work before the boss lady kicked us out.

For the next few hours, we worked on cleaning the store and checking inventory before Skylar said goodbye. She had to work early the next day, so she hadn't planned on joining us to meet Penelope.

"Alright, babe, I'll see you tonight. Be safe, and tell Penelope I said hi." She pulled Drea in for a sweet kiss before leaving.

We spent the rest of the night helping customers and dancing like weirdos to disco music when the store was empty.

When the last customer left, we locked up and headed out.

We walked in silence for a few blocks while Drea checked on some work emails. I swore that woman never took a day off.

She eventually put her phone away and turned to me. "So, how are things with your new neighbor? Have you seen her since the party?"

"Well, I haven't left the house until today, so no. I did see her on my way here, but she was across the street when I left." I didn't find it relevant to mention I ran away like a coward. Some things were better left unsaid.

"That's good, right? I'm sorry she had to ruin the night."

I scoffed. "Yeah, it's a good thing. And I am, too. It was a great party until she showed up."

"It really was! And what about Cara? She told me you had quite the chat at the party after you were whisked away to a mysterious dark corner—which you came out of all flushed and smiling, I might add." She grinned.

"Yeah, I mean, she's cute, and the kiss was hot, for sure. But I don't know. I had a lot to drink, and she left with a group of people." I knew she'd bring up Cara again—she'd been trying to set us up for weeks.

"So you *did* kiss. I knew it! She also told me she asked you out?" she asked.

I smiled. "Oh, yeah, she did, but I'm not expecting her to want to go through with it or anything."

"Well, I'm sure you'll see her around, so you never know."

"Yeah, okay, Drea." I rolled my eyes and linked our arms together as we kept walking.

When we got to the bar, Penelope was already at a table waiting for us. She was wearing her curly hair down to her shoulders, and her brown eyes were sparkling underneath her gold eye shadow. She wore a black tank top tucked into dark blue skinny jeans, which she paired with black sandals.

"There's Pen." I nodded my head in her direction.

"Hey, bitches!" Penelope sang when we sat down at the table.

"Hey!" We laughed.

When the waitress came over, I ordered a Screwdriver, Drea ordered a whiskey neat, and Penelope ordered a Strawberry Daiquiri.

"So, ladies, what's new? Feels like it's been ages since we've been out together," Penelope said.

"Did you already forget my party?" I shook my head with laughter.

She sent me a glared expression. "That doesn't count."

Sighing, I went on. "Well, Drea is freaking out about the book signing."

"I said what's *new*." Penelope laughed.

"I am not freaking out, I'm just stressed. You heathens try owning a business!"

"Okay, Dre, relax. We're sorry." I placed a hand on her shoulder.

"Yeah, Drea, sorry. The bookstore is doing great, the book signing will be great—just like they always are, because you couldn't do anything less than perfect if you tried!" Penelope added with a sympathetic smile.

Drea rolled her eyes with a soft grin. "Thanks, love. I'm really glad it's Francesca right now and not... someone else. God, I need another drink." She groaned as she quickly downed her whiskey. I chuckled and took a sip of my drink before waving down our waitress.

We sat drinking and laughing for a good while, and it was nice—until I was mildly ambushed.

"Oh my God, look who just came in!" Drea grabbed my arm and shook me like a pair of Yahtzee dice.

"What the hell, Dre?!" I yanked my arm away and scowled at her.

With the way she was acting, you would've thought a world-famous celebrity just walked in and not a normal person.

I looked up at the door to see Cara coming in. She looked sexy wearing a barely-there little black dress.

I turned back to Drea, who was wiggling her eyebrows at me. "Oh yeah, Cara's here. Cool," I replied with a smile. I didn't have a problem with Cara at all—my problem was with my friends always trying to set me up. They'd waited patiently for about three weeks after my breakup before they started inviting me out, and we "coincidentally" ran into only their single friends.

"Yeah, and she's heading straight for our table," Penelope added.

I really couldn't understand their obsession with getting us together. I was perfectly content being on my own.

"So what?" I turned back to Penelope.

"So, be nice!" Drea said sharply.

"I'm always nice, Dre," I replied.

I vividly recalled being nice to Cara in a dark hallway the other night. A faint smile dusted my lips at the memory.

"And push up your boobs a little." Penelope shook her chest, as if I needed a demonstration.

"Oh my God, Pen." I rolled my eyes. "Will you guys stop? I'm not pushing up my—" My protest died off when Cara reached the table.

"Hey, guys." She greeted us with a wide smile.

"Hey, Cara," Drea and Penelope said.

You would think with the way they swooned at her, they wanted to set themselves up with her and not me.

Cara turned to look at me, and her smile grew flirtatiously large. "It's nice to see you again, Fallon. You look really good."

When she bit her bottom lip, a slight blush colored my cheeks, and I knew my friends were staring at us, which made the color darken further.

"Hey, Cara. Thanks, so do you." That was the thing about her—she always looked good. Even at a simple house party, she managed to light up the whole room.

"Great party the other night. Thanks again for inviting me. I had a really good time," she commented with a wink. Her voice was low and sultry, and I blamed the alcohol for the warmth that spread through me —and for the thought of wishing we'd stayed in that dark hallway a little longer.

"I'm glad you enjoyed yourself."

She stared at me for a moment longer before someone's throat cleared. "So, Cara, what are you doing here?" I turned to Drea, who had the biggest grin on her face.

"I'm meeting some friends." She motioned to a group of women at a table in one corner of the bar. "But I saw a beautiful woman, and I couldn't resist coming over to talk to her." Cara didn't take her eyes off of me while she answered. "I hope that was okay," she added softly.

"It's more than okay," I replied with a flirtatious tone.

Where did that come from? I had to stop drinking around pretty women. I seemed to always say stupid shit.

She finally turned away from me and focused on Drea and Penelope instead. "Well, I better go. It was nice to see all of you again."

"Yeah, you too, Cara," Penelope said with a grin

"Oh, and Fallon? I hope I'll see you later… in a more private setting." Cara winked and walked away, leaving me at a loss for words— and a little flushed, if I was being honest. Drea stared at me, mouth open and speechless, which was a first for her.

I cleared my throat and took a long drink, avoiding any direct eye contact with my friends and pretending everything was normal, like I hadn't just gotten turned on in the middle of a bar. Totally normal.

After what felt like hours of feeling their eyes on me, I couldn't take it anymore. I slowly turned back to Penelope, and then finally to Drea who was gaping at me with wide eyes.

"What?" I thought I might have missed something. I wasn't sure why they were still staring at me. It wasn't like I had taken her on top of the table or anything.

"Oh my God, she wants you!" Drea barely kept her voice low as she punched my leg.

"Ouch! Okay, seriously, I'm going to need you to stop abusing me!" I rubbed my leg as I scowled at her.

"She's right," Penelope added. "She's got it bad for you. If you could get pregnant with one look—"

"Oh my... not you too, Pen," I whined. "I barely know her."

That's not to say I wouldn't mind getting to know her, but I was perfectly happy where I was in life at that moment.

"That's why you need to go out with her. Get to know her and have some fun, love. What could it hurt?" Drea added.

I took a drink and shrugged. "Yeah, we'll see."

Maybe it wouldn't be such a bad idea. It's not like there was anyone else lined up at my door right now. Not to mention, I hadn't had sex with another person in over two...

Maybe going out with Cara would a good thing. And I guess I could do a lot worse. She was intelligent, interested, and knew how to wear a dress.

The dress hugged every curve and accentuated every asset, leaving little to the imagination. She knew how to leave an impression. I wondered if she knew how *not to* wear a dress just as well.

I bit my lip... a date was a good idea.

Chapter Four

MACKENZIE

I took full advantage of my day off from work. It was my first day off in about a week, and it felt amazing.

I caught up on some reading and even went to the gym—which, I'm ashamed to admit, was the first time in weeks—before heading to the store.

After I put all my groceries away, I decided to take advantage of the cool weather and go for a walk. It was my favorite time of day—mid-afternoon. The brightness of the day was gone, but the sun hadn't set yet, casting a yellow-orange tint over the world. I'd been taking these walks at least once a week since I moved into my building two years ago.

On my way back home, I stopped in front of this little bookstore. I'd seen it a dozen times, but there was a flower in the window that caught my eye. On a round wooden table sat a white vase, and inside the vase were two pink dahlias. They were next to a book titled *Passionate Petals*. It was a queer romance novel. I'd never read it, but my friends seemed to have liked it.

The store was closed, but I wanted to come back to take a look around. I knew it was a queer bookstore—or at least queer-friendly—because of all the equality and various LGBTQIA+ stickers on the windows, but I'd never given it a second glance until today. "*Open Book*, clever," I said aloud as I read the sign.

When I got home, I grabbed my mail before heading to my apartment. The mailboxes were inside the lobby, and mine was filled with mostly junk mail.

I got off the elevator and turned the corner, coming to a halt.

My new neighbor was standing at her door, and as if she sensed I was there, she stopped fidgeting with her keys and turned to me.

I cleared my throat and continued down the hall. I didn't care that she was there, or what she was doing.

She turned back and unlocked her door, neither of us saying a word. I opened my door and paused as she cleared her throat.

"Hey." Her tone was light and friendly. I slowly turned and straightened up.

"Hello," I replied. I wasn't really in the mood for a conversation, but apparently, she was.

"I wanted to apologize for the other night," she said softly, playing with her key ring. "I was drunk, and I feel like we got off on the wrong foot. I never got the chance to introduce myself. My name is Fallon Bennett, and I just moved here from Portland." When I didn't say anything, she spoke again. "Uhh... anyway, I'm really sorry."

I snorted, and a few beats passed before I answered. "Yeah, I could tell you had been drinking."

Her brows narrowed. "Look, things got out of hand, I admit. I had a lot to drink, and the whole situation was handled poorly—on both sides of the door."

I raised my eyebrows. "Both sides?"

She scoffed. "Well, yeah. You were banging on the door like a lunatic, and you were a little rude."

"You were having a rager in the middle of the night, and I was rude?" I questioned.

"What are you, ninety?" She rolled her eyes. "We didn't have a rager! It was just a little party. And you didn't have to insult me, you know. You could've just knocked calmly and asked us to turn it down."

I laughed. "Like you would've heard a knock anyway. And just a little party? I'm pretty sure you could've heard the music down the street. Also, I didn't insult you. I was simply stating facts. It was obvious you could barely stand. If you were offended, that's your problem."

"Jesus Christ, what is your problem?" She scoffed. "Didn't your parents ever teach you the concept of human decency?"

I ignored her and turned around, walking into my apartment and shutting the door behind me with a sigh.

"Unbelievable," I mumbled.

That was only the second time I had spoken to that woman, and I already wanted to bang my head against the door.

I let out a long breath and went into the kitchen to make something to eat. I was so irritated and I needed to relax.

While I waited for my food to heat up, my phone rang, and I quickly answered without seeing who was calling.

"What?!" I snapped at whoever was on the other end.

"Try that again, Mackenzie Isabella Thompson." My sister's stern voice—along with the use of my full government name—extinguished my rage, if only slightly.

"Sorry, Harper. Hello."

"That's better. Hello, dear sister. Is something bothering you? You sound a little tense."

"No, it's just been a day. What's up?" I let out an exaggerated sigh. My social limit for the day had peaked, and I was not in the mood to talk about anything related to Fallon.

"I just wanted to make sure you were still coming over for dinner next Thursday?"

Dinner at Harper's had been the only constant family thing in my life for a long time, and I always looked forward to them.

My sister was a few years older than me, and had been married for seven years to her husband, Grant. She had long auburn hair and hazel eyes—I always thought the she was the prettier one out of the two of us.

"Of course, Harp. You know I'll be there. I wouldn't miss it for anything."

While we talked, I pushed my food around on my plate, no longer interested in eating it.

She went on to tell me about work, and I heard something about Grant, but I couldn't pay attention. I was too busy thinking about an infuriatingly attractive redhead across the hall, which pissed me off all over again.

Irritation was boiling deep within me at the thought of her. How dare she insert her unwanted opinions into my life, like she had any right, like she had any idea. She knew nothing about my life or how I was raised.

I supposed it could be hard to find "human decency," as she put it, when the ones who were supposed to guide you in life didn't display much of it themselves.

"Hello? Are you even listening to me?" Harper's voice cut through my thoughts.

I blinked and shook my head, bringing myself back to the present. "What? Oh, sorry. Yeah, of course I was listening."

"Really? What did I say, then?" I swore, Harper could sniff out a lie three days in advance.

I ran my hand through my hair, trying to come up with a reasonable answer she'd believe. "Um... something about Grant?" I took an educated guess. I'm pretty sure I wasn't too far off, but I doubted she bought it anyway.

"Something about Grant?" She scoffed. "What's going on with you?"

I sighed. "Nothing, I'm sorry. I'm fine." I dumped my plate in the trash, no longer feeling hungry. I sat on the couch, massaging the bridge of my nose.

"It doesn't sound like nothing, Boog. Do you want to talk about it?" she pressed.

I scoffed at the mention of my childhood nickname. You go to school one time with snot on your shirt, and all of a sudden, you're plagued with the nickname "Boog." I blame my parents for that. I was ten years old. They could've warned me!

"Not really, Harper." I paused for about three seconds before giving in. "It's my new neighbor. She's just so..." I groaned. "She's infuriating."

The line was quiet for a minute, and I thought she had hung up. "Okay, Kenzie. What happened?" she asked cautiously.

"I've only seen her twice, but... she just moved here, and she's already driving me crazy." I paused with a sigh before continuing. "The other night, after I came home from a shitty day, I was relaxing with a book and a glass of wine."

She hissed. "Oh, sweetie. Did you get drunk and get into a fight with your new neighbor?" *Lucky guess, Harper...*

"Not a physical fight. She was having a loud ass party, and I asked her to turn it down." I paused again, raking my hands through my hair. "I may have insinuated that she looked too drunk to be capable of anything."

"Jesus, Mackenzie!" Harper yelled. "What is wrong with you?"

"I was drinking, okay, and so was she!" I closed my eyes. I wanted to forget that night ever happened.

I knew I shouldn't have insulted her. I guess it was a little harsh, but I wasn't thinking clearly.

"Kenzie, you need to apologize. Tell her you were drunk and weren't thinking. Even if she doesn't know you, she should have no problem believing it. She's new and doesn't need your bitchy ass making things difficult. She probably could use a friend. Do you even know her name?"

I exhaled, trying to release the tension building in my chest. "Her name is Fallon. She tried to apologize earlier—well, she did, but—"

"You didn't accept it, did you? You are such a stubborn ass!"

"Could you stop, Harper? Honestly, why do you keep doing that?!"

She laughed. "No, I can't. I'm your sister, I know you! So why the hell not?"

"I don't know. She started saying how it was partly my fault, too—"

"Which it was, since you started it."

"I just asked her to turn it down, Harper," I defended myself.

"Yeah, and I bet you didn't say please before you insulted her, did you?"

My only response was a groan.

"Exactly. Mackenzie, you need to apologize. Try to be nice for once —it'll do you some good. Listen, I have to go make dinner, but I love you, okay? Shall we see you on Thursday?"

I closed my eyes. "Yeah, yeah, love you, too. See you Thursday."

I hated it when my sister was right.

Chapter Five

FALLON

I was able to avoid my new neighbor for a few days, making sure it was clear before leaving the house. After the last time, I had no interest in going back and forth with her again.

I had the day off, so I managed to get a good amount of cleaning done around the house. Before I took the trash out, I wanted to take a shower and do some laundry.

Peeking through my peephole, I bolted out the door when I saw it was clear. This was going to get tiring after a while, but for now, I did what I had to do.

I said a quiet thank you when I got to the laundry room and saw that it was empty. The last thing I wanted was to run into my neighbor. It was bad enough she was in my damn thoughts all the time.

The laundry room was on the first floor of the apartment building and was decently sized, with three washers and dryers lining the wall. On the opposite wall, there was a long table for folding clothes.

I had just started the washer and turned around when someone walked in. Before I could see who it was, my heart stopped and I jumped. I couldn't deal with her right now. I was having a relaxing day, and had no intention of letting her ruin it. But when I finally saw who it was, my shoulders relaxed and I let out a breath.

Grateful didn't even begin to cover the emotion I felt when I saw it was just my friendly neighbor, Robbie. Robbie was a 65-year-old man who lived with his wife, Debbie. He was retired, but he was home less often than I was. He was always out walking or picking flowers to bring home for Debbie. Every day, he brought her a single flower, and it was never the same kind.

"Oh, hi, Robbie. You scared me. I thought you were someone else," I said with a smile, trying to catch my breath.

He frowned. "Hey there, Fallon. I'm sorry to scare you. I'm a little concerned for you, though. With a reaction like that, who were you expecting?"

I sighed. "No one as lovely as you, I'm afraid. How's Debbie?"

He smiled at the mention of her name. "Oh, she's as beautiful as the day I met her. She's upstairs reading one of her dirty books."

I could have done without that image… "Oh, well, good for her."

He laughed. "Yes. Anyway, are all the washers taken tonight?"

I looked toward the laundry room and shook my head. "No, I'm just using one, so you're right on time. The rest are all yours."

"Perfect. Thank you, Fallon. So, how are you doing besides worrying and waiting for someone terrifying?"

I laughed. "I'm not waiting on anyone. I was hoping to avoid them, but I'm doing pretty well. Enjoying my day off and having some time to myself."

I was hoping he would stop prying. I didn't want to talk or even think about her.

Why *was* I still thinking about her? I needed to just shake it off and move on. I couldn't let some uptight stranger affect me, even if I could have drowned in her ocean-blue eyes.

"Well, I'm sorry, and I'm glad you're enjoying yourself today. See you at drying time." He waved and headed to do his laundry.

"Yes, see you then. Tell Debbie I said hello." I waved goodbye and left.

When I closed my apartment door behind me, I set a timer on my phone and made dinner. I had leftover steak and potatoes from the night before, so I popped them into the microwave and made some red rice.

I was stirring the rice when my phone rang. I wiped my hands and swiped the screen, putting it on speaker. "Hey, Pen, you're on speaker. I'm cooking."

She laughed. "Oh shit, don't die, please."

I rolled my eyes. "Excuse me, I'm an excellent cook, okay?" I mean, I wasn't Rachel Ray or anything, but I was decent. I used to cook with my mom all the time when I was younger.

"Yeah, well, what else is going on? Have you fully recovered from the party yet?"

I groaned. "Yes and no. I mean I'm not hungover or anything, but mentally, I'm drained."

"From your neighbor? She really did a number on you, didn't she? You were drunk, you need to let it go."

The remaining irritation from a few nights ago was starting to resurface. "She was the worst! And yeah, I know. I think she was drinking that night, too, to be honest, I don't know. It just rubbed me the wrong way, but I don't want to talk about it anymore." I didn't want to think about her either, even though my brain protested and did anyway.

"Fine, fine, I can take a hint. So, what are you making?"

I continued stirring the rice and told her. Of course, she continued to tease me, but I ignored her.

"Okay, but how are you, Pen? Drea told me what happened with Gregory. Are you still staying at your parents' house?"

She sighed. "Yeah, I don't think we've ever been apart this long. I'm just so mad—I can't stand to be anywhere near him right now. But I'll be fine, babe."

It broke my heart to hear her so upset.

Penelope's husband thought it would be a brilliant idea to cancel their plans together so he could go play golf with the guys—on their tenth anniversary. I knew she would forgive him at some point, but my heart still hurt for her.

"Okay, just take it easy, and don't let him suffer too long. I love you."

"I won't. I love the idiot too much, you know that. And I love you, too, Fal."

When we hung up, I took my plate of food to the couch, propped one leg up, and grabbed the remote, scrolling through Netflix for a good thirty minutes until I found a movie I actually wanted to sit through.

Caleb and I used to watch *Stuart Little* at least twice whenever I babysat. It was his favorite movie. Watching it now, even though I was alone, made me feel connected to him, like he was still with me, even though we were miles apart.

I didn't regret moving away, not for a second. Sometimes, though, it was hard being away from my family.

When I went to dry my clothes, Debbie was there with Robbie. She gave me a warm hug and we chatted until the dryers went off. I asked about the romance novel she was reading, and she was excited to talk about it with me. Robbie just rolled his eyes, smiling as he read a magazine. I tried not to think about how much of her books they re-enacted.

I returned with my clothes and put them away as I finished the movie. I tried to take a little nap, but my mind wouldn't stop running.

My past kept creeping back into my head—the good and the bad. I thought about my mom and stepdad, wondering what they were doing and whether they were working or spending the day with Caleb. Then I thought about my little brother.

He was only five, but I wondered if he was upset with me for leaving. He was my little shadow, following me around everywhere and clinging to my legs like a sloth to a tree branch. I smiled and wiped away a stray tear before it hit the pillow. I knew moving to Seattle was the right decision, but that didn't mean it was easy.

Then I remembered how I ended up where I was to begin with. My ex and I had been together for so long, I thought I had finally found my happy ending. The only thing I found was betrayal and heartbreak.

When I found out she cheated on me, I didn't think I'd ever leave my room. I moved out and back in with my mom for two years before I moved to Seattle.

I wallowed for too long before I started to rebuild myself. I still had doubts that I wasn't responsible for pushing her into someone else's bed. I must have done something wrong—she sure acted that way. She acted like I didn't even matter, like what we had, or what I thought we had, meant nothing.

When I confronted her, she turned it around on me and acted like I was the one who was texting someone else. She now has a new "baby" she goes home to every night. I thought I was her home, but I guess things changed.

It had been over a year, but some days were harder than others. I had definitely moved on, and I didn't want anything to do with her anymore, but it still hurt to know I wasn't good enough for someone.

I shook my head, exhausted by all these emotions, and closed my eyes until sleep took over.

Chapter Six

MACKENZIE

I swore I was not allowed to have one nice day off! If I was gone for one day, the aquarium turned into chaos.

I spent hours chasing down a penguin that had somehow gotten out. I finally found him at an ice cream stand—go figure. That was probably one of the weirdest days I'd had at work.

After the longest day of my life, I was walking home and had just gotten off the phone with Harper when I saw Fallon down the hall.

I took the stairs to avoid running into her at the elevator, but apparently, that didn't matter. She must not have seen or heard me on the phone because she didn't stop. *Or maybe she didn't stop on purpose because you were an asshole.*

Once she went inside, I continued my walk home and decided to clean up a bit. I needed something to do—something to distract me.

After I cleaned around the kitchen, I grabbed the trash and headed downstairs to take it out. The distance wouldn't have been so bad if I hadn't lived on the fifth floor *and* halfway down the hall from the elevator, but my load was light, so I managed okay.

When I got there, it seemed I wasn't the only one with the idea of cleaning up. Fallon was tossing her trash as I walked up to the dumpster.

She was wearing white shorts and a plain black T-shirt. The shorts were borderline illegal in length, and I couldn't look away.

When I finally did, my eyes caught on the colorful bundle of decaying flowers in her hand—dahlias, from the looks of it. A mix of purples, pinks, and whites, with a black one thrown in. She was also holding an empty bag of butterscotch candies.

My eyes eventually traveled *slowly* to her red hair, which glistened in the moonlight. It was mesmerizing.

Wait, no it wasn't, dammit!

After she tossed her trash into the dumpster, she turned around and froze when she saw me. I couldn't make out her expression, but it looked like her mouth opened slightly, as if she was drawing in a breath or wanted to say something.

After a moment, she looked down and walked past me without a word. I should've ignored her and not provoked her, but something inside me couldn't let the moment pass.

"Did you have another wild party?" I asked.

She kept walking and didn't say anything as she wrapped her arms around herself, most likely because of the slight chill in the air. *Okay then.*

"Lovely night, isn't it?" I didn't know what my goal was with that. I was just trying to get some words out, I guess.

Still nothing.

I sighed. "Listen, Fallon, I'm sorry, okay?"

She finally turned around. "You're sorry? Sorry for what? You know what, it doesn't matter." She turned back around and walked away.

"Fallon," I called, but she didn't stop.

I didn't know why I was even trying to apologize. It's not like I cared anyway.

I *didn't* care, but Harper's voice echoed in my head.

You need to apologize. Try to be nice for once. She could probably use a friend.

Get out of my head, Harper!

She didn't know what she was talking about. Fallon wanted nothing to do with me. And that was fine by me.

I didn't want anything to do with someone as irritating as her, even if she looked hot in plain shorts, had great taste in candy, and had an eye for beautiful flowers.

When I walked back to the lobby, Fallon was waiting for the elevator. I walked up and stood next to her, not saying a word.

"Oh my God, you have to be kidding me." She groaned and threw
her head back.

I laughed. "Wow, so ladylike. You just saw me, so I don't know why
you're acting so surprised."

"Fuck off," she whispered, so quietly I almost didn't hear her.

I chuckled softly. "Such a dirty mouth."

Nope. I was not going there. I was not going to think any kind of
thoughts about her mouth at all...

Her eyes shot to me. She opened her mouth to say something, but
then closed it.

The elevator doors opened, and we both stood on opposite sides in
silence.

I sighed. "Look, I'm just trying to apologize, here, okay? Like you
said, we both weren't in a clear headspace and we handled the situation
badly."

When she didn't say anything, I tried again. "Anyway, my name is
Mackenzie... Thompson."

She turned to look at me. "That's what you call an apology? And I
didn't ask what your name was."

"Well, then." I chuckled. "You told me your name, so I thought it
was only fair that you knew mine. Excuse me." I threw my hands up in
surrender.

She scoffed. "I should've taken the stairs."

I frowned. "Yeah? Why didn't you, then?"

"Because I shouldn't have to," she replied.

The doors opened to our floor, and I motioned for her to step out
first. She gave me a half-smile in return. "I'm not going to run and hide
every time I see you. I'm just trying to stay out of your way and get on
with my life. I was hoping you'd extend me the same courtesy and not be
a total bitch every time we run into each other."

"Yeah, except for earlier, when you ran away down the street
pretending to be on a phone call, just to avoid me? And that's the
second time you've called me a bitch. I'm starting to think you don't like
me." I put my hand to my chest, pretending to be heartbroken.

She stopped and looked at me. "You... you heard me." It wasn't a question. She almost looked embarrassed before quickly adding, "Well, you were acting like one. And I don't know you, but I can't say I'm a big fan so far. Also, I was on the phone with... my boss." She stumbled over her words, and I tried to suppress a laugh. It was a little too fun getting her all riled up.

"Right." I smirked at her and kept walking.

"You're insufferable, you know that?"

I unlocked my door and opened it, turning to face her. "Am I?" I asked.

"Yes, you really are." She stood at her door, facing me, and took a deep breath. "I think it's a good idea if we just keep our distance and try to stay out of each other's way, okay?"

"Fine by me. Goodnight, *neighbor*." I smiled and shut my door. I stood there for a moment, just long enough to hear a loud groan and the slam of a door.

I gathered myself and went to the kitchen to heat up some leftover lasagna.

"That went well. Thanks for the outstanding advice, Harper," I said to myself. I took my food out of the microwave and headed to the couch.

I sent Harper a lovely text message, thanking her for sending me into the lion's den:

> Me: Thanks, Harp!

It took about five minutes for her to reply, obliviously to my sarcasm:

> Harper: You're welcome. I'm glad I could help! ☺

> Me: The only thing you did was help to ensure I was right. She doesn't want anything to do with me.

Harper: What? What are you talking about? What happened?

Me: I took your great advice and tried to apologize.

Harper: Did you insult her again?

Me:  No. You know, your confidence in me is really sweet…

Me: I actually tried to apologize. I admitted I was wrong and she wanted nothing to do with it.

Harper: Well, damn. I'm sorry. Maybe give her some space and time?

Me: That might be your best advice yet, sis!

Harper: 🖕

Me: Love you too, sister dearest. ♥

I plugged my phone in and closed my eyes, trying to bring the next day closer.

I tried to extend an olive branch, but she broke it down and threw it into a fire pit. It was probably best that I took Fallon's advice and kept my distance. Nothing good could come from being around her more than necessary.

Chapter Seven

FALLON

"Shit, shit, shit! I'm so late!" I jumped out of bed, ripped my clothes from my closet, and ran to the bathroom. I got ready at an alarming pace and grabbed my bag, shoving my phone inside as I ran out the door. *I cannot be late on my first day!*

I pushed the elevator button when I realized I had forgotten to lock up.

"Of course." I ran down the hall, turned the corner, and crashed to a stop.

"What the fuck?!"

My stomach was in my throat, and I couldn't believe this was happening. Of all the people in the world, I had to run into Mackenzie.

It was my first day at work, and I was already on the verge of running late. *Why do you hate me, universe?*

"I am so sorry! Are you okay?" I said, rubbing my face, wishing I was anywhere else.

She looked at me, her bright blue eyes darkening as the seconds went by. "Do I look okay? You made me spill my goddamn coffee!" She glared down at her once-white blouse, now stained a coffee-colored brown.

My gaze traveled down to the stain. My eyes lingered without my permission, but I quickly shot them back up to hers, which were accompanied by perfectly polished raised eyebrows.

Did she see me checking her out? Of course not, because I *wasn't* checking her out. Oh my God, I was. *What the hell is wrong with me?*

"I'm sorry, I didn't see you," I said.

"Yeah, I can see that. I'm already running late, and now I have to change. So no, Fallon, I think it's safe to say I am *not* okay!"

I was at a loss for words, so I did the only thing I could think of—I blinked.

She scoffed and leaned down. I followed her to the stack of papers scattered across the hallway floor. This was my nightmare.

"Shit. Here, let me help." I bent down to gather some of the papers.

I felt awful. I spilled her coffee and made a mess of what looked like some important papers, probably spilling some coffee on them in the process. Drea would've gotten a kick out of this situation, but I was on the verge of tears.

We both reached for the same paper, our fingers brushing slightly, causing us to pause and look at one another. There was a glint of a sparkle in her eyes before it vanished, and her breath seemed to catch at the same time mine did.

I should've moved, but something was anchoring me down, paralyzing me. I had no idea what to do or say. I'd never felt such an intense spark from touching someone before. It was just friction from the carpet, right? Obviously, that's all it was. It had to be.

She was the first one to break the contact, removing her hand and clearing her throat. "I think you've helped enough, thanks. Who runs around a corner? What if it had been a frail, old lady in the hallway? You would've killed her!" Her tone was unnecessarily harsh.

I laughed at her ridiculous dramatics. "She would've, at most, broken a hip. She wouldn't have died. Don't be so dramatic."

She scoffed. "Just leave. Go, fuck, I don't care, anywhere else. You've helped enough!"

I looked at her, shaking my head. "Wow. I guess it's true when they say the third time's a charm," I muttered softly to myself.

"What?" she bit out, picking up the papers.

I took a deep breath and stood up. "You've heard me call you a bitch twice now, well, guess what, Mackenzie? The third time's a goddamn charm. *Why* are you always such a fucking bitch?!"

She stopped and scowled at me. "Maybe because you keep showing up, making me act like one. First, you turned your apartment into a fucking rave in the middle of the night, and you were so drunk I'm surprised you could even—"

"Would you give it a rest, grandma? It wasn't a rave!" I cut her off with an eye roll. She just couldn't let it go.

Ignoring me, she continued. "Then I tried to apologize because I was drinking too, and you didn't even want to hear it."

"I apologized first, and you blew me off. You don't even acknowledge that, do you?" I lowered my brows.

"Whatever. And now you run down the hall like a damn lunatic, and you want to ask me *why* I'm such a bitch?"

I gaped at her, speechless, my mind drawing a blank. The nerve of that incredibly attractive, infuriating woman.

I was simmering with rage, mixed with surprise and a touch of something else.

Hurt? I scoffed at myself. No. I was not hurt. I wouldn't let her hold that kind of power.

"Wow, nothing to say, huh? Color me surprised." She scoffed. "I'm going to change. Try not to run anyone else down out here."

I groaned, walked to my apartment, triple-checked the door, and headed to work.

My first day at the hospital, and I was already running late. Not to mention, I couldn't find a parking spot, so I had to park three blocks away and haul ass just to be ten minutes late.

Luckily, my boss assumed I had gotten stuck in morning traffic, and wanting to put the morning behind me, I didn't correct her. The rest of the day went smoothly, but I was glad when it was over. I wanted to go home and forget the whole day ever happened. It would've been too soon if I never saw Mackenzie again.

The next morning, I woke up an hour early to make sure my second day wouldn't start as badly.

I set my clothes out the night before and made bacon and eggs for breakfast. I made sure I had plenty of time to grab coffee before work.

My favorite coffee shop, *Brewed Awakening*, was just down the street from my apartment. It was one of the first places I discovered after moving to Seattle, and it had been my daily caffeine stop ever since.

Not only was the coffee phenomenal, but the barista was a delight. She always gave me a little more espresso than she was supposed to.

She was around the same age as me, with blonde, wavy hair. She had a sleeve tattoo with different roses, leaves, and stems on her left arm. I've complimented it on more than one occasion.

"Hey!" she said when I walked in. "I'll be right with you."

I waved my hello. "No rush!" I had at least forty-five minutes before I needed to leave for work, so I didn't mind waiting.

"Hey, Fallon, what can I get you?" When I reached the counter, she looked exhausted from the morning rush.

"Hey, Rylee. Can I please have an iced coffee? Extra espresso and hazelnut? Thanks."

"No problem." She smiled.

She started making my coffee before she spoke again. "So, what's new? Last time we talked, you were about to start a new job. How's that going?"

"It's okay. Yesterday was my first day, and of course, I was late. It was a horrible morning, and that's putting it mildly." I groaned.

"Oh no, what happened?"

I sighed. "I woke up late, which wouldn't have been a problem, but the universe thought it would be the perfect time for me to run into my new neighbor, Mackenzie."

"Oh... you live at the apartments down the street, right? *Cedar Cove*, I think, is the name." Her eyes growing a little wider than before.

"Yeah. I can't believe you remember that." I told her when I first came in months ago. I was sure she saw hundreds of people daily, so it said a lot about her if she remembered something as trivial as that.

"I have a pretty good memory." She paused. "So, I take it you don't get along with Mackenzie?"

I didn't know what I said, but her smile seemed more forced when she handed over my coffee. "Not in the slightest. She is such a..." I took a deep breath. "Anyway, thanks, Rylee. Have a good day!" I smiled and took my coffee.

"Yeah, you too," she said.

I went to open the door when someone was coming in. "Oh, excuse me, sor—"

I stopped when I looked up to meet a pair of ocean-blue eyes. My lungs felt too tight in my chest, and my heart was doing somersaults.

Mackenzie, looking irresistibly sexy in a low-cut white tank top and jeans, stood in front of me. And there I was in my scrubs, with my hair in a librarian-style bun. *So sexy...*

"Excuse me," I said dryly. She opened the door even farther so I could pass.

I walked by without a word, but I only got a few steps before I heard a sarcastic voice. "You're welcome."

I whipped my head around, shooting her a glare as I forced a fake politeness in my voice. "Thanks." I turned back and continued walking away.

The past week had been nothing short of horrible. Almost every day, I ran into Mackenzie in one way or another—whether in the elevator, the laundry room, the hall, or my favorite coffee shop. She was everywhere I went.

I needed a distraction, and I needed to get her out of my head. So, I texted Drea and Penelope—one of them was bound to be free:

Me: Desperate for a girl's night tonight. Who's in?

Penelope: Why, what happened? I wish I could but I gotta work early. ☹

Drea: I'm in! What happened?

Me: I got 99 problems and a bitch is all of them! And sorry, Pen. 😔

Me: Perfect Drea! Swing by around 7?

Drea: Sorry Pen, I'll pour one out for you!

Penelope: Thanks, guys. Next time! Later, xx

Me: Xx

Drea: Later, love.

A few minutes later Drea sent me a private text:

Drea: What happened, girl? You finally bang her?

Me: Never going to happen! Had another run-in.

Me: This one was really bad. Tell you about it tonight.

Drea: KK see ya soon!

"So, where are we going tonight?" Drea said as I opened the door to let her in.

I laughed. "Well, hello to you too. I'm almost ready. I was thinking about dinner and drinks at *Neighbors*."

Her eyes grew wide. "What?! You want to have dinner with your hot neighbor? What did I miss?" She grinned. She damn well knew what I meant.

"You're so funny. The bar down the street, smart-ass."

Neighbors was a casual sports bar. It was low-key, but it had the best mojitos in the city.

Drea made herself comfortable on the couch while I finished up my makeup—I was going for something light. I put on a black, above-the-knee dress with short sleeves and paired it with black wedges.

Since it was the weekend, we had to wait about thirty minutes when we arrived. I didn't mind, though, because I needed to use the restroom.

We finally got seated, and I ordered two mint mojitos. "Saving a trip," I told the waitress when her eyebrows shot up.

She turned to Drea as she spoke. "I'll have a whiskey, neat, please."

"Okay, Fal, spill. What is going on?" Drea said after the waitress left. I knew she wouldn't leave it alone, but I didn't want to think about Mackenzie anymore.

"It's just been a stressful week," I replied.

I didn't want to get into it. I wanted to drink and forget about my problems, at least for one night.

She looked at me with raised brows. "Is it work? I thought things were going good?"

"No, they are. I mean, I'm still adjusting, but it's great so far. I was late on my first day, but they were understanding. They assumed I got stuck in traffic, which was partly true," I said.

"Then what—" She stopped when the waitress came back with our drinks.

I thanked her and ordered our food. I went with a bacon cheeseburger and onion rings, and Drea got a steak with shrimp, which, of course the classy bitch did.

She waited until the waitress left again before speaking. "Is it the bookstore? Do you need to change your hours?"

I chuckled. "No, sweetie, I love working at the store. Are you joking? I can't thank you enough for helping me!"

She smiled and we raised our glasses. "To new beginnings."

Drea had been there for me through everything—from my parents' divorce to my breakup. Even when we were miles apart, she was always there for me, more than anyone else in my life. I would never be able to fully express just how much she meant to me.

We clinked our glasses, and mine was empty before she even brought hers to her lips.

"Okay, what the hell is going on with you?" She looked at me with a stunned expression.

"It's Mackenzie. She's driving me nuts!" The words tumbled out with a sigh.

"Who the fuck is Mackenzie?" Drea's face twisted in confusion.

I groaned. "Oh yeah, I didn't tell you. That woman I argued with at the party—my neighbor? I've run into her a few times since then. Her name is Mackenzie." I took another drink, this time a little less desperately.

She looked skeptically at me. "Okay? So, what did she do to get your panties in a twist?"

I scowled. "My panties are not in a twist!"

She looked at me and didn't respond to my outburst, knowing I just proved her point.

I sighed. "Okay, maybe they are. I ran into her the other day—literally, Drea. I rounded the corner and bumped right into her, spilling her papers and coffee. It was a total accident, and I felt awful about it. It was my first day at work, and I was already running late."

She winced. "Oh, shit. So, what happened?"

I rolled my eyes at the memory. "I tried to apologize and help her pick up the papers she dropped on the floor."

I left out the part where our hands touched, and it felt like my heart stopped for a split second. She would've turned that into a whole thing, and I wasn't in the mood to have that conversation. It was nothing— that's why I hadn't thought about it since then... not once.

"After that, she yelled at me. She also insulted me, again! Oh, and by the way, she did hear me call her a bitch the night of the party. I was so embarrassed, I almost had a damn heart attack."

She laughed. "Well, damn!"

"But I made sure she heard me this time, when I asked why she was such a fucking bitch!"

Drea nearly choked on her drink. "Goddamn, Fal, I honestly didn't think you had it in you."

"Yeah, me neither, but she seems to bring it out in me. Every time I try to make peace or ignore her, one of us says something, and it just ends up being a shitty situation. I don't know how much more of this I can handle. I mean, she lives across the hall, so avoiding her isn't really an option. But it's clear we aren't meant to be friends. I don't know what to do." I groaned in frustration and tried to force the tears to stay away. It was ridiculous to be upset over something that seemed so insignificant, something that shouldn't have affected me as much as it did.

"Well—" she started, just as the waitress was bringing our food. We smiled politely until she left.

"Well, darling, I think you just need to fuck her senseless. You never know, what if she just needs to get laid? Lord knows you do."

I snorted at the absurdity of her suggestion. "Yeah, right. That's the worst idea I think I've ever heard you come up with. That is definitely never happening! Next?"

That *was* the worst idea I'd ever heard, even if my body might not have agreed with me.

She laughed, seemingly oblivious to the low heat simmering inside my body. "Listen, sweetie. You can't let her bully you into moving, okay? Just try and talk to her. Like, really talk to her. Or just ignore her. Shit, I don't know, maybe kick her ass?" She shrugged.

"I don't want to move, but I don't know if I can handle feeling awkward every time I see her. Surely, as adults, we can find a way to exist in the same building."

She frowned, her expression shifting from lighthearted to serious. "I know. Like I said, either try and talk to her or just don't let her affect you. Just fake it until you make it."

"Such great advice, Drea, but I get what you're saying. I've tried to make amends, and it clearly didn't work. So maybe really ignoring her is the best alternative."

We paid our tab and headed out. She linked our arms together as we started walking toward the bookstore. Drea had a little couch set up there in the back room, and she slept there when we went out so she didn't have to drive home.

"Thanks for coming out with me. I really needed this," I said, laying my head on her shoulder as we walked.

"Of course, love."

"I'm sorry I complained about Mackenzie the whole time." She was the last person I wanted to talk about.

She nudged me and laughed. "Oh, honey, I'm sorry you have to deal with that. Your move wasn't supposed to start off like this. But it will get better, I promise. Hopefully you guys can come to some sort of civil agreement. Or maybe she'll move?" She shrugged.

"I doubt it, but thanks. Enough about me, let's talk about you. How are things with Skylar?"

Her eyes glistened at the mention of her partner, but she quickly brushed any trace of tears away. "Things are the usual. We fight, we make up—for hours—and then do it all over again."

"Babe, when are you going to lock that down? You two are so in love, it's kind of sick. And you fight over the dumbest things, just because you're both too stubborn!"

She scoffed. "Excuse me, I am not stubborn." I shot her a glare because, yes, she was!

"And that word is so..." She made a face like she'd just smelled something disgusting at the mention of love. "We're just existing, Fallon."

They had been "existing" together for three years. I couldn't help but smile at my best friend. She was in love, no matter what she told herself.

"You're delusional, but fine, I'll drop it—for now."

She smiled at me. "I would expect nothing less from you, darling." Her expression grew oddly serious, as she admitted quietly, "I don't want to lose her."

"I know, Dre. She knows too, but you need to get your shit together and stop being so hard-headed. If you don't want to lose her, pick your battles. You have to compromise sometimes. You gotta break the back and forth cycle, it's not healthy." I spoke as if I had any clue about what made a healthy relationship.

She rolled her eyes, but I saw the slight glossiness in them. "I know." Not missing the crack she tried to clear away, I squeezed her tighter.

"Good, and thank you for this, Dre. I love you. Now, go call your woman!"

She laughed and gave me a tight hug. "Things will get better, I promise. This move was not a mistake," she whispered.

I forced the tears away before I pulled back and looked at her with a smile. "Goodnight."

I wasn't entirely convinced she was right, but I kept that thought to myself.

Chapter Eight

MACKENZIE

Cheers to the fucking weekend! The past week had gone by in a blur. After the penguin incident at work, everything stayed in its place. Unfortunately, I couldn't say the same about things outside of work.

That's why alcohol was invented—to forget about the bad parts of life—at least for a few hours. Tonight, I was meeting Harper and her husband, Grant, to do just that.

We were meeting at *Queer Quarters*, one of my favorite bars. I might have been a little biased, since my best friend, Rylee, was one of the bartenders. She worked there some nights and spent her days as a barista at *Brewed Awakening*. On top of that, she ran her own photography business, *Lens and Light Photography*.

"Hey, Kenzie!" Rylee shouted from across the bar.

The bar was pretty packed, as it usually was on a Friday night, but she still made time to acknowledge everyone she knew.

"Hey!" I shouted as I slid onto an empty barstool. Rylee was finishing up with a customer when she spotted me.

When she came over, she poured a tequila shot and slid it toward me. "On the house, hun," she said with a grin.

"Thanks, Ry. I really needed this." I smiled and knocked it back. "Jesus, I'll never get used to the burn!" I all but gagged at the taste of liquid needles sliding down my throat.

She shook her head. "Hey, uhh... I saw you talking to Fallon at the coffee shop the other morning. I didn't get a chance to ask because you left, but do you know her?" She was pouring a whiskey shot for another customer.

I groaned. "Oh, yeah, she's my new neighbor. We don't get along, but how do you know her?" I paused. "Wait, don't answer that. We were at a coffee shop where you work, of course you know her. You're the friendliest person I know." I rolled my eyes at myself, embarrassed.

She laughed as she walked over to my side of the bar and refilled my empty shot glass. "She comes in almost every morning and orders the same iced coffee. I always give her a little extra espresso. She is the sweetest. How do you not get along with her?"

I scoffed. "To you, maybe. But according to her—several times, to be exact—I'm a bitch." I shook my head and took the shot Rylee had poured.

I needed everyone to stop bringing her up. I'd done a great job ignoring her all week after the coffee incident.

"I mean..." she said, and I glared. "Kidding. Well, sometimes you can be a little harsh, but what happened?"

I sighed. "The first night we met, I guess I was kind of being a bitch, but I was tipsy, okay? Anyway, it's been a little rocky ever since."

"Hey, sis!" Thankfully, Harper came up and threw her arms around me, interrupting the tense conversation I didn't want to be having. "Hey, Ryl."

Rylee looked at me like she knew I had just gotten lucky. She could be as stubborn as Harper when it came to getting information out of someone.

"Hey, Harper. Hey, Grant!" Rylee greeted them with the same warm expression she always wore.

Grant grinned widely. "Hey, Rylee, nice to see you. Hey, little sister," he said, giving me a tight hug.

"Okay, okay. Jesus, I can't breathe, Grant."

Harper smacked his arm. "Honey, I think she knows you missed her. Let her go, please."

He laughed and finally let go. They took the stools next to me and ordered drinks while we talked and laughed for a while.

I had to force down tears a few times. I sat there smiling, but behind that smile was an overwhelming sadness that threatened to consume me.

I was grateful for how my life was going and for all the people in it, but I was especially grateful for Harper. After our mom died, she was all I had. She kept me standing when all I wanted to do was crumble into the earth.

There were days when I didn't want to leave my bed, but I always made sure to talk to Harper—even if it was about something as mundane as what we were having for dinner. I needed to know she was still there.

I honestly don't know where I would've ended up if she had decided to side with our parents that night.

By the time I left my sister and Grant at the bar, it was a little after ten. I loved seeing my family, but I was tired and ready to go home.

Literally running into Fallon had set the whole week off. I was already running late and in a shitty mood that morning, and I may have snapped.

Okay, I did snap. It was just that every single time I saw Fallon, I didn't know what it was about her—the awkward walks down the hall, the elevator rides. You could've cut the tension with a knife.

The past few weeks had been a nightmare. I'd seen her almost every day, whether I was taking out the trash or coming home. I honestly tried to ignore her. And some days I succeeded. But some days I couldn't help it. I made jokes when I was uncomfortable, and standing in awkward silences made me uncomfortable—not to mention she looked so damn cute when she was mad.

But then I'd get mad too, like when she ran me down. I was already in a horrible mood, and I flew off the handle. I felt bad for insulting her again—that time, I really was being an asshole.

Okay, maybe the other times I was too. I wanted to apologize again a few other times, but I stopped myself each time. She didn't want my apology; she made that perfectly clear, and I couldn't exactly blame her.

I was grateful when I came home and didn't run into her. I wanted one day without seeing her or bickering with her—one day without all these thoughts of her running through my mind.

I got on the elevator and let out a breath of relief when I saw it was empty. Just before the doors could close, a hand slipped through, stopping them and making them slide open again.

A voice came through on the other end, asking me to hold the elevator, and as the doors fully opened, I tensed.

Fallon.

Neither of us spoke, but her stunned expression spoke volumes, and it said the same thing as mine: *Shit.*

The doors shut, and I turned to face her. I was having a nice night and wanted it to end that way. I kept thinking about what Harper said, and I knew I was going to regret saying anything, but I just...

I cleared my throat. "Uh, hi."

I shouldn't have been surprised when she didn't answer, so I waited a few seconds before calling her again.

"Fallon?"

She didn't respond or even look in my direction.

"Hello? Fallon?" I waved my hand, as if I thought she couldn't see me.

When she still didn't answer, I sighed. "You can't ignore me forever. As much as I'm sure you'd love to, we see each other too much, and I'm very hard to ignore."

She scoffed. "Sure I can, and yes, we do. Way too much."

I laughed. "Oh, come on. You know you love running into me. I bet it brightens up your day."

She turned to me and scowled. "Oh, please, Mackenzie."

For some reason, I really liked the way she said my name, even though I shouldn't have. "Oh, so she's a beggar?"

She rolled her eyes and turned away. "Look, I'm sorry, I'm just trying to lighten the mood," I said.

But of course, she stood staring at her phone as if I had never said anything at all.

"Okay, fine." I threw my hands in the air and let it go.

We rode the rest of the way in silence. We were almost to our floor when—

"Oh, shit," she said, holding on to the railing as the elevator lights flickered and it came to a screeching halt.

"Well, isn't this perfect?" I muttered as I walked over to the phone.

It rang a few times, and I spoke with the person on the other end when they finally answered. "Hi, yes, my name is Mackenzie. We're stuck in the elevator on the fourth floor. Okay, thank you." I hung up and turned back to Fallon.

"He said someone should be up shortly—about thirty minutes at the most."

"Great," she replied dryly.

Of all the people to be stuck on an elevator with, it just had to be the most beautiful, infuriating woman. Just. My. Luck.

We sat there in silence for a good ten minutes. Fallon sat in one corner, and I sat in the other. We both had our knees pressed to our chests, and our hands wrapped around our legs. She had her head in her lap, I had mine tilted back against the wall with my eyes closed.

The only sounds in the elevator were our breathing and the thoughts cycling through my head. The silence was killing me.

I was about to say something when Fallon spoke first. "This has been the worst week ever!" She threw her head back against the wall, closing her eyes.

"I'm sorry." I wasn't only talking about the elevator.

She turned her head toward me and scoffed. "Oh yeah, I'm sure you are. This is your fault, anyway."

I frowned. "How exactly is it my fault? Yeah, I totally broke the elevator on purpose just so I could be stuck in here with you."

"I wasn't talking about the elevator, smart-ass! I was talking about my shitty life this whole week."

I chuckled. "So you're an ass woman, noted. But please, enlighten me—how is your shitty life my fault?"

"Because it was just fine until I met you!" she snapped. My eyebrows shot up in surprise. "I've been looking forward to moving here since I was a kid. I finally got the courage after a really bad breakup, and all I wanted was to celebrate with people I care about, but no, that was just too much to ask for."

She stood up at this point, fully prepared to let me have it, and I was going to let her give it to me—

"Then, after only a few weeks of moving in, some pretty, angry loner—"

"You think I'm pretty?" I asked, grinning widely.

She rolled her eyes and continued. "Who doesn't even know me, decided to ruin it and insult me. You use every chance you get to insult me."

I raised an eyebrow at her, but she didn't stop.

"On top of that, you make it impossibly tense every time I leave the house. I try my best to avoid you or ignore you, but we always end up bickering. And for what, Mackenzie? What is the point? Why does my presence piss you off so much? Either attempt to be nice, or at least civil, or fuck off, because, frankly, I'm over it!"

I stood up and walked over to her. She was in the middle of the elevator, and I stopped a few feet away.

"Have you been holding that in a while?" I asked. Her only response was a scowl, so I kept going. "Is it my turn now? Or do you want to keep running that pretty little mouth?"

She raised her eyebrows in what looked like a challenge.

"Good. First, you have some nerve. In case you forgot, I tried to apologize. We both drank too much, and neither of us handled it well. Things got out of hand, and I tried to make things right, but you wouldn't even hear me out." I took a deep breath before continuing, as she stood there without a word.

"Second, we live across the hall from each other, Fallon—or did you forget? Too busy getting plastered and running people down in the hall-way? As much as I would love nothing more than to avoid you, it's just not possible. Your 'presence' pisses me off because, as much as I want to ignore you, I can't. Even when you're not around."

Her brows knit in confusion, but I kept going, not elaborating on that last part.

At this point, I was talking just a little bit louder, and her face was turning red, but the words were spilling out. It was like a waterfall, and I couldn't stop it. All the anger and frustration that had built up—I couldn't take it anymore. I didn't know who I was more angry with.

Was I angry at her for yelling at me? For coming into my life and messing up my peace? For taking over my thoughts and making me crazy? For being so beautiful it physically hurt? For having a voice that made my insides knot every time I heard it? For having a sassy-ass mouth I wanted to taste? For being so infuriating?

Or was I more angry at myself for acting out of drunken anger and insulting her? For being in a pissy mood and lashing out at her, even after she apologized? For being a total bitch? Or for having all of these thoughts and not being able to do a damn thing about them, even if I wanted to?

I stepped a little closer so that we were connected toe to toe. "As far as being nice, you don't deserve my *nice*. Frankly, sweetie, you don't deserve an ounce of my anything. I'm not the reason for your shitty life—that's all on you. Maybe if you got your head out of your own ass, your friends wouldn't need to drink just to be around you. Maybe, if you partied a little less and actually did something useful, your life would be a little better." Shit. The words came out before I could stop them.

Fallon's eyes turned hazy and tears swelled up behind them.

I opened my mouth, about to apologize, but closed it. It was too late to take it back, and I doubted she'd want to hear anything else from me.

She was silent for a long while, and I could see in the way her jaw ticked that I hit a nerve.

"Fallon, I—"

"I hope you feel better about yourself, Mackenzie. Screw you." It was barely above a whisper, but the impact of her words reverberated against the elevator walls like a scream.

I didn't feel better, and honestly, I had no idea why I said any of it. She just infuriated me, and it wasn't only the music. I didn't care about the party. That night, I was tired and irritated because I just wanted peace, but after that?

I didn't want to have any feelings or thoughts about her. I didn't want to find any part of her sexy, especially not those freckles—or the way her eyes got darker when she was angry. What was it about those damn freckles that made all my thoughts disappear?

I blame it on the elevator. Being trapped in tight spaces can mess with your brain. Not to mention, she kept going off on me. My fight-or-flight senses kicked in, and in that moment, I chose to fight.

I was really trying to fight this feeling, hoping if I kept my distance, it would make things easier, but it seemed to be making things worse.

I didn't want to make her cry, though. That wasn't part of the plan. I just didn't want to get too close or too friendly. I could never get too close to anyone again—not after the last time.

But it was inevitable. All the tension built up over these past few weeks—I guess neither of us could take it, and it took being trapped in a tight space to let it all come crashing out.

Still, aside from the anger, I felt heat swimming within me, and I couldn't tell if it was the closed space or the fact that I was stuck with this woman I'd really upset. I also felt a little bad. Okay, really bad. I definitely shouldn't have said any of that. I didn't know why I even cared. Maybe I should've apologized, but I knew she wouldn't want to hear it.

She silently looked at me for a moment. Her arms seemed to flex at her side, and I wouldn't have been surprised if she was thinking about slapping me.

There was something in her eyes that I couldn't quite figure out. Did she have more to say? Was she actually going to slap me? Would I deserve it? It was taking everything I had not to grab her and kiss her— *Where did that thought come from?*

I just royally pissed her off. Kissing was not on her to-do list, and it shouldn't have been on mine either. It *wasn't* on mine, and I needed to get the hell out of that elevator.

Fallon and I weren't meant to be anything more than neighbors, that much was made clear.

Still, I wished I knew what she was thinking, or even what I was thinking. All I knew was that I fucked up, and for some reason, I didn't feel good about it.

She opened and closed her mouth a few times, as if debating what to say, and a single tear slid down her cheek before she turned away and walked toward her corner of the elevator. She sat back down, knees drawn to her chest, and angled herself toward the elevator walls. She turned to stare at them, not moving again.

I stood there for a few minutes, about to return to my corner, when the phone rang. I picked it up after the third ring and let out a long sigh before answering. "Hello?" I said. "Oh, okay, and how long will that take? Thank you."

I went to sit in my corner, laying my head back against the wall. "Well, they said it'll be another forty-five minutes to an hour. Something about getting a part they don't have here. I don't know."

She didn't even turn when she responded. "Great." It came out soft and sad.

We sat in silence for what felt like days.

Finally, I managed to find my voice and cleared my throat. I couldn't stand the silence anymore, and the guilt gnawed at me. "Fallon?" I said, but she didn't look at me.

"Fallon?" Nothing.

I sighed. "Okay, I know you probably won't believe me, and you have every right not to, but I'm really sorry. It's just…" I wasn't sure anything I said could've made it better.

She slowly turned to face me, her voice barely a whisper. "You're right, I don't believe you." Then, without another word, she turned back around.

"It was a dick move and I shouldn't have said any of that."

She looked over to me and shifted a little, a small smile playing on her lips. I wanted to rip the doors open and run out of there. That smile was more dangerous than anything else I could've imagined.

"Yeah, it *was* a dick move, and no, you shouldn't have, but you did. You might think you do, but you don't know me at all."

"I know, and I know I can't take it back, but I really am sorry."

We looked at each other for a few minutes. I opened my mouth to speak when the elevator doors opened.

"Listen, Fallon—"

"Oh, thank God!" Fallon jumped up and ran out the door. I stayed back for a second, giving her time to get home. I didn't have it in me to have another minute of awkward silence.

Chapter Nine

FALLON

I could not have gotten home fast enough! As soon as those doors opened, I wasted no time getting the hell out of there.

What the hell was that? I was still trying to process what happened.

All I wanted to do was snuggle in my blanket on the couch and watch some trashy television. I exhaled rather dramatically and sank into the couch. I turned on the TV, fully prepared to relax and escape from the day, but nothing happened.

I didn't do anything except stare at the damn thing. Losing the motivation to watch other people's dramatic lives, I turned it off and dropped the remote onto the table. Huffing, I got up and went to my room.

I was in such a sulking mood that I didn't bother changing out of my clothes or taking off my makeup. I threw myself on the bed and stared at the ceiling.

The day started out so well. I needed the time I spent at the bookstore and getting drinks with Drea. But all good things must come to an end, especially when Mackenzie's involved.

I came home from a great day, only to get trapped in an elevator with the last person I ever expected.

I went off on her, which felt great, but then she insulted me again, and that didn't feel so good.

I was so close to slapping her, but I knew that would've hurt me more than it would've hurt her.

All the anger and tension had built up, and I lost it. I'd never done that before, but it didn't feel as good as I thought it would.

I'd be lying if I said I didn't want to kiss Mackenzie in that elevator. It didn't make sense. She'd just insulted me, and I was still fighting back tears. But the way the air between us thickened, the way the silence screamed at me... I was both furious and drawn to her at the same time.

It took everything I had to turn around and ignore the impulse running through me. Could she tell I wanted to kiss her? What the hell was happening to me? The tension was so damn heavy, I could hardly breathe. I closed my eyes, but I couldn't stop the tears from falling.

This move was supposed to be the start of something amazing. I'd only lived here for a few weeks, and I already had an enemy?

She wasn't wrong, though. I couldn't completely blame her for the way my life had been going, but she hadn't exactly made things easier, either.

We might have had a sliver of a moment in the elevator, but it fizzled out as soon as those doors opened. For the rest of the night, I stayed in bed, trying to push the tears away.

I woke up the next morning and texted Drea:

Me: Thank you for the girls night! xoxo

Drea: You're welcome, did you take my advice?

Me: What advice?

Me: Oh God! No, I didn't fuck her.

Drea: ☹

Drea: Fine, did you see her?

Me: Yeah I saw her. Ran into her on the elevator.

Drea: Ohh, spicy!

Me: 🫠 Hardly.

Drea: Did you kiss her? Kill her? Do I need to help you hide the body?

Me: Lol no I didn't kiss her.

Me: Didn't kill her, but it's still early. I'll keep you on speed dial.

Drea: Lol so what? Did you just sit there in silence? Awkward…

Me: Well not exactly…

Drea: …

Me: There was silence.

Me: Then yelling.

Me: Then more silence.

Drea: Interesting, can I get a little more detail?

Me: Ugh. Well, there was yelling, then she insulted me again and I was seconds away from slapping her. Basically she said if I wasn't useless I wouldn't have a shitty life and my friends wouldn't need to drink to be around me. ☹

Drea: Fucking bitch!

Drea: Sorry that it's your life. Don't listen to her, you know we love you!

I tumbled out of bed and jumped in the shower, desperate to wash away the memories of last night. But as the water ran over me, I couldn't stop thinking about Mackenzie.

Something had to give. I couldn't go around every single day on edge, trying to avoid her. We were neighbors, for crying out loud—it's not like she lived on a different floor where I could actually keep my distance.

While eating breakfast, I started missing my brother, so I called my mom to talk to him and take my mind off things.

Excitement filled his voice as he talked about the new dinosaur toy he got for his birthday and how school was going. His favorite part, he told me, was doing science experiments and watching things change colors. He was such a vibrant little man.

When he asked when I was coming home, I had to clear my throat to keep from getting choked up. "Really soon, bub. You can show me your new dinosaur, and maybe we can do an experiment together," I told him.

"Okay, but real soon, though. I miss you, sissy. Okay, Mama. Bye, sissy. I love you."

The line went quiet before my mom's voice came through on the other end. We said our goodbyes and hung up. Caleb had to get to school, and I needed to get ready to leave, myself.

I was headed to get coffee when a thought made me pause.

Maybe I should try to apologize again. I didn't want to keep living with the awkwardness or the anger, and one more attempt couldn't hurt. She had apologized, so maybe this time wouldn't go so terribly. Maybe.

My phone rang as I was getting closer to *Brewed Awakening*, and I smiled when I saw who it was. "Hey, Pen, what's up?"

"Hey, Fallon. I just wanted to make sure you were alright. Drea told me what happened with Mackenzie."

I groaned. "Oh, yeah, I'm okay. It was an intense situation, but I'm glad it's over now."

Maybe the fight in the elevator was the first step toward making amends. As strange as it sounded, maybe it needed to happen to open the door to something new.

"Do you need me to come kick her ass or something, sweetie? I will leave the house right now!"

I couldn't help but appreciate the thought. It wasn't exactly comforting, but knowing I had my best friends in my corner made me feel a little better.

"No, Pen. I'm fine, but thanks. As angry as I was, I shouldn't have even let my thoughts get to that point. I don't want to be like... I can't..." I trailed off, unable to say the words out loud.

Luckily, Penelope knew me well enough that I didn't have to. "You will not be like him, do you understand? You are nothing like him. You didn't do anything. It's not like you punched her—Shit. Sorry, Fal."

I cleared my throat. "It's okay, Pen, I know you're right. Listen, I'm heading in for coffee. I'll talk to you later, okay? I'm alright, I promise."

I ended the call and stepped inside the coffee shop. The scent of brewing coffee and freshly baked pastries wrapped around me, instantly easing the tension in my shoulders.

Scanning the room, my eyes landed on Rylee, who stood behind the counter with a bright smile.

"The usual, Fallon?" Rylee asked as I approached her.

"Surprisingly, no. I'm not here for me." I was already starting to regret this brilliant plan of mine.

I had gotten into another fight with Mackenzie and called her a bitch at least three times. I was delusional if I thought a cup of coffee would make all my problems disappear, but that didn't stop me from trying.

"Oh? Okay, what can I get you, then?"

"Well, I'm not too sure. I wanted to see what you'd recommend. It's for my neighbor, Mackenzie—I think I've mentioned her once or twice." Or every time I've gotten coffee since I met her.

"Anyway, I kind of spilled her coffee the other day, and I wanted to apologize. We haven't exactly been friendly toward each other, and last night was... bad." I groaned, shrinking into myself at just the memory of what happened.

She blinked. "Oh, um... well, I know she's a big fan of mocha, so how about an iced latte with extra mocha?"

"That sounds good." I smiled, but then confusion hit, and I frowned. "Wait, does she come in here a lot?"

She laughed. "Sometimes, but Mackenzie is one of my best friends."

Horror washed over me. I had complained about her friend—a lot. Her best friend.

"Oh my God, Rylee, I had no idea. I'm so sor—"

"Don't worry about it. I know she can be a lot sometimes."

I was tempted to agree but thought better of it. "Well, like I said, I wanted to apologize. I'm not sure it'll go well, and I don't even know if she works today or when, but I thought I'd try."

She smiled. "She does work today, but not for another hour or so, so your timing is perfect. Let me get her drink started."

"Thanks, Rylee, and again, I'm so sorry."

"It's alright, Fallon, really."

I felt awful. I wouldn't have been surprised if Mackenzie already told her everything that had happened between us. Hopefully, the coffee would be the first step toward making amends.

I didn't know what I'd do if it wasn't. Maybe I could move to a different floor? The idea of moving sounded horrendous, though.

"Can I ask what happened between you two?"

I rolled my eyes. "We got into another big fight."

She looked at me with wide eyes. "Oh?"

I sighed. "Yeah. We both said a lot of hurtful things. Anyway, I'm hoping this will be like a peace offering."

"Wow... well, I hope it all works out. And I'm sorry things aren't going great with you guys."

"Me too." I shrugged.

"Well, I hope things get better for you. Here you go, Fallon."

"Thanks. Have a good one." I took the coffee with a smile and headed out the door.

"Good luck!" she yelled as I was leaving.

I turned around. "Yeah, thanks. Bye!"

The whole walk home, I couldn't stop fidgeting with my fingers. What if she yelled at me again? What if she threw the coffee or slapped me? It would be well-deserved, that's for sure.

There was no way this would end well. It couldn't. She'd probably think I was trying to hit on her or that I was pathetic. I didn't know which was worse.

We saw too much of each other to keep fighting or ignoring one another—not that I'd been able to ignore her anyway. She was everywhere, even when I didn't see her.

I debated knocking on her door, but every time I tried, I chickened out.

The last time I saw her was in the elevator, and a feeling of dread buried itself in the pit of my stomach.

Instead of knocking on her door, I decided to wait outside like a creep. A few people walked by, but I pretended to be on the phone.

Finally, after about ten minutes, her door opened, and she stopped when she saw me.

My heart was racing a million miles a minute, and I wanted to abandon the whole idea.

"Hi," I said with a half-smile.

She looked me up and down, like a predator sizing up its prey and contemplating its next move. The action made it feel like the coffee might slip from my hands.

"Good morning," she said dryly. There was no emotion in her tone or on her face. Her expression was unreadable, and it made me want to run away. Maybe this wasn't the best idea.

"I, uh…" I cleared my throat. *Breathe, Fallon. Take a deep breath. You can do this.*

"I got this for you." I held out the cup of iced coffee.

She didn't take it, and a hint of confusion crept onto her face.

"It's not poisoned or anything." I tried to sound reassuring, but it came out sounding creepy instead. *Why would I say that? Now she probably thinks it is poisoned.*

"Why?" she asked with a furrowed brow.

Deep breaths, Fallon. Do not give up unless she starts yelling. Then, you can throw the coffee in her face!

"I spilled yours, and I wanted to replace it."

She still didn't take the coffee or say anything at all. She just stood there like I hadn't spoken. I was half-tempted to set it on the floor and bolt.

Literally. In that moment, I wouldn't have been above sprinting down the hall like a crazy woman.

"It's from *Brewed Awakening*, obviously." I turned the cup to show the coffee shop's logo. "Rylee said you two are friends. I wasn't sure what to get you, but she told me you like mocha. Will you please take it?" I pleaded, desperate to get this over with.

"You asked Rylee what I like?" she asked slowly, as if trying to process my words.

Her eyebrows lifted in surprise. By what? I wasn't sure. Was she insulted that I talked to her friend? That we talked about her?

Whatever it was, it made my heart pound a little faster, and I caught myself chewing on my bottom lip.

This was not going how I had hoped, and I felt nauseous. To be fair, I wasn't sure what I was hoping for exactly.

I wished she had taken the damn drink so I could've left.

"Yeah." I shrugged. "I wanted to apologize for ruining your morning, and for... everything else. I know, it was a stupid idea. I just..." I sighed. "I'm really sorry."

She smiled—she genuinely smiled—and I didn't know how to handle it. "Well, thank you." She finally reached out to grab the cup, and our fingers grazed.

My breath caught in my throat as our eyes met. The heat of her touch sent an electric current through my body, and the fire in her stare spread throughout me. *Get it together, Fallon. Jesus!*

I reluctantly let go of the coffee, watching her take a sip. She smiled as she pulled the cup away from her lips. "Rylee's drinks never disappoint." Her tone was warm and genuine.

"I'm glad you like it."

We stood there, not saying anything for a few seconds.

After what felt like a lifetime of silence, she cleared her throat. "Well, I'd better go. I have to get to work. Thanks again for the coffee." Her smile faded, and before I could say anything, she was already gone, leaving the space colder than before.

"Right, well, you're welcome!" I yelled down the hall, feeling like a pathetic loser. I think that went okay, but honestly, I had no idea. Hopefully, it was the start of something better.

Chapter Ten

MACKENZIE

I could hardly get any work done the past few days. My mind was still in that hallway.

I was shocked to see Fallon standing outside my door, holding a coffee. After the elevator incident, I didn't think I'd see her again anytime soon—let alone see her bringing me something.

When our fingers touched again, and I felt a spark surging through my entire body, I knew I had to leave.

I called Harper to see if she could come over after I got off work. I missed my sister, and we rarely got to spend time together outside of our monthly dinners.

She was always busy with Grant and with her work as a divorce lawyer, just like our parents had been with theirs. I'd already disappointed them long before I decided not to follow in their footsteps, so I didn't feel guilty about choosing my own path.

"I'm so glad you invited me over, Boog. I feel like I never see you!" she grumbled. She plopped down on the couch and made herself at home.

"I'm just sorry you can't stay longer. I freaking miss you, Harper!"

"Ugh, I know. I miss you too, but it's date night with Grant," she sais, smiling.

Harper and Grant had been married for seven years, but they still acted like they just met. It was nauseatingly cute.

"I know, I get it. I'll take any time I can have with you!"

"So, what's new? How's the aquarium?" she asked.

I took a sip of my wine and grinned, my mind racing through memories of all my favorite animals at the aquarium. Honestly, who wouldn't love sea otters doing flips or penguins waddling around like little tuxedoed businessmen?

"It's really good. They've been giving me a little more responsibility lately—overseeing the bigger corporate events. It's been hectic, but I've been enjoying the learning experience."

I was the head coordinator for all the events and promotions at *The Coral Cove Aquarium*. I started as a gate attendant about seven years ago, and worked my ass off to get where I was in the company.

"That's great." She took another sip of her water and remained unusually quiet.

I knew my sister well. She loved gossip, and I could tell she was itching to talk about a certain redhead who had been the center of our last conversation. A redhead who seemed to be the center of a lot of our conversations lately.

"So…" she said, adjusting herself on the couch. *Wait for it…*

"How's it going with your new neighbor? Fallon, right?" she finished. *And there it was.*

"Wow, you waited a solid five minutes. I'm impressed," I said, checking my imaginary watch.

She shot me a glare, and I let out a sigh. "Nothing's going on. We either ignore each other or argue."

I wasn't about to tell her anything about the brief moments of electricity I felt anytime we were inches apart. She would've jumped on my couch like Tom Cruise and analyzed every detail that wasn't there.

"Rylee told me you two had a moment at *Brewed Awakening*?"

A moment? We barely said five words to each other. What kind of moment could we have possibly had in that timeframe? There wasn't even any smiling happening, except maybe the forced kind.

"Hardly. She was leaving as I was coming in. I let her pass. No moment," I said.

"Well, is she cute?" she asked.

"Why would that even matter? We can't stand each other."

"I don't know, Kenzie, but is she?"

I sighed again, trying to keep my frustration in check. I wanted nothing more than to move on from this line of conversation.

Why was it so much easier to talk to animals than to humans? Houdini would never make me think about the way my breath got lost in my throat when I first saw her sparkling gray eyes, or how utterly adorable she looked when her cheeks turned the same color as her hair.

"I guess, but it doesn't matter. It's not happening. Can we talk about something else, please?" She wasn't just cute, she was so much more than that.

The first thing I noticed were her freckles. They reminded me of tiny constellations that were scattered across her cheeks and nose. It was like the universe decided to leave a map of stars.

And when she smiled—man, it was like the sun breaking through after a stormy day.

But her freckles and smile together... I shook away the warm feeling in my chest.

She shrugged. "Fine, have it your way."

We sat and talked more about her gushing over Grant and how work was going. After about an hour, it was time to say goodbye.

"Well, I better go. Grant is waiting to get his ass kicked at Monopoly." She hugged me and headed for the door. "I love you, sis. I hope everything works out."

"Love you," I replied, my voice quieter than I intended. I hoped so, too, but the thought of talking about it more was exhausting.

After Harper left, I refilled my wine glass and started heading out the door. I needed some fresh air, and a space to think.

Not to my surprise, I didn't see Fallon. It had been radio silence. Ever since she apologized, I hadn't seen or heard from her. Not that I was actively looking for her, of course.

I went down to the elevator. I took it to the top floor and headed toward a door all the way down at the end of the hall.

Through the door was a set of stairs that led to my favorite spot in Seattle—the rooftop.

The roof had a few tables and chairs set up all around. The tables were made of rustic wood, and I loved the cool, laid-back vibe they gave off. Surrounding the tables were two chairs with orange cushions.

There were potted plants scattered around, and twinkling string lights strung across the space.

I'd sometimes go up to the roof to think and escape from life. I mostly went up at night—watching people on the street or looking at the stars when they were visible. It was my peaceful space away from the noise of the city below.

I opened the door and was so surprised that I forgot to prop it open. "Oh, shit!" I turned around as soon as the door slammed shut.

Fallon quickly turned to glance at me before looking back down toward the street.

"Hey. Sorry, I didn't mean to scare you," I said.

She didn't turn back around or say anything.

"Okay then," I muttered quietly to myself.

I walked over and took the spot next to her, leaning against the railing.

She held a glass that looked like it was filled with white wine and was slouched over the ledge.

She wore a pair of red silk shorts with a matching long-sleeve shirt, the white buttons running all the way up. Her hair looked wet, as if she'd just taken a shower.

Great, now I was thinking of her in the shower. That was definitely not what I needed to be thinking about—at least not with her right next to me.

I shook the dirty images out of my mind and turned to face her. "Good evening," I said with a wide smile.

I remembered the coffee in the hallway and assumed we were the best of friends—ready to french braid each other's hair and eat a gallon of ice cream. Okay, not really, but we were at least on speaking terms, right?

She let out a soft sigh. "Hi, Mackenzie."

"Don't worry, I'm not here to fight."

She looked at me with a slight smile before turning back to look down at the street, and my shoulders relaxed slightly. That was a good sign. "Good, me neither. What *are* you doing here, then?"

"I come up here to think sometimes. It can be pretty peaceful. And how do you know about this place? Do you have other friends in the building I don't know about?"

She chuckled softly. "I don't think I'd consider us friends. And there's a lot you don't know about me."

"You bought me coffee, and we aren't friends? Ouch, Sunshine." I put my hand to my chest and gave a dramatic pout.

She rolled her eyes. "I'm sure you'll survive. Besides, it was an apology, not a friend request."

"Well, then. I'd ask you to leave, but it seems we're locked out, so it looks like you're stuck with me for a while."

She snorted. "I wouldn't have left anyway. I was up here first, and last time I checked, you don't own the roof. But if you plan to push me off, do it quickly."

I grinned. "The thought crossed my mind, but I *pushed* it away." She turned to look at me, and I winked, causing her to roll her eyes and grin.

"I'm teasing," I added, holding up my hands in surrender.

She was still smiling when she turned back toward the street, so at least we were making some sort of progress.

"So, tell me, what troubles could you possibly have? Don't tell me you're thinking of jumping off?"

She scowled at me. "You'd love that, wouldn't you?"

I raised an eyebrow. "Only if you make a dramatic exit, like in the movies."

She shot me a sideways glance, rolling her eyes. "You're unbelievable."

"Okay, okay. Give me *some* credit. You really think I'd want that? I guess you *do* think I'm a bitch." I smirked.

"I don't know what you want. And what makes you think I have troubles?" she asked, raising an eyebrow at me.

"Well, I definitely wouldn't want *that*. And because you blamed me for your terrible life."

"I should've done a lot more than just yelled at you," she said with a grin. I wished I could've read her thoughts.

I quirked an eyebrow. "Oh yeah? Like what? What else did you want to do to me?"

She smirked through her wine glass without a word, and my mind started running with all the things I imagined her doing...

I shook my head, clearing the thought. "I guess opposites attract, huh?" I raised my glass of red wine, and she glanced between our cups before looking away.

"Anyway... people usually come up here to think or have sex, but seeing as how you're alone, I figured that wasn't the case. Unless..."

She whipped her head toward me, and I smirked, wiggling my eyebrows. My stomach did a different kind of wiggle at the mental images I pictured, and my smirk grew wider.

"Oh my—grow up!" She scowled, but her cheeks turned the slightest shade of pink.

I laughed. "Hey, don't let me get in your way. Please, continue." I motioned around the rooftop.

"You really know how to talk to a woman don't you? You know, I'm surprised you're still single." She smirked. "Actually, I'm not surprised at all. You can be a bit of an ass, you know that?"

My expression turned serious. "You think I'm gay?"

Her smile fell and the pink on her cheeks darkened to a crimson. "Oh... I'm sorry, I didn't mean to—"

"I'm just messing with you. I'm definitely a lesbian." She let out a breath and I couldn't help but laugh. She was just too damn cute.

"That's... I am, too—not that you asked or anything, but..." She shook her head. "You really are such an ass, you know that?"

I chuckled. "I'm an ass? Now who's being rude? And who said I was single?"

She laughed. "You wear many hats, and I've never seen you bring anyone home or come home super late."

"Do you watch me, Fallon? How sweet. I'm touched, really." I placed a hand on my heart, trying to keep my tone light.

"Ha! I'm just observant, that's all." She laughed.

"Well, I do very well for myself, thank you."

"I bet you do," she said, turning away and looking down into her glass. It could have been wishful thinking, but her tone sounded like a mix of wanting and envy. I caught the subtle shift in her gaze and couldn't help but wonder if there was more to her words than she let on. I quickly pushed the thought out of my mind. I was being ridiculous, and it was probably the wine getting to me, causing a warm feeling inside.

"Aww, don't be jealous," I teased, leaning in just a little closer, my grin widening. "I'm not that hard to keep up with, you know."

She glanced up at me, her eyes flickering with something I couldn't quite place. "I'm not jealous," she muttered, but there was a challenge in her voice, like she was daring me to dig deeper. "What could I possibly be jealous of?"

I turned to face her, slowly crawling my hand down the railing. She looked down at the movement, and I stepped closer to her. "Oh, I don't know..." I mused.

She took her gaze off my hand and turned to look straight ahead, avoiding any form of eye contact. I didn't know if it was the wine, but a slight blush appeared on her fair cheeks.

"Maybe, that I do just fine for myself?" I brought my mouth down until it lightly grazed her ear. "Or are you jealous it's not with you?"

"Oh, please... get over yourself." She rolled her eyes and stepped back into her comfort zone, taking a sip of her wine. But the red tint on her cheeks betrayed her. "If you have to brag about how great you are, you probably aren't."

"Is that what you think? Well, if you ask nicely, I can rip those little shorts off that nice ass of yours, and show you precisely why I do so well for myself." I was desperate to have her on my couch and on her back. I wanted Fallon screaming my name as I made her come so hard, she could describe even the smallest detail of any star.

She let out a slight gasp, and I could tell her heart rate had picked up. When I leaned away, she turned to face me, her cheeks flushed pink.

"You wish." Her voice was breathy, and goddamn!

"Mm, my mistake." I smiled and turned to lean over the railing, looking at the people on the street below.

She cleared her throat. "I don't have any troubles other than you. I just wanted some peace. I wandered around... and here I am."

"Yes, you are," I said softly, keeping my gaze on the pedestrians below us. "So, what about me is troubling you?" I turned to face her again.

"I mean, where do I even begin? How much time do you have?" She grinned.

"I've got all the time in the world. We could be out here for a while." I winked.

She shook her head. "You're rude, for one."

I took a minuscule step toward her and raised my eyebrows. "Am I?"

She looked at my hand on the railing and back into my eyes. I could have cracked under the heat of her stare.

"You can't be serious. Yes, you are. Did you forget the first night we met? Or the elevator? Or the hallway? I mean, anytime, really." She wasn't yelling, but her words still stung as if she were.

My smile fell. "I could never forget the night we met, and I couldn't forget the elevator, either."

She paused, her fingers tracing the edge of her glass before she spoke. "You can't take a simple apology, and every little inconvenience seems like the end of the world to you."

"Hey, now. I took the coffee, didn't I? And I said 'thank you!' I think that counts as accepting an apology." *Another step closer.*

My hand was inches away from hers, and she didn't take her eyes off of it. I wanted to reach out and grab her hand—to feel her skin against mine in any way possible.

"You... you insult me every chance you get, but you don't even know me. And you call me 'Sunshine,' but I don't think it's a compliment."

"Oh, but it is," I whispered as I put my glass on the table. "So, is that all?"

"Huh?" she asked, but the word came out breathless and short.

She looked up at me, then back down at the railing as I finally gave in to temptation and caressed her fingers with mine. She gasped at the touch, but didn't pull her hand away. Her hand was soft and delicate, like the slightest movement would've caused it to break.

When she still didn't pull away, I waited for our eyes to meet again before I spoke. "Is that all that's bothering you?"

"Well, the night is still young..." She pulled her hand back, just slightly. Her gaze flickered to my lips and back to meet my eyes.

"That is true, but do you know what I think, Fallon?"

"I don't really care," she said in a hushed tone. She tilted her head down to look at the floor, avoiding me altogether.

"I think you do, but..." I stepped closer, so close I could feel the heat radiating off her.

I grabbed her chin and gently tilted her head up to meet my eyes, causing a sultry gasp to escape from her lips.

Taking the wine glass from her hands, I sat it down on the table next to mine. "I think what's really bothering you is how badly you want to hate me, but you can't. You're bothered because you can't get me out of your head, and every time you see me, you wonder if I'll kiss you. You may not like me, sure, but you can't deny how much you want me." I released her chin to push a strand of hair back behind her ear, and her breath caught slightly. I took a small step back, but her eyes never left mine.

"That's not true," she said in a shaky whisper.

"It's not? Hmm. So, in the elevator, you didn't think, even for a split second, about kissing me? About what our lips would feel like together? When you spilled my coffee, your eyes didn't go to my chest when you thought I wasn't paying attention? I know that you couldn't help but look down for a few selfish seconds. I don't know a lot about you, Fallon, but I do know that much. And do you want to know how?"

I placed my hand on her waist, pulling her closer. She inhaled softly, instinctively grabbing my arm. Her touch burned against my skin, sending a jolt of electricity through me, igniting a deep desire.

"I... uh, no?" Her dismissal sounded more like a question. She cleared her throat as her cheeks turned a blazing shade of crimson.

I moved my mouth to her ear and whispered, "Because, Fallon, these are all the thoughts I have, too."

"You don't know what I want." Her breathing was uneven and I gazed into her eyes as she stared back at me. Looking into her eyes was like looking at the moon and the stars. They were drawing me into another galaxy, and I didn't know if I would ever find my way out.

"Maybe you're right. So, tell me I'm wrong, Fallon. Tell me I'm an insufferable, arrogant asshole, and that you'd rather jump off this roof than to even think about kissing me. Tell me, and I'll walk away right now."

She stood there for a while and didn't say anything, indecision written all over her face.

I leaned in closer, my lips almost grazing hers, when the door swung open.

"Oh shit, sorry. I didn't mean to interrupt. I didn't think anyone would be up here." A deep voice shattered the moment, pulling us apart.

Fallon cleared her throat. Our eyes were still locked, and I felt her slowly pull away from me.

"I better go," she whispered, her voice barely audible. She turned to the man who'd just interrupted, her focus shifting entirely back to reality. "You're not interrupting. I was just leaving. Uh, we got locked out, so make sure you prop the door open." She walked toward him, then paused at the door, turning back to face me. Her expression was unreadable, but then, without a word, she was gone.

"Yeah, thanks," the man said as she left, checking her out the whole way. He propped the door open and whistled, turning to me. "You are one lucky woman. Your girl is so hot."

I fought the urge to gag and forced a tight smile. "She's not... she's just my neighbor."

I gave him a quick nod and turned on my heel to walk away, quickening my steps as I headed back to my apartment, my face burning with frustration. I needed a cold shower. What did I almost do?

When I turned the corner toward my apartment, I saw Fallon at her door. She was getting her keys out when I approached, pausing for a brief moment without looking up.

"That's the second time we got trapped together. I'm starting to think the universe is trying to tell us something." I laughed.

She shook her head and unlocked her door. When she opened it, I grabbed her wrist, stopping her. "Wait, Fallon."

She stopped and turned to face me. "What do you want, Mackenzie? Do you want to insult me or fuck me? Do you want to insult me while you fuck me? Because I'm sorry to disappoint you, but being degraded is not my kink."

I let go of her wrist. "So, you aren't opposed to other types of kinks?" I smirked. "Kidding, obviously. I was just teasing, okay? I'm sorry, Fal—"

"Look." She stopped me with a sigh. "I don't know if that was some sort of game to you, or—"

"Fallon, it wasn't a game," I said, frowning at the assumption I would play with her in that way.

"Whatever it was, I don't think it's a good idea, Mackenzie. I...

goodnight." She turned away and closed the door before I could say another word.

I went inside, and let out a long breath. "Fuck." I rubbed my face and groaned, hitting my head on the door.

When I went to the roof, I was expecting to be alone. I wanted space to think and get Fallon out of my head. What I didn't want was to be trapped out there with her, and I definitely wasn't expecting to be tempted to kiss her.

I wasn't playing any games, though. Everything I told her was true. I didn't know what was wrong with me. I shouldn't want her. I couldn't.

It was the first day we didn't argue or insult each other, and I tried to kiss her? *Pull it together, Kenz!*

I shook my head. That was a mistake.

I started walking to the bathroom, but I paused. Maybe I could go back out there and knock on her door. Get her out of my system?

No! I had to force myself to keep walking and go to bed. I definitely did not need to be thinking about kissing anyone in this building.

I needed to move my legs, take them to my bed, get in, and go to sleep. I did not need to turn around and…

I sighed, accepting the inevitability. "Shit." I tossed my head back in defeat, turned around, and walked out the door.

I knocked on her door, but there was no answer. I should've gone home.

I knocked again, but still no answer. I should've taken it as a sign from the universe to walk away and leave well enough alone.

I knocked again, but this time, I kept knocking and didn't stop until the door flung open.

"Jesus Christ, what the—" She stopped when she saw me. "Mackenzie? What—"

I took a step toward her, not saying a word. Grabbing her waist, I pulled us closer together. Her face was flushed, and my heart raced.

"What are you doing?" she breathed out.

I had no fucking idea, but I couldn't seem to walk away.

"Tell me I shouldn't kiss you," I said.

"You *really* shouldn't kiss me," she whispered slowly, shaking her head.

"Then tell me not to. Please, Fallon," I begged. I needed a reason not to kiss her. I needed a reason to forget about what I was feeling and turn away.

"I need you to tell me to walk away because I'm having a very difficult time listening to myself when it comes to you right now." I waited a few seconds for her to say something—anything—but she didn't.

She looked at me with heat in her eyes, and her breathing was fast and heavy. Her gaze flickered from my eyes to my lips a few times before landing back on my eyes.

With one hand still on her waist and the other cradling the side of her face, I leaned in, only to pull back slightly just before our lips connected.

"Fallon—"

She gripped my shirt, tugging us closer. "Jesus, Mackenzie, just kiss me, please." Her words were barely above a whisper, but I heard them loud and clear.

I brushed my lips over hers lightly. As soon as I did, I knew it was a mistake—because once I felt her lips on mine, I never wanted to lose that feeling.

Her lips were soft, tasting sweet like cinnamon and vanilla. And her tongue... God, her tongue sent a tingle through every nerve in my body.

She ran her fingers through my hair, pulling us closer, deepening our kiss.

I slowly moved my hand off her face and down her back, drawing her closer. She gasped, and I grinned at the seductive sound.

I moved my hands down to her ass, and squeezed. I needed to know how it felt. If only she knew of all the inappropriate things I fantasized about when I thought of her.

She let out a gentle moan, and I swear I almost shattered. There wasn't a kiss I'd ever shared with anyone that came close to the one I experienced with Fallon. It felt as if our lips were made perfectly for each other. Every swipe of our tongues, every touch of our lips, sent a bolt of electricity through me. I couldn't get enough.

It took everything in me to force myself to end that kiss.

She looked at me with flushed cheeks and dark, hungry eyes. "Wow, I..."

"Goodnight, Fallon." I said, panting.

"I... goodnight," she whispered.

Chapter Eleven

FALLON

OH. MY. GOD! Oh my God, oh my God, oh my fucking God! I just kissed Mackenzie! How did that happen? Why didn't I stop it?

She practically begged me to say no, and yet I ended up begging her to kiss me.

I *wanted* her to kiss me. And what a kiss it was... Wow!

Our mouths molded together perfectly. Her tongue did things to my body I didn't even know could happen.

My knees almost buckled when I felt her hands grab my ass. Holy shit! I had never felt a want for someone so intensely.

I brought my fingers to my lips, still feeling the vibration of her kiss against them. Why did she stop? Why did I let her stop? Why didn't I stop her sooner? *This is so not good.*

I hit my head against the door and sighed. That should not have happened, and I shouldn't have wanted it to happen again.

I slumped onto the floor and closed my eyes.

A few minutes later, my phone went off with a text alert:

Drea: Hey, love, just seeing if you can pick up a shift tomorrow?

. . .

A distraction, good! *Perfect timing, Drea...*

> Me: Hey! Yeah, of course, no problem. Everything okay?

> Drea: Thanks a million! Yeah, Kaia has some family stuff going on.

> Drea: So, what's going on?

Oh, nothing Drea, you know, just over here making out with hot neighbors!

> Me: Nothing just got home, you?

> Drea: Were you out partying??? 😄

> Drea: Ugh, I just got into a fight with Skylar. Of course. 🫠

That comment about partying stung with the memory of Mackenzie's harsh words, but I knew Drea didn't mean it how she had.

Drea and Skylar were always on and off again. They were hopelessly in love and had been for over three years. Drea was stubborn and refused to admit it, but Skylar—despite everything—loved her and was incredibly patient. Drea didn't handle labels well, but without Skylar, she'd be a wreck.

> Me: Lol hardly. I was on the rooftop. Relaxing, well trying to anyway.

Although, a twisted part of me kind of wanted to. That kiss really messed me up.

When I plugged my phone in on the nightstand and got into bed, my body was still buzzing from the kiss. The feel of her lips on mine, her hands on my body. I could still feel the phantom touch of her, and I wanted to go back for more.

I tossed and turned for about twenty minutes, trying to get her out of my mind, with no such luck. Every time I closed my eyes, I saw her. My traitorous body could still feel her, too.

The need was too heavy to resist and I finally caved, slipping my hand in between my thighs. I was already soaked from only a few thoughts of her.

I closed my eyes and tried to picture anyone that wasn't Mackenzie, but of course, nothing worked. My mind kept creating images of her laying naked in front of me.

Every stroke of my hand against my throbbing clit was her hand. Every plunge of my fingers in and out of my needy pussy were her fingers, curling inside me. Every nipple pull, every caress of my breasts, they were all *her*.

I could feel the orgasm building up and getting closer.

Her name was just a whisper on my lips, but the desire for her was a scream. "Mackenzie." I couldn't hold it in as her name came out in a breathless moan.

When my orgasm finally came, I rode the wave of my ecstasy until the high finally dissipated. Then a wave of shame quickly washed over me.

I just... to Mackenzie...

"Fuck."

When I got to *Brewed Awakening* the next morning, Rylee asked how things were going with Mackenzie. I apologized a million more times and told her things were okay.

She asked how the apology went, and I told her it went better than I expected. I left out the part about the kiss. I felt like that wasn't my story to tell, and I didn't really want to relive it, *especially* what came after... that was the wrong choice of words.

The whole situation was messed up. How did I go from hating her, to kissing her, within a matter of days?

After my talk with Rylee, and getting coffee, I walked to the book-store and smiled when I saw Drea at the register getting cozy with Skylar.

"Looks like you two made up," I said as I walked toward them.

"That we did. Thanks for telling her to get her head out of her ass." Skylar smiled when Drea swatted her arm playfully.

"That's what I'm here for. What was it about this time?" I glared at Drea, knowing she had somehow started it.

"Look, we don't need to rehash the past, alright? Let's just move on."

Skylar laughed and shook her head. "Let's just say she thought she was complimenting her favorite part of me, but she definitely wasn't. Luckily, she *really* knows how to apologize." She winked. "Anyway, I'll let you two get to work out here. I'm headed to the back. I need to finish taking inventory so I can place the order for the truck." She kissed Drea goodbye and disappeared.

After Skylar left, Drea turned to me. "So, tell me about the roof. What happened?" She nudged.

"Oh." I groaned. "Nothing happened. We got locked out for a little while and talked, it was…" I had to search for the right word. I didn't want to give Drea too much ammunition. "Tolerable."

"Tolerable. That sounds better than horrible, I guess."

"Yeah, I guess," I said vaguely.

"Hmm… well, I would've done a lot more than just talking, if you know what I mean."

A slight blush slowly crept up my cheeks. I wasn't about to tell her the real story of what happened. The unexpected run-in with Mackenzie on the roof left me feeling so confused.

Mackenzie might have been right, but I was too afraid of getting hurt again to do anything about it.

Still, I couldn't help fantasizing about what she would look like underneath her clothes. Or how her perfect breasts would feel in my hands. And the kiss when she cornered me outside of my apartment? It took everything in me to stop myself from inviting her inside.

I hadn't been able to process any of these feelings yet, and I wasn't about to tell Drea about our kiss. I hated that Mackenzie was right—a part of me wanted her, and I hated myself for it.

I couldn't help those feelings, though. She made it difficult not to want her. Besides the fact that she was gorgeous, she wasn't necessarily a terrible person, and she actually had a great sense of humor. We got off on the wrong foot, and we both said things we shouldn't have. I didn't know what was going on, but I knew I needed to shake this feeling—it wasn't good for my mental health.

Luck was on my side as the bell above the door chimed, and Drea looked up and greeted whoever had just come in.

"Saved by the bell," I thought, thankful that I was able to avoid an awkward conversation.

"Hey there, welcome to *Open Book*."

"Hey, thanks." A familiar voice echoed through the empty bookstore, causing me to look up and freeze. *What is she doing here?*

My cheeks turned red, and embarrassment was written all over my face. The reason for my weak knees had just walked through the door, and any concept of knowing how to use my senses vanished instantly.

Mackenzie had only walked into the bookstore, and I felt as if my whole body was on fire. My legs were paralyzed and I couldn't move or think.

She wore the same Guns N' Roses shirt from the night we met, and I only hoped she was wearing shorts underneath. Because if she was naked under there—God, help me. *Get it together, Fallon. Of course she's not naked under there!*

She gave me a confused look, but smiled slightly before turning away and continuing to walk around the store.

"What is she doing here?" I whispered. When I said I needed a distraction, Mackenzie walking into the store was not what I had in mind.

"She is hot, do you know her?" Drea asked.

I narrowed my eyes at her and let out an irritated groan. "Yeah, that's Mackenzie."

"Wait, hot, bitchy neighbor, Mackenzie?" She gasped. "No freaking way!" Drea was having way too much fun with this, while I, on the other hand, wanted to crawl into a hole and die.

"What the hell is she doing here?" I closed my eyes and pressed them into my palms.

Drea shrugged. "I don't know, but you better go find out."

I groaned. "Can't I just pretend I'm not here? She'll leave eventually, right?"

"Be serious. She saw you already. And the way you talk about her, she doesn't seem like the type of person to ignore you. Just grow a pair and go talk to her."

I glared at her. "I don't talk about her that much." Drea shot me an "oh please" look in response. Okay, so maybe I talked about her a little.

I wasn't sure why I was even entertaining this ridiculous idea, but before I could stop them, my feet were moving toward her.

She was reading the back of a book from the fantasy section. The fact that she had good taste in books, didn't help with the problem of wanting her.

She looked up at me and wore the most heart-stopping smile when I stopped next to her. "Good morning, Sunshine. What a pleasant surprise."

"I'm not sure about pleasant yet, but a surprise, yes." I smirked, crossing my arms. "What are you doing here?"

"I've walked by a few times, and I wanted to check it out. I could ask you the same thing."

"I work here. My best friend, Drea, is the owner." I motioned over to the counter, where Drea was staring at us—not at all subtly either. "I work here part-time when I'm not working at the hospital. I'm an ER nurse, so I do have a job—two, actually."

"I see that, my mistake."

"Yes, well, enjoy your..." I turned the book to see the cover. "Kinky vampire book. If you need anything, please don't hesitate to ask Drea." I turned and walked away.

"Hey," she called after me, causing me to stop. "About last night..."

I froze, the memories of our kiss surrounding me. Why would she bring it up? I turned back around to face her. "Last night was a mistake, okay? Last night never happened."

I couldn't give her the satisfaction of knowing how much that kiss affected me. It was just a kiss. Surely people were left dazed and breathless after a kiss all of the time.

It was totally normal to stay awake all night wondering how someone's tongue would feel on a different set of lips. Or how their fingers would feel curled deep inside you... right?

I swallowed hard, desperately needing a gallon of water.

She narrowed her brows. "Is that what you think? That it was a mistake?"

"Well..." I sighed, trying to gather myself and search for the right words. I nervously twirled a loose strand of hair between my fingers, trying to regain my composure.

"I mean..." I cleared my throat, but no words came.

She smirked slightly and nodded. "Interesting."

Damnit! I hated that I was letting her get to me. She was just a woman, and it was just a kiss. I shouldn't have been so affected by a damn kiss!

With that reasoning, I finally found my words. "Look, it was a good kiss, okay? I'll give you that, but—"

"But it was a mistake. We got caught up in the moment, right?" she finished for me.

"Yeah, right." I sighed.

She nodded and put the book back, acting like she was unaffected by my response.

Was she really unaffected? Was the kiss not good for her? Did she not think it was a mistake, or did she agree with me that it was?

"I'm glad we're on the same page, then." She smiled. "The kiss was... okay, anyway."

I gaped at her. "Excuse me?"

She couldn't have been serious. The way she acted during that kiss told me something vastly different.

She winced. "I'm sorry, It's just... I've had better, to be honest, and—"

I took a step closer until I was inches from her. "That's bullshit," I whispered.

"I'm sorry, Fallon. It's true, I—"

I kissed her, stopping her words and letting it consume me. She tasted of strawberries and citrus, and I couldn't get enough.

When she gripped my arms and brought our bodies closer together, I let in a sharp breath.

Her mouth was claiming mine, and there was nothing I could've done to stop it.

She played me, I knew she did, but I couldn't find the energy to care. I had to taste her again.

I desperately wanted to lift her shirt and find out exactly what was underneath. My grip tightened on her shirt, pulling us closer, but it still wasn't close enough.

Eventually, reality intruded on our heated bubble, and I broke the kiss. My body still buzzed from it, and I waited for air to return to my lungs. I tried—and failed—to steady my breath while our eyes locked.

She brought her fingers to her lips, and my cheeks burned. "Was that a mistake, too?"

"I... uh..." I couldn't form words. Seriously, what was wrong with me?! Had I lost all common sense?

"Well played, Wildcat." I scowled, but it wasn't very convincing.

She laughed as she brought her hand to my face and wiped at my bottom lip with her thumb. I couldn't move. I was frozen in the moment, unsure of what to expect next.

"Well, I'd better go. Tell your friend she did a good job with her store. I'll see you around, yeah?"

I spoke softly, still confused by what just happened, and not trusting my voice to hide how I was feeling. "Yeah." *What just happened?!*

She turned and left, and my head dropped into my hands.

I turned back around to see Drea and Skylar staring at me, their mouths and eyes wide open. When did Skylar even get back?

"Don't!" I said, holding a hand up.

Drea mimed zipping her lips, and I went back to work.

What was wrong with me? I fell right into her trap, and the worst part was, it didn't bother me.

I spent the rest of the day in a haze, partly focused on work, partly confused and asking myself what the hell had happened.

The next few weeks were just plain awkward. The kiss had definitely shifted our dynamic. We used to bicker and throw insults, but after the kiss, it was... different. We would smile at each other politely, not saying anything aside from a few words.

There was one instance in the elevator where it was a little crowded and our fingers touched. We both looked down before quickly moving them away. Maybe I was crazy, but I missed her touch. I knew I wasn't ready to cross that line again, so I told myself to erase those thoughts from my mind.

It had been a long, hectic day by the time I got home from work, and I was ready to curl up on the couch and watch some reality TV.

I locked my car and headed inside, stopping before I got to the mailboxes.

Mackenzie was standing there, wearing the tightest pair of jeans I had ever seen anyone wear. The way her ass was being hugged... I blinked the thought away and checked my mail.

She must have sensed someone next to her because she stopped, but didn't say anything or look up.

When I turned to open my mailbox, she cleared her throat. "Hi."

I looked at her and smiled slightly. "Oh, hey."

"How are you?" She turned back, continuing to get her mail.

"I'm good," I said slowly. "How are you?"

This is so awkward.

I tried to calm myself and take a deep breath, but the scent of her overwhelmed my senses. She smelled like cinnamon and something that was just... her. It was erotic and way too dangerous.

She laughed. "I'm good."

"That's good." We started walking to the elevator, the sounds of our breathing filling the hall.

We rode in awkward silence, and she spoke once we stepped off. "Thanks again for the coffee, and I'm sorry for how I reacted in the hallway that morning. I wasn't in the best mood to begin with. I know it's not an excuse, but..." She trailed off, shrugging.

I blinked. "Oh... uh... you're welcome, and I get it. I should've watched where I was going."

She smiled. "It happens." When she got to her apartment, she stopped to face me again. "Well, bye, Fallon."

She looked as if she wanted to say more, but must have thought better of it as she turned to open her door.

"Yeah, bye," I said, and went inside.

That was...

Chapter Twelve

MACKENZIE

That was... okay. There was no fighting and no kissing. That kiss... wow.

When I decided to check out the bookstore, I wasn't expecting to see Fallon, and I couldn't hide my shock when I did.

She looked incredible in a short hunter-green dress paired with black wedge sandals. When she walked over, I did my best to play it cool—I couldn't let her see how much she affected me.

The last thing I was expecting was for her to kiss me. She claimed every part of my mouth with that kiss. I may have lied about the kiss being anything other than amazing, but I didn't expect that reaction from her.

A few hours later, after I showered the memory of our kiss away, I was sitting on the couch talking on the phone with Harper when I heard the fire alarm going off in the hallway.

"Shit, I gotta go. The damn fire alarm is going off. I'll call you tomorrow," I said as I stood up and headed for the door.

"Yeah, okay. Love you, Kenz."

"Love you, too," I replied and hung up.

When I opened my door, I saw Fallon closing hers. She looked at me for a second and smiled before starting down the hall.

Once we were outside, I took a spot next to her. I turned to look at her, but she wouldn't look at me. She stood facing straight ahead.

I wondered if she was still spooked from our kiss the other night. I couldn't blame her if she was—I was, too. I didn't know what I was thinking; I just couldn't take the tension anymore. I gave her the chance to say no, but when she kissed me back, everything changed. In that moment, I knew she wanted me just as much as I wanted her.

Running into her at the bookstore the next morning felt like a twist of fate. I hadn't expected to see her again so soon—if anything, I'd been hesitant about seeking her out in the first place. I couldn't figure out where I stood with her, or where I wanted to stand.

I didn't think she would kiss me again. It was incredibly hot seeing her take charge like that, and when she grabbed me by the shirt and claimed my lips with hers in front of the whole store, I knew that anything with Fallon was going to end terribly.

Fallon seemed a little relaxed standing next to me, but when I cleared my throat, she stiffened.

"Well, you look... comfortable," I said with a smile. She turned to glare at me, but I still caught the slight smirk she was wearing.

"I was. I was trying to sleep."

She was wearing a blue crop top and a white pair of underwear. Even though it was a chilly August night, inside my body could've been well over one hundred degrees. The way the sides of her underwear hugged her smooth legs, I could barely stand it. *Someone help me...*

"I see that." I laughed. "You didn't think to grab pants, at least? You're going to freeze."

She chuckled. "I was thinking that I didn't want to go up in smoke if there really was a fire in the building. Are you complaining? If it bothers you that much, you don't have to stand here, you know. There are plenty of other places you could go."

I turned to face her. "Nope, I'm not complaining at all." I winked.

"Good," she replied, but then she got a cold chill and shivered.

I chuckled and put my blanket around her, shaking my head.

She tried to resist at first. "I'm fine," she insisted while shrugging the blanket away.

I glared at her. "You're not fine. You're shivering."

Her eyes sparkled and she smiled. "Okay," she said, and I put the blanket back around her.

"Stop being so stubborn, Sunshine—it's not a good look on you. But this?" I smirked, letting my gaze dip to the sliver of skin where her belly button peeked out before meeting her eyes again. "This is very nice."

I tried not to let my thoughts drift lower, but I was failing miserably. My lips itched to find hers again.

Her cheeks turned a slight shade of pink. "Aren't you a charmer?" She smirked.

We heard sirens blaring, and I was thankful we could go back inside soon. I hoped there wasn't a real fire and that no one was hurt.

After what felt like hours, building management said it was all clear to go inside. They said there wasn't a fire and someone probably pulled the alarm by mistake.

"See you around." I smirked and started to walk back inside.

"Hey!" she yelled after me. "Take your blanket."

I turned to face her and paused. "Keep it. I'm not cold." I didn't need her to know that I was, in fact, freezing my ass off.

She smiled before I turned to keep walking.

When we got back inside, I opened my door and she cleared her throat. "Hey, Mackenzie?" she said, standing at her door.

I turned to face her. "Yeah?"

She walked toward me, but stopped halfway. "Thank you for the blanket, and not standing somewhere else. You're one of the only people I know here, so it was nice not to be alone or whatever."

I snorted. "You're welcome, or whatever. It would look bad if you died of hypothermia standing next to me. I'm sure the neighbors know we aren't exactly best friends, so it wouldn't be that difficult to pin your death on me."

She rolled her eyes and smiled. "Yeah, well, anyway, thanks." She reached out to hand me the blanket.

She frowned when I didn't immediately take it. "Please take the damn blanket, Mackenzie."

I should have. I really should have, but—

"You can give it to me inside... over tea?" I said instead.

I didn't know why I was inviting her in. It was a horrible idea, we both knew it.

"Oh." She cleared her throat. "I don't know if that's a good idea, Mackenzie. I mean, it's kind of late, and we really—"

"It's just a cup of tea. Unless you don't like tea, then I can find something else."

Her face was still, her expression blank.

She was right, it wasn't a good idea, and the time wasn't the only reason. That didn't stop me from hoping she would say yes, though.

"It's a peace offering, Fallon. I can leave the door open so you know I won't murder you or anything crazy," I added.

She grinned but didn't say anything.

"Look, obviously you don't *have* to. I just wanted to extend the invitation."

"No, I know. I'm just..." She sighed. She was silent for a good while before she spoke again. "Okay, yeah, sure. Thanks."

I smiled and motioned her inside.

"But *just* tea. Then you take your blanket and I leave. That's it."

I laughed, then planted a mock serious expression on my face. "Yes, Ma'am."

"Please, sit down, make yourself comfortable." I pointed to the couch once we got inside.

She sat down, and I went into the kitchen and started boiling the water. I took two water bottles from the fridge, walked over to the couch, and handed her one, sitting a few cushions away from her, making sure there was plenty of distance between us.

"Thanks," she said.

"You're welcome."

She took a sip of her water and I watched her, completely mesmerized by the way her lips glistened after the water coated them.

Maybe it wasn't the best idea, but I wasn't ready to say goodbye.

She caught me looking and she blushed before I turned away.

I cleared my throat. "So, what an eventful night, huh?"

She laughed. "Yeah, I feel like it's always like that when you're around. It's always something." She sat stiff, like she was uncomfortable.

I couldn't blame her. I hadn't been the friendliest person to be around, and we were still essentially strangers, but that didn't stop the sight from giving me a sharp pain in my chest.

"Well, that can be a good thing, though, right?"

She looked at me and grinned. "Sometimes."

The tea kettle whistled, and I stood up. "I only have chamomile, is that okay?"

"Yeah, that's fine, thank you."

"You're welcome, Sunshine."

She rolled her eyes, but she couldn't stop the smile that appeared on her lips.

While I made the tea, I just watched her. She still sat stiffly, but she was looking around, taking in her surroundings. I really hoped she didn't think I was going to hurt her or anything. That was the last thing I wanted to do.

I walked over to the couch, and handed her a cup. "It's hot, so please be careful."

"Thank you." She took the cup and sat it on the table.

I took my seat back on the couch. "So, tell me something about you," I said.

Fallon was right, I didn't know anything about her, but something was telling me I needed to.

She looked up with narrowed brows. "We don't have to do this, Mackenzie. I can just drink the tea and leave."

"Indulge me, please," I replied, smiling.

She sighed. "Okay, what do you want to know?"

"Anything you want me to know. Like you've said, I don't know you. Let me get to know you."

She cleared her throat. "Well, let's see, I just moved here a few months ago. I was living in Portland with my mom, stepdad, and little brother, Caleb. Before that I lived with an ex for a few years, but it didn't work out, clearly."

She took a sip of her tea and I just watched her, something I could've done all night.

The way she could sit there, bare-faced, hair a sleepy mess, in just a shirt and underwear, and still look like the most beautiful woman in the world—I would never understand it.

"Oh, I love to paint, and I love to ice skate. I've been doing it since I was little. I like arcade games, board games, any type of games, really, reading, and coffee. But other than that, I don't know... I'm kind of boring, I guess." She laughed.

"Not boring at all. I'm sorry it didn't work out with your ex."

"Thank you. That's mainly why I moved here. To get away and have a fresh start, you know?"

I nodded. "Yeah, I get it. So, how do you like working at the bookstore?"

Her smile only grew. "Oh, I love it! Drea is my best friend, so it doesn't really feel like work—except when she gets stressed. Then she turns into a crazy boss lady, but I can usually calm her down quickly. She's been so busy with a book signing coming up, but I make her go out with me at least once a week to have fun and relax. The bookstore is my favorite place to be, even on my off days. I love getting wrapped up in another world, even if just for a little while." Her eyes sparkled the entire time she talked about Drea and the bookstore.

I grinned, enjoying how animated she was becoming. "That's really awesome, Fallon. I'm glad she has someone like you looking out for her, and I'm glad you have a space like that."

She took the blanket off and adjusted herself on the couch. It felt good to see her getting a little bit more comfortable around me.

"So, tell me about you?" she said.

"Me? I'm boring. Probably more than you."

"Bullshit. Even though you crashed my party, you're hardly boring. Every time we're together, there's been *some* kind of excitement."

I laughed. "Well, I work at the aquarium, and I've lived here my whole life. I also love ice skating, oddly enough. I used to take lessons as a kid, and I try to go at least a few times a year. I moved into this building two years ago after I went through a really messy breakup. I have a sister, Harper, who I have dinner with at least once a month. She's the only family I have left. My mom passed away a few years ago."

I didn't know why I was telling her any of this. I didn't talk about my family life. Ever. I hardly knew her, and yet...

There was something about her that was so warm and inviting. I felt like I wanted to tell her every thought I'd ever had.

She frowned. "Oh, I'm sorry. What about your dad?"

I shrugged. "He hasn't been around since I came out. It's just been me and Harper."

She sat quiet for a moment. My fingers tingled at the memory of feeling her soft curls between them, the same red curls that were being twisted and wrapped around her own fingers as we sat together. "Will you tell me your coming out story?" she asked softly, as if she was afraid to voice her question.

"Like you said, we don't need to do this, Fallon," I said. "It's not like we're really friends or anything, right?"

She frowned. "Indulge me, please?"

"Are you sure? It's not a pretty story."

She set her cup down and scooted closer to me. "Tell me anyway."

I inhaled deeply and took a drink of my tea, wishing it was something stronger. I put my mug down and finally looked at her.

"Well, right before my eighteenth birthday, I decided I would tell my parents. I had always known, even before then, that I liked women. I mean, have you seen them lately?" She laughed and lightly nudged my shoulder. I pushed past the heat from that touch.

"I didn't want them to hear it from anyone else, but I wasn't sure how they'd react. I wasn't around a lot of queer people when I was younger, and I'd never heard my parents speak their opinions on it. I had no idea what would happen, but I knew I was their daughter, and I knew their love would have no limits."

She stared at me for a minute, as if she knew where I was going with my story, but she didn't. She wouldn't have any idea where it was going.

"I came home from school one day, the rare day both my parents were home, and knew that would be the day. I was in love, or as in love as a young kid could be, and I wanted them to know. After we graduated, we wanted to get married. Her name was Alexis."

I paused for a moment, gathering my thoughts. "Harper was in her room, visiting from law school. My parents and I weren't particularly close. I knew they loved me, but they didn't show it often. They were always busy with work. Both of them were lawyers. Well, my dad still is." I went on as her eyes locked with mine and never left.

"I asked them if they could sit with me in the living room, that there was something I wanted to talk to them about. They were reluctant at first, busy with work, of course, but I insisted. I told them it was important and couldn't wait. I sat them down and told them about Alexis. How I knew this wasn't a phase, how I had known for a long time, and how we were in love and wanted to get married after graduation. Her parents loved me and were so welcoming of me into their lives."

She took a sip of her tea. "And what did they say?" she asked.

"Well, my dad just sat there at first and said nothing. My mom looked at me, then at my dad. She took his hand and looked sad. For me or for him, I'm not sure. My mom was the first one to speak. She asked if I loved Alexis. I opened my mouth to tell her, yes, I really did, but my dad answered for me. 'No, she doesn't love her. You're too young for love, too young to think these things.'"

She frowned, but I pushed on. "His voice got louder, and I noticed Harper sitting on the stairs behind them. I told them I was almost an adult, that I knew in my heart this was who I was, and that Alexis was the person I loved. My mom was trying not to shed tears, but my dad kept yelling. He kept saying, 'It's a mistake! I didn't raise you like this! I didn't give you and your sister everything just for you to grow up to be —' My mom tried to cut him off, but he stood up, still shouting until..." I trailed off, looking down, ashamed to admit the truth.

Fallon put her hand on my leg. The warmth of her touch caused my breath to catch, and my head to tilt up to look at her. When I did, I couldn't stop the tears in my eyes. "Until what?" she asked with a sympathetic expression.

I exhaled loudly. "Until he slapped me and said, 'we did not raise you to be a fucking Dyke.'"

At this point, the tears wouldn't stop, but I couldn't look away from her. Her eyes were the only thing holding me together in that moment.

"Mackenzie..." Tears started forming behind her eyes, but I shook my head.

"Don't cry for me, Fallon. I don't deserve your sympathy." It was true. I hadn't done anything to deserve her kindness.

She frowned but didn't push. "What happened after that? What did your mom do? Harper?"

"My mom was crying, but she didn't say anything. What could she say? I was crying—not from sadness for disappointing my dad, but for the loss of him. I knew we couldn't recover from this. He walked away, and I didn't go after him. Harper was on the stairs, crying. No one could move. None of us knew what to do or where to go from there."

"Mackenzie, I don't even know what to say." Fallon started caressing my thigh and in that moment, the memories of my past didn't sting so bad.

"I didn't see him after that, except at my mom's funeral three years ago. We didn't speak and he didn't look at me. After he kicked me out, I moved in with Alexis and her family until I started college. Harper still refuses to talk to him. She said it was unforgivable, no matter how close they used to be. She wouldn't talk to our mom for a long time. I didn't blame my mom; she was married to him and couldn't say much to change anything. But Harper, she just couldn't let it go. The fact that our mom sat there and did nothing to defend me."

She removed her hand from my leg, and I missed the reassuring warmth of her touch. "So after graduation, you and Alexis?"

I laughed. "Oh, no. I was the only one in love in that relationship. I went off to college and, well, here we are."

"Yeah," she said quietly. "I'm sorry about your mom."

"Thank you." I smiled.

She looked down at her cup, looking sad, and I couldn't help but wonder what was going on in her head.

"So, how's the tea?" I asked, abruptly changing the subject.

She looked up at me. "Oh, um... it's good, thank you."

"You're welcome." I took a sip from my own cup.

She looked around my apartment. "Your place is really nice. Although, I was expecting more dark colors to match your soul."

"You think my soul is dark? After I shared my blanket with you? The disrespect! I want it back." I reached out my hand and she laughed. She gave me the blanket and I flung it over the couch.

"I'm teasing, just a little," she said. "So, are you going to give me a tour before I go?"

That was unexpected. I raised an eyebrow. "You want a tour? Why, are you planning on casing the joint?"

She laughed. "Damn, you foiled my plans! You don't have to, I'm just nosy."

I chuckled. "It's not much, but if you really want a tour, sure." I stood up and offered her my hand. "Follow me."

She took my hand and smiled back. I wanted to stay in that position for as long as possible—as long as I got to keep looking at that smile.

I pulled her close to me. "No funny business," I whispered.

She let out a slight gasp. "Not a chance," she whispered back and I grinned.

"Well, there's the patio. Nothing fancy, yet." I pointed to the patio doors.

It was a basic looking patio with two black metal mesh chairs that had tan cushions and a matching black metal table. There was a single bamboo plant in the corner in a white vase.

I let go of her hand, as I walked toward the window. "This is where all the magic happens," I said, gesturing to the window. "This is my favorite area."

The bay window had a white bench with a green-colored cushion, and gray pillows with white vertical stripes.

She laughed. "I thought your room would be your favorite area, since you 'do well for yourself.'"

"Don't be jealous." I winked and gently brushed my shoulder against hers. She rolled her eyes.

"Seriously, though. I sit here every day, reading or just looking out the window. It brings me peace on the days my mind is loud," I admitted.

"I love it," she said looking out the window.

"And this is the kitchen, clearly."

The kitchen stood directly across from the front door. A white marble-topped island sat in the center, surrounded by wooden cabinets and three bar stools. A removable gold backsplash accented the counters.

"I love this island," she said as she slowly ran a hand across the top.

I gave her a devilish grin as an idea came into my head. "You can sit on it if you want."

She glared at me. "You're funny."

"Don't you have one?" I was sure every unit looked the same.

She shrugged. "Yeah, but it's not this updated one. They haven't had a chance to come in and change it yet.

"Oh, well, moving on… you've met the living room, the couch, blah

blah. Down there is the bathroom and my room," I said, pointing down the hallway. "It's small, but it does the job."

"Nice, nice." She looked down the hall and nodded. Her gaze seemed to linger for a bit, before she turned away.

"Did you..." I sighed. "Did you want to see them?" I asked. I didn't want her to think I had ulterior motives or anything, I was just trying to be a good hostess and give a proper tour.

She paused and turned around. "If you want me to see them, sure."

I cleared my throat. "Right this way." I gestured for her to lead the way down the hall. "Here is the bathroom."

There was a walk-in shower with a sliding glass door, and a small rectangular cut out that I used as a shelf. I added a fresh Eucalyptus plant there as well. I read in an article somewhere that the scent would help with stress relief, which I really felt like I needed.

The shower had sleek black fixtures with a rainfall shower head. The sink was made of white marble, with black wooden doors beneath it. Above the sink hung a simple rectangular mirror. On the counter, a black cup held my toothbrush and toothpaste, along with pecan pie-scented hand soap. I loved the comforting scent of fall—it reminded me that the holidays were just around the corner.

"Wow, it's beautiful," she said, smiling. Fallon's view on the world was exceptional to me. I'd never known someone who saw a basic apartment bathroom as beautiful.

I stopped when we reached my room. "And, this is my room." I was nervous to show her, and I didn't know why.

She hummed and grinned as she walked past me and into the room. "Oh. Okay, do come in," I said with narrowed brows and a smile.

"It's nice," she said as she walked around.

Above my queen bed, a collection of Polaroid pictures hung on the wall. Some were candid shots of me and my sister, others with Harper and Grant, and a few with my friends, Rylee and Roxxy.

The bed sat in the center of the room, topped with black silk sheets and a black-and-white plaid comforter.

"I mean, yeah, it does the job," I said, laughing.

She turned around and walked toward me, stopping in front of me where I stood at the door. "Thank you for the tour."

"You're welcome," I replied.

Her fingers danced across my wrist as she cut the distance between us. "And thank you for lending me your blanket." She brought her hands to my waist and rested them there, causing a slight hitch of my breath when she pulled us closer together.

"Fallon…" I tried to make it sound like a warning, but it came out in a hushed breath.

"And thank you for inviting me over and sharing your story with me. I know that couldn't have been easy," she said softly.

I placed my hand on her arm and pushed a hair behind her ear. "You're welcome." I cleared my throat and looked into her heated eyes. "Uh… no funny business, remember?"

"I'm very serious, Mackenzie," she replied. Her eyes were dark and her breathing had become ragged.

"Fallon." I brought my thumb up to sensually brush her bottom lip.

"Kiss me," she whispered. "Please, Kenzie."

I smiled, and my mouth crashed onto hers, settling there and getting comfortable. She moaned as I let out a gasp and pulled her closer, which proved to not be nearly close enough.

Our tongues were intertwined and dancing together. I felt a surge of heat through my body, a tingling all the way down to my throbbing, aching clit. It was begging for her after only a kiss.

She slid her hands from my waist, slowly moving up to my shoulders. Her nails grazed down my back, sending shivers through every part of me. I moaned, tilting my head back, and she took the invitation, pressing her lips against my neck.

My knees almost buckled at the sensation of her tongue licking the side of my neck, and I felt as if I could faint. I wanted to feel her tongue everywhere at once.

After a few seconds, she broke the kiss, and our eyes met. Her eyes were dark and heady, filled with so much need, and I could barely form a coherent thought when I looked into them.

"Fallon, what are we—" That's all I could sputter out, and it wasn't much longer before our lips met again. The first kiss was scared and timid. It was sensual and gentle. But the second one? It was hot, primal, and sexy. Our lips had a mind of their own, and it felt as if they needed to be fused together.

I led us into my room, our lips never parting. When we reached the edge of the bed, I paused, her gaze never leaving mine. She slipped my shirt off, and I followed, tossing hers somewhere in the room. I didn't care where they landed. In that moment, nothing else mattered as I stood there, staring at her, unable to tear my eyes away.

"Fuck," I moaned, a little louder than I meant to. She smiled sweetly and blushed.

"You," I said, as if I was stunned—which, in a way, I was—but it was the only word I could find.

"Yes." She laughed.

Her perfect pink nipples were pierced with simple gold bars that had little gold balls on both ends.

I am in so much trouble, holy hell.

"Oh my God, Sunshine. You are perfect." I grabbed her face and kissed her hard.

I gently lay her back on the bed and settled beside her, never breaking the kiss. Her breaths came quicker as our lips parted, and she looked up at the ceiling, giving me the opportunity to trail my kisses down her neck. I was obsessed with feeling her skin under mine.

"Mackenzie." She gasped. I grabbed her chin to turn her head slightly as I licked her throat, circling and flicking like it wasn't her neck my tongue was on at all.

I started leaving a trail of kisses down her neck, but I kept going back up to those soft crimson lips. I placed a kiss on top of her chest, caressing gently with my hand and drawing circles around her left nipple.

"Fuck!" Her moans fueled my desire, and I came back up to kiss her lips once more.

"Mackenzie, I... Oh my God." She moaned when I gently circled her nipple with my tongue. "I... I think we should stop." She was breathless.

I stopped kissing her and looked at her. "Yeah?" I asked.

She nodded.

"Yeah, okay." I reluctantly sat her up, handing her shirt back as I put on my own.

"I'm sorry, I just... I don't think it would be a good idea," she finally said, breaking the silence.

"Yeah, of course. I agree," I replied with a ragged breath, not confident in my agreement.

"Trust me, it's not that I don't want to. I do, but I mean, we're neighbors, Mackenzie." She looked at me, both of us still trying to catch our breaths.

I looked at her, unable to grasp how we had gotten here. It was taking everything I had to not lay her on the bed again.

"Yeah, I know. And not that I'm complaining, like at all, but you started this, so why did you stop it?"

Her smile fell and her shoulders sagged. "I did start it. I don't know why I did, I just... I needed... I wanted..." She shook her head, as if searching for exactly the right words to say. "I stopped because I knew if I didn't, I would've gone a lot farther than I should've. I wouldn't have wanted to stop, and I don't think you would've either, but it would've been a mistake. I think we both know that."

"Right. So, what happens now?"

"Well," she started as she stood up and took my hand. "I'm going to go home."

"And I'm going to force myself not to follow you," I added with a small smile.

She kissed me on the cheek, and I wanted to beg her to change her mind. "Goodnight, Mackenzie," she whispered as she turned around and headed toward the hallway.

I'm not sure what compelled my next words to come out. "Go out with me, Fallon," I called after her. "Tomorrow."

She paused at the bedroom door, slowly turning back around and looking at me nervously. "Like a date?"

I shook my head. "It doesn't have to be, no. Just two people hanging out, doing an activity together, and enjoying each other's company. No flowers, no end-of-the-night kiss. Just friends... if that's what we are?"

"Friends." She spoke the word as if it was the first time, testing how it felt on her lips. "I don't know about that, but I won't say no to a free activity."

I laughed. "Oh no. It's not a date, therefore, I'm not obligated to pay." I winked.

"Always a charmer." She laughed.

"Go on, you better get home." I smiled, nodding toward her apartment.

"That sounds like a good idea." She walked over to me and pressed our foreheads together. "I'm an idiot, aren't I?" she whispered.

I caressed her cheek. "No, Fallon, you're not an idiot. You're thinking smarter than I am right now."

She straightened up. "Right. Well, tomorrow, then?"

I nodded. "Tomorrow."

She smiled before she turned around and walked out, and I didn't stop her.

"I'm the idiot," I mumbled. I heard my front door close, and I threw myself on the bed.

She was right, though. I wouldn't have stopped us. If she would've let me, I would've taken her on that bed. I wanted to see those red curls sprawled across my silk sheets.

But it would've been a huge mistake. Still, there was a part of me that wanted to make that mistake.

Chapter Thirteen

FALLON

"Hello? Do you have any idea what time it is? Some of us—"

"I almost slept with Mackenzie!" I screamed into the phone.

The line went quiet for a minute, and I seriously thought she hung up on me. "Hello? Drea, did you hear me? I said—"

"I'm sorry, who is this? Surely this isn't the name on my phone. That person said they would never hook up with Mackenzie."

I rolled my eyes. "Drea, I'm serious. I almost slept with her! What is wrong with me?"

"You called to tell me you *didn't* sleep with someone? Thanks for the update. Goodnight, sweetie."

"Wait!" I yelled. "What do I do?"

She laughed. "What do you mean, love? You didn't actually *do* anything, and even if you did, who cares? You're both adults."

"We're neighbors, Dre. We're not even really friends at this point—just kind of friendly sometimes. It'd be way too weird. Also, I think we have a date tomorrow."

"That's even better. You don't have to go far to get some." She chuckled. "Hang on, you're going on a date with her?"

"Well, not really, but I guess? She said it wasn't a date, but it sounded like a date invite to me."

She sighed. "Honey, do you want to go?"

I paused. *Did* I want to go? She said it wasn't a date, but... would it be so bad if it was? Two people could hang out without it meaning anything. Right? But did I want it to mean something? Shit.

Too many feelings, too fast. I had no idea what to do with them—how to handle any of this. My head was spinning, and I couldn't breathe.

"I don't... I mean, I do, I think, but—"

"Exactly. Stop thinking for once, and just live."

I groaned. "You know, you sound like Penelope. I can't be into my neighbor, Drea. Did you forget how we met? Not the best of terms. And every time we ran into each other after that, it was awful. It's finally not so terrible, and I can't go back to the way it was before—I just can't."

"It sounds like you already *are* into her, love."

Shit, was I? I mean I kissed her, and I *did* try to sleep with her. I was totally into her!

"This is so fucked! We see each other almost every day. What if we started something, then it ended badly? It would be so awkward and eventually one of us would've to move. It'd be too—"

"Fallon, honey," she started, "take a breath. Get some sleep, and see what happens, okay? Let yourself enjoy this. You are not the same person you were when you broke up with—"

"Yes, Dre. I know." I cut her off. I knew I wasn't the same person. That person was a pathetic shell of who I was now, and I would be damned if I ever went back to her again. Which was exactly why anything with Mackenzie could not happen.

She sighed. "You have to move on, honey. It's been a really long time. You deserve to be happy. Even if it's just from having a fling with your hot neighbor. Stop being so serious, okay? I love you."

I smiled. "I love you, too, Dre. Goodnight."

"Goodnight, Fal." She hung up and I padded down to the bathroom, in need of a cold shower. I knew she was right, but I had moved on.

Okay, maybe not completely, but it wasn't like I'd ever want her back. She had destroyed our relationship, and my self-worth, leaving me feeling worthless. I had worked too hard to heal my shattered heart, and I refused to be that naïve girl again.

My head and my heart both wanted different things, but I knew Mackenzie would be a mistake. A very good, but very bad mistake.

I stood under the cold spray of my shower for a few minutes, hoping it would cool me off, but it didn't.

My heart knew what it wanted, and right now it was telling me to go back to Mackenzie's apartment and finish where we left off. With her soft lips kissing their way down to my needy, throbbing... *block it out. Don't think about it. Block it out!*

I couldn't stop thinking about what almost happened—how I craved her touch again. How I wanted to feel her lips on mine, on my skin. How I craved her tongue everywhere.

I hated myself for stopping it. I hated even more that she let me go. If she would've stopped me from leaving, I would've stayed. I would've taken her on the couch, and on the kitchen counter she told me to sit on.

I let out an audible groan. The shower wasn't helping. I couldn't stop thinking about her, and my body was starting to catch up with my thoughts.

No! I was not going to go there, not again. I shook my head and turned off the water, grabbing my towel when my phone went off with a text notification.

Drea was already sleeping, and Penelope had been long asleep, so who the hell was texting me so late?

After I dried off, I picked up my phone from the sink and saw who it was:

Mackenzie: Don't forget our non-date tomorrow, bring your wallet! ☺

I already regretted giving her my number.

Me: 😵 Sure thing.

108

Mackenzie: You roll your eyes a lot. Why don't you come back over here and finish what you started, and I'll show you how to roll them the right way. 😉

A crimson tint painted my cheeks. That was dangerously tempting...

Me: In your dreams, Wildcat. Where are we going tomorrow? I could still change my mind. You better be nice to me.

Mackenzie: You could, but you won't. How do you feel about arcades? 😊

Me: I mean, you know I like arcades. I haven't been in years, though.

Me: How about a friendly little bet? I'll go. But if I win the majority of the games, you buy dinner.

Mackenzie: And when I win, you buy dinner?

Me: Haha you're cute! Deal or no deal?

Mackenzie: I knew you thought I was cute! Yes deal. So I'll see you tomorrow, about noon? Meet you in the hall. Goodnight, Sunshine.

Me: Goodnight, Wildcat.

I smiled, plugged my phone in next to my bed, and went to sleep, fighting the urge to go back across the hall.

Chapter Fourteen

FALLON

I woke up a little after eight to a text from Mackenzie. A smile landed on my face when I opened it:

> Mackenzie: Good morning, Sunshine. ☀️ Ready to get your ass kicked today? 🏓 I'm already hungry! 😜

> Mackenzie: For food!! Not your ass. Although, if that's what you're into... 🍑

> Me: Omg! 🤭 Nothing is happening to my ass today, other than rolling on the floor laughing when you cry because I beat you!

> Mackenzie: Haha! I'll see you at 12, yeah? Don't miss me too much. 😉

> Me: 🙄 Don't worry, I won't. See you soon, Wildcat.

I grinned and headed to the kitchen. I wasn't terribly hungry yet, so I settled for a simple protein smoothie. I wanted to save my appetite for the free dinner I was going to win.

After finishing my smoothie, I got ready. I opted for a more casual look—a green babydoll shirt, the most form-fitting skinny jeans I owned, and a pair of black Converse. I wanted to look nice, but not so nice that she'd think I was trying to impress her, because I wasn't.

When I opened my door, Mackenzie was already in the hall, leaning against her door like a cool kid.

"You didn't think to eat before we left?" I asked, glancing at the iced coffee and pastry bag in her hands.

"Oh, I did eat. I had eggs and pancakes, and it was delicious." She grinned. "This isn't for me."

She handed me the cup and bag with a smile. "Banana bread and an iced coffee—extra hazelnut, extra shot of espresso."

I stared at her in awe. What the... "You got me breakfast? And how did you know how I like my coffee?"

She laughed. "You got me coffee, so now we're even. Also, Rylee told me you go there a lot. I asked her what you usually get, and she said this was your favorite. She also said sometimes you get banana bread, and I thought you might be hungry. I had her warm it up for you."

I was stunned—truly stunned. This wasn't the same woman I met weeks ago. I was half-tempted to pinch myself, just to make sure it wasn't a dream and I wasn't asleep.

My response was almost a whisper. "You asked her what I like?" I was unsure as to why I couldn't speak at a normal decibel.

"Well, yeah. I wanted to get you something you would actually want." If she kept pulling stunts like that, I was going to keep making bad decisions.

"Well." I cleared my throat. "Thank you, and you..." I trailed my eyes from her head to her toes. "You clean up nice." That was a bold-faced lie. She cleaned up *really* nice.

She chose a natural makeup look with a subtle smokey eye that made her blue eyes even more captivating—something I didn't think was possible. Her brown hair was tied into a sleek high ponytail, with a few strands framing her face. It was, in my opinion, the sexiest hairstyle known to exist. Gold hoop earrings and a simple gold choker matched the hoop septum piercing she was rocking instead of her usual tribal one. Her green criss-cross crop top showed off her cleavage just right, and she had on black faux leather high-rise skinny pants with white Converse.

"Thank you. You look amazing, Fallon." I blinked. Twice. What?!

"Thank you." I furrowed my brows. "Are you sick or something?"

She laughed. "No, I'm just being nice."

"I know, that's what's scaring me!" I took a step back for emphasis.

"You're the one who told me to be nice or fuck off. So here I am, being nice. Just take the damn compliment, please." She grinned.

I gave her a skeptical glare, but didn't press it any further. "Thank you. Shall we?"

"After you." She motioned down the hall and kicked off the wall. I smiled and we headed to the elevator in silence.

Once we got in the elevator, she turned to me. "You look really good."

I raised my eyebrows and grinned. "You already said that."

"Well, it's true. You look good, not that you don't always look good, I mean—"

"Thank you." I laughed, resting a hand on her shoulder. She glanced at it, then met my eyes. I cleared my throat and pulled my hand away. "You look really good, too. But I already said that, didn't I?" What was wrong with me? I'd been on plenty of dates before, and never acted this weird. Was this a date?

"So, what arcade are we going to?" I asked as we stepped off the elevator and headed outside.

"*Five Starcade*. I figured we could walk?" she replied.

"I've heard that place is good."

We started walking down the street toward the arcade, passing the bookstore. My heart started racing as I glanced inside. When I didn't see Drea, I let out a breath of relief. The last thing I needed was for her to put her nose where it didn't belong.

We didn't talk much on our walk. It was still weird after the night before, and neither one of us had brought it up since.

"Why did you choose an arcade?" I finally asked.

"I don't know, I thought it would be fun. Better than dinner and a movie, don't you think?"

I narrowed my brows. "I thought this wasn't a date?"

She smirked. "It's whatever you want it to be."

"Well, I mean, I—"

She stopped walking and turned to me. "Will you relax? It's not a date, okay? No funny business." She raised her hands in surrender. "Unless you want it to be. Or it can just be two friends who want to bone each other but won't." I shot her a look. "Friends who are going to play some games and eat food in the same building. Sound good?"

I smiled and gave her a playful nudge. "Thank you for inviting me, Mackenzie. You know, after…"

"Thank you for saying yes, you know, after saying no." She gave a soft smile and I felt my heart sink.

"Mackenzie—"

She shook her head. "It's fine, seriously. Come on, let's go."

It wasn't fine, but I didn't say anything more as we started walking again.

We walked in silence for a few minutes before she reached for my hand. I hesitated for a second, but then I gently laced my fingers with hers.

A bolt of electricity shot through me the second our hands touched. I wanted to pull away—but at the same time, I didn't. I wanted the feeling of her skin on mine. Friends hold hands all the time, right? Like when they go to the bathroom together in a crowded club?

I was so deep in thought, I hadn't realized we arrived at the arcade until Mackenzie spoke. "Well, here we are," she said as she opened the door for me.

"Right. Thank you." I walked in, and she followed close behind. I made a point to walk extra slow, hoping she'd be checking me out.

"I can't believe I kicked your ass! You started out on top. How did that happen?"

We spent hours playing arcade games and laughing like little kids. We played two rounds of laser tag, which was a mistake for Mackenzie. She was so cute trying to keep up with those kids—she really tried.

"Well, I always start out on top," she said with a devilish grin. "But, you're just a lot better than me, I guess."

"I guess. Do you need a nap? You look a little winded." I grinned when she scowled at me.

She nudged me. "Hey, those eight-year-olds were definitely undercover military personnel—I don't care what you say. The blonde one 'accidentally' tripped me, and I swear I still have a bruise," she added, rubbing her hip.

"A bruised ego, maybe!" I snorted. "Well, if you're not late for bingo, I believe you owe me dinner? I did win after all."

She smiled. "You sure did. How about *Reid's*? It's right down the street."

My grin grew wider. "That sounds perfect."

We walked down the street in a comfortable silence. Our fingers didn't connect again, and I hated to admit I missed the contact.

When we got to *Reid's*, she opened the door for me. I narrowed my eyes but thanked her anyway. I was pretty sure we were on a date. Did I want it to be a date?

The hostess led us to our table, and I slid into one side of the booth while Mackenzie took the other. The hostess set a basket of rolls on the table before leaving to get our waitress. Once she was gone, I started scanning the menu.

Every so often, I looked up and saw Mackenzie staring at me. She would smirk and go back to her menu.

After the third time, I dropped my menu and glared at her. "Can I help you?"

"What?" She set her menu down and folded her hands on the table, looking like the picture of innocence.

"You keep staring at me. Is there something on my face?"

She laughed. "No, there's nothing on your face."

I furrowed my brows. "Then what's your deal, Wildcat? Why do you keep staring at me?"

She opened her mouth to say something but didn't get the chance before the waitress walked up.

"Good evening, ladies! I'm Brooke, and I'll be your server tonight. Can I start you off with something to drink?"

"I'll have a vodka and Red Bull, please," she answered, never glancing at the waitress.

"I'll have the same. Thank you," I responded.

"Am I not allowed to look at you?" she asked once the waitress had left.

"Mackenzie, seriously," I demanded.

She sighed. "I just really like looking at you, is that a crime? You have to know how beautiful you are."

I smiled and tried to hide my blush. "No, it's not a crime. You're just creeping me out a bit. And thank you, Mackenzie. You look really good, too."

I'd already said that, so why was I saying it again? Why was I so nervous? This wasn't a date. I didn't even like her.

She smiled. "Thank you."

When the waitress brought our drinks we thanked her, never taking our eyes off each other.

"So, tell me something, Mackenzie," I said once our waitress left again.

"Anything," she replied.

"Why did you let me win?"

She looked at me and almost choked on her drink. "What?"

"You heard me. Why did you let me win at air hockey, *and* skeeball?"

She laughed. "Whatever do you mean? Are you accusing me of being a cheater?" She gasped dramatically.

"I sure am! You didn't even move your puck, and you looked away the whole time we were playing skeeball! If you're going to cheat, at least be good at it!"

"I am sure I don't know what you are referring to." She winked.

"Yeah, sure. Well, I want a rematch!"

"Okay, deal." She laughed.

"So, about last night." I had to change the topic of conversation. We needed to talk about it.

"My invitation still stands." She winked. "I can be a really good teacher."

I raised an eyebrow. "I'm serious, Mackenzie. I wanted to apologize, I shouldn't have kissed you."

Her smile faded. "You want to apologize? Why? You wanted to, and you did. What's wrong with that? I'm not complaining about it. I personally really enjoyed our evening."

I rolled my eyes. "What's wrong, is that it was a mistake, and if it wouldn't have stopped..." I trailed off, thinking about exactly where it would've led.

She frowned. "Why do you keep saying that?"

I sighed. "Because we're neighbors, Mackenzie. Because it would be weird, because—"

"Because you don't want to."

Groaning, I rubbed my hands over my face. "I do, and that's the problem!"

"You're right. Wanting someone is a problem." Her sarcastic tone was doing little to soothe my nerves.

"I'm serious! Once we take that step, who knows how it will end? I like how things are now, and I don't anything to change," I replied.

"Who said I liked you to begin with?" She smirked. Her expression grew serious when she noticed I wasn't laughing. "Fine. I'm just sitting here with a friendly neighbor who looks sexy as hell all the damn time. It's actually quite irritating, to be honest. But I have to admit, I do enjoy your company, and I'm glad you agreed to have spend the afternoon with me."

I rolled my eyes. "You are something else, you know that? You know I'm right."

She let out a breath of resignation. "Yeah, I know. So here's... to friends?" She raised her glass.

I smiled and connected my glass with hers. "Yeah, Wildcat. Friends."

We spent the next few hours talking and drinking. We talked about everything, and nothing, and it was nice.

When the bill came, I handed it to her, and she rolled her eyes. She paid, and we started walking home, stopping between our doors when we got there.

"Thank you for spending the day with me. Who knew I'd have a good time with you?" She smirked.

"Mackenzie?" I started. "This is a date, isn't it?"

Her expression turned serious. It was kind of scary, to be honest. "Do you think it's a date?"

I sighed. "Honestly, yeah, I do. You've opened my door, complimented my outfit several times, and you cheated to let me win, knowing you would have to pay for dinner.”

“I’m just really bad at arcade games, and I complimented you, not the outfit—although the outfit looks good too,” she said with a smile. “Also, I just wanted to hang out with a friend.”

I laughed. “Well, date or not, thank you, Mackenzie. I had a lot of fun today. I guess maybe I do deserve your nice after all?” I shrugged.

Her lips fell into a frown. “Shit, Fallon—”

I shook my head. “No, Mackenzie, it’s fine, really. I’m just giving you a hard time.”

She grabbed my hand when I started to turn around. “No, it’s not. Look, I know I kind of already have, but I’ve been wanting to really apologize for that—”

“No need. It’s forgotten,” I cut in, still holding her hand.

“Let me say this, please,” she started. I stood there, quietly waiting. “That was messed up of me. I could blame it on my day or the cramped elevator, but there’s no excuse. It was a terrible thing to say. I was right about one thing, though—you don’t deserve just an ounce. You deserve so much more. I’m really sorry, Fallon.”

She let go of my hand, and I immediately missed the warmth of her touch.

“We all have bad days, Mackenzie, it happens. But thank you.” I paused, unsure if I should continue with my next thought, but I decided to be vulnerable and let her in, if only a little. “And you were right, I might have thought about kissing you afterward.”

She beamed widely at me. “I knew it! You do like me, Sunshine.” She winked.

“You’re alright.” I smiled.

“Goodnight, Fallon,” she said as she turned toward her door.

The second she turned around, I didn’t think about my next move, I just acted.

I grabbed her wrist, and stopped her.

She turned around, brows furrowed. “Fallon, don’t—”

I didn’t let her finish as I pulled her close. “Don’t what, Mackenzie? Do this?” I leaned in and brushed my lips against hers gently. Just once.

“Yes. Don’t do... that,” she said in a hushed breath.

"Tell me to stop then, Wildcat. Tell me to turn around, and go inside. Tell me you don't want to kiss me."

"Not a chance in hell. I've never been known to be a liar, and I don't intend to start now." She smiled.

She closed her eyes and kissed me, sliding her tongue across my lips. I parted them, letting her in as our tongues tangled and danced together, our hands exploring each other. My hands cradled her face, and hers rested on my lower back and hips.

The longer we kissed, the more I was losing all of my resolve when it came to her, but I couldn't seem to find the will to stop.

I suppose I didn't have to, because she was the one to break the kiss. "Fallon..."

"Goodnight, Kenzie." I smiled softly, my heart fluttering a little, before she turned and headed inside, the door clicking shut behind her.

Chapter Fifteen

FALLON

I slumped against my door and groaned. What. The. Fuck?! I kissed her again?

It was the alcohol. That's all it was. I just drank too much. I'll go lie down, and tomorrow, this will all be over. We'll go back to friendly passes in the hall. Yeah, staying friends is the best option.

I stood up and dusted myself off. *Now if I could just find my damn keys!*

My purse wasn't even that big. Where were they? *Oh, no... oh, no, no, no!*

"Oh, no!" I whined, hitting my head on the door.

"Is everything okay out here?"

I whipped around to see Mackenzie standing at her door, looking concerned. I groaned, returning to my purse. "Uh, yeah," I replied.

"Shit," I whispered.

"So, not okay, then?" she teased.

I sighed. "I think I lost my keys. Somewhere between the arcade and here. I'm going to walk back there and try to find them." I started heading down the hall when she yelled after me.

"Hey, wait, Fallon. The arcade is closed by now. It's after nine."

"Well, I can at least go to *Reid's* and see if I left it in the bathroom or something," I replied.

Mackenzie shook her head and walked toward me. "No, you can't. It's dark, and It's not safe to go out on your own at this hour. Trust me, I've seen creeps hiding in the alleys at night. Look, you can crash on my couch until tomorrow morning. You can get your keys then, okay?"

I pulled the corner of my bottom lip between my teeth. "That is not a good idea. Like, at all, Mackenzie."

"It's not safe, Fallon."

I laughed. "I know, that's what I'm saying."

"I'm serious! I promise, no shenanigans." She smiled.

I paused for a beat. This was a terrible idea. But did I really have any other options?

She must have sensed my hesitation because she added, "Fallon, it's late. And I don't want you sleeping in the hall or the lobby. You can take the couch, and I promise I won't bother you all night. There are no ulterior motives here. I just want you to be safe."

I sighed, even though I knew it was a terrible idea. "Fine."

When we got inside I walked to the couch.

"Do you want anything to drink?" She asked. "I have water, tea, wine..."

"Uh, wine is good."

Wine was definitely *not* a good idea. We'd already had a few drinks at *Reid's*, and more alcohol wasn't exactly smart—especially if I was staying here. Yet, there I was, accepting a glass anyway. What was it about that woman that made all my common sense disappear?

"Wine it is." She left and grabbed two glasses from the cabinet. She sat down and handed me a glass.

"Thanks," I said as our glasses clinked together.

"So, why Seattle?" she asked.

I turned to her, unprepared for her question. "What?"

"You said you used to live in Portland with your family, so why did you move here?" she amended.

"Oh." I shifted in my seat, I guess we were doing this. I wasn't sure how much information I should share with her, or how much I really wanted to bring up from the past. "After my ex and I broke up, she played the victim, and most of our friends took her side. They stopped hanging out with me and answering my calls. They even blocked me on all social media." I paused, taking a minute to gather my thoughts and shake away the memory.

"I've wanted to live here for as long as I can remember. Growing up, seeing the city in movies and TV shows, I always thought city life was for me. My family was really supportive when I told them I wanted to move, but saying goodbye was bittersweet. I needed a fresh start—staying in Portland would've meant being stuck with memories of my ex."

"And is city life for you?" she asked.

I smiled softly. "Yeah, I think it is."

"What happened with your ex?"

I laughed nervously. There were just some things I wasn't ready to share, not with her. "What's with the twenty questions?"

Mackenzie shrugged. "I'm just making conversation."

"Okay, well, what happened with *your* last relationship?" I deflected.

She flinched slightly, but it was still noticeable. It seemed I hit a nerve. I opened my mouth to apologize, but she stopped me.

"Okay, okay," she said, putting her hands up. "Fair enough. Let's talk about something else. Tell me about ice skating as a kid."

Now *that* I could talk about.

After bouncing between topics—from work to childhood hobbies—we eventually settled into a comfortable silence, sipping our wine.

"Do you want some more wine?" she finally asked when her glass was empty.

I smiled. "Oh, sure, only if you do. Can you handle more?"

"Yes. I think you'll find I can handle quite a few things well," she said with a wink. "Okay, maybe just one more glass."

I grinned. "I agree, I think we can close our tab after one more."

We got up and walked to the kitchen as she made her way to fill our glasses. I propped myself up on a stool at the island and smiled as she poured the wine.

The way her boobs looked in her shirt had my mouth going dry. I tried not to look, but it was impossible. I could've easily reached my hand inside her shirt, and exposed her perfect breasts. I was getting wetter than the wine glasses, and I definitely needed to calm down. I licked my bottom lip and smiled at her.

"What are you smiling at?" she asked.

I laughed. "I think the glasses are full enough." I nodded toward them. She furrowed her brow and looked down to see the wine overflowing onto the counter.

"Oh shit!"

I laughed and hopped off the stool. "Something must've distracted you." I walked around to help her clean up the mess.

"What? No! I—" She stopped abruptly when she caught me staring, not at her face.

"My eyes are up here," she said jokingly.

Shit. I couldn't take my eyes off her chest. I really was a boob woman.

"Yeah, but the wine isn't." I chuckled as I pointed to her very see-through shirt.

"Oh, fuck! Dammit!" She tried to wipe it off, but of course, it didn't help.

I took the towel from her hand and placed it on the island. "Here," I said quietly. "Let me help." Her eyes followed my hand as it grazed the bottom of her shirt. She gasped when my fingers lightly brushed her skin. I grasped the sides and slowly pulled it up.

I should've stopped. I should've said something. Why weren't my lips moving?

Instead of my lips moving, it was her arms. She raised them, letting me lift her shirt all the way off until she stood there, braless. Jesus, this woman!

The piercings. The tattoos. That perfect smile. I didn't stand a chance. Sooner or later, I was going to cave—I just knew it.

She had a tattoo on her right shoulder—a vertical rose, its stem reaching toward the center of her chest. A sleeve tattoo covered her right forearm, a rainbow feather twisting from her elbow to just shy of her wrist.

I tried not to reach out and touch her, but the longer I stood there staring, the harder it became.

My eyes lingered before I finally looked back at her. I was sure she could hear my heart pounding from where she stood.

"B... better?" I asked breathlessly.

She nodded, but didn't speak a word.

I handed her shirt back, watching as she set it on the counter without saying anything.

My pulse was racing, and my blood was so warm, the heat was rushing... everywhere. Wine was the wrong choice of beverage.

I'm not sure why, but I leaned in and gently kissed her lips, just once.

"Where the hell do you think you're going?" she asked as I pulled away. She grabbed my shirt and pulled me to her until our chests were touching. I took in a sharp breath, and I wondered if she noticed how it affected me every time she did that.

She connected our mouths, kissing me deeper. Every time we kissed, she broke down a piece of my defenses. The feeling of her tongue as it swiped my lips and begged for entry was catastrophic to my core. It was like her tongue was connected to my pussy from the second it touched any part of my skin.

Despite my protest, she pulled us apart, and by some miracle, I barely managed to get a few words out. "Um... maybe you should... go, and..."

"Oh. Yeah. Right. I probably should." She licked her lips and I had to stifle a groan. Did she have any clue how sexy she was?

We stared at each other. No one was moving, or breathing. Finally, she turned and went to get a shirt.

When she left, I busied myself by working on cleaning up the mess and I let out a loud breath.

Okay, get it together. What are you doing? You can't lose control every time you're alone with her. Or in a public bookstore! You're an adult, not some horny teenager!

Perhaps staying here was not a good idea, especially with more wine.

"Thank you," she said when she came back. "You don't have to do that."

I looked up at her. "It's the least I can do. I ruined your shirt, again. So, where were we?" My eyes left hers and went back to the spill.

"Well, if I recall, you were talking about how bad you want me."

My eyes shot up to her and she smiled. "Oh, you'd love that wouldn't you?"

She laughed. "I mean, I wouldn't complain."

"I'm sure you wouldn't." I rolled my eyes. She didn't need to know that I did want her. Although, she wasn't stupid, so I was sure she already knew.

We walked back over to the couch and she handed me a glass as we both sat down.

"Thank you." We crashed our glasses together.

"But seriously, last time you were here, I told you about my parents. What's your story?"

I put my glass on the table and looked at her. "About my parents? Oh, uh, I don't know. It's not a pretty one."

She put her hand on my thigh, but when I looked down at the contact, she pulled it away.

She cleared her throat. "Tell me, anyway? If it's too personal I get it, but I'm here to listen."

I took a deep breath. "I was seven when it all started. My parents were always fighting—yelling, throwing things. Then my dad got laid off, and everything got worse. He started coming home drunk after poker nights with the guys—three times a week. Three times a week, he lost so much money and blamed us for it. He was always yelling at my mom, and sometimes at me. Cursing at her, calling her a whore. And sometimes... he hit her. Sometimes, it was a lot worse than just a little slap."

"Fallon, I'm sorry. It's none of my business. If its too much, you don't—"

"No, it's okay. My mom always defended him. She said it was the alcohol, that he was just stressed because of work, and that she didn't make things easier for him. Those were always her answers. She was clumsy—always tripping down the stairs or bumping her eyes and lips on something. I never said anything. How could I? I was just a kid. When I was thirteen, I tried to speak up more, and defend her. She didn't deserve it, and I felt it was my job to protect her if she wouldn't protect herself. I'd try to get between them, but he'd push me aside, and I'd end up on the floor."

Tears formed in my eyes, but I pushed them down. She had shared her hard story with me. I owed her the same in return.

I lifted my shirt to show the scar on my ribcage.

She gasped and I felt the warmth of her hand on my thigh. This time when I looked down at it, she didn't pull away. "He did that to you?"

I took a deep breath and nodded. She grazed her fingers slightly over the scar, and I flinched a little, causing her to jump and pull her hand away. I grabbed her wrist before she could get too far. "It's okay, you won't hurt me," I whispered, bringing her hand back to the scar.

She traced it, and I shivered at her touch. I didn't know why I let her, but she was so gentle, as if I were a piece of thin ice covering a river, and the slightest pressure might crack me open.

"Didn't you see it the other night?"

She shrugged. "I was too distracted with the rest of you." She smirked. "I caught a glimpse, but I felt like it wasn't my place to ask about it."

I smiled and put my shirt down. "I got this when I was fourteen. My dad came home really drunk one night and beat my mom so badly she was borderline unconscious on the couch. I decided I'd had enough—I would be her voice when she couldn't speak. I yelled at him, and he gripped my throat. I tried to fight him—punch him, do anything I could to get away. Finally, I bit him, and he let go. He had a letter opener in his hand, probably from opening another past-due bill. As I ran up the stairs, he caught me and turned me around, I guess not realizing he still held the letter opener. It cut me. He dropped it after hearing my scream. He walked away after that, and we never saw him again. When I was seventeen, she finally filed for divorce. She knew he wouldn't object. Somehow, she knew where to send the papers, and he sent them back— signed—without so much as a phone call. She was terrified when she filed, and I didn't think he would let her. But I guess that night, he finally realized he'd hit his lowest point, and something changed."

"Where is he now? And how is your mom?" she asked as she cautiously wiped the tears from my eyes, letting her hand linger briefly before pulling away.

It felt like she was testing the boundaries of more contact between us, and I was letting her. Keeping my distance was getting harder by the minute. Every second around her pulled me closer to something I wasn't sure I was ready for.

I gave her a sad smile. "I don't know where my dad is, and I don't care. He hasn't tried to contact us since, so I won't curse a good thing." I laughed, trying to ease some of the tension. "As for my mom, she's in a happier place in her life now. My stepdad, Brandon, loves her, and he's so good to her. I tried to talk to her about my dad a few years ago, but she just squeezed me tight and cried. I never brought it up again."

She wiped away more of my tears and started to pull her hand back, but I stopped her, placing my hand over hers. I wasn't ready to lose the comforting contact just yet. "Thank you," I whispered.

"Thank you for sharing with me," she said, softly caressing my cheek with her thumb. "I'm sorry I asked."

"It's okay, really. I don't talk about it much, and it was kind of nice." It oddly felt good to talk about it with someone who wasn't family—someone without an inside opinion. Someone who would just listen.

She looked at me for a moment longer. There was something in her eyes, but I couldn't quite tell what it was.

"What?" I finally asked when she still hadn't said anything. I couldn't take the silence any longer, and her stare was making me itch inside of my skin.

"Nothing," she said. She removed her hand and cleared her throat. "Uh, it's getting kind of late. We should get some sleep."

"Right," I replied softly.

"There are pillows and blankets in the hall closet, and if you need anything, you know where to find me."

I smiled and kissed her cheek. "Thank you for today," I whispered.

"You're welcome. Goodnight, Fallon," she replied, walking to her room without so much as a glance back.

After gathering my arsenal of sleep essentials, I plopped down on the couch and made myself comfortable. I buried myself in a fleece blanket, large enough for two people to snuggle under, soaking up its warmth and security. The blanket wasn't light, and its added weight provided a hug I hadn't realized I needed. I couldn't help but inhale its scent, a small smile dancing on my lips as I did. It was amazing how, even after hundreds of cycles through the washer, it still smelled like Mackenzie.

It still felt a little weird sleeping on her couch, but after the wine and talking about my family, I was exhausted and didn't think about it much. I fell asleep pretty easily.

Chapter Sixteen

MACKENZIE

In the middle of the night I was awoken by a loud scream. I quickly sat up and listened a second longer. It sounded like it was in my apartment and I gasped.

"Fallon?" I whispered.

I threw my covers off and ran to the living room. Was someone breaking in? Were they hurting her? If something happened to her—no. I couldn't think like that.

When I got to the living room, she was still on the couch—thankfully alone and not with a burglar.

I turned on the light and saw her sitting up, breathing heavily. She was rocking back and forth with tears streaming down her cheeks. I hurried to the couch and sat beside her.

"Fallon?" I said, furrowing my brow in concern.

She kept crying and rocking on the couch, not looking my way. Her trembling cracked something inside me, and my heart ached at the sight of her like that.

I reached out, trying to steady my shaking hand as I gently touched her leg. The instant contact made her flinch, and she jumped, her body recoiling as if my touch had burned her.

"Hey," I spoke softly so I didn't startle her further. "It's okay. You're okay. I'm sorry, Fallon. I didn't mean to scare you."

She was still rocking, looking around and trying to figure out where she was. Her eyes finally landed on me and she opened and closed her mouth.

"Sunshine." It was all I could get out before she wrapped herself around me, and started crying again. I held her, not speaking or moving. I wanted her to know she was safe.

After a few minutes, she finally stopped crying, but she didn't pull away. Our bodies stayed connected when she seemed to have found her voice. "Every so often, I have this dream, Mackenzie. It's always the same one." She paused, and I slowly pulled us apart so I could look at her. I didn't say anything, just waited for her to continue.

"I haven't had it in a few months, but..." She paused again. "I guess talking about him brought it back."

I didn't need to ask. I knew who she was talking about. I'd asked about her parents earlier. The fear I felt when I heard her screaming, the concern when I saw her crying—all of that faded and twisted into guilt.

"I'm sorry I asked about your parents. It wasn't my place, and it wasn't my business. We aren't..." I didn't let myself finish. We couldn't be anything.

She looked at me, and a faint smile touched her lips before disappearing. "I know. You couldn't have known, and I agreed to tell you, so you have nothing to apologize for."

She took a breath, and I watched her struggle for a moment. "The dreams started after my mom filed for divorce. I was so afraid he was going to come back and do something far worse than he ever had before. Almost every night, I had the same dream. The exact same one." Her trembling grew more noticeable as she went on with her story. "I'm laying in bed, sleeping. My bedroom door swings open, and a man is standing there."

Her eyes welled with tears, and I softly caressed her hand as she spoke.

She looked down and continued, her voice barely above a whisper. "He... my dad is holding an ax. He doesn't say anything as he slowly walks toward me. I try to move, try to scream, but I just... can't. I'm paralyzed with fear. I always thought it was the house. I thought it was all the horrible memories of him there. After the second night in a row, I asked to sleep at my friend's house. But I still had the nightmare. It was the same scenario, except it wasn't my room anymore. It was hers. No matter where I go, the dream follows me. The only thing that changes is the room I'm in." I just looked at her, unable to find the right words.

"Even if I end up sleeping on a couch, too, apparently," she continued, her voice wavering slightly. "I can't move or scream, not until he's inches from my face. I can't even turn my head until I hear the swing of the ax and wake up, screaming."

She started crying harder and threw herself onto me. I held her tight, drawing delicate circles on her back, whispering, "Shh... it's okay, sweetheart. I'm here. Nothing is going to hurt you, okay?"

I sat there, holding her, not saying anything. I didn't know what to say in that moment. I barely knew her, and yet, there wasn't anything I wouldn't have done to find the man who had caused her so much pain.

After a few minutes, I gently pulled away and stood up, my eyes lingering on her as I did.

"Mackenzie, what—" She gasped as I scooped her up, carrying her toward my room.

"What are you doing?" she asked.

"You just had a nightmare. I'm not letting you sleep alone out here."

Our eyes locked, and she formed a sad smile, wrapping her arms around me. She caressed the back of my neck and whispered softly, "Thank you."

When we got to my room, I kicked the door closed behind me and put her on the bed. She got under the covers and sat up. I got in next to her, hating the way she sat so stiffly. I felt like we were making progress, but now I wasn't so sure.

"I promise I won't... just please try and get some sleep, okay?" I said.

"Okay," she replied, her voice soft. She sat quietly for a moment before letting out a sigh. "I'm sorry for being such a blubbering mess."

I looked at her, scowling. "Fallon, you are not a blubbering mess, do you hear me? You had a terrifying, traumatic nightmare. Your response is perfectly valid, and I don't ever want to hear you talk about yourself like that again."

"I'm sorry, I guess I'm still a little buzzed. I don't know what I'm saying." She laughed and shrugged it off.

"Fallon," I finally said after a few moments of watching her play with a corner of the blanket, "please relax and get some sleep." She smiled and settled into the bed.

I didn't object when she rested her head on my chest. Instead, I reveled in it, gently running my fingers through her hair until she drifted off to sleep.

When she was asleep, I kissed the top of her head and lay there for a little while, feeling her chest rise and fall against mine. It was oddly easy, just being there with her, like I'd been doing it my whole life. It felt natural, like it was exactly what I was meant to be doing. I could've stayed there, listening to her breathe, forever.

After a while, I gently placed her head on the pillow. She stirred for a minute, before settling back into a deep sleep, and I rolled over, just watching her.

I wanted this moment to last for as long as possible. I wanted this vision of her, peaceful and safe, for as long as I could have it.

Eventually, I was comfortable enough to fall asleep next to Fallon. The warmth of her body so close to mine, was the best kind of sleep aid.

I woke up to feel a warm arm across my chest and a leg straddled between mine. I turned my head, opened my eyes, and grinned as the memories of last night came flooding back.

We didn't do anything but kiss, but, God, did I want to. The heat I felt when she stared at me, holding my wine-stained shirt in her hand, was enough to set the room on fire.

I stayed in my room all night, lying next to her, not wanting to leave her side. Even though we eventually fell asleep, I couldn't shake the need to be close, just in case the nightmare returned. Her screams terrified me, and I didn't want to *think* of leaving her alone.

I tensed when I felt her stirring and groaning awake. She was smiling in her sleep, so beautifully, as only she knew how, but when she opened her eyes and looked at me, her smile disappeared and she jolted up, as if the bed somehow electrocuted her.

"Oh my God!" she screamed. I guess she wasn't awake enough to see we were both still dressed, so nothing clearly happened. Still, I let her freak out and wake up.

"Did we..." She was frantic, running her hands through her hair and pacing across my room. I still hadn't said anything, which was probably making it worse, but I figured she had to calm down eventually. Should I have been offended? She seemed to think something had happened, and judging by the way she was creating a tornado with her pacing, she clearly wasn't thrilled about the possibility.

"Well, say something!" She looked at me, but before I could say anything, she gasped. "Oh my God, what were we thinking? I can't believe—"

"Fallon!" I yelled. She stopped and stared at me. "Please breathe. I'm not sure if I should be insulted or not, but look down." I nodded to her fully clothed body. "Nothing happened. I told you nothing would, and I kept my word. Were you really that drunk?" I laughed.

She groaned, rubbing her face. "I mean, a little, but I remember last night. I remember waking up and... Oh God, I'm so sorry!" She covered her face, memories of last night seemingly coming back to her.

I got up and walked over to her, placing my hands on her shoulders. "Fallon. Fallon, look at me, please."

She uncovered her face and our eyes met. "Your eyes are so beautiful in the morning."

The words came out of nowhere, but they were true. She always had beautiful eyes, but honestly, everything about her was beautiful.

I cleared my throat when she furrowed her brows. "You had a nightmare, and I wanted to make sure you were okay. Nothing happened and you have nothing to apologize for." I smiled, hoping it would ease the worry from her face.

"Thank you, Mackenzie. I can't believe I spent the night, *and* cried," she said laughing.

"You better go get your keys. I promised no funny business yesterday, but today is a new day."

She rolled her eyes. "Yeah, I better go."

I rubbed her arm softly, and she gave me a faint smile before she headed for the door. "Please text me when you find your keys, okay? I'll be at work, but I'll have my phone on me all day."

She turned around and smiled. "You got it." And then she was gone.

. . .

About an hour later, Fallon texted me saying she'd found her keys. Apparently, she had dropped them in the bathroom, and luckily, no one had swiped them. They were waiting for her at the bar when she got there. I thanked her for letting me know and sent a sunshine emoji.

Ten seconds later another message came through:

> Sunshine: I'm sorry I freaked out. Have a good day at work. ☺

I smiled at the text, then put my phone down on the bed before hopping in the shower and getting ready for work.

Chapter Seventeen

MACKENZIE

Work, however, was the one thing I couldn't get done.

My mind was not at work. It was at home, with a sad redhead in my bed—

"Hello?!" A loud, grating voice snapped me out of my thoughts. "Kenzie, hello?"

I shook my head. "Sorry, what?" I turned to Roxxy.

She rolled her eyes and glared at me. "Come on, Kenzie, I asked how your date went? The arcade?"

In a moment of weakness, I told Roxxy I was going to the arcade with Fallon. We'd been best friends since fourth grade, which meant we could read each other better than anyone else. We'd started working together six years ago, back before my life fell apart.

I shook the memories out of my head, and tried to get back to work, answering as nonchalantly as possible. "It wasn't a date, Rox, and it was fine."

"It was fine? Mackenzie, every time you've gone out with a woman, it's always ended up way better than 'fine.' What happened?" she asked.

"That's not true," I grumbled, but I couldn't hide my satisfied smirk. Okay, so it was mostly true. Anytime I had shown interest in a woman enough to go out, it usually ended back at my place or theirs.

"Kenzie, what happened?" she demanded again. This time, I sighed. She wouldn't let it go until I gave her something.

"Nothing," I replied. "We went to the arcade, had a good time, and she went home... this morning."

"What the fuck?!" Roxxy yelled.

"Shh. Jesus, Rox! Look, nothing happened, okay?"

She didn't need to know she slept in my bed, or about the wine spill... or the kiss.

"Mackenzie, I need you in my office, please."

"Saved by the boss," I mumbled. I had never been more grateful to be interrupted by my boss than I was in that moment. Roxxy scowled at me but I tossed her a smile, even though I knew that conversation was far from over.

The walk to my boss' corner office was the longest walk of my life. Even though I knew I hadn't done anything wrong, that didn't stop my anxiety from surfacing.

It only took a few knocks before she opened the door, motioning me in. "Good morning, Mackenzie. Please, have a seat."

"Good morning, Claire." I smiled as I sat down in front of her desk. She walked around and took her seat, and my fingers brushed over the fabric of my pants, unable to stay still.

She wore an all-gray pantsuit, and her burgundy hair was always styled in a high ponytail. She had an undercut in the back of her head, designed with three half-triangles. She never spoke of her home life, so I couldn't tell if the undercut was a fashion statement or something more personal.

"I'll keep this short," she began, her voice as steady as it always was. "As you're probably aware, we've been searching for someone to fill the Assistant Director of Operations position. We'd like to offer it to you, starting next month. Amy is retiring at the end of the month, and we've been closely monitoring your work over the past year. We're confident you're the right person for the job."

That was short? I sat there in disbelief, shaking my head. "Wow. I don't know what to say, Claire."

She stood up and came to stand in front of me, leaning against her desk. "You can say yes, for starters. You've earned this, Mackenzie."

"Uhh... yes, of course. Are you kidding?!" I cleared my throat. "I mean—yes, of course I accept. Thank you so much."

"Great. Of course, it comes with a pay raise and you'll have your own office. We will send you the contract and all of the details to look over and sign by the end of the day." She walked me out and I thanked her again.

When I got back to my desk, I started working again, ignoring Roxxy's death stare.

"Excuse me?" She was glaring at me, and I tried not to smile.

"Yes? Can I help you?" I asked coolly.

She groaned. "Can you stop being irritating for one second? What did Claire say? Are you finally fired? It's about time. Honestly, I'm surprised they didn't fire you for taking that new receptionist into the bathroom during your lunch hour. Surely someone knew about that."

I glared at her. "Will you let it go? Nothing happened with Ruby. Okay, we made out a little—well—maybe a little more than that—but anyway... no, I wasn't fired. And you're going to have to find someone else to annoy next month when I move into my new office. I got the promotion."

"Fuck you, bitch!" Roxxy said as she hit my arm.

"Why are you so fucking abusive to me?" I asked, rubbing my now bruised arm.

"Because I love you! But seriously, we need to go out this weekend and celebrate! We haven't gone out in so long."

I couldn't argue with that logic, and I could've definitely used a few drinks.

"Alright, fine, we can go out this weekend." I smiled and went back to work.

It took Roxxy all of five minutes before she brought up Fallon again.

"So, your date, what happened?" She stared at me the way a child looks at bubbles.

"I told you it wasn't a date, and nothing," I said, trying so desperately to let it go.

She narrowed her eyes on me, not wanting to let it go. "Mackenzie, what happened?"

I sighed. "Seriously, nothing. She got locked out and crashed on my couch, okay? That was it."

She groaned. "Boring! But fine, whatever. Still, you should invite her out with us. We want to meet your new friend." She winked.

I rolled my eyes. "She *is* a friend. But sure, Rox."

Introducing Fallon to my friends was the last thing I wanted to do. I loved them, but they could be a lot, and I didn't want her to get the wrong idea and think I was trying to ask her on a date. Though, I wouldn't object to that idea. Fallon, however, seemed adamantly against it. I had to think carefully about how to invite her. I exhaled sharply and texted her:

Me: Good morning Sunshine, how's work?

Sunshine: Oh, you know, people are being stubborn and trying to die and what not. Not on my watch dammit! How's work for you?

Me: Not too bad, today. Got a promotion.

Sunshine: What? That's amazing! Congrats, I can't wait to hear about it.

Me: Well, that's sort of what I wanted to talk to you about. I wanted to see if you would want to go out for drinks with me and the girls?

Sunshine: That sounds good. Who are the girls?

Me: My sister Harper, best friend Roxxy, and Rylee who you already know from Brewed Awakening.

Sunshine: Rylee is the sweetest!

Me: That she is. That's what she tried to tell me about you lol.

Sunshine: Well, she's not wrong!

Me: Haha. I'm slowly learning. So, drinks?

Sunshine: Okay. Meeting friends is okay.

Me: Don't worry, it'll be fine. They've met my one-night stands before, so it's not a big deal.

Why the hell would I say that? Idiot!

Sunshine: Right.

Me: That's not what I meant, they know we are just friends.

Sunshine: Ok.

Sunshine: Sure, sounds fun, ☺ Congrats again!

"Hey now, no sexting!" Roxxy laughed.

I looked up from my phone and gave her a look. "Shut up, Rox!"

"Did you invite Fallon? Is she going?" she asked.

"Yes I invited her. She said she's going. I'll see you tomorrow."

"Work, then drinks!" she sang. "Better bring protection!" she yelled.

I just flipped her off and kept walking with a smile on my face.

When I got home, I got a call from Fallon, and I smiled before picking it up. "Good evening, Sunshine."

"Hey, so I forgot to ask, what is the dress code for this shindig? Dressy, casual, brothel-y?" she asked.

I let out a loud snort. "Hey! Uhh, brothel-y? Shindig? Who are you?"

138

She groaned. "Just help me out, will you!"

She was getting so riled up and it was adorable.

I had to admit, I was getting a little nervous. The more time I spent with her, the more I wanted to spend with her, alone, and preferably with no clothing.

"I'm just messing with you, don't get your panties in a twist." I groaned as soon as the words were out. "It's pretty casual. Whatever you feel comfortable in. We're going to *Reids.*"

"I'm not wearing panties," she replied, and I almost dropped my phone.

"Jesus, woman! You distracted me with the image of you not wearing panties"

That was not the image I needed before being around her in a place where alcohol was present. "Also, can we stop saying the word 'panties?'"

"Sorry, you're just too easy." She laughed.

"So, anyway, how was your day?" I asked, not ready for silence to replace her voice just yet.

She chuckled softly. "It wasn't too bad, thanks."

An awkward silence filled the air, neither of us knowing what to say.

After a few minutes, she spoke quietly. "I've gotta go."

I cleared my throat. "Oh, yeah, of course. Uh, have a good night."

"You, too," she replied. "I'll see you tomorrow. I'm looking forward to it. Goodnight, Kenz."

"I don't think it'd be the same without you. Goodnight, Fallon." She hung up and I wanted to crawl into the couch. That could have gone better.

I spent the rest of the night sulking around my apartment, anxiously waiting for tomorrow to come.

Chapter Eighteen

MACKENZIE

I finished up with work an hour earlier than usual so I could head home and start getting ready. I wanted to make sure I looked good—not for anyone in particular, of course.

Roxxy came to pick me up with Harper and Rylee. Roxxy and Rylee lived down the street from each other, about thirty minutes out of town.

"Aren't you all in a relationship? Why are you guys dressed like that? You two are married!" I directed my question to Harper and Rylee, who were both, in fact, married. They had no business dressing like that. I couldn't deny they still looked good.

Harper laughed. "Maybe you really are a grandma!"

I rolled my eyes. I should've never told her what happened that night I crashed Fallon's party.

"We're adults, Mother, and we look good as hell." She gestured to her low-cut strapless black dress that showed off her chest.

Rylee wore a skimpy red spaghetti-strap dress that highlighted her long legs, while Roxxy opted for black skinny jeans and a red plaid button-up shirt. With her faded pixie cut and piercings, she was the most modestly dressed.

"Yes, you all look great. Can we go now? I really need a drink."

. . .

When we got to *Reid's*, we found a secluded table in the corner. We all sat down and ordered a round of beers. Fallon was meeting us later, which gave me plenty of time to have at least enough drinks to calm my nerves.

We drank as we all took turns bitching about our lives. No one brought up Fallon, and I wasn't about to be the first one. She would get there soon enough, and I was already anxious.

I never knew what to expect with her. I never quite knew where I stood with her. One minute she was kissing me without a care in the world, and the next she was apologizing and saying it was a mistake. She wasn't wrong by saying that.

Anything that happened would be a terrible idea, regardless of how badly I wanted it. That didn't mean I always made good decisions.

"So, then I—" Roxxy was in the middle of talking about her girlfriend, Laura, when she cut herself off and gasped. "Holy fuck shit, who is that?" Her eyes widened as she gaped at something behind me.

"What?" I frowned at her and followed her gaze to a goddamn goddess of a woman who had just walked in the door. "Holy hell," I whispered to myself, struggling to catch my breath.

She looked... well, I didn't have the words for how she looked.

Her red curls were down, blanketing her collarbones. Her makeup was understated, but those crimson lips—the ones I couldn't stop thinking about—were back. She wore a chocolate-brown, low-plunge dress that clung to her curves and stopped mid-thigh. The amount of skin she was showing was enough to make my pulse race. I was fighting every urge to pin her against the bar right then and there. How on earth was I supposed to get through this night?

I clenched my thighs and turned back to Roxxy. "That's Fallon," I said, forcing an even tone, though I couldn't hide the crack in my voice.

"Wow," Rylee said. "She looks... wow."

I scowled at her but excused myself from our table and made my way to Fallon. She hadn't noticed me yet, but when our eyes met, her mouth opened as if to say something, but her expression quickly shifted into a blinding smile.

I kept walking, unable to take my eyes off her. I couldn't have looked away if I tried.

I stopped when I approached her, allowing myself a few seconds to take her all in. I couldn't get enough of her.

What I *really* wanted to do was grab her and kiss those red lips until her lipstick was smeared across her face.

"You look..." I paused, looking all the way from her curly red hair, down to her black strappy shoes. "Abso-fucking-lutely stunning."

She laughed, her cheeks turning pink. "Well, hello to you, too. Are you drunk already?"

Drunk on her, maybe. "I've had a few, but no. You just look... wow, Fallon."

"You look... too," she said, clearing her throat.

I couldn't hide my grin, enjoying the way she looked at me while struggling to keep her composure. She was rarely at a loss for words, so I reveled in this small victory of the night.

I went for a more casual look with a crimson deep-V halter top, black shorts, and white canvas sneakers. Standing next to her, I might as well have been wearing a trash bag.

"You don't look so bad yourself." She cleared her throat. "But it looks like your friends miss you." She motioned to the table, where Rylee, Roxxy, and Harper were all staring at us, waving their hands, and gesturing for us to join them.

"Hey, guys, get over here!" Harper shouted.

"Yeah, I guess they do. Come on, can I buy you a drink?" I asked.

She laughed. "How charming of you. Sure."

I placed my hand on the small of her back, guiding her over to the table. She tensed at first, but by the time we reached the group, she had slightly relaxed.

I introduced Fallon to Roxxy and Harper, since she already knew Rylee. Fallon tried to shake hands with them, but they swatted her attempt away and pulled her into a hug.

"Oh, sweetie, we hug here," Roxxy said with a grin.

Fallon sat down next to Rylee, and I took the seat beside her, leaving Harper and Roxxy across from us.

The waitress came over and I tried to order a round of shots for everyone, but Fallon stopped me with a hand on my shoulder.

"This is your night, Kenzie. This round is on me. Please." I couldn't help but mirror her sweet smile.

The waitress brought our drinks, and I was thankful for the distraction. I'd take anything to keep my mind off all the things I wanted to do to her. I didn't invite her out for... that. I invited her as a friend, and friends don't have those kinds of inappropriate thoughts about each other. But then again, do they show up looking like a fucking wet dream? Because she sure as hell did.

"Kenzie, babe," Roxxy started as soon as the waitress left, "we are so fucking proud of you, and we love you. Cheers to friends." She glanced at Fallon, then smirked at me. I glared in response. "And new adventures." We all raised our glasses and cheered. With a quick tap against the table, we knocked back our shots.

Fallon leaned over to me, gently placing her hand on my arm. "Congratulations," she whispered.

I kept glancing over at Fallon, unable to take my eyes off her. It felt like no one else was there. I desperately wanted to rest my hand on her thigh or her back—to have any form of contact.

After our fourth round of shots, I was definitely feeling the heat of her body next to mine, so I made the smart decision to cut myself off. The last thing I needed was more alcohol adding fuel to the fire—especially when I could cause enough problems on my own. And with Fallon dressed like that? I could've caused all kinds of problems.

"Kenz, you look hot tonight, girl!" Roxxy said.

"Thanks." I laughed.

"You better not leave here alone! There are plenty of hot women in here that would kill for a night with you."

I rolled my eyes in a dismissal, but she kept going, smiling over the rim of her glass. "Seriously, you look too good to let it go to waste. It's been a while since you—"

"Thanks, Rox." I didn't need Fallon to know anything about my sex life, especially how close it was to becoming non-existent.

"All I'm saying is, enjoy yourself tonight, and find someone to play with." She winked.

I turned to look at Fallon. There was a coldness in her eyes I'd never seen before. Her lips pressed into a thin line, and her gaze was narrowed, focused entirely on Roxxy. I couldn't tell if the look sent a thrill down my spine or made my stomach twist in knots. What was going on with her?

"Hey," I whispered, placing my hand on her chair, "are you okay?"

"Come on, let's dance." That was my only warning before she pulled me to my feet and dragged me to the dance floor.

It was a slow song, but she didn't seem to care, so we just held each other and swayed to the music.

I waited until the song was halfway over before asking again, "Are you sure you're okay?" I wanted to talk, just the two of us.

She nodded, a soft smile tugging at her lips. "Yes, I'm fine. Thank you for inviting me out. Your friends seem great," she added, glancing at the group before settling back on me.

"They really are, and I knew they'd like you," I said with a smile.

"They definitely care about you, especially *Roxxy*. She's pretty convinced you should get laid, huh?" she added softly. Her voice was laced with amusement and a hint of something else. I couldn't tell what it was, but I didn't like it. She seemed upset or uncomfortable about something, and that was the last thing I wanted her to feel.

"Roxxy? What are you talking about?"

She opened her mouth to answer, but before she could, the music shifted to a fast-paced song. "Oh, I love this song!" Fallon yelled.

I laughed as we changed our tempo to match the music.

One minute we were swaying slowly to the music, and the next, our bodies were pressed together, moving in perfect rhythm. The warmth of the alcohol mixed with the fire building between us. Our hands gripped each other tighter, our moves getting more intense, and the air felt charged, like it was buzzing.

I opened my mouth to say something, but before I could, her lips were on mine. The kiss was rough but still sensual, full of need that made my knees weak and my mind go blank.

Our tongues moved together, just like our bodies, and for a moment, nothing else existed. Every thought and lingering doubt faded away, lost in the heat of her touch. In that moment, there was only Fallon and the undeniable pull between us.

I let out a sharp gasp when her hands traveled farther down to grab my ass.

"Kenzie." She broke the kiss, my name sounding like a whispered prayer on her lips. "Every time you kiss me, it sends a shock down my body, and I want to beg you to..." She moaned but stopped herself, breaking the kiss and turning red.

"Mackenzie, I..." She pulled away and hurried down the hallway toward the bathrooms. I stood there for a moment, unsure of what to do, unsure of what had just happened.

I finally snapped out of my stunned daze and went after her. I didn't understand how the night had taken such a strange turn. Had I missed something? Did I inadvertently say or do something wrong?

When I caught up to her, she was pacing back and forth. I paused and waited, giving her space.

She turned toward me, and her pacing stopped. Her eyes were swollen and red. There was something in them that made my chest tighten. Whatever it was, it made me want to pull her close and make it go away.

"Hi," she whispered, her voice barely audible.

"Hi." I took a cautious step closer, making sure my tone was soft. She was upset, and I felt an overwhelming need to fix whatever had gone wrong. I reached out, just barely, like I wasn't sure if she wanted the contact, but the distance between us felt too wide. "Fallon, are you okay? What happened out there?"

Her lips parted like she was going to say something, but nothing came out at first.

She took a deep breath, as if trying to collect herself. Her eyes didn't meet mine. "I don't know. I saw Roxxy flirting with you, and then what she said about you not leaving alone, and—"

I snorted. "Flirting? Fallon, God, no. Roxxy wasn't flirting. We've been best friends since fourth grade. Besides, she's a little drunk. Anyway, why would it matter? You and I are just friends, right?"

"Yeah, of course, you're right. I guess I just got..." She trailed off as her cheeks turned red in embarrassment.

"Wait, were you jealous?" I smirked. The idea that Fallon could've been jealous sent a flutter through my chest. We *were* friends, but despite every instinct telling me to walk away, I couldn't deny my attraction to her. And to think she might've felt even a fraction of that? That was a dangerous thought altogether.

"Definitely not!" she blurted out. "I think I've had too many shots... I don't know what I'm saying."

"Right." I drew out the word and gave her a knowing look that said I didn't buy her lie for a second, but I left it alone.

I took a step closer and reached my hand out to fix the strap of her dress. "This dress looks incredible on you," I whispered, "but I'm curious how it'd look on my bedroom floor."

Her cheeks flushed. "You—"

"Wish? I most certainly do, don't I?" I winked.

"Always a charmer." She rolled her eyes with a smile.

I chuckled, ignoring the feelings her eye roll stirred in my gut. "Well, come on, we should probably get back," I said. It was too tempting, being alone with Fallon in the secluded, dark corner of the bar.

She cleared her throat. "Right. We probably should." I held out my arm and she surprisingly took it, linking us together.

We headed back to our table, where everyone was laughing and having a good time. As we walked up, they looked up and waved us over. "Took you two long enough," Roxxy teased, while Rylee lifted her glass with a grin. Of course, Harper sat there quietly, observing everyone.

We sat back down, and she spoke again. "Is everything okay?" she asked, her tone more serious, as if she could sense the tension in the air.

Fallon shot me a quick glance before turning to face her. Lifting her chin slightly, she cleared her throat. "Yes, everything's fine. We were just talking," she said with a smile, taking a sip of her drink.

Roxxy raised an eyebrow, eyeing both of us with a grin. "It's always good to *talk* in the corner of a bar, alone. Can I be next?" she said, her tone teasing.

Harper cleared her throat. "Okay, Roxxy, quit teasing the poor girl before you make her jealous." She laughed, but I kicked her under the table.

"Ouch," she whispered, rubbing her leg before kicking me back.

Fallon almost choked on her drink. "What? I'm not jealous. I mean, yeah, Roxxy, you're gorgeous, but I... we aren't... I mean—"

"Breathe." I laughed, and when I placed my hand on her leg, she finally let out a breath.

Roxxy looked at her, and her expression softened. "Oh, honey, I'm sorry. We were just teasing. We poke fun at each other a lot, and I wanted to make you feel more comfortable. Trust me, Kenzie is not my type."

"Thanks, Rox!" I playfully scowled.

"We've been best friends since we were little. Besides, I am spoken for, maddeningly so. I'm sorry if I made you go all predatory on her ass. You have nothing to worry about." She smiled at Fallon, who returned the smile.

She leaned over to whisper in my ear. "Thank you for inviting me out." She nudged my shoulder.

"Get a room, you two!" Rylee said, and we both laughed.

I leaned over and whispered in Fallon's ear, "That's not a bad idea." I smirked, watching her cheeks flush pink. I sat back, took a drink, and grinned like an idiot.

We sat there for another few hours, drinking and talking. Fallon seemed so comfortable with my friends, and I enjoyed my time watching her laugh and chat with them.

She was just... something special. I couldn't help but wonder if I was the only one feeling something between us.

Chapter Nineteen

MACKENZIE

Four rounds of shots, and a few margaritas later, it was time to call it a night.

When we decided to leave, it was getting close to midnight. Rylee, being our designated driver, was the only one who could still walk in a straight line. The rest of us? Let's just say we were feeling the effects of the night.

We all piled into her car—a steel-gray Yukon that was more like a building on wheels. It was the most massive vehicle I'd ever ridden in.

Harper claimed the front seat, while Roxxy slid into the left side by the window. The right side was taken up by a car seat for Rylee's two-year-old son, Greyson—who wasn't with us, but his seat definitely wasn't going anywhere. That left me crammed into the back row with Fallon, not that I was foolish enough to complain about it.

As Rylee drove us home, she and Harper got caught up in a conversation about the real estate market—not something I was about to join in on.

Roxxy was busy scrolling on her phone, which left Fallon and me in our own little bubble, the hum of the car and the glow of passing streetlights keeping us company. We exchanged glances and soft smiles, our hands occasionally brushing against each other's thighs, creating an unspoken connection between us.

When we hit a sharp turn, Rylee bumped a curb, and Fallon was jolted out of her seat and into me.

"Oh shit, sorry, guys! I'm still getting used to this car." She laughed, and I hoped she wasn't the one driving when Greyson was in the car.

Our eyes met for a second, and maybe it was the alcohol, or perhaps it was the sheer addiction I felt when I looked at Fallon, but I could have sworn we were touching the sun. Heat rushed out of every pore on my body.

"That's why you should be wearing a seatbelt, Sunshine," I said as I helped her sit up, noticing her flushed cheeks.

She ignored my warning and shifted closer, resting her hand on my thigh, her fingers slowly trailing up toward the seam of my shorts, inching closer to the source of my heat. I inhaled sharply and looked at her.

"Fallon," I breathed out in warning.

She pressed her lips to my ear and whispered, "Yeah?" Her voice sent a wave of ecstasy through me. The moment her lips brushed the shell of my ear, I felt like I was burning up.

She moved her fingers lazily across my inner thigh, brushing over the fabric of my shorts. I gasped and bit my lip, stopping the moan that almost escaped. She delicately caressed the side of my pussy and I tilted my head back and closed my eyes. Breathing became a challenge. The heat of her touch was enough to send me over the edge.

"Oh," she moaned in my ear, causing me to smile widely while trying to collect myself.

She was now flicking one of the red balls of my princess Diana piercing. I had gotten the piercing when I turned twenty-one.

"That is so sexy. Is all this for me, Wildcat?" she whispered, moving her fingers and rubbing my sensitive clit.

Yes, I wanted to say, but I couldn't find any words. I was embarrassingly wet from her touch.

A soft moan bubbled in my throat before I swallowed it down. Remembering we weren't alone, I grabbed her hand and pulled it out of my shorts, internally shouting at myself in the process. I really didn't want it to stop.

"Shit," I breathed, "Fallon, my sister is in this car. We can't do that."

She didn't seem offended by my rejection; she only grinned. "Do you want to know what would happen if she wasn't in the car?"

I turned to look at her with narrowed brows, silently answering her question. If I tried to speak, it would've sounded like a plea for her to fuck me in the back seat of my best friend's car—not something I was usually fond of, but with the way Fallon was looking at me, I found it hard to care about anything else.

She leaned in to whisper in my ear, "I would make that wet pussy drip... all... over... this... seat."

"I am in so much trouble," I groaned.

She put her head back against the seat, looking quite proud of herself. With the way her words almost ruined me, she should've felt very proud.

Harper turned around toward us. "Fallon, we hope you had a good time tonight."

Fallon sat up and grinned at my sister, as if she didn't just leave me a horny mess. "I did. Thank you for inviting me."

"It was really great to meet you, Fallon. It takes a strong person to handle this one," Roxxy said, nodding toward me. I rolled my eyes, but Fallon looked at me and smiled.

We made it home without any more incidents, and unfortunately, Fallon kept her hands to herself for the rest of the trip. We said our goodbyes and headed inside. In the lobby, we held hands until we got on the elevator.

We stood there in silence, waiting for the doors to shut. As soon as they did, we looked at each other. After a few moments, the space between us grew smaller until our lips and bodies came together.

I grabbed her waist and pushed her against the wall. She combed her fingers through my hair, drawing a soft moan from me. The way we kissed in that moment, it was like the elevator was stealing our oxygen, and we were each other's only chance at survival.

I heard the ding of the elevator before it stopped. We pulled apart as the doors opened, and my neighbor, Mrs. Thomas, got on. She was a seventy-six-year-old spitfire with fire-engine-red hair that always looked freshly curled, and a mouth like a sailor.

We stood nervously on opposite sides of the elevator, like kids caught making out by their parents. Neither of us moved, staying as still as statues, until we reached our floor.

I said goodbye to Mrs. Thomas, took Fallon's hand, and led her out of the elevator. As I started to unlock my door, she stopped me, gently turning me so I was facing her.

She wrapped her arms around my neck, and I wrapped mine around her waist, pulling her closer. "Thank you again for tonight, I had a lot of fun."

I smiled. "Thank you for coming out. My friends adored you."

"What's not to love?" She shrugged before biting her lip, causing me to grip her a little tighter to hold myself up. "I also *really* enjoyed seeing you in this outfit. It suits you." She smirked as I kissed her nose.

"Do you maybe want to come in?" I asked. "Not to... just to talk?"

She smiled and pulled me closer to whisper in my ear, "If you don't open that door within the next five seconds, I'm going to break it down and fuck you right on top of it, Wildcat."

Holy hell, this woman...

Without hesitation, I kissed her fiercely, not caring if anyone saw us. Once we were inside, she turned us around, pressing me against the door. My hands were over my head, her hands holding mine in place, all without our lips ever parting.

She started kissing my neck, down to my collarbone where she sucked slightly, and I couldn't hold in the moan. She looked at me with a smile and dropped my hands, taking one in hers as she led us to the couch and sat me down before straddling me, making my vision turn hazy.

The feeling of her body beneath my hands, even over the fabric of her dress, had my skin feeling scorched. The restraint I was trying to show in not taking off her dress was impressive.

I remembered how she nervously bit her bottom lip and avoided eye contact after we almost slept together. I wasn't trying to bring back the guilt I felt when I saw the regret on her face.

If this was going to happen, she'd have to tell me she wanted it. If she did, I was going to take my time with her. She deserved more than just a quick one-night stand.

"I've been waiting all night for this." She grabbed my face and kissed me with an urgency I was too happy to match.

I smiled and said honestly, "I've been waiting *weeks* for you."

I grabbed her waist and kissed the top of her chest. She gasped as I brought her close, placing tender kisses along her neck. She tilted her head back, giving me easier access. I traced a line from her chest to her throat with my tongue, biting down lightly, careful not to leave a mark. The low plunging neckline of her dress did little to hide what was underneath, and I reached in to release her gorgeous breasts.

When they came into view, I saw the gold piercings I hadn't been able to stop fantasizing about. Scooping one nipple into my mouth, I groaned. She whimpered and threw her head back. "Oh, shit."

I smirked and took her hand, trailing it down my body, leading her inside my shorts. She sucked in a breath, giving me a devilish grin. "This is what you do to me, Fallon. Anytime I see you or touch you. Hell, even thinking about you. You make me so fucking wet."

She rubbed my clit, causing me to close my eyes and bite my lip. I rested my head on the couch and hissed when she bit my collarbone. "Fuck, Fallon," I murmured.

"Well," she said, before she slowly slipped her glistening fingers out of my shorts, causing a shutter within myself, "why don't you find out how wet *you* make me." Then she brought her fingers to her lips and sucked them clean. The sight of it, along with her words, shot a bolt of electricity down to my core.

Standing, I accepted her hand and pulled her by the waist, closing the space between us.

She took in a sharp breath. "Mackenzie, if you kiss me again, I... I don't think I'll be able to stop," she said nervously.

"I don't want you to stop." I kissed her again, sweeping my tongue in her mouth, tasting all of her. She moaned when I bit her lip, and she returned the favor, causing a similar sound to escape from me.

This kiss was slow and sensual. I was taking my time because I wanted this moment to last for as long as possible. After a few minutes, she hesitated and pulled away. I saw the longing and indecision in her eyes, and as she stared at me, I knew not to push.

"Jesus, Kenzie," she said breathlessly.

I led her into the kitchen and grabbed a couple of waters from the fridge. My mind wandered to the thought of that pretty little ass on my island. I wasn't joking when I told her she could sit on it, but I knew I needed to take things slow with her. As we drank the water, we locked eyes, and as soon as she finished, I gently tugged on her dress, pulling her back toward me.

I cupped her cheek with my hand, pressing a soft kiss to her forehead, then her nose, then her cheek, and finally, those dangerous lips.

"These lips will be the death of me one day," I whispered. She grinned in response.

I brushed my lips against hers. "If you want me to stop, you need to tell me right now." I looked at her for a moment, searching her eyes for a glimpse of protest.

She shook her head. "No, don't stop. Please, don't stop," she breathed. Tilting my head, she kissed my neck, sucking gently before licking her way up to my ear and nipping it. *Did I die and go to heaven, because there's no way this is happening right now. Being this close to Fallon feels too good to be real.*

Chapter Twenty

MACKENZIE

"Do you have any fucking idea how sexy you are?"

Fallon chuckled, a soft sigh escaping her. She had to have known it was true. I had never met anyone who could easily take my breath away, with just a simple smile, like she could.

"I'm serious. You're incredibly beautiful, you know that?" I held her face and kissed her again.

She ran her fingers through my hair, tugging gently, and I let out a soft hum as my hands glided down her arms to her waist. She raked her nails along my back and gasped as I tugged on her dress.

She took off my shirt and pulled away. "God, how is it fair that you look like that?" she said in deep breaths. I smiled, and she kissed me again.

I moved my hands from her waist up to her arms, pushing the dress off her shoulders and down to her feet.

I kissed my way down her hips and legs, feeling the soft curve of her thigh and the warmth of her skin beneath my fingers. Fallon was a dream I never wanted to end.

She tilted her head back, allowing me to start kissing her neck, her shoulders, and eventually making my way back to her lips. Even if I were miles away with no sense of direction, I'd find my way back to those crimson lips, and the freckles sprinkled across her skin like a secret I was desperate to discover.

She turned her body and gripped the counter, leaning back against it. I placed my hands on her waist and lifted her up.

Her head tilted back, but I grabbed her chin gently and forced her to look at me. "Are you sure this is what you want, Fallon? Just one word and it stops."

She looked at me, biting her lip, and nodded. "Yes," she whispered, her voice breathless. "Please, Mackenzie."

Without another word, I kissed her again before licking my way down her neck, lingering in between her breasts. I greedily circled one nipple with my tongue before bringing it into my mouth. She moaned, causing me to smile.

My hands were gripping her hips. Her hands were tangled in my hair. Her mouth was parted. My mouth was in dangerous territory, licking and kissing down her stomach to her waist.

She leaned back and parted her thighs as I kissed them delicately. I licked her inner thighs, teasing her. I traced curvy lines on her skin, taking my time to explore every inch of her.

I wasn't going to make this easy for her. I was going to tempt her until she begged for more. Then, when she couldn't take it, I'd make her come so hard, she would understand why I *did well for myself.*

She jolted when my fingers found her soaked clit, her moans blocking out any other sounds as I blew gently. "Jesus! Please, Kenzie."

"Please what, Fallon? Tell me what you want," I said as I continued to circle her clit.

"I want you to fuck me, right here," she breathed, her sounds shattering the little self control I had left.

"I need to taste you," I said. "Tell me I can taste you." I didn't care that I was begging for it.

"Please, Kenzie." She threw her head back and parted her legs wider.

The taste of her was enough to push me over the edge. Her desire wrapped around my tongue, and I craved more.

I grazed my teeth over her now crimson bud, and sucked. "Oh, wow!" She moaned and smacked the counter, trying to grasp anything she could.

I hummed into her, causing her to feel the vibrations of my pleasure within herself. I took my hands off her hips and interlaced them with hers. As she gripped my hands tighter with pleasure, I eased the pressure of my tongue on her clit, making her swell and beg for more.

Fallon let go my hands, and grabbed my face, pulling me up toward her as she brought our mouths together, getting a taste of her own essence.

She released our lips and I took a step back as she jumped off the counter.

"Fallon?" I asked. She grabbed my hand and led me to the couch.

She stopped once my back was to the couch and kissed me, pushing me back until I was sitting down.

She straddled my lap and kissed me again, my hands feeling the soft skin of her hips, and her lips on my neck. I moved my hands back, and grabbed her ass, bringing her closer to me and causing her to moan.

I began to trail my hands up her spine when she started to rock back and forth on top of me, making me groan and dig my fingers into her skin. I needed more of her. I didn't know what she was doing to me, but I had never craved anyone as much as her.

The sight of her, the thought of her, the smell of her—it was the most addictive drug, and I was desperate for more. I could feel myself losing the ability to think clearly, willing to succumb to the pleasure of the high, even knowing it would eventually come to an end.

She kissed her way up my neck and whispered in my ear, "I want you to know how I taste when you make me come."

"Fuck." The feeling of her panting breath in my ear had me letting out a low whine, wrapping my arms around her, and twisting us until she lay beneath me.

Our eyes locked, my blood simmering with desire. Heavy breaths filled the silence. In that moment, we both knew there was no turning back. It could've been a mistake, or exactly what we needed. Honestly, I didn't care. I was completely lost in the moment.

My lips met hers, and my hands began their slow exploration of her skin. A need to know every inch of her burned inside me—how she felt, how she tasted.

My fingers drifted over the delicate skin of her inner thighs, drawing a sweet gasp from her lips. Feeling her soft skin sent a hum of electricity through me. It felt like my whole body was on fire. With her lips on mine and our bodies only millimeters apart, nothing else seemed to matter.

The kiss deepened, and I teased her bottom lip with a gentle nibble before letting my touch trail further down, stopping to trace around her clit.

She arched into my touch, moaning when I started adding light pressure, forming small circles so delicately she could hardly feel the presence of my fingers.

"You're so wet," I breathed as she grabbed my hand and pressed it harder against herself, demanding more friction.

"Oh my God, Kenzie, please," she begged. I pushed a finger in slowly before pulling out until I was almost out of her completely.

"Tell me what you want, Sunshine." She writhed under me, pushing herself into my hand.

"Fuck me. Now," she whimpered.

"How? How do you want me to fuck you?" I asked. "I need you to talk to me. Tell me exactly how you want this to go." I would do anything she wanted—all she had to do was say the word.

"I want... your mouth on me, and your fingers inside me. I want everything you can give me." Hearing her tell me what she wanted had my pussy aching for her touch.

"Mm, good girl. I love it when you tell me what you want," I whispered, taking my finger out and grazing it against her clit, making her moan. I smiled and brushed my tongue against her lips before we shared another kiss.

She was such a beautiful mess, and we had only gotten started. I couldn't wait to see her trembling beneath me, her perfect red curls clinging to my pillowcases, and my bedsheets soaked with her.

Kissing down her chest, I made my way to her thighs, making sure to take my time. I wanted to be present in the moment and not miss a single sound or shudder she made. She opened farther, giving me permission. I kissed around her clit, before taking it into my mouth, causing her to arch her body. Fuck, she was so perfect.

"Oh, yes," she muttered. I was devouring her as if she were my last meal, licking and sucking until her whole body was trembling. I slid two fingers inside her while my mouth worked her clit. They went in with no resistance, and I ached for the feeling to last. She felt so good clenched around my fingers, and the little sounds she was making that filled the room made me fucking drip.

But her taste was something else entirely. It was sweet and her arousal smelled so incredible, I felt my own pussy tightening with every taste. She was going to make me come without even a touch.

"Fuck, Mackenzie!" she screamed as she exploded with pleasure. I drank up everything she gave me while she gripped the couch and arched her back, her head deep in the pillows.

The sound of her losing control would be burned into my memory for years to come. At that point, if she touched me anywhere, I would've exploded.

I took my time pulling my fingers out while placing tender kisses around her clit, before giving my attention to her trembling thighs.

She lay her head down and closed her eyes, her breaths uneven and unsteady, as though she were trying to gather herself before speaking. "Holy shit." She barely got out the words, and I placed a kiss on her forehead with a smile.

"For the record, sweetheart..." I leaned in and kissed her again, letting it linger. It felt like I was telling her everything I couldn't put into words. I pulled away before the kiss consumed me. "You taste addictive." She smiled and stood up, taking my hand.

She led me to the bedroom and stopped at the edge of the bed. Taking her time, she stripped me of my shorts, like we had all the time in the world. I didn't complain when my underwear went with them and she lay me down. She sat on top of me and kissed me, sucking one nipple while playing with the other, which caused me to close my eyes.

"Fuck," I breathed.

I felt my clit pulse once. Twice. The sight of her alone was enough to ruin me.

This woman was my drug of choice. A naked Fallon and tequila did not mix well. In that moment, though, I didn't care. All I cared about was this. Us.

She brought her lips to my ear, her voice low and gentle. "I want you to get soaking wet for me."

I didn't dare say a word as she led us to the bathroom, turning on the shower and stepping in, motioning for me to follow her. I stopped and stared at her, taking in her fully naked body, soaked in water.

It was Fallon who broke our stare when she walked closer and pressed our lips together. The shower head rained down on us and our bodies glistened with water droplets as we kissed, making the moment blissfully erotic.

She broke the kiss and turned us so I was facing the glass door. She stood behind me and I tilted my head back as she started kissing my back.

As her body was pressed into mine, she reached around, taking my breasts in her hands, and I gasped when she lightly pulled at the nipples.

"Fallon, I need you, please," I begged.

"I knew you were a beggar." She chuckled as she was gently kissing my shoulders. I would've done anything, as long as she never stopped touching me.

"Please, Fallon."

She hummed in approval and walked us forward, pressing my hard nipples against the glass. The coldness of the shower door wasn't the only reason I shivered. She was taking complete control, and I didn't know how much longer I would last.

I gasped when I felt her hand trailing down my body, and she gently massaged my soaking clit. I held myself up against the glass and moaned as her fingers found their way into me. "Oh my God."

"I prefer to go by Fallon, or Sunshine," she whispered. She continued pushing two fingers in and out of me until I was on the edge of coming, before she stopped and slowly withdrew. I groaned in protest, but it was cut short when she spun me around and grabbed my face to kiss me.

"You are unbelievably sexy, Mackenzie," she breathed, breaking the kiss.

My heart was racing and I was panting too much to say or do anything except blush.

She kissed me again, starting from my lips, traveling lower and lower. She kissed in between my breasts, then moved until she was on her knees in front of me.

She took one of my legs and propped it up on the ledge of the shower door and kissed each thigh, causing a moan to escape from my lips.

When her mouth landed on my clit, my head flew back, hitting the glass, but I didn't care. As long as she kept her mouth on me, I didn't care about anything else.

The sight of her kneeling before me, worshiping me with her tongue while the water coated her body, was all that existed in the universe.

When she nipped at my clit, I hissed and tangled my hands through her hair, keeping her where I needed her most.

She licked and nibbled a few more times before I was shuddering and coming undone.

I felt my release coming closer and closer with every touch. "Shit, Fallon. Please don't stop. Fuck, that feels so good, baby," I hissed, seconds away from losing my mind.

When my orgasm came, I couldn't control the sounds that came from my throat. Everything felt too good, and I couldn't find it in me to be embarrassed about whatever was happening inside that shower.

I forced my eyes open when she pulled away, and I was met with Fallon staring widely at me. "What? What's wrong?"

She stood up and kissed me so hard I stumbled back a little. "You... you just squirted," she stammered. "Holy shit, that was the hottest thing I've ever experienced."

We were in the shower for far too long. So long, in fact, the water had run cold, but it didn't matter. I would've willingly froze in that shower if it meant I could've stayed there with Fallon.

I stepped out of the shower first before helping her out and lifting her into my arms. She wrapped her legs around my hips, our wet bodies pressing together again as I carried her to the bed.

I sat her down as I gave her a towel, and headed to the dresser to get some oversized shirts. After we put them on, I quietly sat next to her, my eyes never leaving her as I smiled.

"Why are you looking at me like that?" she asked after realizing I was staring at her. "Is there something on my face?" She began to vigorously wipe her face.

I laughed and kissed her forehead, placing a hand down on the bed next to her side. "I just like looking at you, that's all."

She blushed and nudged me. "Oh," she said softly, leaning in to give me a soft kiss. Just feeling her tongue anywhere on me...

The need for her came rushing back in an instant, and just like that, our shirts ended up on the floor.

Chapter Twenty-One
FALLON

What. The. Fuck! Trying not to believe it was only a little past four in the morning, I turned away from the clock and stared at the ceiling. I had *a lot* to drink last night, but unfortunately not enough to forget... everything.

I looked over at the deliciously naked Mackenzie sleeping next to me, and blew out a breath, remembering the events that happened over the last twelve hours.

Meeting Mackenzie at the bar. Drinking, dancing, and... the sex. Unforgettable, every room in the house, type of sex.

Black Silk sheets barely covered her gorgeous body, and the sight almost wrecked me again. I wanted to get under the sheets and lay there with her, or wake her up and—

"Oh my God!" I mouthed, rubbing my face and trying to forget everything that happened.

I slowly inched my way off the bed and froze when she shifted. She turned on her side and I let out a relieved breath when she faced away from me. I got dressed and got the hell out of there as quietly as I could manage.

As soon as I got in my apartment, I slouched down against my door. "Fuck, fuck, fuck!" I whispered. What was I thinking?!

That was a huge mistake. An amazing, toe curling, multiple orgasmic mistake that couldn't happen again.

I stood up, shaking the memory from my mind, and went to take a shower. I had to get rid of anything that lingered from my night with Mackenzie.

I had never been the kind of person to have a one-night stand and sleep with a complete stranger—that just wasn't who I was, but...

There was just something about Mackenzie. When I was around her, I seemed to lose any sense of rational thinking. But not anymore. What we did would not happen again. It couldn't.

After my ex cheated on me, I swore to myself I wouldn't make the same mistakes again.

Mackenzie *was* a mistake that wouldn't be repeated, even if she was the best I'd ever had.

I woke up in the late afternoon, but just barely. I felt worse than I did after my party, but only parts of me. The rest of my body... it didn't matter. *It's not happening again, stop thinking about it!*

I shook it off and went to make dinner when my phone started buzzing.

At least I had the good sense to turn off the ringer before going to bed last night. But sober me didn't have any good sense at all, because despite seeing who was calling, I picked up anyway.

"Hello?" I said in a groggy voice, almost as if my voice was tired and overused from the night before.

"Hello, love! I have been calling you for at least an hour, where have you been?!" Drea's chipper voice made me want to throw my phone into a fire.

I groaned. "I've been home. Could you lower your voice, just a little?" I rubbed the sleep out of my eyes, squinting from the afternoon sun. "I just got up. I'm not feeling that well today. Sorry if I scared you."

It wasn't a total lie, I *wasn't* feeling well, just not for the reason she probably thought.

"I'm just glad you aren't dead in a ditch somewhere. Do you need me to bring you anything?" The sincerity in her voice made something inside my chest crack.

"No, I'm fine, really. I'm going to take a hot bath and get some rest. I'll call you later, okay?"

"Fine," she relented. "Get some rest, and if I don't hear from you later, I'll send a search party!" With that threat, she hung up. I chuckled and started on my bath.

A hot bath was one of the things that always helped me when I was having a bad day. Lately, it seemed like there were more bad days than good.

My bath time routine was down to a ritual at this point. I had a wax warmer plugged in that also doubled as a night light. I tossed in a few handfuls of lavender salts, and some lavender bubble bath infused with essential oils into a scalding tub. I loved seeing the steam rise from my skin when I left the bath. I turned off the lights and turned on some relaxing music, attempting to float my thoughts away.

I tried really hard to focus on anything but last night. But no matter how hard I tried, it kept creeping back into my mind. Finally, I gave up, climbed out of the water that was filled with memories I didn't want, and headed back to bed.

The following day, I was awoken by a violent knocking on my door. I checked the time, and scowled when I saw that it was the ungodly hour of five in the morning. Common sense told me to stay in bed, but my curiosity got the better of me.

I rolled out of bed and walked to the door. When I checked the peephole, I contemplated not answering, but I knew if I ignored her, I wouldn't have a door anymore.

"Good morning, Dre—" I barely got the words out when she swung the door open and stormed in.

"Please, do come in," I muttered.

"Do you have any idea how worried I was, Fallon Rose?! I was this close to calling the police on your ass!" She whirled around and was talking aggressively with her hands. Subtly was not her strong suit.

"Calm down, Dre. I fell asleep. I told you I wasn't feeling well." The half-truth came out easier the second time. I wasn't about to tell her exactly why I was feeling sick.

She glared at me. "Well, a lot of good that did! You still look like dog shit, love."

I rolled my eyes and flopped onto the couch. "Thank's, Drea. That makes me feel better."

"Well, you do. I'm sorry—are you sure you're alright?" She rubbed my arm, and I tried to hide my emotions—something I was never good at.

I cleared my throat and looked at her. "Yeah, I'm fine. Just a stomach bug, I think. I'm really sorry, I didn't mean to worry you."

It might've seemed silly to an outsider that Drea freaked out over a few hours of no communication, but after my breakup, I hit a rough patch. It got so bad that I turned off my phone for days at a time and barely left my room. I even took vacation days from work because I didn't see the point of leaving my bed. If it hadn't been for Drea, I don't know how I would've survived.

"I just worry about you, you know, after... well, it doesn't matter. I'm just glad you're okay. Is Mackenzie still giving you trouble?"

I looked away at the mention of Mackenzie's name and shook my head. I couldn't tell Drea what happened—not until I could sort through my thoughts about it myself.

"Nope, no trouble." *Except my internal troubles!* "I haven't talked to her, so we're all good there." Technically, that wasn't a lie. I hadn't talked to her. Not since I slept with her, anyway.

I let out a sigh as she headed for the door, but my relief was short-lived when she turned back around. "I'll call you later, okay? And you better answer this time, or so help me!"

"Yes, Mother." I laughed, following her to the door. I just wanted to be left alone with my thoughts swirling inside my head. Regret threatened to consume me, mixing with the desperate need for a repeat of our night together, and I was dizzy from it all.

When I opened the door, I froze. Mackenzie was going into her apartment and my breath caught when our eyes met. Drea looked between us with a question in her eyes, and my cheeks burned with guilt.

"Bye, Drea." I shoved her out the door. She smirked at me as she greeted Mackenzie, and thankfully, she didn't plan on striking up a conversation as she left.

"I..." I started, but quickly shut the door and locked it, hiding like the coward I was. I was afraid of what she would say, and terrified I had nothing to say. If I was being honest, I was afraid she would either say she regretted last night, or she wanted a repeat. Which option I wanted it to be, I wasn't so sure.

Of course, not ten seconds after she left, Drea blew up my phone:

Drea: I felt that tension, what happened??

Drea: Jesus christ, she is still hot! You better take that!

I groaned as I slouched back on the couch. I already had it, and look where it got me!

Me: Oh my God, Drea, seriously? Go talk to Skylar! Remember your devoted partner? I'm going to take a nap.

I turned my phone on silent and hid underneath the covers, hoping everyone stayed away and left me alone for the rest of the day. I royally screwed up...

Chapter Twenty-Two
MACKENZIE

After the hallway incident, I avoided Fallon for the past week. What we did was… well, it was explosive, but it was also a bad idea. And seeing her in the hallway as her best friend was leaving only confirmed she felt the same way.

Which was good, because I definitely didn't want it to happen again. Still, as much as I didn't want to have the awkward conversation, we needed to in order to move past this.

The morning after our night together, I thought Fallon and I had moved past our differences and could start over. I even caught myself fantasizing about making her breakfast in bed. I'd had my fair share of one-night stands, but Fallon felt different.

I woke up before she did and patiently waited for her to open her beautiful eyes. The look on her face told me I was completely wrong about where I stood with her. *What was I thinking?*

A few days ago, I finally got the courage to text her, asking if we could talk. I'd tried reaching out a few more times since then, but every message had gone unanswered.

After waiting around for several days, I decided we had to talk about what happened, and I knew the first place to look if I wanted to find her.

. . .

"Hey, Mackenzie, welcome in." Drea greeted me with a look that made it clear her best friend hadn't filled her in on what happened.

Maybe Fallon was ashamed and hadn't told anyone, or maybe she hadn't had the chance yet. Maybe Drea knew and just didn't care? I really needed to stop thinking so much about it.

I smiled back, my eyes scanning the bookstore for a familiar pair of gray ones. "Hey, Drea." I walked up to the counter where she was finishing up with a customer.

"What's going on? Anything I can help you find?"

"Actually, I'm looking for Fallon. Have you seen her today?" I asked, knowing that if anyone knew where to find her, it was her best friend.

"Oh no, I'm sorry, not today. Is everything alright?"

I smiled tightly. "Uh, I don't know. I haven't seen or talked to her in a few days, and I just wanted to make sure she's okay."

I wasn't sure what Drea knew, so I didn't want to reveal too much about what had been going on. Still, I had a feeling she sensed something was up when I saw her leaving Fallon's apartment the other day.

"Well, aren't you sweet? I'll be sure to send her your way when I see her."

"Yeah, thanks, Drea. Have a good day, alright?"

"Of course. You, too, love."

My last stop was *Brewed Awakening* before taking off for work. I needed to take my mind off things at home, and work was as good of a distraction as anything else.

When I got to work, I noticed a missed call from an unfamiliar number. I shrugged it off, but a few hours later, a text came through from the same number. I dropped my phone as soon as I opened the message and saw who it was from:

Unknown Number: Hey Kenz. It's Rebecca.

Unknown Number: I know it's been a while. I miss you. Can you call me? Please, K?

"Kenzie? Kenzie?!" Roxxy was shouting, but all I could do was stare blankly ahead. The shock of those messages had shattered every part of my senses.

"Mackenzie!" I snapped back to reality as Roxxy shook me.

"I'm sorry, I... what happened?" I closed my eyes, shaking my head as I tried to make sense of what was going on.

"That's what I'm trying to figure out. Kenzie, you look really pale. Are you okay?" She watched me, concern filling her eyes.

I had to sit and blink a few times before I could find the words. "I, uhh..." I cleared my throat. "Earlier, I missed a call from a number I didn't recognize, and they just texted me." I took a deep breath before continuing. "It was Rebecca, Rox. She said she misses me and wants me to call her."

"Are you out of your fucking mind, Mackenzie?! You cannot seriously be considering this!" she yelled.

I rolled my eyes. "Of course not, don't be ridiculous. But what does she want? And why is she contacting me now? It's been two years!"

"Since she fucked some bitch on your couch? Yes, I know. That is exactly why you are not replying back. She doesn't deserve shit from you. I swear, I want to light a firework and shove it up her ass for what she did to you."

I snorted. "That's extreme, but also eerily specific. Have you thought about this at all?"

She shrugged. "Once or twice." The grin on her face was pure evil. I laughed and rolled my eyes. I put my phone away, refusing to respond.

Roxxy didn't need to know the texts from Rebecca had affected me. Every now and then, she crossed my mind, but any desire to reach out to her was long gone. I thought I'd marry her one day—maybe we'd have a few kids and some fur babies. She ruined all of that the moment I caught her fucking someone else in our apartment.

At the time, Rebecca was a business consultant and traveled constantly for work. I didn't think anything of it when we started dating, but after four years together, I began to get suspicious. I offered to fly out to spend time with her on her trips, but she always found reasons why it wouldn't work. When I confronted her about it, she'd turn things around and accuse me of not trusting her. Eventually, I brushed away any doubts, believing the love I had for her was enough.

After a business deal closed, Rebecca was home for a few weeks, and I was so excited to have her back that I left work early to spend the afternoon with her. I picked up her favorite wine and a few ingredients to cook her a romantic dinner and surprise her—but when I got home, I found a surprise of my own.

I quietly opened the front door of our apartment and set the bags on the kitchen table. That's when I heard the loud moans.

Thinking she was probably watching something on the TV, I imagined the ways I wanted to worship her body. Slowly, I walked into the dimly lit living room, wanting to surprise her. But instead, I found her with another woman.

Rebecca was lying on the couch, totally unaware I had walked in. The other woman was underneath her, moaning loudly. I didn't stay to confront either of them. I was so shocked that I backed up and walked right out of the apartment. I cried all the way to Harper's place, telling myself I'd never fall for anyone again.

After work, I wandered into a bar near my apartment. I needed several drinks and maybe an easy distraction, anything to keep my mind off Fallon. Each time I saw a redhead, my chest tightened, and I found myself reaching for another drink.

By the time I left the bar, I had danced with three women—none of them with red hair, coincidentally—and staggered my drunk, miserable ass home. I was intoxicated and in no condition to make any good decisions.

That was the only explanation I had for knocking on Fallon's door well past midnight. I didn't even know what I'd say if she opened it.

After a few unanswered knocks, I gave up. I thought I heard movement inside, but I shrugged it off and went home. She'd been ignoring my calls and texts, so it was clear she didn't want to talk, and that was fine.

Harper called shortly after I got home, but I ignored her. I assumed Roxxy told her what happened, and I didn't want to talk to anyone. I needed to get my thoughts together and get back on track. I went out specifically for a distraction and to forget about the past several weeks, but... I just couldn't.

Before I slept with Fallon, I had no trouble falling into someone's bed and leaving the next morning without a word, but now, I wasn't sure it would be so simple. *Get it together! You slept together one time, and she's ignoring you!*

I shouldn't have been so affected by her. I thought one night was all I wanted. I got what I needed, and I should've been able to move on.

Groaning, I threw myself onto the bed. I needed sleep to suffocate my thoughts.

I couldn't tell if I'd been asleep for a few hours or if it had been days. The clock on my phone told me it had only been six hours, but I didn't want to believe it, so I groaned and rolled over.

"Oof." Apparently, I rolled the wrong way, and there wasn't any more bed to land on, causing me to meet the floor instead of my soft pillow. I hoped the fall was enough to hurt me so I wouldn't have to get up. Sadly, my bladder informed me I hadn't fallen hard enough, and I stood up against my will.

After getting out of the bathroom, I texted Rylee. If anyone could cure a hangover, it was her:

> Me: 💀 Help!

> Rylee: Haha long night?

> Me: You could say that… Can you help please?!

> Rylee: Of course. I'm just waking up so give me like 20 minutes.

> Me: Literal life saver… I love you so much!

I put my hair in a messy bun, not bothering to put on real clothes as I ordered a car to Rylee's.

I was in no mood to be driving, and the driver probably thought I was doing the ride of shame for the way I looked. I felt pretty shameful, honestly. Knocking on Fallon's door in the middle of the night, after she had been ignoring me? Talk about pathetic.

It was Lana's lovely face that greeted me when I knocked on the door. "Good morning, sunshine." She smiled brightly.

It was way too early for her chipper personality, but if Rylee came to the door, she would've been a lot louder than her wife was, and she would've done it on purpose, fully aware of how sick I felt.

I grumbled something that was supposed to sound like a reply, which only made her laugh as she opened the door to let me inside.

"She's in the kitchen making your drink now," she said, closing the door behind me. I shuffled into the kitchen and slumped into a chair at the table.

As much as I loved my sister, her place was the last one I wanted to be when I was hungover. She wouldn't outright judge me, but her mama bear instincts would kick in—followed by a lecture I wasn't ready for. And Roxxy... I adored my best friend, but she'd be cracking jokes the whole time. I needed somewhere peaceful, a place where I wouldn't be judged and could actually start to feel human again.

Rylee turned around, took one look at my disheveled mess of a body, and shook her head with a smirk. "You and Fallon have quite the night?"

I groaned, feeling the nausea creep back up. Maybe I should've just stayed home. Was my life so uneventful that Fallon was the only interesting thing anyone could talk about? I wasn't in the mood to unpack that thought.

A wave of frustration surged through me at the mention of her name. I was in this state because of Fallon. Okay, obviously it wasn't her fault I tried to drink my body weight in alcohol last night.

"I wasn't with Fallon last night. I drank with my other friends— tequila and vodka." I threw my head on the table.

"Okay... my mistake." She turned around and I wanted to cry when she started the blender.

When the blender turned off, she apologized, and I waved her off with a grunt. She handed me a cup of the most disgusting-looking drink, and the urge to vomit was overwhelming.

"What did you make to poison me with?" I asked, blanching at the color.

She laughed. "Just shut up and drink it. You'll feel better, trust me."

Against my better judgment, I held my breath and took a long sip. She rolled her eyes as I tried to keep the drink down. "Will you relax? It's just some pickle juice, a banana, a splash of coconut water, honey, Greek yogurt, and some spinach."

"Are you trying to make me vomit?"

She chuckled. "No, now keep drinking. I have to get ready for work. Are you going to be okay?" She rubbed my arm and I gave her a soft smile.

"Yeah, I just need life brought back into my body."

She gave Lana a quick kiss before heading upstairs. Lana smacked her on the ass, making me cringe at both their cuteness and the drink as I forced another gulp down.

"I don't know what's more nauseating, the two of you or this drink."

Lana laughed as she watched her wife leave the room. "I've had that drink, it's not that bad, so don't insult my wife's amazing skills. Also, I'm not sorry that our cuteness offends you!"

They really were adorable, and despite my grumpy mood, I was happy for them. I used to be jealous of the love they shared. A long time ago, I wanted that too, but I had to learn the hard way that finding true love just wasn't in the cards for me. For the longest time, I thought I had it. I soon realized that love like that is rare and doesn't exist for everyone.

"Do you want to talk about her?" I looked up at Lana's words.

"Her?" I asked, confused. My brows came together, trying to place who she could've been talking about.

She sighed and sat down next to me, giving my arm a reassuring squeeze. "You know who I'm talking about, Kenz. Fallon—the only woman you've brought around."

"I have no idea what you're talking about." Feigning ignorance, I finished the smoothie and went to rinse out the cup in the sink.

"Mackenzie, stop avoiding the subject. You wouldn't have come here if you didn't want to talk about it. So, why don't you tell me the real reason you went out."

I should've stayed home and suffered in peace. "When we went out the other night, I think I screwed up and lost a good friend."

She chuckled. "Friend? I heard about you and your friend dancing the other night, Kenz. I've never danced with any of my friends like that, and I've certainly never made out with them."

I glared toward the stairs. "Fucking Rylee. Look, it doesn't matter, she won't talk to me at all."

"Well I don't know anything about her, or whatever is going on between the two of you, but I do know you, and I can see it's bothering you. You don't act like this after any one-night stand, so she must mean at least something to you."

"Who said we slept together?" As far as I was aware, no one knew about that night. Yeah, we made out, but I hadn't told any of my friends about what happened once we got home.

Her only answer was a look. She either knew me too well, or Rylee assumed something happened. I wasn't about to admit to anything, but it also felt wrong to lie about that night. I would never be ashamed of anything that happened with Fallon.

"Just take some time and see what happens. Don't put too much pressure on the situation," she said, and I was grateful she didn't press the issue further.

"Thanks, Lana." I groaned. "I better go. Tell Rylee her drink is fucking nasty, but I'll let her know if it works."

She walked me to the door and pulled me into a hug. I reveled in the warmth and familiarity of her comfort. "Bye, Kenzie. Feel better, sweetie, and good luck with everything."

The whole ride home, I kept my eyes closed, praying the drink would work and that any thoughts of Fallon would leave my mind.

Chapter Twenty-Three
FALLON

I succeeded in avoiding Mackenzie like the plague for the past several days, mostly due to the fact I only left the building once.

She texted me a few times, but I didn't respond. There was a knock on my door that might have been her, but I wasn't sure. I was too afraid to look, and besides, it was late at night, and I was already in bed.

I couldn't stomach seeing her, and I planned on avoiding her for as long as possible. We could pretend it never happened, right?

I was covering at the bookstore today, so at least I had that as a distraction. Hopefully, Drea was so busy she wasn't in a talkative mood, and I could just get lost in work and not think about anything or anyone.

When I opened my door and found the hallway empty, I let out a breath of relief. I locked my door and started down the hall toward the elevator when I heard a door open and close, followed by a familiar, smooth, knee-wobbling voice calling my name.

"Fallon?" I froze. *Shit, shit, shit!*

There was no reason to turn around to know Mackenzie was uncomfortably close. Ignoring her voice, my steps quickened toward the stairs and straight out the door, pretending not to hear a thing.

That wasn't one of my finer moments, but I didn't know what else to do. I needed more time to get my thoughts in order, and I couldn't do that when she had the eyes she did. Mackenzie and her damn ocean-blue eyes were what had gotten me into this mess in the first place. Whenever I looked into them, all my self-control vanished.

Thankfully, the bookstore was busy. When I got there, Drea was running around like a crazy woman.

"Oh, thank God you're here, love!" she yelled when I came in.

I laughed. "I'm here, so go take a break. I've got it."

She nodded, finishing up with her customer, and I wasted no time jumping in. I didn't have time to breathe for even a second, which was exactly what I needed.

The last thing I wanted was time for my thoughts to run wild. I knew Mackenzie and I had to talk about it eventually, I just didn't want to.

My luck ran out after a few hours, when the store quieted down enough for us to grab something to eat and talk.

"So, how are things?" Drea asked as she sat down with her salad, kicking her feet up on a nearby chair.

"Things are good." I nodded, pretending to be very interested in my chicken fingers.

She glared at me, pursing her lips. "Hmm, good, huh?"

"Yeah, Dre. Good," I replied, looking confused.

She gave me a skeptical look. "Is that why Mackenzie came in the other day, looking for you?"

My eyes widened. "What?! Why? When?"

She laughed. "So many questions, so little words."

Scowling, I tried to collect myself. "She came here, looking for me?" Why had Mackenzie been asking about me?

That night was burned into my memory, her touch still lingered. But it couldn't have meant anything to her, surely. She said she'd done well for herself, after all. It must've been nothing more than a bit of fun for her, right?

"Yeah. She said she hasn't seen or talked to you and wanted to see if you were okay, which I thought was just a little weird, considering you two are neighbors, and you know, live next to each other." She laughed.

No, I'm not okay, I slept with her and I can't stop thinking about it!

I exhaled sharply. "Well, clearly I'm fine."

She laughed. "Fine? Then why do you look so terrible?"

I hadn't really slept well the past couple of days, but I didn't think I looked that bad. My brain wouldn't shut off after everything.

"Gee, thanks, Dre." I groaned. "I went out the other night."

"Damn, and you're *still* recovering?"

I cleared my throat. "Uhh... yeah, kind of. Mackenzie invited me out with her friends to celebrate a promotion at work."

"Ah, so you're avoiding her because you had a date and it didn't go well?" Her eyes lingered on me as she took a sip of her water.

"What's with the third degree, Dre?" I frowned. "We all went out, as a group of friends. It went... okay."

There must have been a look on my face, because she didn't seem to want to let it go.

She set her food down on the table and clasped her hands together like she meant business. "Listen, I didn't say anything when I left the other day, and it looked like something was going on, but I can't hold it in anymore. Cut the shit and tell me what's going on with you two."

"Nothing is going on! Yeah we went out. I met her friends. It wasn't a date, at least I don't think it was. I don't know, the way it ended, it—" I stopped myself.

"The way it ended? How did it end, Fallon?" She raised her eyebrows.

I was looking everywhere but at her. "Come on, Dre. We need to get back to work." She refused to let me stand, grabbing my wrist, which caused me to sit back down with a groan. I hadn't meant to keep talking, but... shit.

"Fallon Rose? How. Did. It. End?" she demanded, each word a little sharper than the last.

I let out a breath and turned to face her. "With me sneaking out of her apartment... in the middle of the night."

She gave me a wide-eyed stare, and I leaned back in the chair, slamming my eyes shut. "What did I do, Dre?"

"You had sex with her, didn't you?!"

I opened my eyes and winced. "Well... yeah, I—"

She squealed. "I'm so proud of you! Was it good? I bet it was. She looks like she'd be phenomenal. Tell me everything!"

Phenomenal didn't even begin to describe that night, but it was over. Every time I took a shower, memories of our night together came rushing back, and I'd have to take care of myself before I could get out.

I covered my face with my hands. "Oh my God, Dre! It was a huge mistake." A really *really* good mistake.

"Have you talked to her since? What happens between you two now?"

I rolled my eyes. "Nothing happens now. I saw her in the hall this morning but I came straight here."

"Was it good at least? Are you guys ever going to talk about it?" she asked.

Honestly, it was the best sex of my life, but I would rather chew on glass than admit that.

"It's over, Drea, and I don't know. I plan to ignore her for as long as possible and pretend it never happened."

"Well, I don't think *she* has the same plan, babe." She nodded to the door, and I wanted to sink into the floor when I turned around.

"Oh, shit," I said, watching Mackenzie walk in. "Why?" I whined.

Drea got up and walked over to her, and I tried to beg the couch to swallow me whole. "Hi, Mackenzie, welcome in. Are you looking for Fallon?" *Thanks Drea! Please say no.*

"Hey, Drea. Thanks. Yeah, I'm sorry to show up like this again. Is she here?"

"Don't worry about it. Yeah, she's here. Hey, Fallon, someone's asking for you," Drea called out, completely blowing my cover.

I sat up and glared at her, but she only smiled and winked, as if everything was perfectly fine.

She said goodbye to Mackenzie and headed to the back. Just before turning the corner, she glanced my way, mouthing, "Good luck," earning herself another glare. *You're the one who's going to need luck when I'm done out here, Drea!*

I made myself busy behind the counter when Mackenzie came up to me. "Hey," she said with a smile.

"Hey," I replied dryly.

Things were so weird and I hated it. Everything had been awkward before, but somehow, I'd managed to make it worse. Maybe if I hadn't avoided Mackenzie or acted like I was invisible, we wouldn't have been stuck with this unbearable tension.

I pretended to look busy. Eye contact was the last thing I could manage. "So, how can I help you?" I asked.

"You can start by telling me why you ran out on me. I felt very cheap." I tensed for a moment at the mention of that night before resuming my shuffle of some random papers. She didn't need to know I had no idea what I was doing. I was just trying to keep my eyes anywhere but on her. I knew that with one look, my resolve would crumble.

"I didn't run out, I... had to work." I couldn't even look up from the counter when I answered.

"At four in the morning? Hm. You can also tell me why you're avoiding me," she went on.

I sighed, not looking at her as I went to stock some books. I didn't place them where they were supposed to go, but I could always fix them later. I just needed something to do. "I'm a nurse, I work weird hours. I'm not avoiding you, Mackenzie, I've just been busy."

I turned to walk away when she grabbed my wrist and I stopped, gasping at the contact. The heat of her touch radiated through me. Her grip was firm, yet gentle, like she was holding me just enough to keep me in place without hurting me. Like she couldn't stand any more distance between us. I wanted the distance; I needed it.

"You're avoiding me, Fallon. You won't even look me in the eyes. Can we just talk for a second, please?"

I straightened up and looked at her. "I told you, I—" I stopped when our eyes met. Those ocean blues pulled me in, and all I could think about was the way they looked that night—full of darkness and lust. I remembered how they raked over me when I walked into the bar. Just thinking about it now, I could barely stand while she looked at me.

I cleared my throat before softening my tone. "I've been busy. Listen, Mackenzie, I need to get back to work. Do you need help finding something, or—"

"No, actually. I was just leaving." She let go of my wrist and turned around, heading for the door. My stomach churned, and I buried my face in my hands, feeling like I'd swallowed something bitter.

"Hey, sweetie," Drea said in a sweet and innocent voice. "How'd it go?"

I glared at the traitor. "How I knew it would. It was awkward and horrible. Thanks for that!"

"I'm sorry, love. I was just trying to help." She seemed genuinely apologetic, but I couldn't find it in me to be accepting just yet.

"What's the point of having a best friend if they can't lie for you?" I scowled.

"You know you're going to have to talk about it eventually, right?"

I sighed. The problem wasn't just that I didn't want to talk about it —I wanted to forget it ever happened. But the worst part? I still wanted it to happen again. "I know. I'm just not ready to talk right now."

"You know I'm here for you, love. No judgment."

I smiled at her warm words. "I know, Dre. Thanks. I don't want to talk about her anymore. Can we get back to work, please?"

She laughed before heading back to the counter as a customer walked in. I groaned, turned back to the books I'd shelved wrong, and finished my shift.

When we finally closed up, I decided to take the long way home, letting my thoughts consume me. It felt good to be alone in the crisp fall air, with only the sound of the wind against the trees to keep me company. Lost in my own head, I hadn't realized I'd forgotten to check my phone all day until the sharp sound of an incoming notification jolted me. The last thing I needed was to see an unread message when I opened my notifications:

Mackenzie: We need to talk, Fallon.

Every muscle in my body tensed, and I groaned, staring up at the sky. I knew I couldn't avoid her forever. That night with Mackenzie had been the best sex of my life. The way she worshiped and explored every inch of me, each touch setting my body on fire. But I had to remind myself it wasn't going to happen again. So why bother talking about it?

In the end, I gave in and texted her when I got home:

. . .

I threw my phone on the bed in frustration. I wanted to crawl under a rock and disappear, but instead, I did the next best thing and took a cold shower, hoping it would snap me back to reality.

We were just starting to be friends, and then I had to go and ruin everything by being attracted to her. She'd given me an out multiple times, and I hadn't taken it. I wanted to stay. I wanted to explore whatever was between us, but I shouldn't have.

I wasn't ready for any kind of relationship, and Mackenzie didn't seem like the relationship type anyway. She was so far out of my league, and it was better to stop thinking about what could've been. No one wanted damaged goods.

The following day, I walked into *Brewed Awakening* and paused when I saw Rylee behind the counter.

I hadn't even stopped to think about what she might know about that night. Did Mackenzie tell her what happened? She must've seen us together. We didn't dance the way friends were supposed to, at all. Not to mention, I kissed her, and then there was what I said to her... oh God!

I raised my chin and walked to the counter. We were all grown women, and there was no reason to run and hide.

"Hey, Fallon! How are you?" she asked with a smile.

"Hey, Rylee. I'm good. Can I get my usual, please?" I said in response. I smiled back, but there was more of an awkwardness in it.

"Of course!" She started making my coffee without another word, acting totally normal. Either she was oblivious to the situation, or Mackenzie told her to act like she didn't know anything.

"I'm so glad you came out the other night, it was so fun." Her warm voice pulled me out of the loop of anxious thoughts I was stuck in.

"Yeah, me too." Despite my current feelings, I was glad to get out and meet new people. Mackenzie's group was so warm and welcoming, and they made me feel comfortable.

"You guys looked like you had fun?" Oh, we sure did...

"Uh, yeah, it was fun. I definitely needed it," I said, trying to sound casual. And it was true. But what happened after the bar? I needed that even more, and to be honest, I wanted it again.

"Well, I'm glad. You two looked really good together. I know she said you're just friends, but I don't think I've seen Kenzie that happy in a long time. It was really nice to see. She deserves it. She couldn't take her eyes off you all night, and it looked like you were having some trouble there as well." The smirk she gave me did nothing to calm my racing heart, and all I could do was blink. I didn't know what to say after that.

We *were* just friends... who happened to sleep together, but a friendship wasn't supposed to cross that boundary. I was the one who initiated everything, and I accepted the consequences because part of me wondered if maybe we were meant to be more than friends. It wasn't just sexual chemistry, either. For a while, I'd felt like something was missing, like Mackenzie could've been that missing piece. How pathetic was I? We slept together once.

I also wasn't sure what we were anymore. We hadn't talked about what happened or what it meant—if it meant anything at all—which was mainly my fault because I refused to even think about it, let alone have a civilized conversation.

The second we addressed it, I knew I wouldn't be able to keep pretending it never happened. I would have to face it, and I wasn't ready for that, but I knew my opportunity to make things right was closing.

"Well, I gotta run. Thanks for the coffee." I smiled as I quickly grabbed my drink and bolted out the door.

"Yeah, no problem, See ya," she replied with a frown.

Chapter Twenty-Four

MACKENZIE

After I cornered Fallon in the bookstore a few days ago, I was sure she thought I was pathetic for trying to get her to talk to me. Maybe I was, but we needed to talk about things. It was driving me insane that she was avoiding me, and I was determined to put a stop to it.

After work, I stopped by *Brewed Awakening* to catch up with Rylee. She had a few customers in line when I walked in, but she still smiled and waved. "Hey, Kenzie! I'm just finishing up here, so give me ten minutes, okay?"

"Yeah, sure. I'll be over here," I replied, nodding to a table by the window.

She finished her shift and came up to me with two coffees in hand. "I'm so glad to be off," she said, handing me a cup before slouching into the chair across from me. "So, what's going on with you? How did that drink work out for you?"

I scrunched up my nose. "That shit was nasty, but effective. Thanks again. And please thank Lana for our talk."

Her smile grew at the mention of her wife. "She told me you talked to her about Fallon. She didn't say what you two talked about, though."

I groaned. "Yeah, well, she sort of forced me to, and I don't want to talk about it."

She frowned. "Okay, I'll drop it, but you know I'm here for you, sweetie. Anyway, how's work going?"

I grinned. "I know, Ry. I love you. I'm still adjusting to the new responsibilities, but I love it. What about you? How are you?"

She smiled. "I'm good. You're one of the lucky ones who has a job she doesn't totally hate. Don't get me wrong, I love bartending, and my photography business is doing pretty well, but working here... I don't know. It's not what I want to do for the rest of my life, you know?" She shrugged.

"Yeah, I know what you mean. Your photography will take off, trust me. You are amazing! And you really know how to make a drink." I smirked, taking a sip of my coffee.

"I hope so, and thanks." She smiled and started to stir her own coffee. "Oh, your girl came in the other day," she added.

I frowned. My what? "Who?"

"I'm sorry. Fallon, your *friend*. I guess she wasn't expecting to see me?" She laughed. "She looked a little confused when she came in. She knows I work here, so I don't know what that was about." I probably could've taken a wild guess as to what it was about, but I kept that to myself.

I raised my eyebrows, trying to mask any emotion at the sound of Fallon's name. "Oh, really? Interesting. What did you two talk about?"

I hadn't told any of my friends what happened. They would've hounded me for details, and try to make it a bigger deal than it was.

"I just told her I thought you two looked good together, and that you looked really happy."

My eyes widened, and I struggled to keep myself from spitting coffee all over the table. "What?!" I groaned. "Really, Ry? Why would you say that?! We *are* just friends. Now she's going to think—"

"Chill, Kenzie." She laughed. "It was the truth. I haven't seen you that happy in a really long time, and it was nice to see. Contrary to what you might think, you deserve to be happy, babe."

"I didn't look any different, Rylee. No wonder she's been avoiding me, she probably thinks I like her or something." I threw my head onto the table.

Playfully kicking me under the table, she laughed, seemingly amused by my turmoil. I was glad one of us could find humor in the situation.

"First of all, drama queen, you *do* like her. You couldn't take your eyes off her the entire night. Second of all, she doesn't think anything, relax."

I rolled my eyes, feeling absolutely mortified. "What did she say?"

She frowned. "She just kind of ran out of here without saying much. It was really weird. Did something happen between the two of you?"

I looked at my cup, suddenly finding it very interesting. "Uh, no." I shook my head. "Nothing happened. Maybe she was late for work or something?"

Thankfully, if she didn't buy the lie, she didn't call me out on it. "Maybe. Well, I wish I could stay, but I need to head out—I picked up a shift at the bar tonight."

When I left the coffee shop, I texted Fallon to see if she was home:

> Me: Sunshine. Are you home?

> Sunshine: No, working.

> Me: When are you off?

> Sunshine: Late probably.

> Me: Okay, well let me know when you're off. We need to catch up.

> Sunshine: Idk yet.

She had a way with words these days. There was no denying she was avoiding me—but not for long. I had all the time in the world, and she'd have to come home eventually.

When I got home, I decided we were going to talk about what happened, and it was going to happen today. I sat down against her door and waited.

I hadn't been sitting there long when she finally came home. As soon as she saw me, I stood up and leaned against her door.

Even in the most basic black scrubs, she still managed to be the most radiant presence in any room. I could've stayed frozen in that moment, our eyes locked, until the end of my days... I really needed to pull it together.

She halted briefly in the middle of the hall, before hesitantly walking toward me. "Mackenzie, what are you doing?" she warned. Even when she was irritated, she was so damn sexy.

"I was in the neighborhood." I smirked. "Can we talk?"

She glared. "I've had a long day, can we talk later, Mackenzie?"

"Sure." I smiled and stepped aside.

I probably looked pathetic, following her around and begging for a spare second of her time. I felt pathetic, but I didn't know what else to do.

"Thank you." She went to shut her door, but I put my foot in the way, blocking it from closing.

She opened the door and glared at me when I didn't move. "It's later, Fallon. We can either go somewhere and talk, or I can come in, but we are talking about this," I said firmly.

"Excuse me?" She scoffed. "Kenzie, I just got home. I don't have time for this."

"You've been avoiding me for a week. Like it or not, we're talking about what happened. The longer we wait, the weirder it's going to get." I crossed my arms, keeping my foot in place to block the door.

She sighed. "It's already weird, but fine. You want to talk? Go ahead, talk."

"Can we go somewhere a little more private? Maybe the roof, where it all started?" I winked.

She shut her eyes before opening them again. "We don't have to do this, Mackenzie. We can just pretend it didn't happen, okay?"

I offered her my hand, softening my tone as I cleared the humor from my voice, asking her instead of demanding. "The rooftop, Sunshine. Please?"

She hesitated before accepting my hand, and I led us up to the roof.

I made sure to prop the door open this time, and we sat in the lawn chairs that were facing each other.

Something about the way she was sitting didn't feel right. She looked just as uncomfortable as she had that first night on my couch, twirling a piece of hair between her fingers, bouncing her legs, and never letting her eyes land on anything in particular. It felt like for every step forward we took, we fell three steps back.

"Hello, Fallon. How was your day?" I started casually.

"My day was absolutely wonderful. Were you going to say something important, or can I go now?" She glared.

I sighed. It was worth a shot. "Right. So, the other night was amazing." That got her attention, and she shot her head up to meet my eyes.

"But..." I continued, "we both know it was a mistake. We weren't thinking clearly."

A look of ease washed over her face. "Yeah, we definitely weren't thinking clearly. Mistakes happen, and I'd really like to move on from this," she said, exhaling a breath of relief.

I smiled despite the gnawing feeling in my stomach. Hearing her call that night a "mistake" didn't sit right with me. "Definitely. We had a good thing going, and I'd hate to lose a friendship over a misunderstanding."

"I completely agree. We had a rough start at the beginning, but we get along pretty well now, and it's best to stay friends. A momentary lapse in judgment doesn't have to change that, right?" She sat up, easing her way into a more relaxed state.

"Right. So, do we agree then? It was a one-time thing, and we'll stay friends?" I reached out my hand to shake hers, unsure why I was being so awkward with her.

She laughed and slapped it away. "Agreed."

It was nice to sit and talk with her on the roof. We stayed there for a while, watching the stars before saying our goodbyes.

As amazing as that night was, it couldn't happen again, and I was glad we agreed to stay friends, even if I didn't feel particularly happy about it in the moment. I was sure I would tomorrow.

Chapter Twenty-Five

MACKENZIE

"Hello?" The voice on the other side of my phone was so soft and sultry that it sent a shiver through me. I could almost picture the cute little crinkle in her freckle-specked nose as she strained to hear me.

"Well, hello, Sunshine." I smiled.

She laughed softly. "You know you live ten feet away, right? You could've just knocked on my door."

I grinned even though she couldn't see me. I wanted her to hear the smile she put on my face. "If you wanted to see me, all you had to do was ask."

She huffed out a laugh. "What do you want, Kenzie? You're interrupting my dinner."

I wondered what she was eating. Did she cook dinner, or did she have it delivered? Did she eat super healthy, or just whatever she was craving at the time?

"Oh no, how ever will you go on? I just wanted to see if you were busy tomorrow." I was always nervous about asking her to hang out, expecting her to come up with some excuse to say no.

I could practically hear her scowl. "Why?"

"I was thinking of going ice skating. Want to come long?"

The line was quiet for a moment, and I was preparing myself for the reason she didn't want to go. "You want to go ice skating? And you want me to come with you," she finally said, her voice soft.

"That was the idea when I told you where I was going and asked you to come." I laughed.

"Okay, smart-ass. You know I love ice skating. Sure, that sounds fun."

The breath I let out was full of relief and excitement. I couldn't wait to see Fallon, not just to spend time with her but to watch her do something she loved. I was determined to do whatever it took to put a smile on that perfect face.

"Great! So, I'll pick you up tomorrow, say eleven?"

She laughed. "In the hallway? Sure. Goodbye, Mackenzie."

"Bye, Fallon."

The next morning, I was embarrassed to admit just how excited I was. I loved ice skating, and honestly, I would've made any excuse to see Fallon. She was becoming a good friend, and I really enjoyed having her around.

"Hi," I said with a smile, waiting at my door with a bag of banana bread and her favorite coffee. My eyes drifted to the small baby-blue duffle bag slung over her shoulder. "Do you plan on spending the night?" I asked, teasing lightly.

She rolled her eyes. "It has everything I need. Ice skating is serious business."

I laughed. "Okay then."

Her gaze drifted to the items in my hand, and I shrugged. "Sorry I didn't get you anything," I said with a grin.

Her smile was bright when I handed her the bag and the coffee.

"I'm starting to feel spoiled." She laughed, her cheeks flushing slightly as she accepted the coffee. "Thank you."

"You should. You deserve to be spoiled," I replied honestly, my voice softening. Her smile faltered for a brief second, like she wasn't used to hearing that. It made me want to say it again, to make sure she believed it. "You do, Fallon."

We walked down the hall in comfortable silence until we stepped into the elevator. "You clean up nice," I said with a smile.

She laughed. "I'm getting déjà vu from the last time we went out, but thank you. So do you."

"Well, stop looking beautiful, and I'll stop saying it. Although, I don't think that's even possible," I replied with a wink, causing her cheeks to turn pink.

We rode the rest of the way, stealing glances and smiles without a word. It was quiet, but not awkward.

"I can drive if you want," I offered.

She shrugged. "If you want, sure."

We got to my car and paused for a moment. "Well, this is me," I said, opening the passenger door for her. It was an all-black Jeep Renegade, the kind of car that looked tough but still had a touch of softness to it.

"Nice car. Thank you." She smiled as she climbed in, and I gently shut the door behind her, the soft click echoing in the quiet parking garage. I circled around to the driver's side, still feeling the warmth of her smile. The whole moment felt unexpectedly easy, like we'd been doing this for ages.

The car ride was quiet, the silence felt awkward compared to the ease of the elevator ride. A few minutes passed before she spoke. "You look cozy." When I scowled, not sure how to take her comment, she added, "I like it."

I went with black leggings and my favorite gray sweatshirt, topped off with a beanie and gloves. Casual, but practical. It wasn't too cold outside yet, but ice rinks were always chilly until you started skating. But her? She looked like an absolute knockout, of course.

Fallon chose a pair of black leggings as well, paired with thick socks that went past her ankles, almost like leg warmers. The socks were black, white, and a hint of gray, soft on the outside and silky on the inside. She insisted I felt them.

"Oh my God, you have to feel this," she said.

"Wow, they are soft," I replied casually, as if it was totally normal to feel someone's foot in your car.

When I asked her why she was wearing a dress, she just shrugged and said, "You have to look the part when you're ice skating."

"I thought you just had to be warm," I said. She rolled her eyes at my clear ignorance on the subject, and I couldn't help but wonder if she knew the thoughts that crossed my mind every time she did.

Apparently, there was a dress code. The dress she wore hit just above her knees, with spaghetti straps and pockets. It was the same shade of green as the shirt she wore to the arcade, paired with a white long-sleeve underneath.

"You are going to freeze," I argued.

She just smiled, her expression softening as she tilted her head slightly. "You'll learn," she said with a playful sparkle in her eye, as if she found my confusion endearing. "Ice skating is not about being warm, it's about how you look. And I won't be cold for long, trust me!"

I frowned. "That is not how it works, but okay. Just at least tell me you brought a sweater or something. I don't need this day to be cut short by a trip to the ER."

She laughed and pulled out a cream-colored oversized sweater from her bag. She definitely looked like a figure skater.

"It's nice to know you care about my wellbeing." She smirked.

"Don't get too excited. I just don't want to spend the day at the hospital," I joked, laughing when she swatted at my arm.

We had similar styles, but there were definitely differences. I was all about comfort most of the time—band tees and black shorts worked for pretty much anything in my book. Fallon, though? She always put effort into her outfits, like she cared about looking good. And, honestly, it worked for her.

"This is the first time I've been in your car. I don't know what that says about me, trusting a stranger with my life." She glanced out the window, her fingers lightly tracing the edge of her seatbelt as a small, playful smile tugged at her lips.

"It can't be worse than letting said stranger fuck you senseless in every room of their apartment."

She let out a laugh, soft and full of disbelief. "You have a very high opinion of your abilities."

I tilted my head, letting a slow smile play across my lips. "And why shouldn't I?"

Her gaze narrowed slightly, a challenge dancing behind her eyes. "Confidence is one thing, but arrogance? That's another story entirely."

"Arrogance?" I feigned offense, letting my elbow nudge her arm just enough to make her shift her weight. "Darling, I prefer to call it... self-awareness. But if you'd like, I'd be more than happy to help you test that theory."

Her brows arched, a laugh bubbling up as she tilted her head. "Oh, is that so?"

"Absolutely," I said, my grin widening. "Though, I can't promise you won't be begging for more."

She rolled her eyes, but a slight blush appeared on her cheeks. "So, where are you taking me?"

It was the beginning of September and the weather was starting to cool a bit, but not enough to skate outside.

"I was thinking... *Kraken Valley*?" I smiled.

"I've never been there. It should be fun."

Kraken Valley was the biggest rink in the city. They had locker rooms with showers, a small food court, a little coffee shop, a game room, and an area to just lounge in, watch the rinks, and get work done.

When we walked in, Fallon's jaw dropped, her eyes going wide as she took it all in. It was like watching a kid in a candy store, the way she lit up.

"The horses are to the left. There's also a spa, if you wanted to start there," I joked, trying to lighten the mood.

"They have horses?!" She looked at me, wide-eyed, and I couldn't hide my grin.

"Very funny." She nudged me with her elbow.

Before reaching the front desk, we decided to grab some drinks. Our session wasn't for another hour, so we had time to kill.

We sat down, sipping our drinks as we watched the skaters. She went for a hot chocolate, and I had an iced gingerbread latte that was absolutely delicious.

I looked at her and smiled. "Warming up your body to prepare for the frost you're going to feel in that outfit, Sunshine?"

"You're so funny." She smiled, turning her attention to the skaters. The kids were holding their parents' hands, stumbling now and then when they let go, but quickly getting back up.

There were some couples holding hands and skating together. Some of the girls were holding on for dear life on their partner's shirts or arms so they didn't fall, and some were holding on to the wall.

After a few minutes, she broke the silence without turning to face me. "So, do you come here often?"

I laughed. "Are you hitting on me?"

She snorted. "I mean here, to this rink."

"I've been coming here a few times a month since I was little. My mom used to bring me and Harper all the time. It's the one place I can find peace, out on the ice, away from everything. I'm not an Olympian or anything, but I stay upright most of the time."

She finally turned toward me for the first time since we sat down. There was something going on with her, and I was itching to find out. Whatever it was, I wanted to take it and hide it away so she would never feel it again.

"What about you? You love skating, so you must do it often."

She shifted in her seat and her smile faded a bit. "Not as often as I'd like. I haven't been since I was a teenager. I took lessons as a kid every week for five years, then my parents divorced, and it was a luxury we no longer could afford. Between working at the hospital and the bookstore with Dre, I just haven't been able to get back out on the ice."

"Oh, I'm sorry." I didn't know what else to say. She shrugged and quickly turned her attention back to the skaters, and I didn't press her for more.

We sat in silence, watching the people on the ice, until I finally cleared my throat, unable to handle the tension any longer. "Fallon, is there something wrong? You've barely looked at me since we got here."

"I just really like watching them, that's all." Her eyes flicked toward me once more, but she turned away just as fast.

There was something going on with her. Something she wasn't telling me.

"This isn't a date, Fallon," I said.

Her brows furrowed in confusion. "What?"

"If that's what's wrong. It's not like the arcade—"

She grabbed my arm and gasped. "I *knew* that was a date!"

I looked down as she removed her hand, and I laughed. "Whatever! Anyway, this isn't like that. I promise."

She smiled and looked away again.

We sat for a while longer, just watching until the hour was up. "Well, it's our time. Shall we?"

She stood up quickly. "Right. Yes, we shall."

"Are you sure you aren't a professional? You're way better than me!" I shouted over the music.

I've seen all kinds of people on the ice—professionals, kids, and those who looked like baby giraffes taking their first steps. Then there was me, wobbling around and occasionally managing to stay upright without clinging to the wall. And then there was her—graceful, breathtaking, elegant. It was like the ice was made for her, following her every move and going wherever she wanted.

I finally caught up to her when she replied, "Yes, I haven't skated in a long time. Guess it's like riding a bike."

"Yeah, I guess." I laughed.

We skated alongside one another for a while, and after a few minutes, I sat down on the benches. My body wasn't as young as it once was, and I was out of breath. It could have also been from the fact that I was watching Fallon glide across the ice, stealing my breath with every move.

"What's wrong, getting too old to keep up?" she joked as she slid in next to me.

"It's a workout!" I said, barely breathing. "I'm sorry we can't all be beautiful angels like you."

"I'm not an angel." she blushed and looked away again, like she was embarrassed.

"Are you sure you're okay?" I asked. I wasn't going to question her again, but she had been acting strange, and I needed to make sure I hadn't done something to upset her. Part of me felt a need to protect her, even if we were just friends.

"Yeah, I just haven't done this in a long time, too long. It feels really good to be back on the ice."

I looked at her. "I'm glad you came, but I feel like something else is bothering you." I waited for a response, and when she didn't give one, I added, "If you're still upset about the other night—"

"No, I'm not upset about that. It's just..." She sighed before continuing, "I'm fine, really. Come on, granny." She smacked my thigh and stood up, offering me her hand. "We're wasting time."

I gave her a questioning glance, but stood up and went with her back to the ice. You're a few years older than someone, and suddenly you're a *grandma*.

We skated for about another thirty minutes. She skated circles around me while I tried not to hold the wall, and practiced my turns.

Eventually, she slowed down, and we skated side by side for a few minutes. Without thinking, my hand reached for hers. She glanced at it for a moment, then took it and smiled. "Not a date, huh?"

I grinned. "Nope. Just making sure if I go down, I pull you down with me."

She glared at me. I winked, but she didn't pull her hand away, and I never wanted to lose her touch.

I wasn't sure how she felt, but for me, this "just friends" thing wasn't going to work. You couldn't get close to someone like Fallon, really get to know them, and not want more. I needed more. Even if I didn't know exactly what that looked like, I was willing to figure it out.

We were doing our last lap when she must've lost her balance and stumbled on an uneven patch of ice. It took her less than a second to begin to fall, almost dragging me down with her. We fumbled, and I quickly pulled her close to me and turned us, so she wasn't the one to hit the ice.

She lay on top of me, our faces inches apart, breaths coming out in heavy pants. We didn't move or speak, just lay there staring at each other. It wasn't exactly how I envisioned her on top of me again.

"As much as I enjoy this position, Sunshine, the ice is really cold," I finally said in a whisper. Unable to help myself, I shifted my hips slightly, causing her eyes to flutter closed for a brief moment. Oh, that was a dangerous move. We needed to get out of here and place some space between us.

She opened her eyes and cleared her throat. "Oh, right. Sorry," she said, her cheeks flushing a light shade of pink. She stood up and extended her hand to help me up.

"Thanks. Maybe we should go?" I didn't want to go, but I knew it was the smarter thing to do. I needed to get away from her.

She nodded. "Yeah, I think our time is up soon, anyway."

The whole car ride home was quiet, maybe even a little tense. I couldn't tell if it was because of the fall or if it was just me, overthinking everything.

We stopped in front of our apartments when she spoke. "Thanks for dragging me along today. It didn't suck as bad as I thought it would."

"You're welcome. I guess I can tolerate you, if only for a few hours."

She laughed and shook her head, walking toward me and putting her hand on my arm. I put my hand on her elbow, drawing circles along it.

She kissed my cheek and whispered softly, "Goodnight, Kenzie." She looked at me, as if she had more to say, but the silence stretched between us.

I brushed my thumb across her bottom lip. "Goodnight, Fallon."

"About the other night," she started.

I looked at her and dropped my hand. "I know, it was a mistake. We already talked about it. I'm sorry I didn't stop it like I should've."

"What? No, Mackenzie, why are you apologizing? I wasn't going to say that, and I started it, remember? I..." she stopped herself but continued with a whisper. "Wanted it. I'm really glad you didn't stop it, but it wasn't—"

"I know... goodnight, Fallon." I smiled and planted a soft kiss on her forehead.

"Goodnight." She gave me a light kiss on the outside of my mouth. She pulled away slightly and stared at me with heat in her eyes.

"Fallon..." My voice was a faint whisper, and as I gazed deep into her eyes, there was no hiding the feelings I had for her.

Her reply wasn't much louder. "Yeah?"

I licked my lips, watching her eyes trail down to see the motion and seeing her own lips parting in a silent breath. "Tell me not to kiss you."

"I can't." Her voice trembled, and the words came out in a breathless sigh.

With a grin, I cupped her face, gently traced her lower lip with my thumb, and brought my lips to meet hers.

I could have gotten lost in that kiss without a second thought. Every touch made me crave her more intensely than before. It was bad. It was so bad.

I was losing my sanity with every exchange. I risked everything when I looked at her. I told myself I wouldn't get close to someone, not after Rebecca. It was just... Fallon.

That kiss was just like our first. It was like I was discovering a whole new world, and I wanted to take my time and soak in every single detail.

My hands moved to her waist and I gripped tight. I wasn't letting her go, not yet. She grinned into the kiss and gripped my shoulders.

When we parted, I took a step back and rubbed my hands over my face. Fuck. She had no idea the power she held over me. Hell, even I didn't know. All I knew was that I didn't want it to go away, and that terrified me. It would break me if I found out the feelings weren't mirrored on the other side.

"What are you doing to me, Fallon?" I whispered. My body lit up with desire, like a wildfire burning only for her.

She laughed nervously. "What am *I* doing? What are *you* doing to me, Kenzie?"

"I think we should..." I shook my head, gathering my thoughts, refusing to say what was really on my mind. "Goodnight, Fallon."

She cleared her throat. "Goodnight, Kenzie."

And then she was gone. I went inside, trying to catch my breath. This woman was incredible, and I was screwed.

Chapter Twenty-Six

MACKENZIE

I was going over to Fallon's for the first time, and I was a little nervous.

She came over last night, but it didn't end on the most certain of terms. I had never had so much fun winning a game of poker, but whatever I said or did clearly upset her, which made something in my stomach turn.

She had invited me to spend the afternoon together, so that had to be a good sign, right? We were just going to hang out, play *Mario Kart*, and binge on pizza, but any time spent with her was a gift.

The last time we were supposed to have a casual day together, we ended up sweaty on my couch, but she made it clear we needed to stop, and I was determined to respect her wishes and not overstep any boundaries. I would rather be sexually frustrated, than get the silent treatment again.

I sent her a text to make sure she was up and to see if she needed anything other than her typical breakfast:

> Me: Good morning! Do you want me to bring over anything later?

Sunshine: Hey, sorry I forgot to call you earlier. Can I get a raincheck today?

Me: Is everything okay? If it's about last night, we can talk about it.

Sunshine: I'm just not feeling my best. I started my period. 😔

Me: Damn that sucks!

Me: Yeah we can hang out another time. Feel better.

Sunshine: Thank you, and I'm really sorry.

Me: Don't be! It happens! 😀

I wondered if she canceled because she thought I'd want to do something besides play a game. The thought had crossed my mind, but I genuinely just wanted to spend time with her. I wholeheartedly agreed when she said we shouldn't sleep together anymore. Okay, maybe I didn't totally agree—but I at least understood where she was coming from.

I knocked on her door a few times before standing back and waiting for her to answer. When she did answer, I couldn't read her face, but she was dressed in fluffy pink pajamas and matching bunny slippers. I swear, even if she was dressed in a trash bag, she'd still be the most stunning thing to exist on earth.

"Mackenzie? What are you doing here?" I couldn't tell if she was happy or irritated to see me. After the way we left things last night, it could've gone either way, to be honest.

I smiled when she looked at the bags in my hands. "Can I come in? This stuff is kind of heavy."

She gave me a confused look and a small grin. "Of course, but Kenzie, I'm fine. You didn't have to do all of this."

"Are you joking? Of course I did, Sunshine. This is what friends are for."

She motioned for me to set the bags down on the kitchen table. Fallon's apartment was vibrant and full of life, just like she was.

Next to the front door was a wooden bookshelf that was filled with various board and card games.

She had a cerulean-colored sofa with black and white pillows and a white throw hanging off the back.

Her dining room table was black and round, with four matching wooden chairs. On the wall behind it were four pictures: two of queer women kissing and two of different musical instruments.

I went through the bags one by one, showing her everything I'd brought to help her feel better. "Okay, so, to start—obviously—I got you breakfast."

She smiled as she took the iced coffee and banana bread. "Thank you, Kenzie, but seriously, you didn't have to go through all this trouble. It's just period cramps. I have endometriosis, so they can get really bad, but I'm fine."

I frowned at her. The only trouble was my attraction to her. "It's no trouble at all. Besides, you can't run away from getting your ass kicked for a second game night in a row!" I winked

She shook her head. "Kenzie, last night was amazing, and I'm sorry for how I left, okay? I—"

I put my hand on her arm, stopping her apology. I didn't need it. "Fallon, stop apologizing for how you feel. I agreed with you, remember? My friend is hurting and I am here to make it better. Now, have your breakfast while I tell you what else is in here."

She rolled her eyes, but smiled and drank her coffee while I went through what I'd brought.

"So, you definitely cannot survive a period without ibuprofen and a heated blanket. I also grabbed some ice cream—but not cookies and cream." I gagged. "I wasn't sure what you liked, so I got a few options: peanut butter with chocolate-covered pretzels—my personal favorite— chocolate chip cookie dough, and rocky road. Oh, and I got you some lavender-scented bubble bath because lavender helps with relaxation, plus some bath salts for muscle pain."

As much as I wanted to offer to help her with the bath, I knew that wasn't what she needed. It was what I wanted, though—to strip every inch of clothing off her body...

I quickly brushed the thought from my mind. Not tonight. Not again—unless she was absolutely sure.

"And you can't have a relaxing peaceful day without a great movie! Now, I don't know what kind of movies you like, but you seem like you have great taste, I mean hello, we slept together." I flipped my hair over my shoulder and she glared at me with red tinted cheeks.

"Anyway, I brought a classic and a personal childhood favorite—*Stuart Little.*" I chuckled. "Obviously, we don't have to watch it together or do anything together, I just..." My sentence trailed off when her eyes started to get glossy, like she was about to cry.

"Fallon, are you okay? Did I say something wrong? We don't have to watch the movie. Or is it the ice cream? I should've asked before—"

"No, no, it's none of that, it's..." Her words faded as a few stray tears slipped down her face.

I had no idea what was going on or what to do, but I followed her into the living room and sat down on the couch beside her.

She played with a piece of her hair before looking at me. She only did that when she was anxious—but why? For the life of me, I couldn't figure out what I had done wrong this time.

"I'm sorry, Kenz, I just... stupid ass period." She sobbed out a laugh and wiped some tears away. "My little brother Caleb and I used to watch *Stuart Little* all the time before I moved. It's his favorite movie."

I wanted to reach out and comfort her, but I thought it was better to keep my distance.

"I can't believe you did all this for me." She smiled, her gaze dropping to her feet.

"Of course I did, Fallon. I was kidding about the game. I just wanted to bring this over and make sure you have what you need to feel better," I said with a soft smile.

I stood up to leave, but she stopped me, grabbing my wrist and standing so we were eye to eye. Her grip was firm, yet her touch sent a warmth through me that I couldn't ignore. I froze, unable to look away as my thoughts spiraled out of control.

Looking into her soft gray eyes, I couldn't tell what lengths I would've gone to just to make sure they always looked at me the way they did in that moment.

"No, Mackenzie. Please don't go. I'm not sure I'm in the mood for the movie right now, but we could still play *Mario Kart* and order pizza. Now that you're here and did all this for me, it'd be rude to send you away without at least enjoying a slice." Her smile was warm and inviting, and I couldn't help wondering if she realized how her fingers were tracing soft circles along my wrist, or how that simple touch set my whole body on fire. How could I ever say no to this woman?

"I won't argue with that. How about I order the pizza while you get things set up?"

She put away the bags while I quickly ordered the food on the app, and I couldn't help but watch her move around the apartment, gathering everything we'd need before handing me a controller.

"Since this is my game, and I'm in pain, I get the best controller, and the best character." She grinned and did a little shimmy in her spot on the couch.

She sat on the left side, which was the same spot she sat in on my couch every time. I thought that was the cutest fucking thing I had ever seen.

"I get the controller, but in what universe do you think *Donkey Kong* is the best character? Haven't you seen the movie, or played any of the games? He is literally the worst!" I argued.

"Because, Wildcat, he is a badass! And he makes the coolest noise when you pick him. Who do you think is the best? I swear to God, if you say—"

"*Yoshi*," we both said at the same time, laughing. "No, I definitely wasn't going to say *Yoshi*. The best is obviously *Lakitu*, because he's cute as hell, and I love saying his name."

"Fair enough, but—" There was a knock on the door that interrupted her thought, and she got up to answer it.

She came back with a piping-hot pizza, and the combined smells of cheese and sauce had my mouth watering. I was a sucker for cheesy New York-style pizza. She set it on the coffee table and sat next to me, her thigh pressing into mine, making me bite back a groan.

Just feeling her bare skin against mine was enough to make me forget the pizza altogether. I had to let that thought go. She was in pain, and she was the one who put an end to things. I couldn't go against that. But I swore, if I had a choice, I'd choose Fallon over pizza any day.

"Oh my God, I'm so full." Fallon groaned as she sat back, rubbing her stomach with her eyes closed, while I cleaned up the half-empty pizza box and empty box of cheesy breadsticks.

"Not to judge, but I only had two breadsticks, and two pieces of pizza." I laughed.

She glared at me. "Fuck off, I'm internally bleeding over here." She turned her head and closed her eyes again, propping her feet on the coffee table. I loved seeing how comfortable she had become around me. We had come a long way since we first met.

I chuckled at her and shook my head. "I'm sorry, you're right."

"Damn straight I'm right! Hey!" she yelled as I grabbed her feet and twisted her, settling her onto the couch with her feet in my lap.

"What the hell, Wildcat? Have you ever heard of asking someone before you give their body whiplash? What are you trying to do, anyway?"

"Do you want a foot massage or not?" I asked with a smirk.

"I mean, I won't say no, obviously, but like, maybe warn somebody next time."

I laughed and massaged her feet while she relaxed into the couch. I intentionally ignored the soft moaning sounds she was making and thought of the most nauseating images my mind could think of.

After a good five minutes, I thought she had fallen asleep, so I slowly started to get up when she stopped me.

"Hey, why'd you stop? I was enjoying that." Her voice was soft and sleepy, freezing me in place. Fuck, if that wasn't the sexiest thing I'd ever heard. Whatever we had, there was no way I was getting out of it in one piece.

I turned to her and smiled. "I'm sorry, I thought you fell asleep."

"Almost, but no. I should get up anyway before I really fall asleep. You're too good with your hands." I laughed when her eyes went wide, realizing what she'd said.

I let her have that one and didn't mention it. "You should get some sleep, it'll help you feel better."

"No, it's okay. I promised you at least a few rounds of *Mario Kart*. Besides, I won't sleep tonight if I take a nap now." I didn't argue any further.

We played two rounds of the game, which I let her win—but I'd never tell her that. Who could blame me? She wasn't feeling good, and I didn't have the heart to add to it. I wouldn't tell Harper about it either. I wasn't ashamed of coming over to comfort her, but...

She would've kicked my ass if she knew I'd purposely lost at *Mario Kart*. I could get dangerously competitive with that game, but for Fallon, I was willing to lose a game or two. Speaking of Fallon...

"Why are you so happy over there?" She was doing her little happy dance, the same one she did when she ate something really good. I was always taking note of the little things she did—the little things that made her... her.

"I kicked your ass, Wildcat!"

I laughed. "Okay, don't rub it in! Congratulations. Maybe we should've placed our bets beforehand." She sent me a glare at the mention of last night, and I winked in response.

It wasn't my fault she lost the bet during our poker game, but if the sounds she made were any indication, I'd say she couldn't have been that upset about losing.

"Kidding. I'm glad you enjoyed yourself."

"I really did. I still can't believe you did all this for me. I'm not sure I would've done the same for you." She grinned.

"It's okay. I'm a giver, not a receiver."

She coughed and nudged my arm, her cheeks turning a bright shade of pink as my words caught her off guard. "Anyway, thank you for taking care of me. Of course, I would've done the same for you."

"Well, thank you for spending time with me, despite not feeling well. I promise, it wasn't my intention to ruin your day." I patted her leg and stood up, but as she started to get up with me, I stopped her.

"No, you lie down. I'm getting your blanket."

She looked at me, confused, probably wondering why I was being so insistent. "Kenzie, what?"

I let out a quiet sigh. "Just lie down, please. Let someone take care of you for once."

I came back with the blanket and plugged it in. "You're going to lie here and take a nap if you want, or watch *Stuart Little* and feel better. I'm going to leave so you can enjoy the rest of your day. Do you want any ice cream before I go?"

She smiled. "Yeah, but you didn't get cookies and cream."

I gagged. "Sunshine! I told you, we don't eat that shit!"

She laughed. "I know. You're too easy. I'll take the rocky road, please."

I shuddered at the thought of cookies and cream anything, but went to get her ice cream anyway. She was so lucky she wasn't feeling well—otherwise, I might've made a bigger deal about it.

"Thank you again, Kenzie, for all of this. It really means a lot to me. I've never had anyone do anything like this for me before. Not even my ex." She smiled softly, and something in her eyes made my chest tighten.

"Of course, Fallon." I leaned down to place a kiss on her temple. When I pulled back, our eyes locked, and I had to force myself not to lean in again.

I tried to back away, but she grabbed my shirt, pulling me closer to her. "Kenzie," she whispered. Hearing my name on her lips felt like a quiet prayer, gentle and pure.

I grabbed the side of her face and caressed her chin. "Fallon..." I took a deep breath and cleared my throat. I needed to get out of there.

It was becoming nearly impossible not to lean in and kiss her, and I promised myself I wouldn't do that anymore. "Feel better, okay?"

She loosened her grip on my shirt and nodded, my gut twisting at the rejection that flashed across her face. I didn't have the strength to question it. If she wanted me, all she had to do was ask, and I'd be hers in a heartbeat—if I wasn't already.

I let go of her chin and stood up, placing a hand on her leg. I still needed some sort of contact before I left. She looked down at my hand and smiled sweetly.

"If you need anything at all, you know where to find me, okay?"

"Of course. Thank you, Kenzie." She smiled, and I couldn't help returning it before turning to walk out of her apartment.

Chapter Twenty-Seven

FALLON

Apart from going to work, I didn't leave my apartment all week. My period drained me, and I was still recharging my social battery.

On top of that, my hormones were all over the place, and I didn't think it was smart to even look at Mackenzie. After everything she did for me when my period started, I didn't want to risk seeing her smile and end up sleeping with her again. I couldn't seem to help it; she was a freaking sex goddess.

Not only with the way she seemed to know my body, but with how she treated me afterward. She always made sure I was taken care of and comfortable. She respected my boundaries like it was second nature, and she had the heart of an angel. I was so screwed.

I was finally starting to feel like myself again and decided a late-night swim sounded perfect, especially since I hadn't visited the pool since moving in.

For a moment, I considered inviting Mackenzie but decided against it. I mean, we were friends, and friends went swimming together all the time. But it was a good idea if we didn't spend too much time together. It also wouldn't hurt to have on as much clothing as possible when we were in the same room.

There were still at least three hours until the pool closed, and it seemed to be a good time to go.

Surprisingly, there were only two other people there. I smiled at them and went to place my towel down on a chair, slipping off my sheer cover-up. I wasted no time getting in.

The pool was heated and the water was the perfect temperature for a much-needed relaxing night swim.

After a while, the couple left, and I was finally by myself—thank goodness—because I desperately needed some time alone. I hadn't had much of that since I moved to Seattle, especially with Mackenzie. We had slept together a few times, but we agreed it wouldn't happen again. It would only complicate things further—not that things weren't already complicated.

Every time we slept together, I told her it needed to stop. She was always sweet about it, agreeing without an argument. Yet somehow, the next time we saw each other, it would happen all over again.

After our steamy poker night, I swore it would be the last time. Spending the day with her, while feeling like death on the first day of my period, only cemented my stance. I respected our friendship too much to risk it over amazing sex. I could find that anywhere—but her friendship? That was priceless to me.

I had hoped that spending some time alone would clear my head. I needed to leave all these feelings behind.

Taking a deep breath, I floated in the pool, letting the water carry me as I relaxed and listened to the sounds of the water moving around me. My hands drifted in and out, the cool water seeping into my skin. It was the best feeling in the world—to feel weightless, almost nonexistent. I could've stayed like that forever, perfectly content to float without a single worry.

After what felt like thirty minutes of floating, I heard the door open. I didn't pay much attention until a voice said, "Well, isn't this a nice surprise?"

Instantly, my whole body tensed. I planted my feet on the pool floor, afraid to turn around. "Fancy seeing you here," she continued. *Please be in sweatpants and a turtleneck. And a hat... maybe even a ski mask. Preferably smelling like a garbage truck. Please don't be here to swim.*

I slowly turned to face a half-naked Mackenzie. My voice was breathy and hushed when I spoke—at least, I thought it was. I could barely hear anything over the pounding of my heart in my ears. "I... uh, wanted to swim," I managed to say.

Mackenzie, of course, looked deadly in the most torturous black two-piece. The top barely covered anything—she might as well have been wearing a belt. And SpongeBob would've been jealous of her bikini bottoms. She had absolutely no right looking that good.

I wanted to untie those straps and feel her hard nipples between my teeth. Untie the ones at her hips and—*Calm down, Fallon!*

I've seen her naked, so I shouldn't have been losing my mind so badly.

I've seen her perfect breasts, and her peach-colored nipples. Her perfect round ass, and her perfectly delicious pink pierced—

I physically shuddered, hoping she'd chalk it up to getting a cold chill. Good God, I needed to leave immediately.

"I see that." She smiled as she walked over to put her belongings in the chair next to mine. I swear she bent down like that on purpose. Dozens of empty chairs circled the pool, and she just had to choose the one next to mine.

I was hyper-aware of how little I had on, and it left me feeling vulnerable. I swallowed, struggling to find words. "I haven't been here since I moved in. I was just in the mood for a swim. Do you come here often?" I asked—only later realizing how much it sounded like a cheesy pickup line. I chuckled.

She sat in the chair and smiled. "Sometimes. I like to come here at night. It's usually empty and peaceful."

I swam toward the stairs and climbed out, maybe a little slower than I should've. Mackenzie definitely noticed. And I definitely didn't do it on purpose.

What was wrong with me? I was playing with fire. I could feel the heat of her gaze from ten feet away.

She looked me up and down, savoring every inch of my skin. When her gaze met mine again, she inhaled sharply. The way her eyes swept over my body, how she tugged her bottom lip in, and the way it made my heart race had my confidence growing just a little. I walked over to my chair, bending down a bit too slowly to grab my towel and throw on my cover.

"Goddamn," she mumbled under her breath. Seeing my arched eyebrows, she cleared her throat. "You should sit down and relax. I won't bother you. I'll be out there," she said, her voice barely above a whisper, eyes locked on mine.

I sighed and did as I was told... which was typical when she was around. And when I was naked—nope! Shutting down that thought, I leaned back in my chair. "Have a blast, Wildcat."

As she walked past, her hand grazed my leg ever so gently, and I was pretty sure she did it on purpose. That touch seared into my skin, and I sucked in a sharp breath.

The second she turned away, I sat up, watching her make her way to the pool. I had always been an ass woman, but hers? That could've turned my legs into jello. Round, perfect, and so damn soft. My hands tingled at the memory of squeezing it in the shower, while my tongue— nope. Not going there.

If I wasn't already sitting, I was positive I would've fallen over. Everything about this woman was pure perfection, and it pissed me off. I almost wished she would go back to how she was when we first met— then I wouldn't have the constant, unbearable urge to touch her.

I shook my head, but my eyes never left her. Watching her slip into the pool was like the best porno I'd ever seen. And suddenly, I was very jealous of the water wrapping around her, making her dripping wet.

I cleared my throat and closed my eyes, trying to gain some type of composure. "So, how's life?"

How's life? What the hell was that? I winced at myself, still not sure how to handle this whole "friends" thing. It felt weird—like trying to wear a jacket that was a size too small.

"How's life?" she parroted back, the laughter in her voice obvious.

Yeah, I know it was a stupid thing to say, Mackenzie. You try looking at yourself right now, and getting any form of a coherent sentence out!

"Life is grand. How's your life?" She smiled.

I looked at her, which was a huge mistake. Her hair was piled up in a messy, wet bun, and her lips glistened from the pool. She licked them slowly, and I swallowed hard, barely managing to keep myself together.

"Life is fine," I said coolly.

"You've upgraded from shitty, I see." She grinned.

"I guess I have," I replied, trying to keep it light, but my mind was already replaying everything that had changed since I'd moved to Seattle. I had a group of friends I adored, two jobs I enjoyed, and I'd even managed to have spectacular sex. Life was better than I'd expected it to be.

"You're welcome," she said like it was no big deal.

I scoffed. "You think you're the reason?" I laughed, keeping it casual. No way in hell was I about to boost her ego by telling her the truth.

She shot me a look, then suddenly jumped out of the water. Her boobs bounced, and I nearly choked on my own breath.

"I like to think so." She smiled.

I had to close my eyes. If I kept looking at her dripping wet body, I was going to lose it. I shook my head with a smirk.

It was quiet for a moment—long enough that I almost opened my eyes, thinking she'd left. Before I could, a rush of cold water hit me.

"What the hell?!" I yelled, snapping my eyes open to find Mackenzie grinning at me, looking way too pleased with herself.

She shrugged like nothing happened. "Oops. Sorry."

"Yeah, I'm sure you are." My pout didn't seem to have the effect I was hoping for, as she flashed me a gleaming smile.

"Come swim with me, Sunshine. You're already wet."

I knew she didn't mean it like that, but that didn't stop my traitorous body from reacting, causing me to clench my thighs.

"Uhh, sure," I said.

I stood up, and as soon as she turned around, I took off, running and jumping right in next to her with a huge splash.

"Hey!" she sputtered, wiping the water from her face.

I just laughed and shrugged. "Oops. I guess now we're even."

She raised an eyebrow. "Okay, okay. Truce?" Her tone was playful. I looked at her outstretched hand, my heart skipping a beat. The way she looked at me—like she was daring me to take the bait—made it hard to catch my breath.

It felt like there was more to that handshake than she was letting on, but I shrugged it off. No point in reading into something that wasn't there.

I took her hand, my fingers brushing hers longer than necessary. "Tru—"

I barely got the word out before she gripped my hand tighter and pulled me closer, grabbing my waist with her other hand.

I gasped. "Kenzie—" I stopped when she brushed a stray hair behind my ear, and kissed me. If she wasn't holding me up, my knees would've given out.

The kiss was gentle, sensual, and so heated. It was like we were starving for each other, yet still trying to take our time and savor every second.

Every time we kissed, it felt better than the last—and that scared me. I shouldn't have wanted her as badly as I did. Hell, I shouldn't have wanted her at all. It was too complicated. But as she kissed me senseless in that pool, I just couldn't seem to care.

She pulled away, clearing her throat. "I should go."

I nodded, as if I wasn't about to pass out from need—as if I didn't want her to set me on the pool ledge and devour me until I could barely think. "Yeah... uh... I should go, too. I've been in here so long, I'm starting to turn into a raisin." I chuckled, and she let go of my waist before climbing out of the water.

We got dressed in silence, not looking at each other, not saying a word. It felt weird, like something was unfinished—but neither of us had the guts to acknowledge it.

We walked to the elevator, our footsteps the only sound filling the air. When the doors slid shut, it was like the rest of the world disappeared, leaving just the two of us.

I kept my hands glued to my sides, refusing to fidget, refusing to let her see how much she was affecting me. I didn't dare look at her. If she was watching me—if our eyes met—I might not have been able to control myself in the empty elevator.

The awkward tension thickened between us until I stopped in front of my door. I turned to face her before unlocking it.

"See ya later, neighbor," I joked.

She smiled and opened her door. "Bye, Fallon."

I stood there for a second, just looking at her. "Wait!" I blurted out.

"Yeah?" She turned around, giving me an inquisitive look. I held her stare for a few seconds, wondering if what I was about to do would be a mistake. In the end, I thought, why not? I was already this deep—might as well go all in.

"Fuck it," I muttered, closing the space between us and grabbing her shirt.

"Fallon," she warned, her voice more breathless than anything. "What are you doing?"

"I have no idea," I said before I kissed her.

Chapter Twenty-Eight
MACKENZIE

"What," I breathed, "was that?" I asked Fallon as she lay next to me, staring at the ceiling.

"That was... well, it was... fuck, I don't know." She rubbed her face.

We really had to stop doing this. The whole reason I left the pool early was to avoid getting tempted—only to end up doing exactly what I was trying to resist.

Clearly, I couldn't outrun whatever this was between us. Especially when she had looked at me the way she did.

I couldn't stop thinking about how she looked in that pool—with her sage green off-the-shoulder bikini top and black bottoms. That color against her red hair? My weakness. Every damn time. When she kissed me, unless she pulled back, there was no way I wasn't dragging her into my apartment. Saying no to her? Impossible. The situation we were in now proved that.

"What were you thinking, Fallon?"

She sat up, scoffing. "Excuse me? I'm pretty sure you were a part of this, too. You're the one who showed up to my peaceful swim, looking so mouthwatering. What was I supposed to do?"

I felt a blush creep up my neck. "I'm sorry. It's not my fault we both had the same idea." Her compliment sent a rush of pride through me, and I sat up a little straighter, purposefully letting the blanket fall just enough so my nipples were almost showing.

She noticed, and I reveled in the way she caught her bottom lip between her teeth. It was a quick moment, but it was there.

Shaking her head, she cleared her throat and tried to scowl again. "Not to mention, that little stunt you pulled—jumping in the water and making your boobs bounce? Come on! That was definitely intentional. And *you* kissed me first!"

"Like your whole bending-over show wasn't? And don't think I didn't notice how slowly you walked out of the pool, all dripping wet, putting your whole perfect fucking body on display. You just *had* to go that slow?" I raised an eyebrow and smirked.

She laughed. "You could've looked away. I was just getting out of the pool. It's not my fault you can't keep your eyes to yourself."

"Have you seen yourself?!" I yelled. "Of course I can't keep my eyes off you! We're getting way off topic here. None of that matters, anyway. Yeah, I kissed you, but I stopped and left, so this," I motioned between us, "didn't happen."

"Well, look how that turned out. It happened anyway." She smirked.

I rolled my eyes. "Seriously, Fallon. You were the one who said we had to stop, which is why I left. I was trying to respect your boundaries."

As much as I didn't want to stop, I respected Fallon, and I didn't want to lose her in my life, no matter what role she played in it.

She groaned, running a hand through her hair. "I know I did. And we do, I just... shit! We really have to stop doing this, Mackenzie!"

I sighed, leaning back against the headboard. "Yeah, I know. But let's be real—neither of us actually want to stop, do we?"

She looked up at me, and for a second, her expression softened. "No, I don't think we do."

"What are we doing, Fallon?" My voice was quieter when I spoke.

She twisted the bedsheet between her fingers, exhaling slowly. "I don't know," she said, meeting my eyes. "But whatever this is, I don't think it's going away just because we keep telling ourselves it will."

I didn't know either, but I didn't think I could stop, even if I wanted to.

We sat in silence for a long while. "My ex royally fucked me, Fallon, and not in the mind blowing way you do. I don't know what you're wanting this to be, but I'm not sure I can go through that again right now. But, I also can't deny that I can't seem to keep my hands to myself when I'm around you, nor do I want to."

She chuckled softly. "Yeah, I can tell. I get it, though. My ex messed me up, too, and honestly, I'm not sure I'm ready for that either."

"So what do we do then? Do we stop and go back to being friends? Do we end our friendship entirely and go back to ignoring each other? Does one of us move?" I asked, my voice trailing off by the end. I didn't like any of those options.

She didn't respond right away. The silence stretched, making my chest feel tight. I knew she was going to put a permanent stop to this, but I wasn't ready to find out exactly how.

I nudged her gently, thinking maybe she hadn't heard me. Then, finally, she turned to face me, her expression unreadable.

"No one's moving, and I don't think we can go back to ignoring each other. That didn't work even when I didn't like you." She smirked. "I think we're two friends who enjoy each other's company... and apparently, fucking each other into oblivion. Why change things?"

I couldn't hide my laughter. "What are you saying?"

"I'm saying, why define anything?" she said, her voice a little hesitant. "I've never done this before—this kind of situation, I mean—and I don't really know what I'm doing. This move was supposed to be a fresh start, something different, so..." She paused, biting her lip for a second. "We both aren't ready for a relationship right now, so let's just keep it simple. Keep it casual, if you want to." She turned to face me, her expression serious. "But I think we should set some boundaries. Some rules, to make sure we're both on the same page with everything."

She wanted to keep sleeping together? Really? I tried, and failed, to hide my stupid giddy smile. "I think I can handle something simple. What did you have in mind?"

"Well, it probably goes without saying, but as long as we're being safe, I think we should be able to do our own thing."

"Of course. Okay," I said. I wasn't sleeping with anyone else right now, but she didn't need to know that. And I certainly didn't need to know if she was.

"We need to be honest with each other," she added, her voice firm. "But we don't have to give too many details if we aren't comfortable."

"Okay, I can manage that. Anything else?" I asked.

She frowned. "Well, do *you* have any rules? If we're going to do this, it needs to be equal."

I thought for a minute. My only rule was to not fall in love, which I didn't think I would be breaking, but I chose a different condition instead. "I don't think we should have sleepovers."

She nodded. "That's fair. Are we agreed then?"

I wanted to tell her no, we were not. This sounded like the worst idea in history. I was already feeling things I shouldn't have been, but to add more sex to the mix? That didn't seem like a good combination.

I looked at her for a minute, then spoke softly. "Yes, Sunshine, just don't go falling in love with me." I winked.

Rolling her eyes, she answered in a sarcastic tone, "I'll try my very best."

"I told you if you kept rolling your eyes, I was going to show you how to do it the right way, sweetheart." That was the only warning she got before I topped her and showed her exactly that.

After a few more hours of eye-rolling and disturbing the neighbors, we took turns cleaning up, and I walked Fallon to the door. I was already regretting the no-sleepover rule. I just wanted to stay in bed with her all night.

"Oh, I wanted to ask you. There's a book signing next week at the bookstore. It's for the author of the book in the window. I have to work it for a little bit, but I was wondering if you wanted to stop by?"

I paused. "I saw that display. It's what convinced me to go inside that day. Sure, that sounds fun. Count me in." I smiled.

She grinned widely. "Thanks, it was my idea."

"Wow, really? You did an amazing job. It's beautiful. Now that I think of it, that makes sense."

"What does?" she asked, looking confused.

"That a beautiful soul created that beautiful display." I winked.

She blushed. "Jesus, you're something else. Well, I only have to work half of it, but Drea's cashier, Kaia will be there to help out all day. Drea gets extra stressed during these things, even though they always work out perfectly."

"Well, I'll be there to help for a bit too, so no worries, darling." I smiled and she planted a kiss on my cheek.

"Thank you. Goodnight, Kenzie."

As she started to pull away, I stopped her, cupping her chin and pulling her in for a real kiss. Now that I could, there was no chance I'd let her leave my sight again without a proper goodbye.

She melted into me, letting out a soft sigh before breaking the kiss. As quickly as it had started, it was over—and she was walking away. The only difference this time was that I knew she'd be back.

Chapter Twenty-Nine

FALLON

It was the morning of the book signing, and I woke up early so I could get to the bookstore and help Drea get everything set up.

I was in the middle of heading out the door when my phone rang. I didn't recognize the number calling me, but I hesitantly picked it up anyway. "Hello?"

"Hey, Fallon, this is Cara," a cheery voice on the other end said.

Cara? Why the hell was she calling, and how did she get my number? "Oh, um, hey, Cara."

"I'm sorry, I know this is so random, but Drea gave me your number."

I scowled. *Of course she did.* "Did she now? Well, how are you?"

"I'm good, I'm good. Actually, I was calling because I wanted to see if you might want to go out sometime soon. I know I asked you at your party, but I was drunk, so I didn't expect you to take it seriously. I just wanted to ask you properly."

I was grabbing my keys from the table by the front door when I paused. *She was serious about going out? Should I tell Kenzie?*

Mackenzie and I were not together, therefore I had nothing to tell her unless she asked, right? We were allowed to do our own things as long as we were being smart about it.

We agreed to keep things casual between us. I wanted to keep things casual, so no one got hurt. More specifically, so I didn't get hurt.

"Sure, Cara, that sounds great. I gotta go, but call me later and we'll work out the details?" We said goodbye, and I ran out the door, heading down to the bookstore.

Drea was running around like crazy when I finally made it. "Drea, relax. Everything will be fine," I said in a soothing tone. "Everything is set up, and ready to go. Kaia and I are here to help, and Kenzie will be here later, so don't worry!"

"I know, I know. I can't thank you enough for your help, love. Also, I'm happy you invited her, but she's 'Kenzie' now? Is there something I need to know?"

I groaned. "Drea, we have more important things to worry about. Do you really want to talk about my sex life right now?"

"You have a sex life now?!" she screamed.

"Drea!" I hissed.

I looked around, horrified as the customers around the store froze to stare at us. I gave them a polite wave and turned five different shades of red.

She winced and lowered her voice. "And you're the one who said to relax. I'm just trying to listen to your advice."

I laughed. "Yeah, okay."

"So?" she pressed.

I sighed. "So, what? There's nothing to tell. We're friends, that's all." She looked at me with a skeptical glare. "Let it go, Dre, there's nothing to tell, don't you have something else to stress about?" I grinned.

"Bitch, we *will* be discussing this later! But yes, I really do." I laughed as she headed to talk with Francesca who just walked in.

Kaia came up to the table where I was unboxing the books. "Do you think she'll ever relax?" I asked her.

She laughed. "Probably not. One bad apple and she thinks the whole basket is poisoned. I don't understand their issues with each other. Blair is always so nice to me when she comes in."

"I know, me too. I don't get it, but I hate how it always leaves Drea on edge for a few weeks. I'll never understand why she keeps agreeing to do them. Maybe for business?" I shrugged.

She started helping me set up the table when Drea and Francesca walked over.

"Thank you so much for coming in, Francesca. I think it's going to be a great turnout." I smiled.

"Oh, thank you for having me. I hope so. I'm always nervous about these things, but the book seems to be doing really well."

"I totally agree. It'll be great, and everyone loves the book." Drea beamed.

I had been standing next to a table, waving people over for a good forty-five minutes, and I was already ready to go home. I was just about to switch places with Kaia, who was at the counter checking people out, when I heard Drea's voice.

"Hey, Mackenzie!" Drea yelled. I turned around to see her walk in, looking absolutely insane. She wore my favorite olive green button-down, leaving the top three buttons undone to show off her exceptional cleavage. The shirt was tucked into a pair of tight black jeans that hugged her perfectly, and she paired it with tan ankle boots. I really wished she would stop looking so damn good!

"Hey, Drea. The place looks great." She smiled and waved before her eyes found mine, and her grin widened.

I returned the smile and went back to work, trying to gather myself before she came over. She walked up to me, standing there with an iced coffee and a pastry bag that most likely had banana bread inside.

"When I have a heart attack from all the coffee you bring me, I'm sending you my hospital bill." I nudged her with a smirk, taking the coffee anyway.

"I'll gladly give you CPR, *especially* mouth to mouth." She winked and kissed my forehead.

There was just something about forehead kisses that made my stomach swim—especially from her. That one little gesture had a way of making me feel like I was all that mattered. Safe. Secure. And even though I knew I shouldn't have felt that way, it didn't stop the feeling from surfacing.

"I'm sure you would. Thanks, Wildcat. I really needed this."

"You're welcome. The turnout looks pretty good."

I was unboxing copies of the books to be signed when she came to stand next to me.

"Yeah, not bad. I think we had about twenty-five people show up."

"That's a decent amount. Has Drea been making you work hard?" she asked. Her fingers delicately grazed mine before she intertwined our hands together.

Just feeling her hand against mine was making my stomach knot. A small smile appeared on my face when she started caressing my hand with her thumb.

I chuckled. "Not really, just waving people over when it's their turn. I've been doing some riveting stuff over here."

"Well, you look good doing it." I felt a light squeeze of my hand, and I returned the gesture, wanting to stay connected like that for as long as I could.

I was wearing a basic floral mini dress with black flats. I smiled and accepted the compliment. "Thanks. You look good, too, but I would appreciate it if you could dress like a slob for one day in your life. It's kind of annoying, to be honest, that you always look so damn good."

She turned her head and grinned. "I'm sorry, I'll try harder next time."

"So, I was thinking, when I'm done here, maybe we could go grab a bite? I haven't eaten all day, and I'm starving." She released my hand, and I looked down at the emptiness.

"Well, I can't stay long, actually," she said, pausing before continuing. "I just wanted to pop in to see you and help out if I can, but... I have a date." She said it almost as if she were afraid to.

I tensed and locked my eyes with hers. "Oh, you do?"

"Yeah." She didn't elaborate, and I wasn't sure I really wanted to know.

She quickly looked away, and I felt like I wanted to be anywhere else.

After a few minutes of awkward silence, I couldn't take it anymore, and I cleared my throat. "Okay, well, have—"

"Shit. Hey, love?" Drea cut in.

"Yeah, Dre?" I whipped my body toward her, relieved for the interruption.

"Can you go to the back for more receipt paper and sharpies? We're almost out."

"Yeah, of course!" I shouted.

I let out a breath of relief, turning back to Mackenzie. "I gotta go, but enjoy your date." I gave her a smile, but it didn't reach my eyes fully.

"Oh, okay. I'll see you later?"

"Yeah, sure," I said, and walked away, trying to ignore the nauseous feeling in my stomach.

She was going on a date? With who? What were they doing? Had they gone out before? I had so many questions... but little desire to hear the answers.

The thought of her touching anyone else made my skin itch. I knew it shouldn't have. This was what I wanted, right?

Still, wanting it and actually living it were two different things, and I wasn't sure I was as okay with the living part as I thought I would be.

Maybe going out with Cara would be a good thing. It seemed Mackenzie was taking advantage of dating other people, so maybe I should, too.

"I really like the view from back here."

I dropped the box of markers and turned around to find Mackenzie grinning at me with her arms crossed, that beautiful smile on full display. She was annoyingly gorgeous.

"Shit, sorry. I didn't mean to scare you." She laughed.

"Jesus, what are you doing here?" I asked, scowling as I waited for my heart rate to return to normal.

"You invited me, remember?" She smiled.

I narrowed my brows at her. "What are you doing *back here*, Mackenzie?"

"You've been back here for a while, so I asked Drea if I could help."

"I thought you left for your date?" I asked, picking up the markers, trying to keep my hands busy and my eyes anywhere else.

"Not yet. I have some time."

Well, good for you! I'm relieved you had time to fit my peasant ass into your busy schedule of going out and finding someone else to fuck in your bed.

"Oh, well, I'm fine." I turned back to the shelf, pretending everything was perfectly normal.

"Fallon, are you upset about something?" she asked. Hell yeah, I was upset! Although, I shouldn't have been.

I snorted. "What? Why would I be upset?"

"I don't know, you just seemed a little tense when I mentioned my date. I just wanted to be honest."

"You're the one who pulled away, but thanks for being honest. I'm not upset—I'm fine."

"Okay..." If she didn't believe me, she didn't show it. She started walking toward me. "So, how can I help?"

"Mackenzie, go, enjoy your date. I'm fine back here," I said dryly.

"I have time. Let me help, Fallon." Her tone was firm, leaving no room for argument. That voice always got me to do whatever she asked.

I sighed. "I can't reach the box of receipt paper, up there on the shelf, next to the cleaner."

"Here," she said, putting her hands on my waist and slowly moving me to the side. Her touch was more than I could physically handle. It felt like a thousand tiny suns burning into my skin. "Let me help."

Her words were soft spoken, and I only hoped she couldn't hear my breath catch. If only she knew what she did to me. The walls of the back room were inching closer and closer, making my breathing uneven.

She got the box off the shelf and put it on the floor next to us. "Have I told you how beautiful you look today?"

"Mackenzie, please. Don't—" The words barely left my mouth before she grabbed me, pulling me close in one swift motion that stole my breath away.

"Jesus. You know what that does to me." The words came out breathlessly.

"Why do you think I keep doing it?" She grinned. "It gets you to stop talking so I can kiss you." She put her hand on my cheek and slid her thumb across my bottom lip. I didn't have time to resist before her lips met mine, and just like that, all thoughts disappeared.

But, if I was being honest, I couldn't have resisted anyway. I could fight it all day, but the moment her lips touched mine, I was completely gone.

I felt her desire for me with every breath, every touch of her lips against mine. It was sensual and caring, yet passionate and filled with so much need, like it was the last kiss we'd ever share.

She backed me into the shelf, causing the cleaners to fall off and roll onto the floor. My squeal was muffled by the press of her lips. I could only hope the noises out in the bookstore drowned out the ones back here because, with Mackenzie, it was never quiet.

She turned us, walking me backward until a chair hit the back of my knees. The kiss broke as she sat me down.

By that point, I was pretty sure the air from my lungs was lying on the floor with the bottles of cleaner as we stared at each other in silence.

After a quick, heated moment, our mouths crashed together again —tongues tangled, hands pulling at hair. It was primal, and holy shit, it was hot.

When she broke the kiss again, she moved down to my neck, biting and sucking on my collarbone as her name came out in a moan.

Her lips were still on my neck as her hand slipped under my dress, cupping one of my breasts.

She lightly flicked my nipple piercing, causing a gasp to be released. "Shit," I whispered, "do you know what you do to me?"

She looked at me and grinned. "I think I have a pretty good idea."

Her hands fell down to the hem of my dress and she lifted it up to my waist, baring myself to her.

I enjoyed the smile that played on her lips when she saw I wasn't wearing underwear. I told myself it was because I didn't want underwear lines, but I think we both knew the real reason.

She kissed my thighs apart, and I threw my head back. "You. Are so. Beautiful," she said between kisses.

"You always say that." I let out a breathy laugh.

"And, it's always true."

She started kissing and licking the crease between my thighs and aching center, and I arched slightly, tangling her hair in between my fingers, desperate to feel her mouth on me.

"You're so needy, baby girl." Her voice was soft, and the way she said "baby girl" almost ended me every time—primal, filled with so much need and desire.

"For you? Always," I moaned. Somehow, she always got me to be so vulnerable and honest during sex. Outside of this, I would never have admitted that so willingly.

She swirled my throbbing clit with her tongue, and I gasped, needing so much more. "Fuck me," I panted. "Please, Kenzie. I need you."

"Anything for you, sweetheart." This woman was going to be the death of me...

She inched two fingers deep inside me, and I let out an embarrassingly feral moan. I swear I could've died in that moment. The way she looked at me, the way she touched me... I never wanted it to end. That moment was the only thing that mattered.

She finger and tongue-fucked me into pure ecstasy, and it felt as if I was on the edge of unconsciousness.

When she lightly nipped my sensitive clit with her teeth, and curled her fingers to hit that perfect spot simultaneously, I knew it was only a matter of time before I shattered into nothing. I could feel my orgasm building and building. I was seconds away from—

"Oh my God!"

My heart stopped briefly, before trying to leap out of my body.

I tensed and quickly stood up, adjusting myself. Mackenzie, though, didn't seem to be in any rush—she stood calmly, not freaking out at all.

A horrified expression crept across my face, my cheeks burning with embarrassment. "Drea! Uh... Mackenzie was just helping me with the boxes." I could barely get the words out.

"Clean this up, and then get the fuck out of my store!" Her eyes were dead set on mine before she turned and walked out of the room.

Drea and I bickered like siblings all the time, but she'd never gone as far as kicking me out of her store. I needed to fix things.

"Oh my God!" I slouched onto the floor covering my face with horror, while Mackenzie just stood there, chuckling.

Chapter Thirty

FALLON

"This is so not funny! What were you thinking, Mackenzie?" I knew she wasn't the only one at fault, but I was so embarrassed, all I could do was place the blame anywhere else.

She scoffed. "Are you joking? You know I'm not to blame here, right?"

I huffed. Of course I knew that. "You're the one who started it!"

She laughed. "Yeah, and I'll start it again... and again... and again." I looked up at her with a scowl.

"Do you think I'm lying when I tell you you're beautiful? Because I'm not, Fallon. I say it because it's true, and I can't stay away from you. I'm sorry we got caught, and I'm sorry you're upset about it, but I'm not sorry it happened. I will never be sorry it happens."

Tears threatened to spill, but I blinked, refusing to let them fall. I knew she was being honest, but this was still just an itch to scratch for her, and I had to remind myself of that. "Thank you, Wildcat. I'm sorry —I'm just mortified." I groaned.

Mackenzie crouched down and grabbed my face. "Fallon, it's okay. Look, I'll clean up, and you can take the boxes out to Drea and talk to her."

That didn't even seem like a possibility. Drea made it perfectly clear she had no intentions of talking about this.

I shook my head. "You heard her. She doesn't want me here. I highly doubt she will want to talk to me—probably ever."

"Fallon, go talk to her," she said firmly. "She's your best friend. She'll calm down eventually."

I nodded in defeat. "I know, you're right. She's going to kill me!" I couldn't blame her. I crossed a line.

We stood up, and she grabbed my shoulders, lightly caressing them. "No, she's not, okay? Just take a deep breath." I inhaled and exhaled deeply, and she rewarded me with one of her magical forehead kisses. "Good girl," she said softly.

And just like that...

"Fuck," I moaned. "You can't say things like that right now! Are you *trying* to get us into more trouble?"

Her words, her voice, her scent were making me dangerously feral. I needed to get out of there, and fast.

Luckily, just thinking about having the conversation with Drea dried me up pretty quickly.

She smirked and lightly kissed my cheek. "Go talk to her."

I left to find Drea at the register with a customer. When I approached, she didn't even look at me. At least I knew she wouldn't kill me with witnesses... probably. This was going to suck! I'd rather get a root canal than have this conversation.

"Here you go, Dre." I waited a few seconds for a response that never came.

I set the boxes on the counter... still nothing. So far, things were not going well.

"Here you are, thanks for coming in." She handed the receipt to the customer, who thanked her and left.

"Have a great day!" I said with a smile. Drea, however, didn't smile.

"Drea, can we—"

"Leave." Her tone was harsh and unforgiving, and she didn't even glance my way.

"Come on," I pleaded. "Can we at least talk about this?"

She still didn't look at me as she answered. "Goodbye, Fallon."

"Seriously?" I frowned. "We always talk our shit out, and now you won't even look at me?"

Fully turning in my direction, the look in her eyes was dark and terrifying. "Get." The word was sharp, leaving no room for argument. "Out."

That was probably a good idea. Drea was usually always calm and easy-going, but when she got angry, it wasn't a good idea to push her.

I sighed, but didn't say anything as I turned and walked away. Mackenzie came out of the back room, and I paused before walking over to her.

I'd been so swept up in the rush of being with her—and then the horror of getting caught—that I'd forgotten about her date. Being reminded of it made me feel sick again.

"You better get to your date. Drea doesn't want our help anymore," I said as I approached her.

"Are you okay?" She tried to place a comforting hand on my arm, but all it did was make me more anxious.

I shook my head. "Not really. She doesn't want to talk right now, but I'm going to stick around and try again. I'll see you later. Enjoy your date."

"Fallon, are you sure?" she asked, and I knew she wasn't talking about leaving me alone with Drea.

I rubbed my face and forced a smile. "Yes, Kenzie. I'm fine, really. Go."

"Okay..." She hesitated briefly before adding, "Good luck."

She leaned in for a kiss, but I turned just enough that she only brushed my cheek. My stomach twisted, and I couldn't bring myself to let her kiss me.

She pulled back, her brow furrowing in confusion. I could see the question in her eyes, but it never came out. Instead, she gave me one last small smile and turned to leave. I groaned and went into the back room to grab my jacket, finally letting the tears fall.

Drea needed space, and I needed fresh air, so I decided to take a walk for a few hours. I'd go back before closing, when the store would be cleared out, and it would be just the two of us.

Although that might not be the smartest idea, hopefully she'd have calmed down by then. I knew I'd fucked up, and I was expecting a lot of silence on her part and begging on mine.

Mackenzie had stormed into my life and turned everything upside down like a damn tornado. On any other day, it might've been the best thing, but today? It just might've been the worst.

I walked down three blocks until I stopped at this little flower shop. They had pink and purple dahlias out on display, and I had to stop and smell them. They were my favorite flowers, especially the pink ones.

Eventually, I found a bench and sat down, watching people pass by. I breathed in the fresh air, taking in the commotion of conversations, the sight of people holding hands, and everything going on around me.

I thought about my life and how grateful I was for my family and friends. In a weird way, I was grateful for Mackenzie, too. She had come into my life and completely turned everything around.

A few months ago, I was in a terrible place, still trying to recover from a breakup. Then, I finally found the courage to move to Seattle, and look at what I found—a great job, an incredible group of friends, and Mackenzie.

Honestly, I wouldn't turn back the clock for anything. I never thought I'd sleep with someone I hardly knew, let alone have it turn into something more. I knew that things with Mackenzie were just casual, but I'd never met someone so thoughtful and passionate at the same time.

As I sat on the bench, reflecting on the past several months, I realized my feelings for Mackenzie might've been more than just casual, and that made me feel certain that accepting the date with Cara had been a good idea. I needed to remember our original set of rules and not blur the lines any more than they already were.

I knew I should've stopped what happened in the back room, but selfishly, I didn't want to. I couldn't accept that Mackenzie was going out with someone else, and I wanted her to appreciate me in any way she chose. I wanted to feel wanted by her, even as she was about to be with someone else. But in doing so, I'd messed things up with Drea.

I never meant for any of this to happen—especially not catching feelings for Mackenzie, and strong ones at that. But I needed to fix things with Drea. She had been my family for too long, and I couldn't lose her.

. . .

It was getting darker, so I knew it was time to head back when I checked my phone. I didn't have any notifications, nor was I expecting any. Drea would probably never speak to me again, and Mackenzie...

My heart twisted at the thought of her going on a date, and even more so at the memory of what had happened between us. I didn't regret it—not for a second. I never regretted sex with Mackenzie. Being with her was like taking your first breath. Every single time.

However, I couldn't deny that I felt a little gross. I knew it was a normal thing between two people who were casually dating, but that didn't stop the feelings from being there.

The walk back to the bookstore felt like the longest of my life, but I didn't rush. I wasn't eager to get back and deal with what I had done.

When I made it back, it was nearly empty except for Kaia, who was still cleaning up.

I walked up to Drea, who was filing away receipts at the counter. She still had the same stressed expression she always did after the signings, but with an added hint of rage.

She barely turned her head to look at me before turning away. "I told you to leave."

"I did leave, but I came back." I smirked.

She glared at me. "Go home, Fallon. I can't even look at you right now."

"No! You think I want to sit here and have this conversation? Fuck, I really don't, Dre! You can hit me if you need to, but I'm not leaving until we talk about this." I crossed my arms and waited.

It only took about three seconds for her to say something. She slammed the drawer where she had filed the receipts and shot me the darkest glare I had ever gotten from her.

"What in the actual fuck were you thinking, Fallon Rose Bennett?! Are you fucking serious? You are so lucky this wasn't Blair's signing! Do you have any idea what would happen if she found out about this? You know how she is, she would make sure I never saw another author in here as long as I lived!" she yelled. Drea *rarely* yelled. And she had *never* used my full name.

I looked over to Kaia, who was just staring at us wide-eyed. I nodded my head toward the back room, and she didn't give it a second thought as she took off to leave us alone.

I turned back toward Drea, whose cheeks turned bright red—I could have sworn I saw actual steam coming out of her ears. I was pretty sure the bookstore wasn't excluded from the list of places she and Skylar had hooked up, so I didn't understand why she was so upset with me. I didn't think anyone had heard us.

"I wasn't thinking, obviously!" I yelled.

"Yeah, no shit! I cannot believe you! Not only did you have sex in my fucking store—while I was here, you pervert—but you had sex with Mackenzie again? 'Just friends,' my ass! What the fuck is going on with you two?"

"I'm sorry. I didn't mean for any of this to happen—especially that." I nodded toward the back room. "I just... I can't control myself when I'm around her. But I really am sorry, Dre."

"I sit in that chair, you know! Now I have to burn it!" she said, scrunching up her nose.

"Don't be so dramatic! You told me to sleep with her, remember? I'm pretty sure you squealed like a little girl when I did." I laughed.

"This is not funny, Fallon! And yeah, I did—but not in my store, and not when I'm literally feet away! You're like a sister to me. Do you have any idea what that was like? It felt like I was walking in on my parents!"

We gagged at the same time. What a gross image. "I'm sorry, Dre, it obviously wasn't my intention. It just sort of happened."

She lowered her voice slightly and let out a long sigh. "I know, love, I know. But, drunken sex, *and* public sex? Honestly, who have you become?" she teased.

I laughed. "I really don't know. She brings out a different side of me."

"You don't have to remind me. I saw a side of you I have no intention of seeing again, thank you very much. So, how many times has this 'just sort of happened,' exactly?"

Not knowing how to be honest, I bit my bottom lip. "Here? This was the only time."

"And let me tell you how thankful I am for that! And, *not* here?"

"Well..." My voice raised about three octaves.

"Fallon." Her tone was stern, like she was scolding a child.

I sighed. She was not going to let me get out of this conversation without the truth. "We've been kind of doing a casual thing, you know? A lot."

"Interesting. From the woman who doesn't do casual, nor would she ever do her bitchy neighbor. Also, the way she looks at you—it doesn't look 'casual' to me." She had a slight smirk etched across her face. I wasn't sure what part of this she found funny—I was so embarrassed.

"I know, it just sort of happened. And she looks at me like any other person, Dre." I scowled.

She scoffed. "Honey, please. She looks at you like every star in the sky was handpicked straight from your eyes. That woman has it so bad for you, babe. And if that kiss from weeks ago is anything to go by, I'd say she's not the only smitten one here."

"You said you wouldn't bring that up anymore! You know how embarrassed I am every time I think about it! I basically groped her in the middle of the store. I still apologize to Kaia every time I see her. She is too pure to witness things like that!"

Her expression softened, and she leaned over to rub my arm. "It's not necessary, but I'm sorry. The point is, there's something there between the two of you, whether you choose to see it or not."

I pushed back the heaviness forming behind my eyes. Surely, she didn't feel that deeply for me. It was just physical, wasn't it? I mean, of course it was—she was on a date with someone else while I was here, feeling mortified about what we had done.

"I'm done with this conversation, okay?" I said, forcing the lump back down my throat.

She glared at me, but smiled. "Okay, fine. But are you happy, love? You know that's all I care about."

"Yeah, Dre, for the first time in a long time, I really am. We're just friends who really enjoy each other's company." I could feel the tint of red creeping up my neck at the thought of enjoying Mackenzie's company.

"Okay," she said with a wince.

I laughed. "Sorry."

She rolled her eyes. "Well, we really are good here. You better get back to your *friend* before she starts thinking you ditched her." She wiggled her eyebrows. "Wouldn't want to keep your *totally platonic* companion waiting."

"She *is* a friend, Drea, and I can't. She has a date," I said dryly, raising my eyebrows at the word.

"Oh, shit. I'm sorry."

I furrowed my brows. "Why? We agreed to do our own things. I'm fine."

She glared at me. "Honey, do you think if you say it enough times you'll believe it?"

I sighed, really thinking of my answer. "I don't know, maybe. It's complicated."

Drea crossed her arms, leaning back against the counter. "Complicated, huh? Just promise me you'll be careful? I hate to see you hurt, and I would hate even more to have to get rid of a dead body."

I laughed, despite myself. "I'll be careful, Drea. I know what I'm doing."

She raised an eyebrow. "Do you? You're not exactly known for making the best choices when it comes to... feelings."

"Thanks for the vote of confidence," I muttered, but there was no heat behind my words. I knew she was right—my ex was a prime example of my bad decisions. I tended to lead with my heart instead of my head, like I should've. But that was the old me.

Drea's expression softened as she pushed off the counter. "I just want you to be happy. And if Mackenzie is going to be a part of that, in whatever way that looks for you two, I want you to make sure you're not getting hurt in the process."

"I promise. Are we okay, Dre?"

She smiled, pulling me into a hug. "Yeah, babe, we're okay."

"Good, but you might want to go check on Kaia, she looked like a scared baby deer," I laughed.

"Yeah, you're probably right. I adore that sweet girl."

"Me too. I'm glad you keep her around. She's good for this store, and for you. She brings a little sunshine to your dark cloud."

"Hey. Rude." She nudged my arm and I smiled.

"I'm teasing. You know I love you, babe."

We said our goodbyes, and I headed home, eternally grateful to have Drea as my best friend.

I didn't hear from Mackenzie for the rest of the night, and even though I wasn't expecting to, I was still upset about it.

I grabbed my phone and stared at the screen for a few minutes, hesitating. It felt wrong to text her, but at the same time, I felt like I needed to reach out—like I needed to hear how her date went. Which was ridiculous, because I didn't care who she was on a date with, or if she was kissing her, or...

My thumb hovered over the messaging app before I decided to pull up Cara's contact information. It was time to start following my own rules about our casual arrangement.

When I made it home and got comfortable, I pressed the call button.

Chapter Thirty-One

MACKENZIE

My date ended several hours ago, but I stayed at the bar for another two hours after she left.

I hadn't heard from Fallon all night, and texting her after my date felt weird—even though we'd done a lot more than that in the bookstore. God, the way she moaned my name unraveled me. Everything about her did, though.

I wondered how her talk with Drea went—if they talked at all. I felt bad for leaving her, but she insisted she was okay. I hated that she was upset. I hated that I had made her upset. But casual dating had been her idea, and I wanted to be completely honest with her, like we agreed— even if it killed me.

I hadn't planned to say yes to the date, but she was nice enough, and I wanted to at least try to get Fallon out of my head. Tonight, I learned that was a mistake. Getting her out of my head was an impossibility.

The date was... alright. She was beautiful and sweet, but she wasn't a curly redhead with freckles. She wasn't the woman whose smile brought me to my knees. She wasn't Fallon.

I finally decided to go home when I knew Fallon would most likely be asleep. The last thing I wanted was to run into her and have the inevitable "How was your date? Not that I care. I mean, we're doing our own thing, so it doesn't bother me at all. Except maybe it does, but I'll never admit it" conversation. Yeah, no thanks.

I didn't care what she said—I knew it bothered her. I just wasn't sure why. It wasn't like I cared who she went out with.

Fallon still hadn't texted me all day, and I didn't want to have that conversation over the phone, so I avoided contact until later that night.

When I got home from work, I saw her getting her mail.

She turned to me and smiled as I approached my mailbox. Not what I was expecting. But then again, I hadn't really expected much.

"Oh, hey. How was work?" Fallon asked.

"Hey. It was good. Glad to be home, as always. How was your talk with Drea?"

"Oh, uh, well... she yelled at me and used my full government name, which is never a good sign. For a second, I really thought she was going to hit me. But we talked it through. I think she's okay now—though she might be bleaching the room as we speak." She shrugged. "I probably owe her a new chair."

"I'm glad she didn't hit you. I'm sorry I put you in that position."

She laughed. "No, you didn't. I was equally at fault. Not that I regret it. Well, I mean... getting caught, yeah. But I can't bring myself to regret what happened between us."

"Good. I don't either, by the way. Thanks for inviting me again, and I'm sorry I got you into trouble."

She laughed nervously. "It's okay."

An awkward pause settled between us as she shifted her mail from one hand to the other. "How, uh... how was your date?"

She glanced at me briefly before quickly looking away, her gaze landing on some random spot on the floor.

I dreaded this. I hated even talking about the date, but I didn't want to hide anything from her.

After going back and forth in my mind about what to say, I finally settled on the truth. "It was fine."

"Just fine?" she pressed, her eyes narrowing slightly. "I didn't hear you come home, and I went to bed pretty late. Not that I was waiting up for you or anything," she added quickly, her words spilling out in a rush. "I was just catching up on some reading, but—"

"Do you really want to hear all the juicy details of my date, Fallon?" I glanced over at her, unable to understand the expression on her face.

There were no juicy details—nothing happened. I couldn't do it. But why did I feel the need to make it sound like there were?

"No, I guess not. So, are you going to see her again?"

I wasn't planning on it. But instead of being honest, for some unknown reason, I shrugged. "I don't know, maybe."

"Oh. Well, okay." She started heading toward the elevators, and I let out a sigh. I was such an idiot. Why hadn't I just been honest? Why couldn't I have told her my date was fine, but it would've been better if I was with her instead?

"Fallon!" I called after her, but she didn't look at me until we were inside the elevator.

"I'm glad you had a good time." She plastered on one of her fake smiles—the kind that never reached her eyes. She was lying.

I frowned. "Fallon—"

"I'm fine." She cleared her throat. "I'm sorry, it's just been a long day. It really doesn't bother me, Kenzie." She shrugged, forcing another smile before pulling me in for a kiss.

I smiled warily and kissed her back. "Okay..." I didn't believe her for a second, but the feeling of her body pressed against mine was too good to interrupt.

When we got off the elevator, she stopped me just as I was opening my door. "So, I was thinking..." She trailed a finger down my chest.

Then, without warning, she grabbed my shirt at the center and kissed me—hard. "How about you come inside and see if I can show you a time that's better than 'fine?'"

"Mmm, I like the sound of that," I moaned as I caressed her hips, guiding us inside. Something was off, though. The way she was taking charge—that wasn't like her. But was I about to complain? Hell no. I had no doubt in my mind that she could show me something I couldn't find anywhere else.

We were lying in bed, naked, and I felt completely spent and satisfied. After a minute, I finally found the energy to speak.

"I'm going out with the girls for drinks on Saturday, and I wanted to see if you wanted to go? I know it's last minute, and I was going to ask you earlier, but I kind of got... distracted." I smirked.

She sat up and scooted away, looking nervous. "Oh, um, thank you, but I can't." Her eyes stayed anywhere but on me, and that alone made something tighten in my chest.

"Fallon, if you're upset, please talk to me about it."

She shook her head. "I'm not upset. I just... I have plans already."

"Oh. Okay, no worries." I smiled. "Another time, then. Anything exciting?"

She sighed. "I have a date."

I froze. A date? Fallon had a date? Why was it so hot, and why was I having trouble breathing?

"Cool," I said, like I was totally okay with it.

"Are you okay?" she asked.

I should've been. It shouldn't have been eating me up inside. No, not at all.

I forced a smile, brushing a stray lock of hair from her face before I kissed her forehead. "Yeah, of course. I'm good. Come on, let me tuck you in before I go. It's getting late."

I moved to get off the bed, but she stopped me by the wrist. "You don't have to go. You can stay, if you... if you want."

I wish I could've. I would've loved nothing more than to have stayed in that bed with her, to just forget everything else for a while. But I knew I couldn't. It didn't feel right, especially knowing she had a date.

"I don't think that's a good idea, Fallon. Our rules, remember?"

"Right," she said, her voice almost a whisper. "Of course." She let go of my wrist and gave me a defeated smile, one that had my heart sinking.

I forced myself to leave, resisting the urge to climb back into bed with her, no matter how badly I wanted to. We had rules for a reason, and as much as it hurt, I knew I'd be smart to remember that.

Chapter Thirty-Two

MACKENZIE

It was Saturday night, and I was sitting at *Reid's* with Roxxy and her girlfriend, Laura, along with Harper and Rylee.

Roxxy had planned this little girls night, with the excuse that she had some news and wanted all of us around. She still hadn't told us anything, but we were all being patient and enjoying our drinks.

"So, Kenzie, what's the deal with you and Fallon?" Roxxy asked.

I hadn't told them anything for this exact reason. I didn't want to talk about my... whatever I had with her.

"Nothing. We're just friends," I replied coolly.

"Just friends? Please, you two were all over each other at the bar, and I saw you dancing with her." Harper smirked.

"And you think I didn't hear you guys in the car?" Roxxy chimed in, laughing. "I had to put the window down, it was getting so hot in there. She doesn't look like it, but that girl is wild!" She winked.

I looked at Harper, who cringed, and I blushed. "Oh God! I'm so fucking sorry!"

They just stared at me, saying nothing.

"Okay so *maybe* we did hook up that night, but we both agreed it was a mistake. We *are* just friends."

Harper glared at me. "Is that what you really want?"

Part of me was saying yes. But another part was screaming... I don't know.

"Of course it is. You know me," I said.

"Yeah, Kenz, we *do* know you. Which is why I bet you two haven't even hooked up since then, right?" Roxxy said, her voice dripping with sarcasm.

I didn't answer. I stared down at my cup and took a sip, hoping the alcohol would somehow drown out the embarrassment creeping up my neck.

"Oh my God, Kenzie, seriously?!" Harper said, her voice incredulous, pulling me right back into the moment I was trying to escape.

I groaned. "Fine! Yes, okay? We're just keeping things casual. It's not a big deal."

They exchanged a look and rolled their eyes, clearly not buying it. I didn't know why they were making a big deal out of it.

"Can we just move on, please?" I sighed, desperate to shift the attention to literally anything else. It was bad enough she was always circling my thoughts, especially tonight, knowing she was on a date with someone else.

The last thing I wanted was to sit there talking about her with my friends. I knew they meant well, but their questions would dig into things I didn't have answers to.

"Fine," Harper said sharply, making it clear this conversation wasn't over. "Let's talk about Roxxy. You've been keeping us in suspense all night—what's your news?"

Roxxy looked at Laura and grinned. "Well, we wanted to tell you all together. I proposed to Laura, and she said yes!" Laura held up her hand to show off the gorgeous princess-cut diamond ring.

A series of loud squeals echoed around the table as we made a toast to the happy couple. It was surreal to see them going through such a big life change.

We'd always talked about getting married in college, but we never thought it would actually happen. It was just one of those dreams everyone had—marriage, a couple of kids, a house with a yard, and a white picket fence.

"I can't believe you're choosing to be stuck with her ass, Laura. Are you sure? It's not too late to back out." I smirked.

She laughed and snuggled up closer to her fiancée. "Yes, I definitely want to be stuck with her forever. I don't know what I would do without this one. My life would probably be sad and boring." Roxxy kissed her temple and I took a long sip of my drink. I was truly happy for my friends, but I was also a little envious.

At one point in my life, I wanted to share my world with someone—come home from work and have someone there waiting for me, excited to share the events of the day. I wanted someone in my bed for more than just a few hours. I wanted to wake up and turn around to see that same person smiling at me, day after day.

But then my last relationship ended, and I accepted that the life I had envisioned wasn't one I was going to live.

Roxxy and Harper were deep in conversation about something, but I wasn't paying attention. I was checking work emails on my phone.

Harper was saying something, but Roxxy cut her off. "Um... Kenzie, sweetie?"

"Yeah, Rox?" I asked, not bothering to glance up from my phone.

After a few seconds of silence, I looked up to see they were both looking at something behind me. "What? What's wrong?"

They silently nodded toward the door behind me. Confused, I turned around to see what left them so stunned—and I wished I hadn't.

A couple had just walked in the door—a blonde with a high pony-tail and a black dress, and a redhead in a burgundy strapless mini dress, her face full of freckles and a smile that could stop the earth from spinning.

"Fallon," I whispered. I swore I literally felt all the air leave my lungs and float straight out of the bar.

Fallon was here. Fine, whatever. But she wasn't alone. She was with... Cara? That's who she had a date with? And this was where her date was? The universe really had a cruel sense of humor.

How did they even know each other? Where did they meet? I felt sick, and I didn't want to know any of those answers. Luckily, she didn't notice we were there.

I couldn't pull my eyes away even if I wanted to. I was drawn to her like a stupid moth to a flame. They chose a seat at the bar and already seemed cozy, giving me the answer I wasn't ready for—they knew each other.

I wondered if this was their first date or if they'd been seeing each other for a while, but it didn't matter. I didn't care who she dated. I just hoped they had a good time together.

Groaning, I covered up my shocked expression and turned back toward my friends, who were still staring at Fallon.

"Fallon's here, so what?" I asked.

"We can go, Kenzie," Harper finally said. "We don't have to stay."

I took a sip of my drink, hiding my feelings about seeing her there. I knew she had a date, and I was totally fine with that—I just hadn't expected to see her with her date.

I laughed nervously. "We don't need to leave, Harp. I told you, we're friends. She can date whoever she wants."

They looked at me like they weren't buying it. "I'm serious! I don't care," I added.

"Okay, Boog. Calm down. We just wanted to make sure you were okay. We can stay if you want."

Hell no, I didn't want to stay and watch Fallon on her date, but if I left now, they'd definitely see me.

I shook my head, trying to clear my thoughts. "I'm fine, guys, I promise. There's no reason to leave."

They shrugged and returned to their conversations. I wasn't sure if I was trying to convince them that I was fine, or myself.

When Harper and Roxxy weren't looking, I would sneak glances over to where Fallon sat at the bar.

They were sitting close—intimate—which was to be expected on a date, I guess.

My jaw ticked slightly when I saw she was touching Fallon's thigh, and I forced myself to look away. I definitely didn't care.

"Do you have any plans for Thanksgiving, Kenz? You know you're more than welcome to come over and spend it with us if you ever get sick of Harper's cooking," Roxxy said.

"What? Oh, uh I'll let you know."

"Wait, you guys aren't coming over this year?" Harper asked.

Roxxy laughed. "Of course we are. I was just trying to get Kenzie's attention. She thinks we can't see her staring holes into the back of Fallon's head."

I whipped my head to Roxxy. I wasn't being that obvious, right? "What?! I'm not staring at anyone. I don't care, remember?" I knew they didn't believe me, but they were smart enough to let it go.

As soon as they looked down at their phones again, I stole another glance at the bar—and my stomach twisted. My eyes narrowed, shoulders locking up so tight it hurt. I had to bite back a scream, my nails digging into my palm. She was touching Fallon—*my* Fallon.

Cara had her hands on Fallon's beautiful, delicate face, caressing her while they kissed. They pulled away, and Fallon smiled—a real smile, not one of those fake ones she'd throw my way sometimes. Then she put her hand on Cara's leg, and I couldn't take it anymore.

"I'm going to the restroom," I said harshly, not looking away from them.

I stood up with my drink and started walking toward the bar, blocking everything else out. I didn't hear anything or see anyone. Rage had cast a fiery red film over the entire bar.

I walked a little faster until I reached the happy couple, and of course, I tripped and stumbled right into her date. Our drinks spilled— mine and hers—soaking her pretty little black dress.

"Oh my God!" she yelled as she stumbled off her stool, but Fallon quickly caught her. Fallon's eyes grew wide when they met mine, and she turned two shades paler, as if she'd seen a ghost.

"Oh no, I'm so sorry," I muttered, my voice tight with frustration. "I didn't see you there." I didn't take my eyes off Fallon, who stood there staring at me, still not saying anything.

"It's fine, it's just a little—Mackenzie?" Cara asked.

I finally looked at her and smiled. Her gaze was frozen in surprise, her lips parted in disbelief. "Oh, hey, Cara. So nice to see you again. Sorry about your dress." I winced half-heartedly. I wasn't sorry about her dress at all.

"Yeah, it's nice to see you, too," she replied hesitantly. "Fallon, this is Mac—"

"Oh, Fallon and I know each other *very* well, Cara."

"Oh, my God," Fallon mumbled.

"I'm so sorry to interrupt your date. I'm just curious how you two know each other. Do you pick up a lot of your dates at coffee shops?" I smirked. I didn't look at Fallon, but I could feel her stare burning into me.

"Not particularly, no. We have mutual friends and have become really close," she said, pulling Fallon closer to her, kissing her temple. I gritted my teeth and finally moved my eyes to Fallon, who pasted a smile on her face that didn't reach her eyes, and she visibly tensed.

I forced a fake smile of my own. "Well, isn't that nice. Since you're so close, I'm sure you already know how she comes harder and faster when you call her 'baby girl'?" At that point, my smile was no longer forced, but when I looked back at Fallon, it fell away.

"Mackenzie!" Fallon said through a clenched jaw. Her face turned fire red, and Cara stared at me, mouth wide open. I admit, that wasn't one of my proudest moments.

"Wow, Kenzie. Uh, no, I didn't know that." Cara took a small step away from Fallon, and inside, I smiled.

"I guess you aren't as close to her as you thought, huh? Oh, and thanks again for the drink last week. I'm sorry it didn't work out."

Cara looked at me and then at fallon. "Oh, uhh... it's okay... it happens." She cleared her throat.

"Anyway, I think maybe you might want to go get cleaned up. That stain is going to set soon." I smirked.

"Yeah, whatever," Cara said, throwing her hands up as she walked out of the bar.

"It was nice seeing you again!" I called after her.

Fallon slowly turned to me, her eyes going stormy. "Wow... I just... I don't even know what to say to you right now!" The anger in her eyes was so intense, I couldn't look at them any longer.

"Excuse me," I replied dryly before walking toward the bathroom.

I passed the table where Roxxy sat, staring at me with her mouth hanging open. Harper was scowling, but I ignored her and kept walking. I stormed into the bathroom and turned on the faucet.

I shouldn't have been upset. We weren't even together. I shouldn't have cared who she slept with. And yet, I did care—too damn much.

The thought of anyone else touching her made my skin crawl, and that only pissed me off more. I had agreed to this. It was never supposed to happen this way. It was supposed to be just sex—nothing more. It wasn't supposed to mean anything. But somewhere along the way, it started to. Maybe it always had.

Not even thirty seconds later, the door swung open, and a furious Fallon stormed in.

Her eyes were dark and her face was flushed. "What the fuck was that, Mackenzie?!"

The door shut behind her, and she stood beside me with her arms crossed over her chest, waiting for an explanation I didn't have.

"What was what?" I asked, avoiding eye contact.

"You know damn well what I'm talking about. You spilled your drink on my date!"

I turned off the water. "I tripped." I dried my face off and turned to her.

"You tripped," she repeated.

"Yeah. It happens all the time," I answered dryly.

She scoffed. "I'm sure it does. Care to tell me when you picked her up in a coffee shop, Mackenzie? Please don't tell me you picked her up at *Brewed Awakening*!"

When I didn't answer, she gasped, coming to her own conclusions. "Was she your date the night of the book signing? After you fucked me in my best friend's bookstore?!" She groaned. "Oh my God!" She covered her face and turned around.

"Technically, she picked me up, but yes," I said. "Also, no, it wasn't *Brewed Awakening*."

She whipped her head back toward me. "Seriously, Mackenzie?"

"Why does it matter? This is what you wanted, right? To keep things casual and be honest? That's what I was doing, and you said you were fine with it. You were certainly fine with it when I fucked you."

Her eyes went narrow and she gaped at me. "Wow. I was—I am fine with it. Date whoever you want, I don't care. That *is* what we agreed to, and that's what I was doing, too, until you came in and fucked..." She sighed. "You know what, you're right. Thank you so much for your honesty, really. Maybe we should go call Cara and tell her more things to do that will make me come!"

Are you fucking for real?! I guess I had that coming. What was wrong with me?

I didn't respond—I didn't have the words. I was too angry to find the right ones.

Angry at myself for feeling this way. Never angry at her. Instead, I just rubbed my face in my hands.

"What the hell was that, Mackenzie?"

I sighed. "A really stupid thing to do."

"Yeah, no fucking shit! You are unbelievable, do you know that?!"

"I know, I just…" I trailed off.

It was nearly impossible to look her in the eyes. She was furious, and she had every right to be, but I didn't know what to say. I couldn't be honest—it was never supposed to get like this.

So, I did the only thing I could think of to drown the fury in her eyes. I turned to her and stepped closer. "I'm sorry, Fallon. Have I mentioned how amazing you look in that dress?"

She scoffed. "No, and you can't get out of this with compliments. You had no right—"

"I know, I know. I'm not trying to get out of anything."

I put my hand around her waist, erasing even more of the distance that separated us. "She wasn't your type anyway," I murmured, then kissed her. For a brief second, I thought she might kiss me back, but she pushed me away, frowning.

"Why, because she's yours?"

"No," I said, grabbing her wrist and pulling her to me again.

"And you think you know my type?" she asked, turning her head slightly when I tried to kiss her again.

"Well, let's see. Did you leave with her, or are you here, desperate for me."

"You don't know anything," she whispered. Then, finally, she let me kiss her. It was brief, barely more than a brush of our lips, but it was enough.

"Really? So if I touched your clit right now, my fingers wouldn't come back, glistening with your need for me?" Her only response was a slight gasp.

"I know you all too well, Sunshine." I smirked as I caressed her arms, causing her to shiver.

"That you do," she whispered.

I grasped the back of her neck and crashed our mouths together. She moaned into my mouth, her arms wrapping tightly around my neck.

Turning us so her back faced the sink, I gripped her hips and lifted her onto the counter. She squealed, her fingers tangling in my hair, pulling me even closer.

Someone could've walked in at any moment, but I didn't give a shit. I was taking her right there. I wanted her to know that she was mine. Even if I couldn't say it with words, I needed her to know.

I slid her underwear to the side and slowly rubbed her clit, not wasting any of the time I had with her.

She let out a moan when I started licking the spot just below her ear. "This doesn't excuse... fuck, Kenzie," she breathed.

"I know it doesn't. I haven't even begun to apologize," I whispered against the shell of her ear.

I slid two fingers inside her and she gasped, throwing her head back and hitting it on the mirror. "Oh my God!" she moaned.

All of a sudden, the bathroom door opened, and I quickly pulled out of Fallon. The woman stopped for a second, her face unreadable, before continuing to a stall and shutting the door. If she was bothered that I was fucking Fallon on the sink, she didn't show it.

Fallon, on the other hand, definitely did. She jumped down and adjusted her dress. "Mackenzie, what—"

"I don't know. Goddammit, Fallon!" I said, rubbing my face. "I'm sorry, I can't... maybe you *should* go find Cara."

She looked at me with narrowed brows. "What? You can't be serious."

I ignored her and stormed out.

"Mackenzie!" She yelled after me, but I kept walking until I was out the door. I didn't even say goodbye to any of my friends, though I knew they saw me leave.

I didn't turn around until I reached the elevators in my building. I wasn't even a little surprised that Fallon hadn't followed me.

I had to get out of there. It was all too much—the alcohol, the fighting, the feelings. Too many feelings making my head spin.

This was just a casual thing. There was no place for feelings—especially not feelings of falling in—no! That was *not* what was happening!

When I got in the elevator, I slumped on the floor and threw my head back. *Fuck, me!*

Out of nowhere, my phone started going off. I glanced at the screen and saw new messages from the group chat. *Well, that was fast:*

> Roxxy: Fallon said you guys got into a fight? Are you okay? WTF?!

> Harper: Sis, wtf?! You just dipped? Fallon just stormed out! What happened??

I groaned and started typing:

> Me: You talked to her? I'm fine. No fight. Sorry I bailed. Not feeling well.

I knew they wouldn't buy it, but I didn't know what else to say. I was hoping if I was short with them, they would drop it.

> Roxxy: We saw you trip into Fallon and her date, Kenzie. That doesn't seem fine.

> Me: I did trip, I didn't see them.

> Harper: 😳

> Me: Goodnight guys.

I turned off my phone and shoved it into my pocket. I didn't want to deal with anyone else.

I felt like such a dumbass. I kept screwing things up because I didn't know how to be honest. Or maybe I did know how, but I just couldn't get the words out. And when I finally managed to say something, it was always the wrong thing. I knew what I wanted, but I was too afraid of getting hurt to admit it.

When the elevator doors opened, I stepped out. But instead of heading home, I kept walking. I didn't stop until I reached the stairs leading up to the roof. I needed fresh air and quiet to clear my head. Too many feelings were swirling around, and I had to sort through them before I talked to Fallon again.

I had no idea what I was going to say—I just knew I had to fix things. I hated seeing her upset, and I hated being away from her.

But I couldn't fall in love with her. I couldn't let myself fall in love at all.

When I reached the roof, I didn't bother propping the door open. I didn't care if I stayed out there all night.

Chapter Thirty-Three

FALLON

As soon as Mackenzie left, I started walking after her, but I didn't get very far. When her friends stopped me to ask what happened, I couldn't hide the tears.

I was breaking down over another woman. That only made me more upset. We weren't even dating—not really—so why did I care so much?

I didn't give them any details as I said goodbye and went home.

When I reached my floor, my steps faltered at the sight of Mackenzie approaching her apartment. I stood there for a second, waiting for her to go inside.

She didn't. Instead, she headed toward the stairwell at the other end of the hall—the one that led to the roof.

Good. I hoped she got locked out. Not really, but seriously, what the hell just happened? We had agreed to do our own thing, and that's exactly what I was doing.

Although I'd never admit it to Mackenzie, I was relieved that Cara had left. The kiss had been good, but she was right—she wasn't my type. She wasn't a brunette with ocean eyes.

Mackenzie had a date last week, and maybe I wasn't as okay with it as I thought I was. Maybe I was just trying to get her out of my head by going out with Cara.

That still didn't give her the right to ruin my date, bring me close to coming, and then storm off. I wasn't sure which part pissed me off more.

I walked to my apartment and took out my keys to unlock the door, but I froze, undecided.

Do I go after her and get answers, or do I go inside and move on? We weren't technically dating, so I shouldn't care.

She should be the one to find me—I didn't do anything wrong!

"Goddammit!" I yelled, squeezing my hands into fists.

I turned and headed for the roof, pissed at myself for always being the one to right someone else's wrong. I wouldn't give in so easily, though. There was a lot of damage control to be done, and I wasn't going to be the one to do it.

I propped the door open and stormed toward Mackenzie, who was sitting in a chair facing the street, her head tilted back like she didn't have a care in the world. The picture of calm. That made one of us.

"What the fuck, Mackenzie?!" I shouted, throwing my arms up.

"What?" She answered so calmly, as if nothing had happened all night.

I stood in front of her, where her feet were propped on a table, and I kicked it out of the way.

"Hey!" she snapped.

"What is wrong with you?! You fuck me in a bathroom at some bar after you ruin my date, and then you storm off without an explanation?!"

She furrowed her brows. "I didn't storm off. And you weren't complaining in the bathroom," she replied.

I narrowed my eyes. "Really? Are you fucking serious right now?! Yes, you did. And you spilled a drink on her."

"I told you, I tripped."

"Bullshit!" I yelled. "And what about calling me 'baby girl'?! Do you have any idea how embarrassing that was, Mackenzie?! You were completely out of line!"

"Was I wrong?"

She couldn't have been serious. I didn't understand what was happening. She was acting as if I were the crazy one here, as if my feelings meant nothing to her.

I glared. "Jesus, Mackenzie! That's not even the point, and you know it!"

She sighed. "I know, I'm sorry. It was a shitty way to go about it. I wasn't thinking, but you looked like you needed saving." She got out of her chair and walked over to the ledge.

Why was she being so calm right now? Acting so weird? Meanwhile, my blood was boiling, and I was seconds away from throwing her off the goddamn roof.

"Saving from what? A good time? Because that's what I was having before you got there, and that is not for you to decide!" I yelled.

She stopped and turned toward me, but I didn't let her get a word out. "You don't get to decide when or if I need saving from anyone. We are not together!" I let out a long breath. "We agreed to keep things casual, remember?"

"I know! How could I forget?" she yelled back. "We're doing our own things... I know I shouldn't have handled things the way I did. I'm sorry. You got upset when I told you I had a date that night."

I opened my mouth to say something, but she kept going.

"And don't tell me you didn't, Fallon. I know you did. And I got upset tonight. Let's just move on. We're keeping it casual, right?"

"Yeah, well, we should've never agreed to that in the first place. I knew it would get like this." Tears started falling down my face, but I brushed them away.

She turned slowly to me, her eyebrows lowering in confusion. "Like what, Fallon?"

"Like this!" I gestured between us. "Weird and uncomfortable... infuriating!" I said through gritted teeth.

"I knew it from the first time we kissed. The second our lips touched, I knew it would be a huge mistake. The first time we had sex, I knew it too. And yet, I wanted to make those mistakes—even knowing it would end badly. In that moment, I didn't care. I couldn't deny my feelings for you any longer, and I was so tired of fighting it."

She looked away, and I shouldn't have been surprised when she didn't say anything.

"I never should've had that party," I said softly. I hugged myself tightly, as if trying to shield myself from the world.

She turned to look at me. "What? Fallon, what does that party have to do with anything?"

"It has to do with everything, Mackenzie!" I started. I turned to walk away, rubbing my face, and then stopped to turn and face her again.

"If I wouldn't have had the party, I wouldn't have met you, and we wouldn't have fought that night. And if I wouldn't have met you, I..." I stopped myself. Now was not the time.

"You would be happy." She said it like it was final. Like there was no room for argument. No room for the truth. How could she really think that? I was up there fighting for us, and she thought I regretted everything?

Her voice was sad, as if she'd already accepted some inevitable truth that hadn't even crossed my mind.

I shook my head. "No, that's not—"

"You wouldn't be up here, fighting with me," she cut in. "You never would've made the mistake of kissing me. You'd be happy, maybe even up here with someone else, not fighting." She turned back to lean over the ledge, staring up at the night sky.

"Is that what you think, Mackenzie? You think I would be happy with someone else if I never met you? You think I would be happy at all if you never showed up in my life?" I scoffed.

This infuriating woman! She had no idea what she did to me, or what she meant to me. Could she not tell by how hurt I was over all of this, just how much of me she really had?

"And I'm the only one fighting here. You aren't saying a damn thing!"

"What do you want me to say, Fallon? You've already said everything! Do you want me to admit that, no, we're not together, but we both got jealous? Is that what you want to hear? That I was so fucking jealous of Cara? That it killed me to see you kiss her and realize I'm not the only one you give your genuine smiles to? I know it shouldn't have, but goddammit, Fallon, it did! Okay? Is that what you want to hear?"

"I am so tired of this back-and-forth bullshit, Mackenzie! We agreed to keep things casual."

"I know," she said softly.

"And we both did that, with Cara, apparently. But I didn't 'trip' into your date and mention very personal things about you."

"I know, Fallon." She sighed, refusing to meet my eyes.

"And the *one* time I tried to do my own thing, Mackenzie... the *one* time I tried to get you out of my fucking head, you had to ruin it. Why?"

"I don't know, I—"

"You what, Mackenzie?" I yelled. "You like playing games? You like messing with my head, making me think you care about me one day, then you don't give a shit the next?"

"What? No, Fallon, that's not—"

"I can't keep doing this, Mackenzie. Keeping it casual doesn't mean getting jealous and making a scene. It doesn't mean feeling like your heart is being ripped out when the other person mentions they have a date with someone else after they've just been with you, making you feel like you're the only thing that matters in this world."

I paused, waiting for her to respond. When she stayed silent, I spoke again, my voice quiet but firm. "What are we doing?"

She didn't say anything. I exhaled, a chuckle escaping my lips, knowing she wouldn't answer. Instead of staying to fight, I turned to walk away. I wouldn't beg someone to love me again.

But before I could make it more than five steps, she grabbed my wrist, and I stopped. "Fallon, please."

She let go, and I turned to face her. "What, Mackenzie?"

"I'm sorry." That was all she said. Did she even know what she was apologizing for?

"Yeah, me, too," I replied, my voice quieter but still heavy with frustration.

I turned back toward the door. Before I could create distance between us, she spoke again. "Don't go, Fallon, please."

"Why?" I narrowed my eyes. "So I can keep yelling, and you stay quiet? Or so I can stay quiet and you start yelling, but we don't actually say anything? What are we doing, Mackenzie?"

She sighed. "I don't know, Fallon. I—"

I scoffed. "I know."

I tried to walk away, but she grabbed my wrist again. "Fallon."

I turned around and started yelling louder, yanking my wrist from her grasp. "I swear to God, Mackenzie, if you stop me one more time, and don't say a fucking thing, I'm going to toss you off this roof! What do you want?!"

"I fucking want *you*, okay?!"

Her words stopped my breath, stopped the blood from flowing through my veins, stopped... everything.

"What?" I said in a quiet breath.

"Fuck, Fallon! Do you have any idea what it did to me, seeing you there with her? Do you know how it felt when I saw you kiss her and touch her? I hate how I reacted—it was so fucked up. I know that, I just..." She groaned as if in physical pain. "I hate the effect you have on me! You're all I can think about, all the time, and I hate it. I don't want to think about your laugh or those goddamn freckles."

I let out a tearful laugh, but she kept going. "I don't want to think about how it feels when you're near me or the sensation of your skin on mine. I don't want to think about how much I just want to be around you and learn everything there is to know about you, but I do." She sighed. "I'm fucking scared, okay? I've never felt anything like this before, and I'm terrified. I want you—way more than I should—and I don't want to. I can't."

I stood there, tears filling my eyes. "It's just a physical want," I said softly. "That's why you agreed to keep it casual, right?"

She laughed, shaking her head. "I agreed because that's what you wanted, and I couldn't stomach the thought of not having any part of you at all."

She took a step closer. "If it was just physical, Fallon, I wouldn't still be here. I wouldn't have cared if you were on a date with Cara or anyone else. I wouldn't have been terrified when I heard you screaming that night. I wouldn't have been so angry that someone made you so scared, and I wouldn't want to do anything—absolutely anything—to make sure you always feel safe. You asked me two questions: what's wrong with me, and what do I want? You are the answer." She sighed heavily and turned to walk away.

"Wildcat?" I wiped a few tears from my face. I was scared, too, but I had to give my heart what it wanted.

She stopped, but didn't turn around. I took a deep breath, forcing myself to be brave for once. "Tell me."

She slightly turned her head toward me, a crease forming in the middle of her forehead. "Tell you what?"

I smiled. "Tell me not to kiss you."

She turned around completely. "What?"

I laughed and took a few steps toward her. "Tell me not to kiss you."

"After everything, you still want me?"

I walked over to her, playing with a stray piece of her hair, and looked into her eyes, silently begging for her to understand. "I don't want to talk anymore tonight. You said you want me, so show me."

"I told you, it's not just physical for me, Fallon."

"I know, and I believe you. It's not just physical for me either. I don't think it ever was."

She smiled. "I don't think so, either. So, what now? What do you want?"

What did I want? I wanted to hold her close and never let her go. "I want to kiss you, Kenzie. Please tell me I can?"

She grinned, cupping the side of my face. "Baby, you can have anything you want."

Chapter Thirty-Four

MACKENZIE

"Baby, I have to go. If I'm late, Harper will kill me, and then who will satisfy you?" Fallon was straddling me, fresh from round two, and already trying to start round three.

She bit my collarbone and I completely lost my train of thought. She knew every button to press, and damn could she press a button in the best way.

"Okay, seriously, baby, I really have to go." I moaned as I reluctantly placed her in the bed next to me. If it were up to me, we would never leave this room.

She pouted and kissed me, making me contemplate canceling on Harper. "Fine, fine. You're no use to me dead. Go, but take one last look at what will be waiting for you when you get home." She pulled the sheets off to the side, and her hand slowly started to make its way down...

She smirked as I groaned and kissed her one last time before getting up to take a shower.

After the best make up sex of my entire life, we had a long conversation about our expectations moving forward. Even though I was terrified of getting hurt again, the thought of losing Fallon felt worse, so I made a promise to myself that I would do whatever it took to not ruin what we had.

When I got to Harper's, they were already sitting down at the table. Harper looked peeved, and Grant looked guilty of something, but I didn't dare ask what happened.

I kissed Harper on the cheek and said hello to Grant. "I'm sorry I'm a little late, traffic was a bitch." It wasn't a total lie. I did hit traffic... after Fallon helped me take a shower.

We ate in silence for about ten minutes before Harper put down her fork and cleared her throat. "So, drinks at *Reid's*... that was fun."

My fork froze in mid-air, and I slowly looked up to meet her hard stare. Her eyebrows were raised, and it felt as though she was looking right through me. She could be one intimidating bitch when she wanted to be.

"Yeah, it was," I said coolly. I glanced over at Grant, who was looking down at his plate, oblivious to the silent fight brewing in Harper's eyes. Lucky bastard. Whether he knew what was going on or not, I didn't want to find out.

She cleared her throat. "It was terrible that you 'tripped' into that adorable couple at the bar."

When she said the words "adorable couple," my cup stopped just before it reached my lips. My eyes twitched, and I narrowed them. "I did trip," I bit back.

"I'm sure you did. And you felt so embarrassed about it that you had to storm off and leave your 'friend' in tears?" she added.

Fallon was crying? A heavy ache settled in the hollow of my chest, and I felt two inches tall.

Her voice had raised a little and she kicked Grant under the table, which caused him to groan softly.

When he looked up at her, she gave him a terrifying glare with gritted teeth.

"Well, I'm going to, uhh... go," Grant said as he stood up. He kissed her cheek and gave me a sympathetic glance.

I glared at him. *Thanks for leaving me alone with her, asshole!*

When he went into the kitchen, I shot her a look. "What the hell, Harper?" I asked.

Her fork clashed onto her plate. "Mackenzie, what the fuck is wrong with you? What happened?!" she yelled.

"Nothing. Like I told you a million times, I tripped!"

She rolled her eyes. "Mackenzie, do you know who you're lying to? I know damn well you didn't accidentally trip. You saw Fallon out with another woman—getting close to her, touching her, and kissing her. You got pissed off and caused a scene. My question is, why?"

A sharp wave of anger shot through me. She smirked, clearly seeing my clenched jaw and white knuckles around my fork. She knew damn well her words had hit their mark.

"How many times do I have to tell you? We are just—"

"Goddamnit! Stop saying you're just friends! I'm not a fucking idiot. You wouldn't have stood up so suddenly and gone to the bathroom—with your drink—if she was just a friend. I might have believed you, had the bathroom not been in the opposite direction of the bar." She glared.

My drink was more interesting than what was being said on the other side of the table. At least, that's what I told myself when I didn't look at her or respond.

"She wasn't just a friend the night of your promotion celebration, and she sure as hell wasn't just a friend that night, either. After you stormed out, she walked by our table and was sobbing, Mackenzie. Friends don't cry over friends like that. That night we met her, we watched you two the entire time. Fallon looked at you like she would stop breathing if she looked away, even for a second. That is not how friends look at each other."

I rubbed my face. None of this was supposed to happen, damnit.

We *were* just friends, and then somewhere along the way, it became more, and now I can't imagine going back to anything other than what we were now.

"I... I didn't know she cried." Guilt twisted in my chest. I had no idea how I could ever show Fallon how sorry I was for what happened with Cara. "We didn't fight—not at the bar, anyway. I just got confused, upset, and I had to get out of there. When I got home, that's when it all blew up."

"Mackenzie, I know you're still getting over your breakup. You're scared, and I get that. But you have to stop lying to yourself. It's not just hurting you—it's hurting Fallon, too, and neither of you deserve that. What are you two doing? Are you still keeping it casual, or is it something more?"

"I don't know, Harper, okay? I don't want to feel this way about her. I don't want to get hurt again—I can't." I dragged a hand down my face, frustration and fear twisting inside me. "It's just... when I'm with her, I feel..."

Harper's voice was gentle, free of judgment. "You're falling for her, aren't you?"

"I think, maybe? Fuck," I groaned, shaking my head. "I just know that when I'm with her, I never want to leave, and when I look at her, I never want to stop. Her laugh... it feels like a part of me, and it's something I don't want to live without."

"Honey." She reached across the table to grab my hand. "You're falling for her, hard. And that's okay, that's *really* okay, but have you told her how you feel? How does she feel?"

I sighed. "I mean, she asked me not to sleep with anyone else, and I'm not, obviously, but I don't know if I'm ready for *that* word yet. I'm not sure if I'm ready to face the possibility of my feelings being one-sided."

She laughed. "Considering she was devastated when *you* left her, and not her date, I think it's safe to say she feels the same way, sweetie."

"God, I'm so screwed aren't I?"

She just laughed. "Yeah, you really are. But in the best way."

Chapter Thirty-Five
MACKENZIE

I made things right with Fallon, so I thought it was time to apologize to Drea. What happened at the bookstore was... I needed to apologize.

Fallon left my apartment early the next morning, so I didn't get a chance to tell her where I was going. I planned on telling her later that night during dinner.

When I walked into the bookstore, Drea looked up and was smiling, so that seemed to be a good sign.

"Welcome to—" The shock on Drea's face quickly changed to one of anger as her eyes grew wide and then narrowed.

"Get out!" She threw a pointed finger toward the door. Okay, so maybe it wasn't a good sign.

"Drea, let me explain..." I said with my hands up.

"Get the fuck out!" she said.

I looked around the store to see wide eyes fixed on me. I threw them an apologetic smile.

Drea just glared at me, silently demanding me out.

Of course, I didn't listen and walked closer to the counter. She quickly came out from behind it and rushed toward me. I stood my ground, but inside, I was terrified.

"I said get out, Mackenzie! You are not welcome here!" She shouted even though she was only a few feet in front of me.

At that point, the store emptied out, except for one woman with her nose stuck in a book, like she was in another world. She was lucky. Drea was yelling at me, and I started to become uneasy.

"I'm not leaving until you let me explain, Drea," I interrupted.

She glared at me, and didn't say anything.

"I came to apologize about the book signing. We didn't mean for that to happen, and it wasn't Fallon's fault. I'm the one who started it."

"I'm not talking about the book signing. We've moved past that, and we are *never* talking about that day again! I know about your little outburst at *Reid's*! Fallon is my family, Mackenzie! What were you thinking? You have the world's biggest lady balls to show your face in my store after that!"

"I tripped." I shrugged. "Why does everyone keep making a big deal about that? She forgave me—why can't you?"

"I don't give a shit if she forgave you or not! And what about your 'baby girl'? I suppose you're going to tell me she tripped and landed on the sink? You clearly had no issue disrespecting her date while you fucked her in the restroom—on top of saying that to Cara?! What is wrong with you? Neither of them deserved that!"

"She told you what happened?" I winced. I was so embarrassed. I regretted everything about that night—well, everything involving Cara, anyway.

I sighed. "Look, it was really shitty of me, okay? I apologized, and we talked it out. Well, she yelled, and then we talked. I didn't mean any of it, and she knows that. Things just got out of hand that night. I'm really sorry, Drea."

She glared at me. "Of course, she told me—all of it. She called me in tears, Mackenzie! She may like you, but I sure as hell don't. My best friend calls me crying, and you think I'm just going to let that slide? You're lucky I promised her I wouldn't strangle the shit out of you! Honestly, Mackenzie, what the hell were you thinking?"

"I don't know what I was thinking! Maybe I was thinking about how it made me physically sick to see her out with someone else, to watch her kiss someone else. Maybe I was thinking that I'm so damn crazy about her it makes my head spin. Clearly, I wasn't thinking at all— I can never think when I look at her! I guess I tried to push her away, only to realize I'm the one who can't stay away, the one who doesn't

want to stay away! Or maybe I was thinking that I'm so insanely in lo
—" I stopped, the weight of the truth hitting me like a freight train. I
couldn't bring myself to say it out loud.

I wasn't in love with Fallon...who was I kidding? Of course I was.
My world didn't make sense if she wasn't in it. God, I sounded pathetic.

She smirked. "How does it feel to tell the truth, Mackenzie? The
whole fucking world knows how you two feel about each other, but for
some reason, you can't admit it."

"Listen, I'm scared, but I'm trying. I got jealous seeing her with
Cara, and I was more angry with myself for the way I reacted. I've been
hurt before, and I'm so damn scared. I can't go through it again, but I
can't seem to stay away from her."

"We all have fucked-up pasts, Fallon included. Her ex really altered
her in a negative way, and she's finally coming back from that hurt. And
I *really* hate to admit it, but I think part of that is because of you,
despite what happened at *Reid's*. I've never seen her look at someone the
way she looks at you. The way she talks about you makes it easy to see
what her feelings are."

I didn't know a lot about her ex-girlfriend, just that she cheated on
her and basically forced her to leave her old life behind. I didn't know
the woman, but I hoped for her sake that we never ran into one another.

"Look, Kenzie, I can see you really care for her. I see it in the way
you look at her, how you light up when you talk about her, and I can see
it in how you risked your life to come here. I still can't forgive you for
what you did, not yet, but please promise me you won't hurt her. If you
hurt her again, I can assure you, you will regret it. She is my family, and I
can't stand seeing her upset."

"You have nothing to worry about, trust me. The last thing I want
to do is hurt her, Drea. She means more to me than I can admit."

"Good." She smiled slightly.

"Well, I'd better go, but I'll see you around, Drea. And again, I'm
really sorry about everything—the signing and—"

"We are not talking about that, remember? But, yes, see you
around."

. . .

I waited until Fallon came over for dinner that night to tell her about my talk with Drea. I wanted to have the conversation in person.

"So, I had an interesting day today," I said

"Oh yeah?" Fallon replied. She had made a delicious stir fry with a salad for our dinner.

I nodded. "Yeah. I went on a nice little walk and went into a cute little queer bookstore."

She froze. "Really?" she asked, not making eye contact.

"Yup, I sure did. I wanted to apologize to my beautiful girlfriend's best friend for the book signing incident, and she had some interesting things to say."

Fallon looked up slowly. "Um..."

"You told her what happened at *Reid's*? Fallon, seriously?"

"She's my best friend, and I was upset—for a good reason, might I remind you. Look, I'm sorry. I told her we worked it out."

"I know, you did have a good reason, but I'm not so sure she believed you."

"Why wouldn't she?" She frowned.

"Because she yelled at me, babe! She's scary!"

She laughed. "Yeah, she really is, but she means well. I'm sorry."

She caressed my face and I smiled, folding my hands over hers. That one touch could've made anything better.

"I'm not, I definitely deserved it."

She kissed my cheeks, and when she went to pull away, I grabbed her face and kissed her sweetly. "All better?" she whispered.

"Definitely," I answered and kissed her nose.

"So, is she still mad?" She winced. "I really did tell her everything was okay."

I laughed. "After she tried to kick me out, we talked, and I think I might be allowed back there. But to be safe, I'm going to maybe give up reading for a while. She also told me you called her crying? Harper said the same thing when you left the bar."

She looked down at her plate. "Oh, um... yeah, kind of?"

I grabbed her chin, tilting it up to me, and kissed her so she could feel the truth in my words. "I am so sorry I made you feel any kind of sadness. Those beautiful eyes weren't made to shed a single tear."

She cleared her throat. "So, what else did she say?"

"Well, she asked what the hell is wrong with me, which seems to be a popular question among both of our friend groups." I laughed.

"I'm sitting on the edge of my seat. What did you tell her?"

"I told her that I'm so damn crazy about this woman, and how I got jealous because I want to be the only one who can touch her or kiss her." I leaned in to kiss her and show her exactly how crazy I was about her.

Chapter Thirty-Six

FALLON

The bookstore wasn't busy at all by the time I made it in a few days later, so Penelope stopped by to hang out and talk about our weekend plans.

We had been trying to find a time when we were all free to get together, and this weekend was turning out to be the perfect opportunity.

"Okay, ladies, where are we going this weekend?" Penelope asked. "I really need a night out. Greg has been keeping me so busy. I need a break!" We all laughed.

She'd finally forgiven Gregory for missing their anniversary, and he'd been making up for it ever since.

"Well, you know I love *Queer Quarters*. Rylee makes the best drinks." I smiled, thinking it had been far too long since we had all been out together.

Drea nodded. "I definitely agree. Pen, what do you think?"

"Sounds good to me!" she said, propping her feet on a coffee table, before Drea gave her a look that had her swiftly removing her outstretched legs.

Drea looked over at me and sat up. "Oh, why don't you invite Mackenzie, love? I know she likes it there, too, and we haven't all been out together."

I turned to her, furrowing my brows in confusion and shock. "Wait, you *want* me to invite Kenzie?" I asked nervously. I felt like it was some sort of trap.

"Yes, love." She sighed. "I've had time to process everything after she came in to talk to me, and you seem fond of her. If she's good enough for you, then she's good enough for me. But if she hurts you again, you'll be filing a missing persons report." Her expression softened, and she smiled. "In all seriousness, though, invite her, love."

"If you're sure?"

"Yes, I'm sure. She's come in a few times, and we are okay."

I smiled and told her I'd ask her tonight. But if I was being honest, I didn't think she would want to go. She told me what happened when she went to talk to Drea, and if the roles were reversed, I would've been a little terrified, too.

Several hours later, I knocked on Mackenzie's door and she opened it with a sexy smile and a sports bra. "If you let the neighbor's see you looking like that, we're going to have a big problem!" I said.

"Then you better get in here and do something about it." She winked.

I rolled my eyes but walked in anyway, losing my breath when she spun me around and pulled me close to her. "Jesus, Wildcat, you can't even make it down the hall?"

She played with a loose hair and tucked it behind my ear. "Have you no shame?" I teased.

"Not when it comes to you." She leaned in and kissed the air from my lungs. "The weather is nice tonight. What do you say to wine on the patio?"

I smiled, leaning into her touch. That sounded heavenly. "You spoil me. That sounds perfect."

We stepped out onto the patio, and as soon as Mackenzie sat down in a chair, I claimed my usual spot in her lap. If I didn't, she'd just move me there anyway.

"So," I said, wrapping my arms around her. "I'm going out with the girls this weekend, and I want you to come."

She paused her gentle massage of my sides and nuzzled into my chest. "I don't know, Sunshine. A whole night with Drea? That sounds a little risky, don't you think?"

I laughed. "You'll survive, Wildcat... probably." She didn't find it funny at all, which only made me laugh harder. "It was her idea to invite you. Obviously, I want you there and would've asked, but I thought it might be awkward. She said you two were okay, though."

She sighed. "I mean, I guess so. If you want me there, I'll be there. I would risk my life for you." She smiled, grabbing my face and kissing me, leaving me a mess. It was amazing how she could make me forget everything with just one kiss.

"Maybe we should take this insi... okay," I breathlessly protested when she slid her hand between my legs.

"I think you're right, sweetheart. Any longer and the neighbors might file a noise complaint," she whispered in my ear.

"You and your inflated self-opinion," I teased, letting out a squeal when she smacked me on the ass as I walked inside. She followed close behind, and the seductive look in her eyes left no question about what was coming next.

It was finally the weekend, and I was beyond ready for a girls night. I had just stepped into *Queer Quarters* when Mackenzie texted, saying she was finishing up a work call, and would be meeting me shortly after.

"Hey, Fallon!" Rylee called from behind the bar when I arrived. I was surprised to see her. I was hoping I would, but I rarely saw her outside the coffee shop.

"Hey, Rylee. I didn't know you worked tonight."

She smiled while she was pouring someone a drink. She looked at her the whole time she worked. Maybe they knew each other?

She had long, wavy brown hair that framed her face, and her dark brown eyes held Rylee's stare just as fiercely. A beauty mark rested above the left side of her lips. She wore a dark blue blouse with the sleeves casually rolled up, paired with white skinny jeans that completed her look. She was gorgeous.

"I picked up an extra shift." She smiled.

I grinned and sat down next to the stranger. "That's good for me then. I know the drinks will be great!"

She waved off the compliment. "Are you here alone tonight?"

I shook my head, glancing around the bar. "No, I'm meeting Kenzie. She should be here soon."

"Oh, awesome. Well, Fallon, this is my wife, Lana. And Lana, this is my friend Fallon—Kenzie's girlfriend."

I gave a small wave to Lana, noticing that Rylee introduced me as her friend and not just "Kenzie's girlfriend."

"It's nice to meet you, Lana." I reached out my hand with a smile.

She returned the smile and swatted my hand away, going in for a hug. "It's so good to finally meet you! I've heard Rylee and Mackenzie talking about you nonstop!" Her words caused a blush to creep its way onto my pale face. I finally knew how Mackenzie felt about me, but it was still nice to hear it from someone else.

"Okay, honey, don't embarrass Mackenzie when she isn't here to defend herself. And let her go, you'll suffocate her!"

She laughed and released me. "It's okay, I'm pretty fond of her best friend," I replied.

"Speak of the devil. Hey, Kenz." Rylee grinned.

"Hey, Ryles." Mackenzie put her arm around my waist and kissed the top of my head. "Hey there, beautiful."

Turning to face her, I smiled and pressed a kiss to her delicious-looking lips. "Hi."

"You look amazing," she said. I blushed at her compliment and felt warmth as she caressed the sides of my body gently.

I cleared my throat, hoping the feeling I got when we were together would never go away. "Thanks, baby, you look hot." She leaned in for another kiss.

"Okay, you two, this is a public place. Keep it in your pants." Rylee laughed. She handed us two shots and went to tend to the customers at the far end of the bar.

"Thanks, Rylee," I called, and she waved us off. We clinked our glasses together and threw back the shots.

"Let's go find a table, sweetheart," Mackenzie said.

"Okay, babe. Lana, it was so nice to meet you."

"It was so good to meet you, Fallon. Don't be a stranger. You guys have fun and stay out of trouble." She winked, and I chuckled softly.

With Mackenzie, that was easier said than done, if the book signing was anything to go by.

I hopped off the barstool, and she placed her hand gently on the small of my back, guiding us to a table.

Turning to her, I couldn't stop the smile that was trying to break free. Every time I looked at her, it felt like I was replaying all of our happy moments, and I couldn't believe where life had brought us.

When we got to our table we ordered another drink. She was sitting there, nervously playing with a straw wrapper, and kept looking up to the door every few minutes.

"Don't be nervous." I grabbed her thigh under the table and her shoulders dropped slightly. "It will be fine, I promise." At least I hoped it would be. After talking more with Drea on my way to the bar, she assured me everything was okay, but I still had my doubts.

"I know, we just haven't really been in the same room for a long period of time. I mean she's been nice to me anytime I go to the book-store, but that's her place of business, so she has to be."

"You forgot what happened when you apologized already?" I laughed as she threw her head onto my shoulder and groaned. "She doesn't have to be nice at all—she's choosing to be. Besides, I'm here as a buffer, and Penelope will be here, too, so you're not alone. Everything will be fine."

"I know, you're right. You know her better than I do. I'm sure it will be fine."

"I'm always right, haven't you learned by now?" I winked.

She took my hand and kissed the top of my knuckles sweetly. "I'm learning so many new things with you, darling, and I hope to never stop."

Drea and Penelope approached our table, giving me an excuse to shift my attention away from the woman who was currently making me blush. "Hey guys," I said as they came to sit down.

"Hey, Fal. Hey, Mackenzie, it's nice to finally put a face to all the stories we've heard about you." Penelope smiled.

"Oh my God, Pen," I covered my face, feeling embarrassed. I blushed as Mackenzie put her hand on my leg, squeezing gently.

"Hey, Mackenzie, glad you could make it," Drea said with a smile. Whether she was being nice for my sake or not, I appreciated it.

"Yeah, me too. Thanks for inviting me." Under the table, her fingers brushed against my thigh, and I had to resist the urge to let my eyes flutter closed. I'd only had one shot, but the heat from her touch was already spreading to places it shouldn't have been.

"Of course. Everything's cool, Mackenzie, really," Drea smiled, and I could feel Mackenzie's shoulders relax, just a little.

"Well, would you look at this gorgeous group of ladies?" Rylee had just walked over to our table and was smiling brightly. I looked over to the bar, seeing her wife wear the same smile.

"Hey, kiss ass," Mackenzie laughed.

I swatted her arm, and she kissed me on the cheek. "Be nice!" I demanded.

"Only for you, darling." She sent me a wink, and I playfully rolled my eyes.

"God, you two are too adorable. Alright, what can I get you guys?"

Penelope ordered the first round, and I told Rylee I had the next.

"Um, excuse me? I don't think so." Mackenzie handed her card to Rylee. "I have the next one, Rylee. Don't take any of her money!"

I rolled my eyes but smiled anyway. "Wildcat, I don't deserve you."

Rylee walked away shaking her head, and Mackenzie turned to me and smiled. "You're right, you don't. You deserve so much more."

"Mackenzie Isabella..." I grabbed her face, pouting dramatically. "How dare you say such a thing about my sweet, very sexy girlfriend? You have no idea just how much you mean to me." I smiled and pressed a soft, lingering kiss to her lips.

How did I get so lucky to find someone who cared for me as she did? I wanted my friends to see why she was so special to me, and why she meant the world to me.

It made my heart happy to see my friends include Mackenzie in the conversations, and it seemed like they genuinely wanted to get to know her. They were all talking and having a good time, and I saw an opportunity.

I shot Penelope a look and nodded toward the bathrooms. "Well, I'm going to go to the restroom. I'll be right back."

"Do you want me to come with you?" Mackenzie asked, her eyes filled with concern.

"No, I'll be okay." I glanced at Penelope again, raising my eyebrows.

After a moment, she finally got the hint and stood up. "I have to go too, actually, so I'll go with you. I'll look out for her."

I smiled at Mackenzie, who stared at me with wide eyes. Leaning in close, I brushed my hand over the top of her thigh. "Don't worry, I'll make it up to you later."

I went to kiss her cheek, but she turned at the last second and I caught her lips instead. She cupped the side of my face, and I deepened the kiss. For a moment, I wanted to forget everything else, and just lose myself in her.

But then I felt the weight of everyone's stare on us, and reluctantly broke the kiss.

"Oh, I know you will," she whispered breathlessly.

I grinned and walked with Penelope toward the bathroom, trying to shake the heat still simmering between us.

"What was that about?" Penelope asked when we got to the restroom.

"I wanted them to have time to talk alone. She's nervous about being here with Drea. Maybe it wasn't the best idea to leave them alone," I said, laughing, even though I was pretty sure Mackenzie wouldn't find it funny.

"Oh, she'll be fine. She really shouldn't be nervous at all. Drea and I talked about it on the way here. She said she's fine with her, as long as she makes you happy. We really like Mackenzie, sweetie, aside from what happened with Cara. We haven't seen you this happy in a long time, and it's been good to see."

"Thanks, Pen. I'm really happy. It's crazy to think about how this all started, but I couldn't be more grateful for where we ended up. It feels different than how it was with my ex. I know it's only been such a short amount of time, but I feel safe with her."

We went back to the table, where Mackenzie and Drea were grinning like idiots.

"Oh God, what?" I asked, looking between the two troublemakers. I was glad they weren't fighting, but I wasn't sure if this was any better.

Drea laughed. "Nothing, love. We're just happy to see you."

I scowled at her but sat down anyway, trying to ignore them. "You guys are so weird." I snuggled closer to Mackenzie.

"How did it go?" I whispered when Drea and Penelope were in their own conversation.

"Not as bad as I thought. I think everything is really okay, at least for now."

I smiled, feeling her reassuring words settle something inside me.

The ride home felt like the longest thirty minutes of my life. I think she could tell I was getting anxious, because she kept asking me if I was okay, but I brushed her off every time. I was nervous, but I knew we had something to talk about.

"Baby, are you sure you're okay?" Mackenzie stopped me as soon as we got inside her apartment. "Please talk to me. I can tell something is bothering you."

I sighed and walked to the couch, hating, in that moment, how well she knew me already. "I'm going home for Thanksgiving, and I would really like it if you'd go with me." I anxiously played with a loose strand of the blanket draped over the back of the couch.

She came down and sat next to me. "You want me to meet your parents? That's a big step, are you sure?"

I frowned. "Do you not want to? You don't have to if you're not comfortable, I—"

She pulled me in for a kiss, effectively stopping any future anxious ramblings and calming my nerves.

"Fallon, of course I want to meet your family. They're important to you, so they're important to me. I just wanted to make sure this is something you're sure about. It's a big step, but it's one I am ready to take if you are."

I smiled, warmth spreading through me, and snuggled up to her. "Yes, baby. I would really love for you to be there. I know you always go to Harper's, so I understand if you can't."

"Shit. Harper. Let me talk to her. I'm sure she'll understand. Come on, let's get to bed. It's getting late, and there are a few loose ends I've been dying to tie up before then." She winked, and I swore my body temperature rose thirty degrees. My clit throbbed, anticipation building for what was surely going to be a long night.

Chapter Thirty-Seven

MACKENZIE

"You really need to stop getting me drunk!" I said as the curtains opened and the blinding light threatened to shatter my corneas.

"Me? I'm sorry, you're the one who insisted on taking shots!" Fallon laughed and ripped the covers off. "Just get up, buttercup. Breakfast is calling." She smacked me on the ass, and I let out an involuntary moan, jumping up to glare at her.

"What?" she asked, staring back.

I smirked ever so slightly and whispered, "Run, Sunshine."

And she did—laughing and shouting down the hall to the kitchen until I jumped onto the island and landed right in front of her.

"That's cheating," she said in between breaths as I pulled her close and kissed her.

She pushed me off and turned around to grab the cooked bacon from the pan. As she placed it on a plate, I stood behind her, wrapping my arms around her waist and nuzzling my nose into the crook of her neck, peppering it with kisses.

"You know, I think I could get used to waking up with you half-naked in my kitchen everyday."

She hummed as we started naturally swaying back and forth slowly. This was a life I could've gotten used to if I wasn't careful.

After a few minutes of watching her cook, I spun her around and started slow dancing with her.

"What are you doing, babe? There's no music playing."

"Your voice is the only music I need." She rolled her eyes, and I kissed her nose.

"Jesus, you are so lame."

"Yeah, but you like me anyway." I winked.

She grinned from ear to ear, and I swore her smile never failed to almost knock me out. I never wanted these moments between us to end. I really was becoming lame, but I was oddly comfortable with it.

"For now, if you're on your best behavior." She giggled.

"I know it's breakfast, but I think I would much rather have dessert instead." I winked.

She playfully punched my shoulder. "Keep it in your pants, for now. Sit, sit," she said, pointing to the stool by the island.

I pulled it out and sat down. She turned around, holding two plates of food—bacon, sausage, and pieces of toast with eggs and cheese in the center. It smelled absolutely delicious.

I took a bite and moaned so loudly she gasped, turning pink.

"Should I be jealous that I was sitting over here when you made that sound?" she asked, biting her lip.

"I'm sorry, it's just so good!" I said, with a mouthful of food and embarrassment on my face. "I'll make it up to you later."

We spent the whole day lounging around the house, talking more about spending Thanksgiving with her family. It reminded me that I needed to call Harper. I went into the other room so Fallon wouldn't distract me —she was a professional at that by now.

"Hey, sis," I said cheerfully, hoping she'd match my energy.

"What do you want?" She sounded suspicious. "You sound too happy. What's wrong?" Damn my sister!

"Why do you always assume something's wrong? Can't I just be happy to talk to you?"

She sighed loudly on the other end. "Alright, alright. I'm glad you're in a good mood. What's up?"

I took a deep breath. "Well," I said, my voice a few octaves too high. "I wanted to talk to you about Thanksgiving. Do you have a minute?"

"Yes," she said slowly. "What about it? You're still coming over, aren't you?"

I really hated this. I was more scared of disappointing my sister than anyone else in my life. "That's what I wanted to talk to you about. I haven't said yes yet, but Fallon invited me to spend Thanksgiving with her in Portland, and obviously, I want to go, but I wanted to run it by you first."

I sat there while the line was quiet for so long, I honestly thought she hung up.

"Boog, I love you. You know that, right?"

"Yes?" I said hesitantly. Where the hell was she going with this?

"I can't even express how happy I am for you that you've found Fallon. Of course, I'm sad and want you here for Thanksgiving, but that's selfish. If you want to go, then I think you should."

"Are you sure? I know how important family time is to you, especially on holidays."

"Kenzie, seriously, go! Family *is* important, and it sounds like you're finding a second one, which is equally as important."

I smiled sweetly. "I don't know if I'd go that far, but maybe. Her family is so special to her, and if she wants me there, I want to be there. Thank you for understanding."

"Thank you for talking to me about it. It means a lot that you wanted my opinion. I love you, Boog."

"I love you, too. Oh, and Harp?" I felt a nervous flutter in my stomach, but I needed to tell someone.

"Yeah, Kenz?"

I took a deep breath and whispered so Fallon couldn't hear, "I think I'm going to tell her how I feel. She needs to know."

I think I knew I was in love with Fallon long before that first night we went out. I knew I felt something for her that was more than just friendship, but because of my past, I was so afraid to admit it—a part of me still was. But I couldn't let that stop me from going after what I wanted, and that was Fallon.

"Yeah? Honey, that's amazing. We've all known for a while, but I'm glad you finally figured your shit out. And don't worry, that woman loves you more than the air she breathes."

I cleared my throat. "I better go, she's waiting for me. I love you, Harp."

"Love you, Kenz."

I hung up and went back out to Fallon, who was on the patio.

"I'm sorry, babe. Sisterly talk. She's chatty."

She smiled when I came out and handed me a glass of wine. "It's okay. I wanted to give you your space. I know family is important to you, which is one thing I... really like about you."

I looked at her with raised brows. "Anyway, she was sad I wouldn't be there, but she understood some things are just too important to pass up," I said with a smile. "Speaking of... I was wondering if I could take you out on a date?"

"What do you mean? We've been on dates."

I smiled. "True, but not a real one as an actual couple. I want to properly take you out."

"Well, I guess I can't argue with that, can I? Fine. What did you have in mind?"

"Oh, it's a surprise." I winked.

"Is that so? I'm sure I can find some way to get it out of you." She walked over to my chair and straddled me.

My body surged with heat, and I was convinced she could get anything out of me without saying a word. But I would never tell her that.

"I'm sure you could try," I said, caressing her hips as she kissed below my ear and down to my neck.

She spent the rest of the night trying to make me tell her about the date. I would've never told her the truth, but she could've gotten anything she wanted with just her smile.

Chapter Thirty-Eight

FALLON

I woke up the next morning, angry with myself. I'd spent all night trying to get the surprise out of Mackenzie, only to forget to ask her again after we were finished. I'd fallen asleep in her arms instead. She had a way of distracting me—when I was with her, she was all I could focus on.

Mackenzie refused to talk to me or see me until our date, saying she had a few things to take care of first. I'd be lying if I said I wasn't a little upset about it. We'd only been apart for a few hours, but I already missed her. Fuck, I was in way over my head with this one.

I wasn't surprised when she showed up later that night with goodies from *Brewed Awakening*. She was always doing things like that. I swore, every time I saw her, she had an iced coffee in one hand and a bag of banana bread in the other.

"How did you even get this? They closed hours ago." I laughed, taking the coffee and pastry bag.

She kissed my forehead as we started walking. "I know people." She winked, and I knew she'd enlisted Rylee's help.

"Thanks, baby. You're too good to me." I took a sip and did a little happy dance. "Perfection, every time."

I blushed when I heard the faintest whispered, "Yes, you are."

I turned to her as soon as we got into the elevator and wrapped my arms around her neck. "You clean up really fucking nice, Wildcat."

"You look pretty damn perfect yourself," she said with a wink. I was wearing a floral sundress with sandals.

We walked down the street for a few blocks, pausing every once in a while to share a knee-buckling kiss. When we stopped in front of the bookstore, I turned to her, confused. It was closed, and Drea never stayed past closing, so I wasn't sure why we were there. "Why are we stopping here? It's closed."

"Is it?" she asked with a smirk.

I narrowed my brows. "Yes, it's nine o'clock at night, first of all, and there's a sign that clearly indicates the store is closed," I said, dramatically pointing at the obvious "Closed" sign.

She laughed, stepping closer to the door and reaching for the handle. "Have faith, it might be unlocked."

I furrowed my brow and tilted my head, trying to piece things together. "Drea never leaves the door unlocked. It's not..." My words trailed off as she turned the knob, and the door opened.

"What the hell? I need to call her and check around to see—"

"Fallon, relax, okay?" She took my hand and led me inside.

Relax? How could I possibly have relaxed? What if we'd been robbed or something had been damaged? I couldn't see anything except for a glow coming from the back of the store.

"What the hell is that?" I whispered. "Kenzie, I'm scared."

"Don't be scared. Just trust me." She grabbed my waist and pulled me closer, shielding me from whatever unknown danger surely awaited us.

I still had no clue what was going on. When she locked the front door, my panic grew. Not only was it dark, but now I was locked in— what if something *did* happen?

"Look, if you're planning on killing me, just give me a heads-up so I can at least prepare for it."

She turned toward me, cupped my face gently, and pressed a soft kiss to my temple. "Fallon, I'm not going to murder you. Will you relax?" She took my hand and led me toward the glowing light.

When we got there, I stopped and gasped. "What... what is this?"

My voice came out weak. Right in front of me was the most romantic setup I'd ever seen.

In the corner of the bookstore, she had arranged a cozy little picnic. A large blanket covered the floor, surrounded by soft pillows. A spread of fresh fruit, crackers, and even a damn cake had been laid out beautifully.

String lights twinkled around the setup, and a laptop sat on a chair, ready to play a movie.

When I saw what movie she had picked, I nearly started crying. "*Stuart little?*" I turned to her and smiled.

"I wanted our first date to be something special. This is your favorite place to be, so I thought it was the perfect destination for our date. Do you like it?"

I couldn't form words. I was too stunned to think of any.

It was the most thoughtful thing anyone had ever done for me, and it was taking all my willpower not to burst out into tears. I was such an emotional wreck.

"I... how did you do all of this?"

She grabbed my waist and pulled me close. "I know the owner."

"You were in cahoots with my best friend behind my back?!"

She laughed. "Cahoots? And you call me old! We talked while you and Penelope were in the bathroom. I told her my idea and she was more than willing to help. I just had to promise her that we would lock up when we were done. Do you like it, Sunshine?"

I gave her the warmest smile as she wiped the tears away. "It's perfect," I whispered before I kissed her softly. "Thank you."

We devoured the fruit and crackers while watching the movie, along with half of the most delicious chocolate cake.

It was the perfect night, better than anything I could've asked for. I couldn't believe she'd done all this for me—and even got Drea to help. No one had ever done anything half as thoughtful. I wanted to tell her how much she meant to me, but I was scared. Scared she wouldn't say it back. Scared she would. Scared I'd lose everything.

Instead, I just lay there, soaking in the moment, feeling safe and at home. There was nowhere I'd rather be than in her arms. It didn't matter where we were or what we were doing, as long as I could lose myself in her eyes.

We stopped watching the movie halfway through, and I had to force myself to pull away. We were kissing like teenagers, but I wanted more.

"Baby, we better go. Drea might actually kill us if we have sex in her store again."

She laughed softly, her hand drifting down to my thigh. "Don't worry, I got permission to defile you—as long as she never hears about it." She winked. "That's why I brought the blankets. No mess to clean up."

"You really thought of everything, didn't you?" I smiled and placed a gentle kiss on her lips. "Come on, I'll help you clean up, then we can make a better mess after we leave."

Her hand stopped dead in its tracks and she looked at me. "Why are you so fucking perfect?"

My cheeks turned two shades of red. "I'm far from perfect."

I sat up, and she furrowed her brows. "Darling, I wish you could see what I see when I look at you. I see the most beautiful, kind, and amazing woman."

My gaze drifted to the side as tears began to form. I couldn't hold in the sadness that had been weighing on me since I left Portland. I stood and turned away, quickly wiping the tears streaming down my face.

"Fallon, are you okay?" Mackenzie asked, concern filling her voice as she stood and wrapped her arms around my waist from behind. "Did I say something to upset you?"

She turned me around and placed a light, tender kiss on my lips as the words I'd been so afraid to say finally started to pour out. "Kenzie, I know you care for me, and I'm so thankful you came into my life after my breakup. But I have a long way to go before I can fully trust that you won't break my heart."

Mackenzie's eyes seemed to shine, but behind them was a sadness that made my chest ache. Her voice trembled as she spoke. "I'll never forgive myself for how badly I treated you when we first met, but you have to know I would never do anything to hurt you."

"It's not about how we met," I said, my voice quiet, almost distant. "I've been broken for a long time, and trusting people isn't easy for me. It wasn't just my ex who did that to me... I still think about my dad. It's hard to hate someone you once loved, you know? If the person who was supposed to love you no matter what can hurt you like that, how do you trust anyone? How can I be sure a stranger won't do the same?"

We stood there for a moment before Mackenzie finally broke the silence. "Fallon, I can't even begin to tell you how sorry I am for everything you've been through. I wish I could've been there to stop it. But please know that I'm here now, and I will always protect you. I'm always here to listen, whenever you need to talk about it."

She gently kissed my tears away, and in that moment, with every part of who I was, I knew I loved Mackenzie Thompson—body and soul.

Chapter Thirty-Nine

MACKENZIE

We were lying in bed when I finally got the courage to say what I'd been feeling for a while. I couldn't find the right words until now. Seeing the hurt on her face as she told me one of her darkest fears earlier, I knew I couldn't go another day without telling her how I felt. She needed to know how safe she was with me.

"I'm really sorry for everything, Fallon. My past relationship has really fucked me up, and I'm so thankful for you, but I'm still learning how to get over the trauma she left. I know it's not an excuse for how I acted, but I promise I'll spend every day you let me, making sure I never do anything to hurt you."

I held her, rubbing delicate circles on her hips, my gaze fixed on the beauty I was lucky enough to share my bed with. In that moment, she was utterly perfect, and she was completely mine.

She smiled, and I kissed her softly, feeling the warmth of her lips. "We've all had our share of heartbreak and bullshit," she said with a gentle laugh. "You don't need to explain. I have my own things I'm dealing with, too, and I'm scared, but it's okay, really. I have no idea what's going on in that sexy head of yours," she paused, her fingers brushing over my hand, her gaze holding mine with an intensity that made my heart race. Did she feel anything I felt for her? "But I do know I really like you, and I've enjoyed every second of being with you," she continued, her voice steady. The soft sincerity behind her words made my decision easier.

I was so in love with this woman, and it was time she knew. Every part of me wanted to say it, to let the words spill out, but I held back for a moment, letting the weight of the feeling settle in my chest. I had to explain my past, to make her understand why I was so guarded—but also why I was still willing to give her everything.

"My ex and I..." I started, struggling to find the right words. "We broke up a few years ago."

"You don't need to tell me, it's okay," she interrupted, her voice gentle.

"No, it's not, Fallon. I know it's not an excuse, but I want to share it with you. I don't want any secrets between us." I paused, looking into her eyes, trying to make her understand how important this was. "You deserve the truth, even if it's hard for me to say. You shared your truth, so please let me share mine."

She nodded and I continued, "We lived together for three years, before..." I took a deep breath, "I found out she was cheating on me and it felt like my whole world shattered after it ended. We were together for four years, and she was living this whole other life."

She sighed. "I'm so sorry, Mackenzie." She didn't question it any farther after that. "Cheaters are the fucking worst!" I laughed in agreement.

"I know. I'm sorry, Fallon," I whispered, wishing it could be enough to undo the past and wipe away the scars—for both of us.

I could feel the rhythm of her breathing beside me, and I was still trying to find the right words—the words to convey just how much of myself belonged to her.

Kissing me again, she lay down on my chest, getting comfortable as I played with her hair and held her close. I never wanted to be anywhere else.

"You know, I'm still trying to figure out how I got here," I said softly, stroking her hair.

"What do you mean?" She turned to look up at me.

I smiled as I played with a strand of her hair. "I went from not knowing you existed, to not knowing of any universe where I would be able to exist without you."

"What are you saying, Kenzie?" Her words were quiet, her voice cracking as a tear rolled down her face.

My expression softened as I looked into her perfect gray eyes. "I'm saying that being in love with you feels like coming home to a place I never knew I needed to be, and a place I never want to leave."

"You... love me?" she asked, several tears sliding down her face. She sat up, inching closer but still hesitating. Her eyes searched mine, like she was trying to find the answer in them.

"Yes. I'm so fucking in love with you, Fallon." I wiped her tears away, my heart pounding as I tried to convey everything I felt in those few words.

"Do you remember what you told me, when we first started sleeping together?"

I remembered every detail about that night. "That you taste addictive?" I winked, trying to keep the mood light. "I still stand by that statement."

She shoved my shoulder and rolled her eyes. "You told me not to fall in love with you."

"Yes, I remember." I smirked, my heart racing even more.

"Well, I failed. So fucking hard." Her voice was a mixture of a laugh and a sob, and I could see the vulnerability creeping in. "I guess I'm not a very good listener." She shrugged, but the weight of what we'd both been through was sitting heavy between us.

I reached for her, pulling her back down to me, my hands cradling her face gently. "Say it, Sunshine."

Her breath hitched, but she didn't pull away. Instead, she closed her eyes for a moment, taking a slow breath before whispering, "I'm so fucking in love with you, Mackenzie." She kissed me again, and I swore I wanted to stay like that. Having her love felt indescribable. It didn't compare to anything in the world.

"How did I do for our first date, baby?" I asked, my voice soft and teasing, with a hint of vulnerability.

She looked up at me, her smile so sweet I could've melted. "Best first date ever."

"Well, it's not over yet, sweetheart." I started kissing her as my hands caressed her sides. I wanted the feeling of her body against my skin. I ached for the contact.

"I don't know what I did to deserve you," she murmured. Her breathing was rapid and she became eager as I started kissing my way down her neck. I was obsessed with the way she could get so desperate. One flick of my tongue, one perfectly measured touch, and I could've had her begging for me.

She moaned when I bit at her collarbone, and I had to force myself to take it slow. My fingers itched to be inside her, and to feel her come apart around them.

Sex with Fallon had always been passionate. Even before I accepted my feelings for her, something had always been there. Tonight was no different, and I wanted to savor every minute of it. I wanted to show her how much she meant to me and that I'd do anything for her.

"It only took one smile for me to realize I was yours," I whispered.

Her cheeks turned pink, and she playfully rolled her eyes. I smiled, brushing my lips across hers, enjoying the warmth of her skin beneath mine.

I looked into her eyes, hoping she knew I belonged to her. I softly pressed my palm down, and massaged across her chest, making sure to barely graze her pierced nipples. The more I massaged around them, the more they hardened, and it sent a shock of pleasure between my legs.

"Close your eyes. I want you to be fully relaxed when I make you come."

"Yes, baby," she whispered. I could never handle the way she called me "baby." That voice could get me to do anything.

At this point, I was so wet with need for her, but I pushed it away. Tonight wasn't about me. It was about her pleasure, and what she needed.

I leisurely massaged her chest for another minute or so before moving down to her stomach, using the palm of my hand. My touch was soft and deliberate, every movement made with purpose.

"That feels so good," she moaned with her eyes still closed. As I massaged her stomach and around her chest, a warmth passed through me, and not only from the touches I was giving her. I honestly loved her, and I would've done anything for her. I wanted to take a mental picture of her in that moment, to remind myself of the best place on earth.

I started massaging lower and around her thighs and back up again. "You are so fucking perfect."

"I need you, please," she begged. I could tell she was starting to get needy, and I resisted the urge to glide my fingers inside her.

Instead, I trailed back down her stomach and slowly began to rub her clit with my palm.

"Kenzie, please," she moaned.

Fuck... I was fighting with my inner thoughts not to give her what we both wanted. Instead, I massaged up and down her thighs, and around her hips.

"Relax, Sunshine," I whispered. "Don't think, just feel. Feel my hand rubbing your swollen clit. Feel your orgasm building and building." I stopped and trailed my hand back up to her breasts. "Feel my hand against your hard nipples."

"Fuck," she whined. The sound almost caused my resolve to crumble.

I went back to massaging each of her thighs, not touching where she needed it most.

Fallon opened her legs farther when I finally moved my movements to her clit. She arched into my hand to beg for more.

Her moans grew more frequent when I slipped my thumb in between her thighs, and started stroking her clit in small, slow circles.

"Oh my God... Kenzie."

I grinned as I felt her arousal grow with every pass of my thumb. She let out a whimper when I stopped massaging her clit, but it was cut short when I finally gave her what she had been begging for, and slowly inserted a finger inside her.

"Yes, baby," she groaned. I swore her sounds could've shattered me.

"I love feeling how wet you are, Fallon." Just feeling her need surrounding my fingers had me so soaked, I wanted to crumble into oblivion. The things she was able to do to me, without even trying...

"Only for you," she panted as I pumped in and out of her, whining in protest when I pulled out.

"That's right. I'm the only one who gets to feel you like this."

"Why did you... oh fuck!" She seemed to have lost all thoughts as I replaced my finger with my tongue and tortuously rolled it across her swollen clit. Her taste caused me to moan against her, and I could've come right then.

Her breathing became frantic and her moans became louder when I alternated massaging her clit with my thumb and tongue.

"Kenzie!" Her hands were gripping the sheets, and I slid two fingers into her while my tongue massaged her. I knew she was getting close, so I curled my fingers at the same time my tongue curled around her clit, and lightly nipped.

"Right there, shit! I'm gonna come," she moaned. She sat up slightly and my eyes found hers for a split second, before her eyes rolled, and she was coming apart all over me. She threw her head down on the pillow and lost all control.

"Fuck," I whined as I slowly pulled out of her when she came down. I wanted to stay like that for as long as she would let me, and I was forever grateful that I would have my chance over and over again. I lost her once, and I had no intentions of losing her again.

When I sat up and kissed her forehead, she gave me a warm smile. "I love you," she whispered.

"I love you, too, sweetheart. And you still taste addictive," I winked.

"Hm, well…" She sat up and settled herself on top of me, and I let out a whimper when I felt her wetness on my skin. She leaned down to kiss the side of my neck and circled one of my nipples with her fingers.

"Sunshine, you know what that does to me." I wasn't going to last long if she kept it up. I was already a mess, just from feeling her.

She smirked. "Oh, I do. And I fully intend to taste what it does to you."

"Fuck, baby girl."

She groaned and kissed me, and I lost all train of thought. Nothing else mattered but her. "That's exactly what I plan to do."

Her hand traveled down my stomach and to my thighs, and I had to tell myself not to arch into the touch. I wanted this moment to last for as long as possible. I never wanted to lose her touch.

I hissed when she flicked my piercing. God, I was going to lose it. "Please, Sunshine. Fuck me, hard. I need you."

"Yes, baby," she whispered in my ear. She knew just what that did to me.

She felt what it did to me when her hand finally reached where I needed it the most, and I moaned. She circled my clit a few times until she curled two fingers inside me.

"Fuck." I let out a breath as she hit that perfect spot. She thrusted her fingers in and out a few times, harder every time.

"Fallon... don't stop, fuck." She slowed down, but didn't pull out as I felt her tongue circle my clit. My eyes shut and my fingers found themselves curled in her hair.

"Oh my God!"

She sucked my clit, and heaven help me. As much as I didn't want this to end, I knew I wasn't going to last much longer. She knew my body like the back of her hand, and she knew exactly how to get me to fall apart.

Her tongue was lapping my pussy, and her fingers were pumping in and out of me so fiercely, I didn't know how to exist outside of this moment.

She moaned her approval as I felt warm liquid streaming out of me. Her sounds, along with my orgasm, seemed to have turned on something inside of me, because it kept coming out. I was squirting for her, and fuck if she didn't suck harder.

God, this woman! I was coming, and I was coming hard. Harder than I ever had before, and I never wanted it to end.

"Fuck, fuck, fuck!" My orgasm came rushing out, and I shut my eyes, selfishly riding her face. When I finally came down, she slowly relented and released my clit.

She was panting when she removed the fingers that were still inside of me, and I threw myself back on the bed, trying to catch my breath.

She came up and lay her head on my chest, and I wrapped my arms around her, kissing the top of her head. "Holy shit, you were ready for it, huh?" she teased.

I laughed. "I'm always ready for you," I said in between breaths. She smiled and gave me a soft kiss. "I love you, Fallon Rose," I whispered softly.

"I love you, too, Mackenzie Isabella."

She lay there while I played with her hair until she dozed off. I wrapped the blanket around us and fell asleep with a smile on my face and my love on my chest, realizing this was home.

Chapter Forty

FALLON

As the sun began to rise, there was no way I wanted to let Mackenzie leave the bed. I wanted her to spend the day worshiping my body, until I carved my name into her back. I didn't care if the neighbors heard me scream her name until I lost my voice.

But unfortunately, we had a flight to catch, so we couldn't stay in bed all day. "Come on, Kenz! We have to leave now, or we're going to miss our flight."

We were almost to my car when she stopped walking, and I could have sworn I was going to run her over. "Mackenzie?!"

"Fallon, my love." I couldn't help but smile every time she said that word.

She was in love with me, and I was madly, head-over-heels in love with her. Except when we were trying to leave. "We need to go! Now!"

"Honey, please relax. If we leave now, we'll still have three hours before our flight takes off. We're not going to be late," she said with a laugh.

I didn't find it funny, but I was thankful she kept walking. "You never know how traffic will be or how long the security line will take!"

I knew we'd have plenty of time. I was just anxious for this trip. I sighed. "I'm sorry. I know you're right. I'm freaking out again, aren't I?

I'm just nervous. I haven't seen my family in months, and I miss them like crazy. Not to mention, I'm bringing someone home this time."

The last person I brought home was my ex, and they didn't like her from the start. I should've taken that as a sign. I really hoped they loved Mackenzie as much as I did.

"I know, baby. Just relax, okay? Here, I'll drive, and you can over-think peacefully." I rolled my eyes but smiled because she knew me too well. That was exactly what I would do until this trip was over.

My feet were frozen on my parents' doorstep several hours later. I knew I needed to knock sooner or later, but I couldn't get my hands to move.

"They might not know we're here until you knock, sweetie."

I sighed. "I know, I'm just nervous. I want everyone to get along. I'm not saying you won't, I'm just..." I shook my head and knocked on the door. It was now or never.

My stepdad, Brandon, answered with a wide smile. "There's our girl!" He pulled me into a tight hug, and I had to beg him to let go.

"I missed you, too, Dad." I cleared my throat. "Uh, Dad, this is my girlfriend, Mackenzie."

He looked between us, confusion written on his face. "Girlfriend? Your mom didn't tell me you were bringing someone home. Either way, it's nice to meet you, Mackenzie."

"It's nice to meet you, sir." Mackenzie held out her hand, but he waved it away.

"Sir? That makes me sound old. Please, call me Brandon. Well, come inside—your mom and Caleb are in the living room."

When we got inside, he set our luggage by the stairs. I took Macken-zie's hand, and she squeezed it three times before we started walking to the living room. I looked at her and smiled as I squeezed hers four times in response.

"Sissy!" Caleb threw his cars down and ran over to me, almost knocking me over.

I smiled, and Mackenzie let go of my hand so I could pick him up. "Caleb, you've gotten so big. I missed you, little buddy."

"I am big! I'm five now, didn't you know? I missed you!"

I smiled. "I did know. That is so big—wow."

He let go of me and hugged Mackenzie's leg. She stood still for a minute, but patted his back cautiously. "Hi, buddy."

"Momma, Sissy is here, and she brought a friend. Momma, who's her friend?" He ran over to my mom, who was staring at us with tears in her eyes.

"Hi, Mom," I said, clearing my throat. I was trying not to cry as I walked over and hugged her.

"Hi, baby," she said through a sob. Apparently, she didn't care to keep it together, which made me lose it in return.

"I've missed you so much, honey. I'm so happy you're here," she whispered.

"I've missed you, too, Mom. So much." I gave her one last squeeze and forced myself to let go.

She wiped her tears and turned toward Mackenzie. "I'm so sorry, where are my manners? You must be Mackenzie. Fallon has told me so much about you. I'm Marie, Fallon's mother."

"And I'm Caleb. I'm five, and my sissy is the bestest sissy!" Caleb shouted.

We all laughed and my mom walked over to Mackenzie and said something I couldn't hear before she hugged her. By the look on Mackenzie's face, I assumed it was something good.

"Momma, who's sissy's friend?"

She picked Caleb up and held him as she walked to show us to our room.

I told her we could sleep in separate rooms if that made her more comfortable, but she insisted she wasn't oblivious to "young love," as she called it. I wanted to vomit, but decided not to argue.

"Why don't you ask her yourself, honey."

"Sissy's friend, who are you?" I laughed, and Mackenzie looked at me for reassurance. I nodded, finding it adorable how nervous she looked.

"My name is Mackenzie, but you can call me Kenzie."

"Okay. Hi, Kenzie. I live here. Let's go upstairs."

She laughed. "Hi, Caleb. It's cool that you live here. Can I come upstairs, too?"

He scratched his head and thought seriously for a moment. "Well, upstairs is only for family, but momma always said if you're welcome here, you're family. Momma, is that okay? Can Kenzie come with us?"

My mom looked at me and smiled. "Of course, baby. She is welcome here."

After Caleb demanded he show Mackenzie his room, we got settled in before meeting everyone downstairs for dinner.

We were unpacking when I stopped and turned to her. "I can't thank you enough for coming with me."

She walked over to me, giving me her signature grin, and I had to remind myself that my parents and innocent baby brother were downstairs. I couldn't jump her in my childhood bedroom. "Of course. I don't want to be anywhere else."

I smiled and gave her a hug, wrapping my hands around her neck. "I love you." I kissed her. "So, so much." I kissed her again.

"I love you, too, baby." She smiled, and we finished unpacking before heading down to dinner.

"Remind me to never bring you near my family again!" I shouted as soon as we got back upstairs."

She rolled her eyes and laughed. "Come on, it wasn't that bad. I think your parents like me."

"That's the problem! They like you too much… probably more than me. Not to mention, Caleb! Listen, you can have Brandon and my mom, but leave Caleb alone!"

She came up behind me and kissed my shoulders. "Baby, they're like me—they could never love anyone more than you."

I turned around, still pouting, but a faint smile lingered despite my best efforts to get rid of it. "Yeah, yeah, whatever. I'm glad everyone's getting along, though."

My parents adored Mackenzie, which I was happy about. I wasn't happy, however, when they decided to show my baby pictures. Why do parents do that?! Babies are cute and all, but I looked like a fluffy Michelin baby—so embarrassing! My mom insisted on giving Mackenzie a copy, and I'll probably never hear the end of it.

Chapter Forty-One

FALLON

We were sitting in the living room the next day, feeling stuffed after Thanksgiving. Brandon was sitting on the chair's arm my mom was sitting in, and I was sitting on the couch next to them.

Caleb had kidnapped Mackenzie, and they were in the middle of the floor, playing with a train set.

"Okay, so the train goes this way, not this way." Caleb was giving Mackenzie strict instructions on how to play trains, and I just sat there smiling, watching them play together.

The two of them had been going at it for at least a few hours, and I was still in awe of how she was powering through. The longest my ex played with him was maybe thirty minutes, then she would make an excuse to leave the room until he got distracted with something else.

"Got it. Which train is your favorite? I don't want to take the wrong one," she replied.

"This red one is mine, but you can have it. I'll take the blue one." He smiled and handed her the train.

My mom nudged my arm and I looked over to her. "It seems you might have competition over there."

I smiled sweetly. I couldn't have been more content than I was in that moment, watching two of the most important people in my life spend time together and thoroughly enjoy themselves. "For which one? Caleb or Mackenzie?"

Brandon laughed. "For both, it looks like. Caleb has been stuck to her side all day, and she hasn't shown signs of wanting to escape. She's a natural. I bet you can't wait until you have your own little trouble-makers running around."

"Dad! It's way too soon to talk about that!" I laughed, but I could already picture it. "But I know, I kind of feel left behind today."

As if she heard me, Mackenzie looked up at me and smiled. I returned her smile, even when Caleb caught her attention before they went back to playing.

"She's pretty great, I guess," I said. She was more than great.

"You really like her don't you? I'm happy for you, baby, I really am. You deserve to be happy."

I cleared my throat, trying to force down the tears that threatened to surface. "Yeah, Mom. She's amazing. I'm so glad I found her."

She rubbed my arms, sending warmth through me. It had been too long since I felt the comfort only a mother's touch could provide. "She seems really good for you, sweetie. I can see it in the way you two look at each other. Hold on to that feeling, there's nothing in the world like it. You know she's welcome here anytime, with or without you." Brandon laughed when I rolled my eyes.

I didn't know what it was about my mom's house, but something about it always made me feel completely at ease. I sat there for a few moments staring at Mackenzie, thinking of what our future would look like.

I hoped it would somewhat mirror what my mom had with Brandon. What man takes in a woman with a child, not to mention, heavy baggage from a previous marriage, raises them as his own, and loves those two women with his whole heart?

I quickly blinked away the tears that were beginning to form in my eyes. I loved Brandon as if he were my biological father, and I was thankful to have him in my life.

"Fallon, honey, are you alright? You seemed to be a bit lost in thought," my mom asked.

"Oh, sorry, Mom. Yeah, I'm alright. I was just really comfortable. I think I was in the middle of a food coma," I said, trying to play it off.

"Come help me in the kitchen. Let's catch up while Mackenzie's playing with Caleb." I looked over at Mackenzie, who shot me a wink.

As I walked into the kitchen, I noticed the pile of dishes in the sink and the dirty pots and pans all over the counters. "Oh my God, Mom! Did a tornado pass through here?" I joked.

"Fallon, don't act surprised. You know how hectic it gets in here. Stop yapping and start on those dishes while I pack the leftovers," she said in the most loving way possible.

After an hour of washing dishes and cleaning the counters, we left the kitchen looking spotless. "That was a workout!" I stretched my aching arms.

"How about some wine for your poor, delicate arms? I hear it works wonders," she chuckled.

We had a few glasses of sparkling pink moscato and talked about work, friends, and life. It felt good to spend this time with her.

Maybe it was the wine, but there was a burning question I'd never had the chance to ask. "Mom, I hope this doesn't bring back bad memories, but... Did Dad ever try to contact you after the divorce? I know this is coming out of nowhere, but my nightmares are coming back, and it made me think about it."

She hesitated for a moment and set her glass down on the counter. "He sent me a letter a few years ago to apologize for all the things he ever did to us. I didn't respond back, but his letter indicated he found the help he needed."

Her response left me speechless. I honestly thought he would've been in prison or possibly worse by now.

"You know, I never told you the story of how I really convinced him to sign the divorce papers. After the incident when he... hurt you." Her voice cracked. "He was terrified that I had gone to the police, and maybe I should've, but he agreed to meet with me and talk about it. I waited until you were in school to meet him, and I told the neighbors to call the police if I didn't return in an hour. I brought the divorce papers with me and agreed to meet him at a coffee shop near the house. He thought I was ready to take him back. I served him the papers and threatened to go to the police if he ever came near us again. He didn't believe me, but I looked him dead in the eyes and said, 'If you ever come near us again, I will make sure you spend the rest of your miserable days in prison. You will never hurt her again.' Fallon, you have no idea how afraid I was. I didn't have a backup plan if he called my bluff." Her eyes filled with tears, and I wished I could've taken that pain away for her.

That part of her story was hard to hear. I never realized how brave my mom really was until now.

"Thank you for telling me that, Mom. For the longest time, I've lived in fear that he'd try to get revenge on us, and I think that's where the nightmares come from. Lately, I've been thinking a lot about that night. Knowing he found help does bring some closure, but it doesn't change the fact that I don't want him to be part of my life."

"I understand, Fallon, and no one is asking you to do that. Brandon has shown me what unconditional love looks like, and he's helped me heal in so many ways. I'm sorry your nightmares have returned. Mine still come back from time to time. I truly hope Mackenzie can help heal your heart. I can see in her eyes how much she loves and cares for you."

"Thanks, Mom. You always know what to say. I've missed this so much." I put my glass down and hugged her as tears streamed down both our faces.

After wiping away our tears and finishing the wine, we made our way back to the living room.

I was relieved that my family seemed to approve of Mackenzie, because I wasn't planning on letting her go anytime soon. I was about to tell her I was heading to bed when I heard Caleb speak a little louder than usual, as if he was excited about something.

"Hey, Kenzie?" Caleb asked, setting down his train and turning to face her.

"Yeah, buddy?" Mackenzie stopped what she was doing and gave him her full attention, and it warmed my heart to see.

"Do you love my sissy?" I sat up a little and glanced at my mom and Brandon, who both shrugged, looking just as confused as I did.

If Mackenzie knew I was listening, she didn't show it. She kept her focus entirely on Caleb. I already knew the answer, but waiting to hear her say it out loud still made me nervous.

"Can you keep a secret?" He nodded excitedly, and she smiled at him. "Don't tell anyone, but yes, I do. I love your sissy very, very much. Is that okay?"

I was seconds away from crying. Hearing how sweet she was being with my little brother, and being so honest with him, was doing terrible things to my heartstrings.

He didn't answer for a second, and I worried about what his response would be. He looked over to me, and I smiled sweetly, mirroring his own smile. Finally, he turned back to Mackenzie. "Please don't hurt her feelings, okay? I love her so much. I want her to stay here. Can you guys stay here? I'll share my room with you."

She smiled softly at him. "I promise. I'll never hurt her feelings. I wish we could stay; I'd love to share a room with you, but we live somewhere else, and we have to go back so I can love her more. But we can visit, okay?" He frowned but nodded.

She put a hand on his arm. "Hey." He looked up at her. "Your sissy loves you—way more than she loves me. She'll always come back to see you, okay?"

"I don't know. Momma told Daddy that she's head over... heels for you. Whatever that means."

I glared at my mom, whose smile was anything but innocent.

I spent the rest of the night with my family, falling even deeper in love with Mackenzie.

Chapter Forty-Two

MACKENZIE

It had been a long week, but tonight was date night. After our Thanksgiving trip, Fallon seemed happier. I still hadn't asked her if she'd heard my conversation with her brother. Honestly, I wasn't expecting a five-year-old to give me fatherly advice.

I loved her family. They were so warm and welcoming, just like their daughter, and they made me feel right at home.

The workweek had been hectic. Getting back on track after being off for two weeks took a lot out of me, and I was ready to spend some relaxing time with Fallon.

She was bringing over dinner from our favorite Thai place, *The Lucky Lotus*, after she got off work, which left me in charge of picking out the movie.

Fallon definitely had the easier job between the two of us. She was the pickiest person when it came to movies.

I was setting everything up when I heard a knock on the door. I opened it, expecting to see Fallon with our food, but when I swung it open, my smile instantly fell.

"Rebecca." I was left breathless.

Out of all the people who could've shown up at my door, she was not even remotely on that list.

"Hi, Kenz," she said with a shy smile. That smile had once promised so many things, right before that same smile broke them all.

I didn't know why she was here, but I knew I didn't want her to be. There wasn't anything she could want that I was willing to give her.

"What are you doing here?" I showed no emotions, indicating there wasn't an ounce of happiness at seeing her.

"Can I come in, please? I just want to talk." What on earth could she want to talk about?

I hadn't seen or talked to her in over two years, and now, all of a sudden, she shows up wanting to have a chat?

All of her texts and calls had gone unanswered for a reason. There was nothing left to say between us.

"We have nothing to talk about. You lost your chance to talk when you fucked someone else on my couch."

She furrowed her brows. "That was so long ago. You know she didn't mean anything."

"Right, because you're selfish and only care about satisfying your own needs." I rolled my eyes.

"That's not true, I care about you. You meant everything to me. Let's just talk inside, please?"

I meant everything to her? She had a really funny way of showing it. I went to say as much, but stopped. There was no use in arguing with someone like Rebecca. It wasn't worth even half a breath.

I reluctantly opened the door for her to come in. I had a feeling I wouldn't want the neighbors to witness any of what was going to be said.

"I missed you, Kenz. You look really good."

"How did you find me, Rebecca?" I said in warning, ignoring her fake compliment.

"What? I don't even get a hello? I haven't seen you in so long. I thought we could catch up." She walked toward me, and it took everything I had not to laugh at the hurt expression on her face.

She had the audacity to come into my life unannounced after all the pain she caused? What did she think? That she could just fuck someone else and come back like nothing happened? If she honestly thought this situation would play out in her favor, she was more delusional than I thought.

"Rebecca," I bit out, stopping her with a hand up.

She sighed. "Well, I went by your work, and your boss—"

"You went to my work?!" I said through clenched teeth. "What is wrong with you?!"

"You weren't answering any of my messages, Kenz. I wanted to see you"

"Why would I, Rebecca? I mean, seriously, why would you think it was okay to show up at my work? Do you have any idea how unprofessional that makes me look? I don't know why I'm even having this conversation with you. What did you say to Claire?" I pinched the bridge of my nose, where a small migraine was starting to form.

"I told her I had something personal of yours I wanted to give back to you. She said she would bring it, but I insisted. I told her it was from your mom, and I wanted to make sure it got to you safely."

I needed to pinch myself. I was convinced this was all a horrible nightmare, and this two-faced, narcissistic, cheating-ass bitch wasn't actually saying all of this to me right now.

I let out an irritated laugh. "So, let me see if I got this right. You pretended to love me for four fucking years, then cheated on me in the place we shared, ruining everything. And then, years later, out of the blue, you start texting and calling like nothing happened? Now you're telling me you lied and used my dead mother as an excuse to see me? Are you fucking serious?"

I took a deep breath. Shouting never got me anywhere with her. "What do you want, Rebecca?"

"I miss you. I miss us. I wanted to talk to you in person and try to work things out. We were always so good together. We can have that again."

I scoffed. "We were good together. Is that why you cheated on me? What ever happened to your couch buddy? Does she even know you're here?"

She waved me off, walking toward the living room. "She... well, that didn't work out."

"Let me guess—she caught you cheating on her, too? What a surprise."

She laughed. "The past is the past, Mackenzie. What matters now is that I'm here, with you, and I still love you."

"You need to leave, Rebecca. There is nothing left between us. There hasn't been for a long time. Like you just said, the past is the past." I started heading for the door to open it, but she stopped me.

"Oh, come on, Kenzie." She took a step closer. "Don't say that. Don't you remember how good it felt when we were together. I know I made you feel so good, baby. You can feel like that again. Let me help you remember." She started playing with a lock of my hair but I shook my head, removing her hand.

"I am not your 'baby,' and I don't need to remember anything. You need to go," I said firmly. I gasped when she grabbed my waist and pulled me to her.

"Remember how good we were?" She pushed a hair behind my ear. "We can have that again. There is no one else for me, Kenz." She was rubbing her hands up and down my sides.

Before I could back away and tell her to leave, she pinned me to the wall. Then, she cupped the side of my face and crashed our mouths together.

In the past, I would've felt a warmth surge through me—what I thought was love—and I couldn't get enough of that feeling. But all I felt now was disgust and hatred for Rebecca. It wasn't like when I was with Fallon, who I—

Fallon... I had to stop this.

"Okay, babe, I'm sorry, but they didn't have—" I broke away from Rebecca when I heard Fallon's voice. She was standing at the door, and the food dropped from her hands.

"Fallon..." My heart raced a thousand miles a minute, and I couldn't catch my breath.

"Rebecca?" Fallon's voice wavered, a mix of confusion and disbelief. "What... what the fuck?"

She looked at Fallon, her eyes going wide in surprise. "Fallon, hi."
Wait, they know each other?

"Can someone tell me what the fuck is going on?" Fallon asked, looking at me with hurt in her eyes. I couldn't bear to look at her any longer.

"Fallon, this is—"

"Her fiancée," Rebecca cut in helpfully.

"Fiancée? What... you... wait, what?" Fallon asked, her voice breathless.

"Rebecca is my *ex*-fiancée," I corrected, still avoiding her. I couldn't look her in the eyes.

She huffed out a laugh. "Really? Well, that's not what it looked like when you had your tongue down her throat."

"No, Fallon, I didn't—"

"Fallon, it's good to see you. You look well," Rebecca said, standing with her arms crossed and a faint smirk on her lips. The way she eyed my girlfriend made something protective flare inside me, and I had to fight the urge to step in front of her.

"I look well? That's what you want to fucking say to me right now? I guess some things never change. Unbelievable."

"Okay, I'm sorry, but how do you two know each other?" I looked back and forth between them, trying to piece together what was happening.

Rebecca shrugged, as if we had all been having a simple conversation —like nothing was wrong. "Funny story, actually. Fallon was... what did you call her, Kenz? My 'couch buddy'?" She smirked.

Fallon and I stared at each other before I turned back to Rebecca. "Wait, she was the one you had sex with on my couch?"

If their roles had been reversed—if Rebecca hadn't been on top, I would've seen that red hair, and this whole time, I—

"Couch buddy?" Fallon's enraged voice sliced through my thoughts of what-ifs. "We were together for two years, and all I was to you was a fucking 'couch buddy'?" She laughed, shaking her head. "Unreal."

She looked at me, tears filling her eyes. "Engaged?" she whispered, her brows furrowing. Hurt was etched into her features, and it made me want to cry.

I opened my mouth to speak, to say anything, to try to explain, but Rebecca cut in. "Well, this is a little awkward. Listen, I was just stopping by to talk to your friend, Fallon."

"Fallon is my girlfriend, Rebecca." I explained. I was growing more angry by the second, and I just wanted to be alone with Fallon.

Rebecca narrowed her eyebrows. "Girlfriend? You didn't mention you were seeing someone?" She brought her thumb to her lips and brushed the lipstick smear away, making the situation worse.

"I *was* her girlfriend," Fallon said, not looking at me.

I could tell she was trying so hard not to let the tears fall. I felt like the worst person in the world, and I didn't know how to make it better.

I stepped toward her, but she put up a hand and shook her head. "What? Fallon, please just let me explain," I pleaded. I needed to get Rebecca out of here and fix this mess she'd put me in.

"No." Her voice sounded soft and broken. "There is nothing left to say, Mackenzie."

She turned to walk away, but I grabbed her wrist. She yanked it back and slightly turned to me, but her eyes didn't move up to meet mine. "Don't. You don't get to do that anymore," she whispered.

She looked at Rebecca and shook her head before finally looking at me. "Just me, right?" She scoffed. "I am such an idiot."

"Fallon, please," I begged, but she turned and walked out the door, not looking back, not saying a word.

I turned to Rebecca and took a deep breath. "You better be gone by the time I come back," I demanded in an eerily calm voice.

She narrowed her brows. "Mackenzie, you can't be serious. You're choosing her? Look how easily she gave up on you. She'll never love you the way I do. She's just a pair of tits, and that's all she'll ever be. Now, let me take you to your room and remind you what you've been missing out on." She grinned seductively.

My rage consumed me as the love of my life walked away. I stepped into Rebecca's space, my voice turning into something unrecognizable. "Do not ever talk about Fallon like that. I will never want you again, do you get that? You're insane and delusional, and you need to understand that we are done. If you ever come looking for me, or Fallon again, I will make sure everyone knows what a disgusting, worthless piece of shit you are. And trust me, I'll stop at nothing to make your life a living hell."

Rebecca's face turned pale as she lowered her gaze, and I didn't wait to see if she left. I slammed the door behind me and ran after Fallon.

Chapter Forty-Three

MACKENZIE

I followed Fallon down the street, yelling for her to stop, but she didn't turn around.

She ignored me for almost four blocks before I finally started to catch up. I couldn't let her walk away from this, away from us, without at least trying to explain. I had to get her to talk to me—away from Rebecca.

"Fallon, stop," I said, out of breath, grabbing her wrist to pull her to a stop when I caught up with her.

She stopped walking and wrenched her wrist out of my hold. As she faced me, tears were flooding down her face. "Engaged, Mackenzie? I can't believe you never told me! Did you know she was my ex? Is this some sick joke to get back at her for cheating on you? And don't even get me started on what the fuck just happened back there! After everything I told you, everything she put me through. You promised you wouldn't hurt me." She shook her head and took a step back. "You promised Caleb," she whispered.

Hearing her mention her brother, and the genuine hurt in her voice, made me want to cry right alongside her. I never meant for any of this to happen. I wasn't supposed to fall in love with her, with her family. I should've told her about Rebecca from the start. Maybe things would've been different.

"I'm sorry, Fallon. I didn't... I didn't mean to hurt you. I love you. Please, just let me explain. I swear, I had no idea she was your ex. She just showed up out of nowhere."

The hurt in her eyes was enough to break me. I couldn't take it, so I had to look away.

"Explain what? Why you didn't tell me you were engaged? Why you kissed her, knowing I was coming over? How could I have been so stupid? I don't want to hear another excuse." She wouldn't look at me.

"I'm sorry I didn't tell you about being engaged, okay? I wanted to forget that part of my life, but I should've told you anyway. I don't want any secrets between us."

She scoffed. "It's a little too late for that now, isn't it?"

"Sunshine, please—"

"Don't." She cut me off with a sobbed laugh. "Don't you fucking dare call me that."

"I'm really sorry. Please, just look at me and let me explain."

Our eyes met, and she scowled, crossing her arms. "Okay, explain why you didn't tell her you had a fucking girlfriend, Mackenzie?" The hurt in her voice was unmistakable.

"I did, Fallon. You heard me tell her."

"Yes, I heard you. After. After you kissed her. You let her believe you were single and ready to be taken when you kissed her. You knew I was coming over. Is that why you asked me to pick up dinner?"

I shook my head, looking confused. "What? No, of course not. I didn't even know—"

"Was that your plan the whole time? Did you want me to catch you with her, so you didn't have to be the one to break things off for whatever reason? Well, congratulations, Kenzie. It worked. You got what you wanted."

"This is not what I wanted. You are what I want, Fallon." I tried to take a step toward her, but she closed her eyes and shook her head, tears falling down her face.

"Just stop, please. I can't stand to look at you or be near you. I can't believe I let myself trust you." She wrapped her arms around herself and took a few steps back.

"Sunshine, please—" I started to walk toward her again, but she stopped me with one hand.

She scoffed, wiping the tears from her eyes. "Sunshine? Fucking Sunshine. I'm not your Sunshine, Mackenzie. Not anymore."

"Don't say that, please. Just let me explain. I didn't kiss her. Well, I did... I mean, she kissed me, but I didn't kiss her back. She—"

"Save it! This is exactly why I said we should've stopped after the first time we slept together. I knew I would get hurt again. I knew we would be a mistake!"

I stumbled back a step, feeling like she'd punched me in the gut. I knew where she was going, and I didn't want to go there.

"Fallon, don't," I started.

"No, Mackenzie, I can't. I just... I have to say this, please." She paused and took a breath before continuing, "From the second I thought about kissing you in that elevator, I knew it would be a mistake. And then, after we kissed, I knew for certain. I kept telling you that, Mackenzie. But somewhere along the way, I fell for you, and I stopped thinking about the reasons we shouldn't be together. I wanted to make those mistakes because I hoped I'd stop seeing them that way. I knew anything between us would be a mistake, but I made them anyway because I trusted you. You made me feel like nothing and no one else mattered. Like, when you looked at me, I was the only person you ever wanted to see. I never knew what that kind of love felt like until I found you."

She played with a string on her sweater, and I wanted to do anything to erase the sadness radiating off her. She was walking away from what we had, and there was nothing I could've said to stop it.

I had to hold back the tears as she continued shattering my world with just a few words. "Out of all the mistakes I've made in my life, I didn't expect my biggest one to be falling in love with you, Mackenzie."

"Fallon, please..."

Her gaze never wavered as she broke my heart. I missed the softness in her eyes—the love I once saw there. Now, all I could see was mistrust and anger.

I did this. I broke us. I broke her. And my punishment was watching her slowly lose the love she once had for me. I deserved it.

She took a step closer and raised her arm, as if she was going to touch me, but she thought better of it and pulled back. "First Cara, and now Rebecca? I can't do this. I won't be anyone's second choice—not anymore. Goodbye, Mackenzie." She met my eyes for the briefest moment before turning and walking away.

"Fallon!" I yelled after her, but she didn't stop. She kept walking—right out of my life.

I stood there for what felt like an eternity, watching her walk away, hoping she'd turn around. She never did. I stayed until she disappeared around the corner.

Eventually, I made the long walk back home, but I stopped before reaching my building. Rebecca was standing on the front steps, staring at me. I took a long, steadying breath before walking up to her.

"That was a dramatic exit, don't you think?" She smiled and I swore I could've smacked it off her smug face.

I rolled my eyes. "Go home, Rebecca. This isn't a game. I meant every word."

"Don't be like that, Kenz. Now that she's gone, we can go back inside and—"

"Enough, Rebecca!" I took a step closer, my voice steady with resolve. "Jesus! I just lost the best thing that's ever happened to me, all because of you. Listen closely—since you clearly didn't hear me the first time—we are done. There will never be anything between us again. Even if I lose Fallon for good, you'll never take her place. Do you hear me? Leave. Now."

She took a step back like I threw a punch at her. "Wow, Kenz. After everything I've done for you? Whatever. Good luck with her." She rolled her eyes and finally walked away.

I went back inside and slammed the door. The sound must've cracked something inside me, because as soon as it closed, the tears started pouring out, and I couldn't stop them.

I lost her. I lost Fallon, and I didn't think she was ever coming back. I stood at the peephole for what felt like hours, waiting for her to return.

My calls went straight to voicemail, and my texts remained unread. I didn't know why I expected anything different, but I had to try. I would've done anything to fix what I broke.

I couldn't believe she was gone. How could I have been so stupid? I should've sent Rebecca away the minute I opened my door and saw her.

Accepting defeat, I dragged myself to bed. I lay there for hours until I finally found sleep, which didn't last long.

I kept waking up throughout the night, feeling like something was missing. I'd reach over to the other side of the bed, hoping to find Fallon still sleeping safely next to me, only to feel an empty space beneath my fingers. I was all alone, and that's how it would stay. It was what I deserved, anyway.

Eventually, I had no choice but to let the darkness consume me, and I cried myself to sleep.

Chapter Forty-Four

FALLON

As soon as I turned my back on Mackenzie, tears started flooding out. What I thought was the best part of me was gone.

I walked away, unable to turn around no matter how much I wanted to. My feet carried me to the first place that came to mind—the only place I knew I'd be safe. I texted Drea when I arrived at the bookstore, thankful she'd given me a key:

Me: Hey Dre. I'm at the bookstore.

Drea: Please don't fuck in my store again. You know I have cameras, right?

Drea: Lucky for both of us, I didn't have them in the backroom. Now I do thanks to you horn dogs! 😛

Me: Sorry. And you won't have to worry about that again.

Me: I'm staying here tonight. Stay with me? I don't think I can be alone.

When I got to the bookstore, I locked the door and didn't bother turning on any lights. There was no point in shining a light on the situation. I went straight to the back room, but stopped when I reached the door. The last time I was back there... it was with her.

I shook the memory away and sat down on the couch in the far back, intentionally avoiding the chair—and everything it reminded me of.

After a while of sitting alone, with only my thoughts surrounding me and a dim light on, I heard Drea calling out, "Where are you, sweetie?"

"I'm back here." I had to summon every ounce of strength to get the words out loud enough for her to hear. My voice sounded like I'd been screaming for days.

I was curled up in a blanket on the couch. When she came to the back, she walked slowly toward me, as if I were a delicate baby deer, and she was afraid I'd flee at any sudden movement. "Honey, what's wrong?" She noticed my red eyes and the puffiness that circled them. "Talk to me, babe. What happened?"

For a moment, I couldn't say anything, but as soon as I felt her caress my arm, I leaned into her and started crying all over again.

"I... she." I couldn't get the words out. I didn't want to believe any of it was real. I fell so hard for that woman. Despite all my reservations and resistance in the beginning, I fell anyway.

Who would've thought the person who made me build the walls before Mackenzie would help rebuild them? Three seconds—that's all it took to ruin everything.

Drea sat there, letting me gather my thoughts. When the tears stopped, I sat up, my face solemn, my tone defeated. "Mackenzie and I..." It was impossible for me to get the words out. I didn't want it to be true. "We broke up."

"I will kill her! I will hunt her down, and—"

"Drea, stop. Please. I love you, you know I do, but I don't need the dramatics right now. It's been a long, horrible night."

"You're right. I'm sorry, sweetie. Do you want to talk about it?"

Not really, but I knew she wouldn't let it go. And, honestly, it probably wasn't healthy to keep it all bottled up.

I took a deep breath, swallowing the new tears that threatened to start coming up. "Tonight was supposed to be a date night... with dinner and a movie. I was in charge of dinner, which was probably her plan the whole time." I let out a soft chuckle at the ridiculousness of the situation.

She sat next to me, listening and patiently waiting for me to go on. "When I walked into her apartment, she was kissing someone else." I put up a hand to stop whatever profanity and threats she was about to start shouting. I could see it in the way her mouth hung open, and how her eyes got wide, that she was about to explode. "Unfortunately, it gets a lot worse."

At this point I couldn't tell if I was laughing or crying, or a combination of the two. I probably looked like a lunatic.

"I walked in on her kissing her ex... her ex-fiancée," I said, shaking my head when I saw her eyes widen. "She caught her ex with someone else on their couch a few years ago. The messed-up part? *I* was that someone, but I didn't know it at the time. Want to hear the best part? Her ex is Rebecca. Yes, *that* Rebecca. I didn't think anyone walked in on us, and I had no idea she was engaged and living with someone else." A bitter laugh spilled out. "How could I have been so stupid, Dre?" I collapsed into her arms, sobbing again.

I once thought she was my happily ever after, but then I met Mackenzie, and she proved me incredibly wrong. What I had with Rebecca wasn't love at all. Mackenzie showed me what real love was, and how I deserved to be treated.

Before I walked out of her apartment for the last time, I thought I knew in my heart that Mackenzie and I were meant to be—that there was no one else in this world who could ever compare to her.

But it turned out our feelings weren't mutual. Our love was one-sided, and once again, I wasn't good enough for someone. For the second time, I gave my heart away, only for Mackenzie to slap a "return to sender" label on it.

When would I learn that I'd never get my happy ending? Was I really that horrible of a person, that I didn't deserve love? My dad never loved me, Rebecca didn't, and Mackenzie—clearly, I was just a joke to her. Maybe I never should've answered the door that night we met.

Maybe I was destined to spend my life alone. This was the second time I'd let myself be consumed by love, only to have it blind me to the red flags. Rebecca had torn me down—body and soul—until I began to believe there was something wrong with me.

When I initially moved in with Rebecca, I accepted her hectic work schedule and her long trips out of town. After a while, part of me knew something was off, but I chose to ignore it because I didn't want her to leave me if I questioned her about it.

One day, when she came back from a work trip, I started getting suspicious. She was always on her phone, getting text after text, but wouldn't tell me who it was. So, when she went into the shower, I decided to check her phone. I knew I shouldn't have, but something told me I had to. And what I found, destroyed any future I thought we might have.

She was sending dirty texts to a bunch of different women and had a few dating apps on her phone. Honestly, I had no idea how she kept everything straight without mixing anyone up. None of the contacts had their full names displayed.

When I confronted her, she accused me of violating her privacy. She told me she was seeing other people because I "changed" after we moved in together. Then she called me jealous, manipulative, and said all I did was argue with her whenever she came home. It was all lies—but what if I really was being too needy?

That night, I packed up my things and moved back in with my parents. I tried calling a few of our mutual friends for support, but either they didn't pick up, or they sided with Rebecca.

She'd convinced them that I was jealous, mentally abusive, and that she ended things because I was crazy. Maybe I was crazy, to believe we had something special together.

. . .

Drea let me pull myself together before she finally found her words. "First of all, if I ever see Rebecca again, I swear to God, that home-wrecker is going to need a nose job. Also, honey, fuck, Mackenzie, okay?"

I let out a chuckled sob, but she went on. "Seriously, though, I told her what would happen if she ever hurt you again, and I meant it."

"I appreciate you, but you cannot kill her. I can't lose you, too. I want to forget about her and forget this night ever happened." I knew it would be a long time before that ever happened—if it did at all.

I didn't know who I was more furious with—myself, for being so careless and giving my heart away just to have it shredded again, Rebecca, for messing everything up in my life for a second time, or Mackenzie fucking Thompson, for coming into my life, making me fall in love with her every single day, and then breaking it all within a matter of minutes. I think it was a twisted combination of all three.

"Is there anything you need, love? Just say the word, and I will go over there right now!" She stood up, but I sat her back down.

"Seriously, Drea. I just want to sleep this night off and have a few days to figure out what I'm going to do next." I didn't know what I was going to do, but I knew I couldn't hide out in the bookstore forever.

"Fal, you know you can stay here for as long as you want. I'm really sorry you're going through this, babe. If it means anything, I never liked Mackenzie, anyway."

I forced a small smile. "Thanks, but you loved her, Dre." I loved her, too. Who was I kidding? I still did. Fuck her and this whole situation!

She sighed. "Yeah, I kind of did. Get some sleep, love. I'm going to call Sky. She was working when I left, so she doesn't know where I am, and I don't want her to worry. I love you, sweetie." I nodded, and she kissed my forehead.

Forehead kisses from Mackenzie used to be my favorite thing. Now, receiving one from Drea only brought me sadness, leaving me feeling hollow and empty.

Chapter Forty-Five

MACKENZIE

I hadn't left the house since Fallon walked out of it four days ago.
My solitude was coming to an end, though, because family dinner
wasn't up for negotiation.

The last thing I wanted, was to face Harper and admit I'd screwed
everything up. Honestly, locking myself in my room and avoiding
daylight forever sounded like a solid plan. But knowing my sister, she'd
barge in, find me, and haul me out by the ear.

Stepping into the hall, I noticed Fallon's door was open. Her apartment looked bare, moving boxes scattered across the floor, like she was
in the middle of packing up her life and starting over. The sight was
miserable, and knowing I was the reason behind it hit me hard.

I felt my chest tighten when I saw her walking toward the front
door. I wanted to go back inside or start walking away, but my feet
wouldn't move. She paused when she saw me, and it took her a good
while before she started walking again.

When she approached me, I could see the tears starting to form in
her eyes, and I had to force my own away. She didn't deserve to feel the
pain and heartbreak I'd caused.

"Mackenzie. Hi." Her voice was soft.

I glanced over her shoulder, then back at her. She looked so sad
holding a moving box, and I had to clench my jaw to keep it together.

Even with her hands full, I could tell she was uncomfortable—the way her eyes never landed on mine, the way she chewed her bottom lip. I knew her too well to miss how she really felt.

I swallowed hard. "So, you're really leaving?"

She turned to her apartment filled with boxes. "Uhh, yeah. I'm going to stay with Drea for a while."

I couldn't stand this. A few days ago we were happy and in love. I would've given anything to have that back. "Fallon, you don't need to do this."

She blinked as a few tears escaped, and I had to force myself not to reach out and wipe them away. I wasn't in a position to do that anymore.

"Yes, I do. It's too hard, I..." She shook her head, clearing her throat. "This is the best thing for both of us."

"This is not what's best. Please stay and let me explain so we can move past this," I begged.

She sighed. "Mackenzie, please don't, okay? This is already hard enough for me. I have to go." Her voice cracked, and so did my heart.

For the last time, I looked away from the love of my life. I couldn't stick around to watch her leave—it hurt too much.

Despite myself, I went to Harper's for our monthly dinner, plastering on a fake smile as I sat across from my sister. With Grant at work, it was just the two of us—not exactly an ideal scenario.

Being alone with my sister meant talking, which would lead to opening up when I didn't want to, and that would inevitably end in a breakdown—the last thing I wanted.

"I love my husband, but sometimes I want some quality sister time. Cheers to a partner-free night." She raised her glass of wine, and I lifted mine.

"Cheers," I said with a faint smile.

I took a long drink and looked up to see Harper looking at me with an arched eyebrow.

"What? I was thirsty." She didn't answer right away, just studied me, like she was waiting for me to crack.

"You're not fooling anyone, you know," she said softly, setting her glass down. "You've been quiet all night, and the way you just inhaled that drink tells me something is bothering you."

My chest was starting to feel too tight. She could always read me like a damn book, and I hated it. I bit my lip to keep the truth inside. I didn't want to talk about what happened. I didn't want to face the fact that I lost her.

"You don't have to say anything," she added, her voice gentle. "But you can't hide it from me, Kenz."

"Everything's fine, Harper." I smiled and went back to eating my food, desperate for a distraction. "Have you talked to our father?" I knew that would get the attention off me. It might cause a fight, but that was better than facing the truth.

She scowled at me. "Why would you ask me that? You know I haven't."

I shrugged. "I'm just making conversation, Harper. Sorry."

She relaxed her shoulders and took a drink. "It's fine, and I'm sorry, too. You know how I am about him. Anyway, how's work going?"

"Yeah, I know. Work is fine, what's new with you?" I needed her to keep talking and let me sit there quietly.

She started talking about her life and how everything was going. She kept asking me questions and I responded with one or two word answers until she got to her next question, when all the color had left my face.

"Since you aren't very chatty this evening, why don't we talk about something I *know* will get me more of a response? How are things with Fallon? I haven't seen her in a while—I miss her. You should bring her to the next family dinner."

I tensed at the mention of Fallon. "I don't think that's going to happen. We..." I had to swallow the lump in my throat before continuing. I didn't think it would ever get easier. I clenched my jaw, lifted my head slightly, and forced the words out. "We broke up."

Harper froze, fork halfway to her mouth. "Wait, what? What happened?"

I sighed and rubbed my face with my hands. "Uhh, Rebecca happened." I went on to tell her everything that happened that night, only managing to hold back tears a few times.

She didn't say anything for a while, and she took a sip of her wine before she spoke again. "Well, I have a few notes."

"Of course." I nodded my head as she scowled at me. I knew she would've had something to say, which was exactly why I didn't want to tell her.

"Well, for one, that was a fuckload of information."

"Yeah, I know. What am I going to do? She doesn't even want to look at me. I can't say I blame her, but this fucking sucks, Harp!"

"First of all, Rebecca is a dumpster fire of a human. I think that's a communal agreement amongst the population. So, note number two. You are a goddamn idiot. Which I'm assuming you already know, or else you wouldn't be acting like this."

I hung my head in shame and nodded like an insubordinate child. "Yes, I'm well aware."

"What the fuck were you thinking, letting her through the door? And kissing her? Really, Mackenzie? I thought you had more sense than that. I really did!"

I slouched in my chair. "I screwed up, okay? I know that. I shouldn't have let her in. And she kissed me, but I didn't kiss her back! I was about to stop it when Fallon walked in. I begged her to let me explain, but she wouldn't even give me a chance. The whole ex-fiancée revelation didn't help matters, either."

Harper rolled her eyes. "Well, put yourself in her shoes. If you walked in on Fallon kissing someone, then found out you had the same ex—who just so happens to be the one who cheated on you—would you even listen to her excuses? Would you believe her in that situation?"

I paused. She was right. I wouldn't. I wouldn't want to hear anything from her. "But to completely move out?"

She sighed. "Honey, you're only seeing this through your eyes. She did what she thought was best. She needs space, and being neighbors makes things more complicated—it makes it harder for her to get the space she needs to think. You both said from the beginning it would be a mistake, and here we are. You ignored each other's reservations, and now it's biting you in the ass."

I couldn't talk about it anymore. "Thank you for dinner, sis. I love you, but I need to get going." I kissed her cheek and left without another word and she didn't try to stop me.

When I left Harper's, I didn't go home. That was the last place I wanted to be. Instead, I took a Lyft straight to *Queer Quarters*.

Rylee was working and waved at me, but I only nodded and headed for a booth in the corner.

I sat down and started off with three shots. I didn't care what they were, only that they were strong enough to make me forget.

Rylee was the one to bring the drinks and I rolled my eyes, throwing my head back. I should've known she wouldn't let me drink in peace.

"Please don't start. I don't want to talk about it. I just want to drink."

She put the drinks down and sat next to me. "Okay, babe. We won't talk about it right now. These are on the house." She patted my arm and got up.

I took the drinks and almost gagged at the taste. "Perfect," I mumbled.

I ordered two more rounds of shots, and Rylee brought them each time, shaking her head at me as she set them down. "Still don't want to talk?" she asked.

"Nope," I said, waving her off.

A few more shots later, and gravity had become my enemy, so I decided to lie down in the booth for a while.

I had just closed my eyes when I heard a voice. "Thanks, Rylee. Yeah, we got her. Hey, sweetie." I looked up to see four people crowded around me.

"Fuck Ryl." That was all I could get out. I couldn't believe Rylee snitched on me to my sister.

"Kenz, are you okay?" Roxxy number one said in a soothing tone.

Harper number one scooted in next to me and helped me sit up. "OhmyGod. My sissterr. Everyone, thisis my sister, Harvey—"

"Harper," she corrected.

"Yes, right. Harper."

"Mackenzie, we love you." One of the Harper's spoke next.

"What?" I asked in a high pitched slurred voice. "I love you guys, too. So somuch!"

Harper, with a gentle smile, shook her head and said, "We know, kenz. Talk to us, babe."

I groaned and took a sip of either vodka or water, honestly I was too drunk to care which. "I... I fucked up. I fucked up so bad an' I don' know how t' fix it." My words were slurring, but I pushed on. "I love her so much... I feel like nothin' without her. I need her, y'know? She's the best thing in my life. She's my person... like... she's it, y'know? There's... nothin' an' no one after her."

Roxxy number two spoke next. "Jesus, Harper, I think she's lost it. You really have it bad, huh?"

I sighed. "What do I do? I can't go on... without her."

"Yes, you can. You have to," Harper number one said, brushing a strand of hair out of my face. "I know it hurts now, and it's going to take time before it hurts less, but you have to give her space. If you really love her—"

"I dooo... I really dooo! I'd do anythin' for her!" I yelled, swaying a bit as I clutched my glass.

"Then you need to give her space and if she wants to move on, you have to let her go."

I shook my head. "Nooo. Anything, but that. I can't, Harperp. I... couldn't let her go, even if I wanted to."

I knew they were right, but honestly, in that moment, I couldn't even imagine a world where that was an option.

"I... I don't know where to go from here," I mumbled, tears spilling down my face.

Harper number two started rubbing my arm softly and I leaned into the gesture. "I do."

"Of course you do, Harvey! You're the smartest and I'm the dumbest."

She laughed. "You're not dumb, you just did a dumb thing. But what you're going to do is go home. I'm going to help you up, and we're going to get you nice and cozy in your bed." I shook my head in protest, but she pressed on. "Yes, Kenzie. You're going to sleep this off, and tomorrow you'll start with a clear head."

I looked at her, and she wiped my tears away like she was trying to make everything better. "That sounds good," I muttered, sniffling.

She nodded and helped me stand, even though I was swaying a little.

She got me out of the booth, her hand on my back, and it felt nice, like I wasn't as completely alone as I felt.

We didn't talk much on the way to the car—honestly, I don't think I could've even formed a sentence. It felt nice to just have her support, no matter how stupid I got.

Harper was helping me out of the elevator when she stopped, nearly causing me to fall over.

"What the hell—" My words died in my throat when I looked up and saw Fallon down the hall. She stood there, holding a moving box, frozen as we approached. I couldn't take my eyes off her. It had only been a few hours since I'd last seen her, but it felt like a lifetime.

I didn't say anything as we got closer, but Fallon was the first to speak. "Hi," she said softly. She cleared her throat and turned to Harper. "Uh, is she hurt?"

Harper winced. "Only emotionally."

Fallon looked at me and narrowed her brows. "What—"

"I'm fine. I've never been better, actually. We were just out celebrating how fine I really am. Anyway, uhh... I'll be inside." I patted Harper's arm. "Fallon." I nodded and waved as I turned and went inside.

I slouched against the door and rested my head back, fighting the urge to cry. She still looked perfect, even with a thin layer of sweat on her freckled face. I couldn't miss the redness around her eyes, but I told myself it was from a swim. The idea of her crying over me like I had over her? I couldn't handle it.

I sat up when I started hearing voices coming from the hall. "How's she doing?"

"Uh, well, I mean, you saw her. She's not doing the best."

I couldn't hear Fallon's response, but I heard Harper's comforting voice. "Hey, it's okay. Please don't cry. You did what you thought was best. I'm not here to take sides or explain anyone's reasonings. This is between the two of you, just..." I stood up and looked through the peephole when I heard Harper stop talking.

"I know, Harper. It just... sucks. I hate this whole situation, but I think this is the best thing for everyone. I can't stay here. I can't be anywhere near her. It hurts too much." My chest tightened when they hugged, and I hated that I wasn't the one comforting her.

"Take care, okay, Fallon? Take some time, and maybe don't write her off completely just yet? I know she messed up, but she's a good person and she really loves you."

Fallon didn't say another word as she turned and left. I quickly went to the couch and sat down when Harper came in. I didn't want her to know I was listening to their conversation. Honestly, I just wanted to see Fallon one last time.

"How much of that did you hear?" She scowled.

I waved her off and closed my eyes. "Enough."

She came down and sat next to me on the couch. "Give her time, Kenz. If it makes you feel any better, she seemed pretty broken up about the whole thing."

I scoffed. "It doesn't. It's killing me to see her like that, but it's only been a few days. She'll move on... I'm sure."

"I really don't think so, Boog. I think you underestimate the love she has for you. If she didn't love you, it wouldn't hurt so damn much."

I adjusted myself on the couch. "Dad would be happy to see me now, huh? Getting what I deserve for being gay." I laughed.

"Oh, sweetie, don't say that. I mean, yeah, maybe he'd be happy, but he's a piece of shit, and you don't deserve any of this. Yeah, you messed up, but we all do. You still deserve a happy ending. Just give her some space."

"Thanks, Harp. I don't know what I would do without you, to be honest. Mom would be proud of you, that's for sure. You've done a great job of taking over for her." I snuggled up to her while she played with my hair. She looked more like our mom than I did, and I closed my eyes, pretending she was there with us.

"She would be proud of both of us. We turned out pretty decent. Get some sleep, Kenz. We can talk more..." I didn't hear the rest of her sentence as I slowly drifted to sleep.

Chapter Forty-Six

MACKENZIE

Three months later

"Hey, Kenz." Rylee waved me in as I entered *Brewed Awakening*.

"I smiled and walked up to the counter. "Hey, Ryles. Can I get my usual?"

"Of course. How are you?" she asked softly while she started preparing my drink.

How was I? Well, I was out of the house, so that was something. I was doing better than I was a few weeks ago, that's for sure. "I'm hanging in there. Every day is a little easier," I shrugged.

Since Fallon officially moved out, I hadn't seen or talked to her—not that I expected to. That's just how it went when you lost the best thing you had. I stopped going to the bookstore, and I avoided bars that weren't *Queer Quarters*. At least there, Rylee could keep an eye on me and step in if I started spiraling. I'd managed to cut that down to every other week.

I was still nervous to come here, but it had always been my favorite coffee shop, so I took the risk. I hadn't run into Fallon yet, but my heart stopped right before I walked in, just in case.

"How's she been? Have you seen her?" I asked nervously. I knew I shouldn't have, but I couldn't help it. I needed to know she was okay.

She put my coffee on the counter and gave me a sympathetic smile. "She's doing about as well as you, but getting better. She doesn't come in here as often as she did, but she still comes around."

"That's good." I was glad to hear she was at least getting out of the house and doing something. "Thanks for the coffee. I better go, I'm meeting someone."

She gave me a look that told me I better choose my next words carefully. "Mackenzie, please do not tell me you're meeting someone here for a date?!"

I laughed. "You're joking right? You really think I would be even remotely interested in dating someone that wasn't Fallon?"

She shrugged. "I don't know you these days, Kenz. Since the breakup, you've been different. You know we all love you and want what's best for you—both of you. We're not choosing sides on this, and she hasn't asked us to."

I smiled faintly. Fallon would never ask them to do that—it wasn't her style. "I know, and thanks. Anyway, I know I've been a hermit these past few weeks. I needed time to wallow. Still wallowing, obviously. Honestly, I don't think I'll ever get over her. But no, I'm not meeting a date—I'm actually meeting my dad."

She took off her apron and yelled to the back, "I'm taking my break!"

I rolled my eyes as she dragged me to a booth and sat me down. "Okay, repeat that? You're meeting who now?"

"I'm meeting my dad, and no, I haven't told Harper yet. I know she'd make a big deal about it, but I need to do this for me, Ry. He's the only parent I have, and I need closure. Even if it goes badly, I have to move on."

"I get that, honey, I really do. But are you sure this is a good idea? It's been almost ten years since you've said a word to him, and he hasn't even tried to reach out. You're already going through so much, and I don't want to see you get hurt again."

She reached across the table and took my hand. I smiled at the warm gesture, grateful for her effort to comfort me. "I'll be fine, Rylee. I'm not expecting some big, dramatic reunion with hugs and tears or anything. I just want closure."

She looked at the clock and sighed. "Shit, I gotta get back. I'm right here if you need anything, okay?"

I smiled and nodded as she got up and went back to work. I watched her for a second, thankful she was always there for me, even when everything else felt like it was falling apart.

But I was still nervous. Hanging around too long meant risking a run-in with Fallon, and I wasn't ready for that. It was too soon, and just the thought of seeing her felt like ripping open a wound that hadn't even begun to heal.

My head turned every time I heard the door open, wondering if it was Fallon or my dad.

After about twenty more minutes, I turned my head one last time as the door opened, and my heart stopped. It had been so long, but not a lot had changed since the last time I saw him.

My dad looked older, but not too old. He had a dark beard with some gray mixed in, and still had a full head of hair. He dressed like the lawyer he'd always been so proud to be.

I stood up on shaky legs and walked over to him. This was the first time I'd seen him in years, and the nerves were getting to me. I was trying very hard to keep it together, unsure of what to expect.

I cleared my throat before speaking. "Hi, Dad."

I didn't smile, but he gave a soft grin when he replied, "Hey, Butterscotch."

I let out a teary chuckle. "Wow, I haven't heard that one in a while."

As a kid, I used to eat all the butterscotch candies in the house. Eventually, my parents stopped buying them because I'd tear the place apart looking for them. He stopped using that nickname the day I came out.

"Uh, do you want to order something? I already got something to drink, but I have a table for us." I was pretty sure he could see my body trembling.

"I'm okay, thanks. But yes, let's sit down."

We walked past the counter, where Rylee gave us a cautious smile and watched us all the way to our table.

"So, Dad, how are you?" I asked, not knowing what else to say.

He cleared his throat. "I'm doing okay. I've been working from home a lot more since the move. I've been living here since your mom passed away."

My chest tightened at the mention of my mom. "Wow. So, you've been nearby and haven't reached out in three years? Awesome." I nodded.

He sighed. "I know, I'm sorry. I didn't know if you girls would even want to see me after everything." He paused for a moment, looking down at his hands folded on the table. "So, how is Harper doing?" he asked. I'd been waiting for him to bring her up.

I still felt guilty for not telling Harper before meeting with him. I knew she wouldn't understand, and I wasn't sure if I was actually going to go through with it or not.

"Harper's doing fine. She's still working as a lawyer, and she's married now. His name's Grant, and he's an engineer. They met in college and have been married ever since. He's really good to her, and—"

My sentence died off when the door opened, and a pair of the most devastating gray eyes stared widely back into mine.

My breath caught in my throat, and I couldn't move. Out of the corner of my eye, I saw my dad turn toward the door. Fallon's eyes flicked between us, her face full of confusion. She turned and walked out, and when I blinked, he was looking at me again.

I cleared my throat. "Uh, sorry. So, anyway, how's work?" I couldn't find any more words to say. I blinked a few times and looked down at my coffee.

"Who is she?" My dad's voice cut through the silence.

My cheeks were on fire, and I was trying very hard to hold it together. That was the first time I'd seen Fallon since she left, and of course, it had to be while I was with my dad.

"That was Fallon. We used to be neighbors," I said, glancing over his shoulder toward the door where Fallon had disappeared.

He nodded a few times, as if processing the information. "*Just* neighbors?" He raised an eyebrow, silently pressing for more.

I sighed. "No, she wasn't just my neighbor. She was so much more than that." I clenched my jaw, trying to keep the tears from coming. That was the last thing I needed right now.

"I see. And you love her." I looked up at him. It wasn't a question.

"Do you really want to know? I'd rather not repeat what happened the last time I was honest with you about my life."

"Sweetheart..." He reached for my hands.

"Don't..." I murmured as I pulled my hands away, placing them safely in my lap.

He removed his hand. "I'm sorry, Mackenzie. I am trying my best to understand."

I narrowed my eyebrows. "I know it's hard for you to believe, but yes, I did. I do. I've never loved anyone or anything the way I love her, Dad. Without her, I feel like I can't breathe." I couldn't fight the tears anymore.

"I know saying I'm sorry doesn't justify what I did. And while I can't agree with the decisions you've made in your life, I also cannot agree with the ones that I have made either. Your mother would hate this right now, you know? She would hate seeing you like this, and she would hate me for allowing so many years to go by without reaching out, especially after she left."

At the mention of my mom, my world seemed to crash down around me. Tears started streaming down my cheeks—right in the middle of a damn coffee shop. This was definitely not the place for this conversation.

"I'm so sorry I reacted the way I did when you came out. That was wrong of me, and nothing I say will bring back the years we lost. But if you'll let me, I'll spend the rest of the time we have left, trying to be a better father to you and your sister."

"Thanks, Dad." I sobbed out the words. I didn't know where we would go from that, but I appreciated the apology. I had waited years to hear it, even though it couldn't make up for everything.

"I know there's nothing I can say or do that will ever be good enough to earn your forgiveness, but I'd really like to try. I'm willing to take the time to earn it—even if it means dealing with your sister. I'm sure she doesn't think very highly of me."

"I didn't tell her we were meeting yet, so maybe let me talk to her first. Thank you for meeting with me, and I'm sorry you had to see my breakdown."

He reached out for my hand again, and I reluctantly gave it to him. I wasn't ready for a hug yet, and I think he knew that.

"Mackenzie, I don't know what happened between you two, and I'm not sure if I want to know, but I can see this isn't like when you were young and thought you were in love with Alexis. This is real, unfathomable love, and you can't let it go."

I frowned. "What? You saw how she left. She doesn't want anything to do with me, and she has a pretty good reason."

"I know what I saw. She didn't walk away so easily. If you really love her, which I can see you do, then you've got to fight for her. Give it everything you've got until you can't fight anymore, and when you think you've given everything, give more and keep fighting. Don't let her go that easily. Go get her."

I let out a sobbed laugh. "Thanks, Dad."

I stood up and we walked down to his car. We talked about life, and I made a mental note to meet up with Harper later. It was better that she heard it from me in person.

"Your mother would be so proud of the woman you've become, and I'm ashamed I missed the journey, but I hope you'll let me stick around to see where you go next." He smiled, and I did something I hadn't done since I was ten—I hugged him.

"You don't know the woman I've become, but I'd really like you to."

"I'm sorry, you fucking did what now?!" Harper dropped her fork down on her plate and looked at me with dark, furious eyes.

Later that afternoon, I was sitting across from Harper and Grant for our family dinner. I purposefully brought up our dad when Grant was around. I needed witnesses.

"Harper, just calm down and let me explain, please."

"Explain what? Why you not only talked to that piece of shit, but went to see him?! This breakup has really fucked with you head!" I knew she was upset, so I let her harsh words slide.

Grant stood up slowly. "Well, I'm going to—"

"Sit down, Grant!" we both said in unison. I really needed him here for this. He sat back down and stared at his food like it was doing the most interesting dance.

"Look, you're right. This breakup has really fucked me up, and I've had a lot of time to think."

She scoffed. "Clearly not enough. Mackenzie, seriously, what the hell?"

"Just listen, okay?" She sat there, staring at me, waiting for me to continue. I cleared my throat. "Yes, I met with him. He is our dad—"

"Your dad, Kenz. I don't have a dad, remember?" she cut in.

I rolled my eyes. "Harper, come on, it was a long time ago. I'm not making excuses for what he did, but I feel like you shouldn't hate him more than me. And I don't think I do. I know I probably should, and I don't know if we'll ever have a relationship, but if my relationship with Fallon taught me anything, it's that life is too short for regrets, and you have to enjoy what you have." I was trying to keep the tears away.

She was still sitting there with her arms crossed, not saying anything, so I took that as my sign to continue. "He's acknowledged that he regrets what happened and knows that saying 'I'm sorry,' won't fix things, but he said some things that made me realize maybe forgiveness could be a possibility."

"Yeah, and what lying bullshit point was that, Kenz?"

I looked into those angry eyes, and tried to get them to soften. "That mom would hate all of this. She would hate that we lost the love we had for him when we were little. She would hate that none of us have reached out to try and fix things. He's the only part of her we have left, Harper. We all make mistakes, and with what I'm living through right now, I'm no one to judge. I'm not doing this for him, or for me—I'm doing it for mom. Life's too short to hold a grudge."

She had tears running down her face and Grant was caressing her hand.

"I know it doesn't fix anything, but it's a start. I'm so tired of feeling angry, Harper. Aren't you?"

She cleared her throat. "I will say he's right about one thing—she would hate this. And I do, too. I'll forgive him when you do. But don't expect me to talk to him or want to see him right away. I'll need time for that. When did you become the wiser sister?" She stood up to hug me.

I laughed, wiping the tears from my eyes. "When the best thing in my life walked out of it, and made me open my eyes."

She gave me a sad look. "Are you going to be okay?"

"Eventually, yes." I nodded. "I'm taking it one day at a time. Today is dinner with my family, and tomorrow, I'm going to get the love of my life back."

Harper pressed a gentle kiss to my forehead, her hands wrapping around my arms with a reassuring squeeze. She gave me a soft smile, her eyes filled with love. "Go get your girl, Boog."

Chapter Forty-Seven

FALLON

"Okay, so will you please tell me this big, secretive plan you have for my party?"

Drea told me weeks ago she was planning my twenty-fifth birthday party. I begged her every chance I could to tell me what it was, but she wouldn't budge.

"For the last time, no! It's a surprise, love. It means, arrive and find out!"

I looked to Kaia for any sort of help, but she held her hands up in surrender. "I've been sworn to secrecy, sorry. Can we at least tell her where it's going to be, Drea? She needs to know that much, right?"

I nodded in agreement. "Yes, I need to know where it is, and what to wear. Also who will be there, and—"

"Nice try. Just look hot, but not like some lady of the night. It's a small gathering, and no, Cara won't be there. I did invite a few people from your party that you know, but it's low-key, I promise."

"Okay, so you said you're picking me up, but where are we going?!" I needed answers, dammit!

Before I could get those answers, a delivery man walked in the door with the most gorgeous bouquet of flowers.

"Oh, someone's getting lucky tonight!" I yelled at Drea as I ran over to the flowers and smelled them. "Dahlia's, my favorite. I'm so jealous, Dre."

"I have a flower delivery for... Sunshine?" I froze, my nose stuck in the flowers.

Drea came up quickly beside me. "I'm sorry, there's no one here by that name."

"Drea, it's fine," I said softly, standing up and taking the flowers with a faint smile. "Thank you, sir." I tipped the delivery man before he left.

I walked the flowers to the counter and sat them down, taking the card out. Before I could read it, she snatched it from my hands.

"It most certainly is not fine, Fallon Rose. Sunshine died, and she is not coming back. These flowers are for a ghost."

I rolled my eyes reaching for the card, but she kept it just out of reach. "Drea, please give me the card."

"Why? Why do you even need to read what's on there? Would you believe it after everything?"

I sighed. "I won't know that until I read it. I didn't even give her the chance to explain, and when I talked to Harper—"

"Harper is her blood relative! Of course she's going to tell you to hear out her cheating, asshole of a sister—it's her job!"

"I know, Drea. And I know Harper already kicked her ass when we broke up. She isn't taking sides, I just... give me the damn card!"

She relinquished her grip on the card and handed it over, but not without a huff of irritation escaping her. "I swear to all that is gay, if you give her any of your time, I will rip your nipple piercings right out!"

"Ouch." Kaia winced and folded her arms across her chest.

"Drea, you should've opened a theater, not a bookstore. Your dramatic nature is a gift."

I opened the envelope and unfolded the little card inside. Walking over to one of the couches, I sat down when I saw her hand writing and read the first line:

You'll always be the sunshine that brings the rainbow after a rainy day.

I pushed through the rest of the card, barely able to read through the tears. It was just one line, but... it was her.

Seeing her handwriting felt like holding her hand again and reconnecting with a part of her:

I hope there is still room left in your heart for me, and that you'll give me the chance to explain.

I can never say I'm sorry enough for causing you so much pain.

No, I didn't mean for that to rhyme, but I hope it made you smile.

You deserve everything in life and more.

It was always just you, and it will only ever be just you.

Happy birthday, Fallon.

I will love you until my last breath.

Always,

Your Wildcat.

I put down the card and let out a sobbed laugh. Drea came to sit next to me and I put my head in her lap as I let the tears fall. My Wildcat...

"Do you want me to invite her, love?" she grumbled while stroking my hair.

I sat up, wiping the tears from my eyes. "No. I can't see her, not yet. It's just too hard, and I don't know what to say."

I handed her the card and let her read it. "Damn that bitch and her love for you!" she yelled. "I hate her, but I also kind of want to hug her. Are you going to let her know you got the flowers, at least? They're your favorite."

I started crying again. "Fuck her! She knows those are my favorite, and she knows how to make me smile, even when I hate her. I can't talk to her, Dre. Can you please text her or something?"

"Of course, love. For all this emotional damage, I'll give you an early birthday present and tell you where your party's going to be. Drumroll, please."

I laughed as she imitated a drumroll. "You're going to party the night away, at *Pinstripes*!"

I gasped. "What? No fucking way! That's so expensive to rent out! Drea, that's too much."

She waved me off and stood me up. "Hush now. It's you we're talking about—nothing's too much, babe."

I thanked her, and she hugged me so tight I thought my eyes would pop out. "I can't thank you enough, Drea. You've been with me through everything. I don't know what I'd do without you." She smiled and kissed the top of my head before getting back to work.

Later that afternoon, I was heading home from the bookstore after a long day. I decided to grab some Chinese takeout—it was easier than cooking a meal that only I would enjoy.

The best part about my new apartment was the Chinese restaurant, *The Golden Dragon*, just around the corner. Best egg rolls ever!

"Hold on, Mom, I'm just walking in the door."

As soon as I got home, my mom called. Even though my hands were full with dinner, I still answered the phone—I would never miss a call with her if I could help it.

"Okay, I'm inside. How are you?"

"I'm good, dear. How are you? Caleb says he misses you."

I sat on the couch and propped my feet on the table. "I'm doing okay. I just got home from the bookstore. Tell Caleb I love him, and I miss him, too."

I was grateful to see my family over the holiday, but I was starting to miss them again.

"He's in bed right now, but I'll tell him tomorrow. Are you doing anything for your birthday? I'm sorry we can't be there this year. Ticket prices aren't what they used to be, and your brother is starting soccer this spring."

"Drea planned a small party at this really nice place downtown. It's okay, I understand. It sucks you guys won't be here, but we can Face-Time so you don't miss it. My little brother is growing up so much. I can't believe it!"

"That he is, honey. That sounds wonderful. I'm sure you girls will have a great time. Did you invite... you know who?"

I sighed. I had told her what happened during one of our phone calls. She wouldn't stop raving about Mackenzie after we visited for Thanksgiving. I was so angry, and I couldn't take her talking about it anymore. I kind of lost my temper and shouted. I quickly apologized and told her everything.

"Uh, no, I didn't invite her. She sent me a card and my favorite flowers today, actually." I still couldn't stop thinking about the flowers as I looked at them on my kitchen counter.

I stayed with Drea for about a month before I found this small one-bedroom apartment. It wasn't as nice as my last one, but it was livable and in a safe neighborhood.

Drea's house was big enough for me, but I wanted her to have her space back, and I needed my own, too. With Skylar there most nights, Drea's house was too... loud.

I didn't know if I should call Mackenzie or not to thank her for the flowers. I knew it was the polite thing to do, but I was afraid to hear her voice. I didn't know what to say, and after seeing her at the coffee shop, I definitely was afraid to be anywhere near her.

I'd be lying if I said I didn't miss her or constantly want to pick up the phone and call her. Every time I went into *Brewed Awakening*, I asked Rylee how she was doing. I knew I shouldn't, but I needed to know. Was she seeing someone? Did she talk about me? All the questions I had, I was too afraid to ask.

"Oh, well, that was sweet of her, right?"

I smiled. "Yeah, Mom, it was," I said softly.

Aside from the coffee shop, I hadn't seen her since we broke up. She tried calling a few times but gave up after a week when I didn't answer. There was nothing to talk about, and I needed time to figure things out.

"Are you going to call her to thank her for the flowers? I don't want to pry, but you said you talked to her sister. Maybe she was right, and you should at least hear her out and get some closure. It's been a few months, sweetie."

I groaned. "Mom, I'm not going to call her. At least not right now. I need to figure some things out. After Rebecca, I don't know if I want to hear her out, no matter what Harper or the card said."

"What did the card say, honey?" I read it to her, and she let out the longest, "Aww," I'd ever heard.

"Oh my God, Mom, seriously?"

"I'm sorry, honey, but that was sweet. But listen, if you hate her, so do I. I still think you need closure, though."

Did I hate her? I wasn't so sure anymore. After the anger and hurt faded a bit, I started thinking. I tried not to think too much about her, or I'd fall apart all over again. But my mom was right, I still hadn't let her explain. Regardless of whether I knew what I saw or not, I needed to hear it from her to close that chapter of my life and move on.

"Thanks, Mom. I'm still angry, but I don't know if I hate her. The only person I could ever hate is my real dad. Besides, if you want to like her, that's fine. I won't get in the way of that."

"Oh, honey, I loved her, but when she broke my baby's heart, she broke mine too. Oh, listen, I have to go, sweetie. Someone's at the door. I love you, and I'll talk to you soon. Goodnight, baby."

And with that, she hung up. I threw my head back on the couch and groaned.

Chapter Forty-Eight

MACKENZIE

"Mackenzie, Hi. What are you doing here?"

"Hello, Mrs. Bennett. I'm sorry to just drop in like this. Is there a chance we can talk?"

I got on the first plane I could to Portland, and I now stood nervously on the front porch of Fallon's parents' house. She blinked a few times before finally letting me in.

She walked me to the living room, and I took the chair across from hers. "Does my daughter know you're here? Surely not. I just got off the phone with her, and she would've mentioned if you were going to be showing up to my house unannounced." She didn't sound very pleased to see me, and I couldn't blame her.

Her response told me all I needed to know about what Fallon had told her mom. She knew I messed up.

"No, she doesn't know. We haven't spoken in a while, as I'm sure you already know."

"Hmm. Yes, I'm well aware of what's been going on. She told me I didn't have to hate you, but I want to."

I nodded, forcing away my small smile. That sounded like my Fallon. "I know, ma'am, and you have every right to. I fu—I messed up by letting my ex into my house. I know I shouldn't have."

"And kissing her. Don't forget that part."

I sighed, bracing myself to repeat the same explanation I'd already given countless times. "I didn't kiss her. That's what I was trying to explain to Fallon, but she wouldn't listen, and I didn't want to push her too hard. My ex... she's incredibly narcissistic and manipulative. I'm not making excuses for either one of our behaviors. All I'm saying is that I didn't intentionally cheat on your daughter. I love her, and I care for her more than anything in this world. That's why I'm here—to woman up and talk to you face to face."

"Correct me if I'm wrong, but shouldn't you be saying this to Fallon? She's the one you need to explain yourself to, not me." She crossed her legs and folded her arms, her mama bear stance on full display.

I took a deep breath. If I wanted to win Fallon back, I needed to build the right bridges along the way.

"I know, and I want to. That's also why I'm here." I reached into my bag and pulled out three pieces of paper.

"I wasn't lying when I said I love your daughter, Mrs. Bennett. I would do anything for her, and this is only the beginning. I know how much this would mean to her." I pointed to the papers she held in her hands.

She sat there silently, staring at the papers, flipping them over, front to back before she spoke, a single tear sliding down her cheek. "You make it very hard to hate you when you show your heart. You need to do that with my daughter if you plan on sticking around. She's been through enough, and she deserves happiness. So you'd better deliver it."

I smiled. "That's the plan."

She folded the papers and smiled cautiously. "Tell me the rest of the plan."

I stayed for another hour, lying out how I planned to win back the love of my life.

A few hours later, I was on my way home when I got a text. I almost dropped my phone in the middle of the airport when I saw who it was from:

Drea: Those flowers were lovely, and the
card was sweet. Fallon wasn't ready to
reach out, but she thanks you. Your stupid
card made her cry, so I hate you more for
that.

I understood and respected Fallon's decision not to reach out, but I smiled anyway. Drea was as close as I would get to Fallon, and for now, that was good enough.

Me: Thank you. And she is welcome.

Me: While I have you, can I stop by the store tomorrow, preferably when Fallon isn't there?

Drea: Haha! Funny. Also, you don't have anything!

Me: I'm serious, I want to talk.

Drea: At least you're asking this time. I promised her I wouldn't kill you, so fine. Anytime tomorrow. She works all day so she won't be around.

Me: Thanks, Drea.

The next morning, I walked into the bookstore so slowly, anyone walking by probably would've thought I was a sloth.

When I saw Drea look up at me, my heart stopped. I was prepared for anything at this point. She may have promised Fallon no death, but near death was probably acceptable.

"Mackenzie," Drea said, so dryly. At least she wasn't yelling.

I cautiously walked up to the counter. "Good morning, Drea. You're looking lovely today."

She hummed and looked at me, calm and collected. I wasn't sure how to feel about it. Honestly, it was creeping me out.

"Look, I'll spare you the bullshit excuses that you're probably expecting me to give, and how you should strangle me for breaking my promise, okay? I fucked up. I'm well aware of that. I broke her heart, which was the last thing I ever wanted to do. It kills me every day, but it's what I deserve."

She nodded quietly while I spoke, but I kept going, thankful she was even letting me talk. "I'm begging for a chance to explain to Fallon and try to earn her forgiveness. I'm sure she won't, and she has every right not to, but I think she deserves to at least hear me out. I came here to beg on my knees if I have to. You're her best friend, and I am desperate."

I stood there, waiting in silence while she stayed quiet. I didn't rush her or say anything else. If I had to crawl on the floor and beg her to help me, I would've.

After what felt like the longest minute of my life, she finally looked at me. "What a speech. Really, Mackenzie. I'm impressed. Did your lady balls grow over the past few months?"

I rolled my eyes. "Drea, be serious, please."

"What? I am being serious. You think you can walk in here, give me some sob story, and expect me to what, exactly? Welcome you with open arms? That's not happening. I told Fallon, and I'll tell you the same thing—I will not forgive you until she does, and she hasn't even given it a second thought." *Ouch.*

I guess I had that coming. I shouldn't have come here expecting Fallon to be miserable like I was—up all night, thinking about what we had.

I sighed. "I know, Drea. That's why I'm here—to beg for your help."

"Why would I want to help you? Give me one good reason why I should even consider helping you with anything. I swear, Mackenzie, you really have a lot of nerve—"

"Because you read the card. You know how I feel about her. The love I have for her doesn't just go away. It will never go away. You know I'd risk my life for her. I'd do anything for that woman, and that includes talking to her best friend, alone, with no witnesses—begging her to help me have a chance to talk to Fallon. That's all I'm asking for here, Drea. A chance."

"I swear to God, Mackenzie, this better not come back to bite me in the ass. Start talking."

And so I told her everything, including my visit with Fallon's mom. She reluctantly agreed to help me, and I thanked her profusely.

"I have to ask—how is she?" I really needed to know.

She sighed. "She is Fallon. She's strong, she's smart... she's managing. You better not fuck this up, Wildcat."

Chapter Forty-Nine

FALLON

I couldn't believe the night of my party had finally arrived. It had been a long few months, and I was more than ready for tonight. I couldn't have asked for a better group of friends to celebrate my birthday with.

I was hesitant to invite Rylee at first. She was Mackenzie's best friend, and even though I told her not to choose sides, I wasn't delusional into thinking she wouldn't side with Mackenzie.

Although, when I finally left the house and ran into her at *Brewed Awakening*, she wasn't acting any different.

When I invited her, I told her I understood if she thought it would be weird or if she didn't want to go, but I wanted to extend the invitation anyway. She said she wanted to go, but thought it was only fair to run it by Mackenzie, which I respected.

I had to clear my throat to keep the tears away when Rylee brought up her friend. Against my better judgment, I asked how she was. She told me she was doing better, but that she missed me and asked about me often.

The next time I saw Rylee, she said she'd be at the party, and I wondered how that conversation with Mackenzie went. I didn't invite Harper, though. I thought that would be way too weird, and it sucked.

"Holy shit, you look amazing!" Penelope shouted when I opened the door to see her, Skylar, and Drea all smiling at me, with "Happy Birthday" balloons in their hands.

I laughed. "Thanks, Pen. Come on in, I'm just about ready to go."

I decided I wanted a color theme for my party. That was the only decision Drea let me make.

We were all decked out in various styles of black and gold. I wore a sparkly gold spaghetti-strap mini dress, while Skylar and Drea were matching—Skylar in a gold button-up shirt and Drea in a black mini dress. Penelope wore a black strapless dress, and we all had matching black-and-gold high-top shoes. I grabbed a jacket, and we headed out the door.

When we got to *Pinstripes*, there was a line out the door. It had just opened a few weeks ago and seemed to be doing really well.

Pinstripes was a restaurant, but they also had a bar, bowling, and a rooftop patio, which is where Drea informed me we were headed. She'd rented out the whole space for tonight, so it was going to be nice to have a place all to ourselves.

"Holy shit, babe. This is incredible!" I said as we made our way up to the roof. I didn't have any other words. I was speechless. The space was massive. It could've easily fit hundreds of people.

"Do you like it? Sky and Pen helped, of course, but it was all my vision."

Skylar elbowed her. "Really modest, babe," she said, smiling.

Several tables were set up with bar stools, and there was a bar on either side of the roof. The tables all had gold or black tablecloths with little centerpieces, each featuring a tiny "25" balloon. A big sign read, "Happy Birthday, Fallon!" and my favorite flowers were everywhere. There was even a proper DJ station set up, along with a black inflatable photo booth that actually fit in the space.

"I can't believe you guys did all this." Tears slid down my face, but I couldn't stop them. It was all too much. They pulled me into a group hug, and I couldn't help but squeeze tight.

"Happy birthday, babe. You deserve it," Drea said when we all finally let go.

"Yeah, happy birthday, Fal. We love you! Enjoy your night."

. . .

Thirty minutes later, we were a few drinks in when people started to arrive. Some coworkers I had invited showed up, along with a bunch of people from my party and a few authors we had worked with at the store.

Rylee came over to our table and pulled me into a hug, making me fight back tears. "Fallon, I'm so sorry about everything. I'm glad you still wanted me here. You look amazing."

I smiled faintly and wiped the tears away. "Thanks, Rylee. Please, have a drink and enjoy yourself."

"It was nice you invited her," Penelope said when Rylee left.

I shrugged, clearing my throat. "We were friends before I met..." I had to swallow the lump in my throat before I could continue. I hoped that would get easier with time. "It would've been rude not to invite her. Besides, I wanted her here."

"Well, it was still nice that she came. I'm going to get another drink, enjoy your party, babe," she replied.

When Penelope left, I turned to Drea. "Drea, this party is amazing. I can't believe you did all of this. I just wish my parents were here to celebrate with us."

I had spent all day trying not to think about my family. I wanted to enjoy my birthday, but it was hard when all I really wanted was for them to be there with me.

I stayed up most of the night reading Mackenzie's card over and over. If it had been anyone else—anyone but Rebecca—I wouldn't have considered giving her the time of day. And honestly, I still wasn't sure if I would. I wanted a perfect world where we could go back to how things used to be, when we were crazy about each other. But I wasn't a total idiot.

Drea's voice pulled me back to the present—to my party and my amazing friends. "I know, love. I'm sorry they're not here, but you're going to FaceTime them later, so you'll still get to see them. I know it's not the same, but it's better than nothing, right?"

I shrugged. "Yeah, I guess. Oh, I've been meaning to ask if you thanked Mackenzie for the flowers?" I wasn't going to bring it up, but I knew it would eat me up inside if I didn't.

She rolled her eyes. "Yes, love. And I was nice, I promise. As much as I wanted to rip her apart, I held back. I told her you said thank you for the flowers and the card, and she said you're welcome. That was it."

"Oh, cool." I nodded. I guess I was a little upset there wasn't more to it than that, even though I shouldn't have been. As angry as I was, my heart still carried a piece of her, and I didn't want her to be totally unhappy. It would make things a lot easier if I did. If I wanted her to be miserable and get what she deserved, but I just didn't have it in me.

"Forget about her tonight, love. Enjoy your party." She smiled and nudged my arm just as something ran into my leg.

"What the—"

"Sissy!" My heart stopped.

"Caleb?" I hugged him tight and picked him up. "What are you doing here, buddy? How did you even get here?"

I must have been dreaming. There was no way my little brother was in Seattle. I had just talked to my mom when she said they couldn't make it.

"We had a little help." I heard my mom's cheery voice and turned around.

In front of me stood my mom and Brandon. Brandon was beaming, while my mom had tears in her eyes. "Happy birthday, baby."

"Mom! I can't believe you guys are here. How did you even get here? You said you couldn't make it." My mom wiped her tears away, and I leaned into her touch.

"Other sissy brought us. She said it would mean worlds for us to be here. Happy birthday."

I looked at my mom and Brandon, confusion written across my face. "What is he talking about?"

"Mackenzie paid us a visit the night you and I talked on the phone, honey."

I lost the air from my lungs at the mention of Mackenzie. "She what?"

"She wanted to talk to me in person. She knew we wouldn't be able to make it, so she paid for our tickets."

I was speechless. Mackenzie always said she'd do anything for me, so I guess I shouldn't have been surprised. But I never expected it to still be true after we broke up.

I was still standing there, stunned, when Drea nudged my arm. "Why don't you go ask her yourself, love?"

"What are you talking about?" I looked at her, confused, and she nodded toward the patio door.

I turned and nearly stumbled back when I locked eyes with the most intoxicating ocean-blue gaze.

"Mackenzie," I whispered. All of the air from my lungs had vanished, and I wanted to fall over. Mackenzie was here and she was looking... *Shit.*

She was wearing the same outfit from our first "not a date" at the arcade, and my knees felt just as weak as they had that day.

"Drea... how is she here? Why is she here?" I breathed. I couldn't look away from her.

I didn't know what to think or do—I could only stand there, staring. She gave me a slight smile and mouthed, "Happy birthday."

When Drea didn't answer, I finally tore my gaze away and turned to her. "Drea, what the hell is going on?"

She grinned and pulled me into a quick hug. "Go catch your Wildcat."

My heart pounded as I hesitantly started walking toward Mackenzie, hoping she had all the words—because right now, I couldn't find any.

I stopped a few feet away, trying to pull myself together, which became even harder when she had the nerve to smile at me.

"Hi." Hearing her voice for the first time in months made my legs want to give out.

I was impressed with myself for standing there as long as I did without falling apart. I couldn't believe she was right in front of me. My legs were unstable, and I was trying to force the anger to overtake all the other emotions swirling inside me.

None of this was fair. Not her bringing my parents to Seattle, and definitely not her being there—as if nothing had happened between us —and making my lungs feel like they might collapse.

"You paid for their tickets?" was the first thing out of my mouth. I tried to sound angry, but my voice was shaky and it was taking every-thing I had not to lose it. I didn't know if I wanted to slap her, kiss her, or cry. Maybe all three.

She winced. "I'm sorry. That was such a Rebecca thing to do, wasn't it? But I knew how much it meant to you for them to be here, so I wanted to help."

I stiffened at the name, unable to hide my glare.

"Too soon? Got it. I'm sorry. Anyway, happy birthday, Fallon. You look incredible."

And like nothing happened, I blushed at her compliment. "Thank you." I cleared my throat. "You talked to Drea?"

This whole situation was bizarre. We'd broken up months ago, but she was still doing the same things she always did.

The last time she dealt with an angry Drea was after my night out with Cara. Honestly, I was impressed she'd braved that dragon to begin with. But even that couldn't compare to the fire burning in Drea now. Or so I thought...

She groaned. "Yeah, that one was harder to convince. But thanks to her promise to you not to kill me, I made it happen."

"Well, thank you. But what are you doing here, Mackenzie?"

I needed to know what the point of all of this was. Having my family here meant everything, but seeing her again? I wasn't sure how to feel about that yet.

She sighed. "I know I don't have the right to be here, and I shouldn't be. I just... I wanted you to have everything you deserve on your birthday. My words probably don't mean much to you right now, and I get that. I thought maybe my actions would. I wanted to show you how much you mean to me and prove I'd do anything for you. I'd really like a chance to explain. I know what you saw, but it's not the whole story. I'm not here to ruin your day, and I'm not sticking around. I just wanted to wish you a happy birthday. And maybe after the party, or whenever you're ready, we could talk?"

I told myself my makeup was too expensive to ruin with tears. It was the only thing holding me together.

I cleared my throat and looked around. Everyone was having a great time, and when I looked back to Drea and my parents, they all smiled and nodded encouragingly.

"No... you don't have to go. You went through all this trouble, the least I can do is spare you a few minutes. Let's talk inside."

"Thank you, Fallon." She smiled softly and led me to a more secluded area. I trembled as we walked to a table, hoping she didn't notice. She pulled out my chair and sat across from me. I appreciated the fact that she was giving me at least that much distance. I was afraid if we were any closer and accidentally touched, I'd lose my composure, and I wouldn't let that happen, not anymore.

"So, I've been wanting to know, who was that man you were with at the coffee shop?"

She sighed. "Oh, well, that was my dad."

I blinked. "What? You saw your dad?" I asked.

Her coming out story had made me so angry for her. I couldn't understand why she would even want to see him again.

"Yeah. We've been talking, actually. I told him about you. He saw the way I looked at you that day. I hadn't seen or talked to him in almost ten years, and after just fifteen seconds of looking at you, he knew exactly how I felt. But that doesn't really matter. Harper still won't talk to him—not yet, anyway—but I think she's getting there. I haven't forgiven him, but we're working toward... something."

I sat stunned. "Wow, what made you reach out to him?"

She smiled. "To be honest, it was you, Fallon. Losing you was my biggest regret, and I learned not to let the things I really care about slip away. You taught me to see the beauty in life, and by spending time with you and your family, I realized I had to at least try to fight for mine."

I cleared my throat, forcing the tears back down. "Well, I'm happy for you. It seems like you're doing really well, so why are you here? It looks like our breakup helped you grow, so I don't get it."

"It has shown me some things, but that doesn't mean I'm doing well. I'm better than I was a few months ago, but I'm still not complete. The only way I can be complete is if I'm with you."

I scoffed. "Give it some time, Mackenzie, I'm sure you'll get there. It's only been a few months."

"That's the thing. I don't want to get there, not unless you're going with me. If you honestly don't want anything to do with me, if the love you had for me is genuinely gone, then I'll have to learn to accept that someday. But if there is even a little bit of it left, I'll never stop fighting to show you how much I love you and how sorry I am."

"Love has nothing to do with it. Whether I love you or not has never been a question. But I won't be someone's second choice. I can't do that to myself anymore."

"Fallon, you're not the first or the second choice. You're the only choice. I know I fucked up. I never should've let her in. I should've told her I was madly in love with the most amazing woman I've ever known. And I never should've let her kiss me. I didn't kiss her back. I need you to know that, but I should've never let it happen in the first place."

I finally couldn't stop the tears from coming down. I knew I would cry at my party, but I figured it would be from missing my family, not from having this conversation with Mackenzie.

"Kenzie, I saw you kissing her. How do you expect me to believe that you didn't kiss her back?"

"I don't expect you to believe anything I say, but I hope you will, because I love you and I'm telling the truth. I've been nothing but honest with you from the start. No, I didn't tell you I was engaged, and I messed up there, too, but I didn't lie. When she showed up, I was still shocked from seeing her after two years of nothing. I didn't even have a chance to react before she kissed me. The second it happened, I was about to push her away when you walked in. And I promise you, I had no idea you were the one on the couch. Maybe if I hadn't been such a coward, I could've confronted her back then, and we wouldn't be in this mess. But honestly, I don't want that, because if I had, I wouldn't have been lucky enough to fall in love with you. I made a promise to you and to Caleb that I'd never hurt you, and she forced me to break it. For that, I'm eternally sorry. You are the last person I ever wanted to hurt."

"And yet, here I am—hurt and angry. I'm so damn angry, Mackenzie! I fell so hard for you. Do you have any idea what it did to me, to come home and walk in on the two of you making out in your kitchen?"

I had pushed away all the doubts and reservations I had about us because I was so tired of fighting what I was feeling. I let her into my life, into my heart, and she poisoned it.

Mackenzie lowered her gaze to the ground. Defeat was written all over her face, and tears formed in her eyes. It was a struggle for me to hold it together. My love for her hadn't faded since our time apart. The grip she had on me still held firmly in place.

"I trusted you, and I shouldn't have. I should've walked away that night on the roof." The tears were threatening to come out, but I forced them away. I wouldn't let her see the vulnerability anymore.

"I'm so glad you didn't. I fought for us then, and I'm fighting for us now. I will always fight for us. I know I messed up, and I will never forgive myself for allowing her to come in and ruin everything." Her eyes never left mine, and I had to pinch myself under the table, just to force the eye contact to remain.

"There were two sets of lips that ruined everything. It wasn't just Rebecca's."

"Trust me, I know. I'm not putting all the blame on her, and I'll never forgive myself for making you feel like I didn't love you. I swear to you, I didn't kiss her back. I should've been honest about my engagement and that she was still trying to reach out to me. It was dishonest of me to hide that from you. I promise, hurting you was never my intention. You have every right to walk away and never want to see me again, and I'll respect that. I can only hope you'll give me the chance to beg on my knees for your forgiveness. You have to know, somewhere deep down, that I am madly in love with you and that will never go away. How could I think about kissing someone who wasn't you? I don't even want to exist with anyone who isn't you, Fallon."

I rubbed my face in my hands and wiped the tears away. "Fuck you."

She narrowed her brows. "What?"

I sighed. "Fuck you for coming in here, right when I was starting to pick up the pieces of my life. For knowing my favorite flower and knowing exactly what to say to make me smile, even when I wanted to hate you. For bringing my family here, knowing it was all I would've wanted for my birthday. And just... fuck you, Mackenzie, for making it impossible to hate you because I love you too damn much. I really don't want to believe you, but I can't help that I do. If I didn't know Rebecca, I'm not sure I'd believe you so easily, but that doesn't mean I can just go back to how things were before. I'm going to need time before I can trust you again, but I think I want to get there someday."

She choked out a tearful laugh. "I'm so sorry, Fallon. I will spend the rest of my life showing you how sorry I am and how much you mean to me."

I wiped away a stray tear. "I will hold you to that."

She stood up and grabbed my hand, connecting us for the first time in a long time. "Please tell me you still love me, Sunshine," she asked, brushing my tears away with her thumb.

I smiled and leaned into her touch. "I never stopped, Wildcat. But you owe me dinner. You made me waste good Thai food!"

She laughed. "Anything for you," she said, her voice low, her eyes filled with promise.

Before I could say anything else, she pulled me closer, and I let her kiss me, every ounce of frustration and hurt from the past melting away. This wasn't just a kiss—it was everything I'd been holding back. It was a promise, a second chance, and a reminder that love, messy as it was, was still worth fighting for.

Epilogue

Eighteen months later

I'd been on edge all day at work, waiting to get home to Fallon.

She'd moved in eight months ago, and I had been scared to ask her at first, but I'd lost her once and swore to myself I wouldn't lose her again. Every day, all I wanted was to get home to her, and I never wanted to take that for granted.

It was the best feeling in the world—going to sleep with her in my arms and waking up with her leg straddled over mine.

We were lying on the couch, finishing up *Stuart Little*, which had become a routine date night at least once a week. I was getting sick of that damn mouse, but Fallon loved every second of it, so I suffered through it for her.

The movie was nearly over when I hit pause. "Okay, I love you, but that's enough mice for today. I need some fresh air, so let's go," I said with a smile.

"Baby, I'm already comfy, and I was enjoying snuggling on the couch with you. If you really need fresh air, go to the patio. I'll be snug right here." She tried to bury herself further into the couch, but I took her hand and stood up.

"I don't want to go to the patio. I want to go to the roof, and I want you there with me. So, come with me, please." I winked at her with a smile, my heart racing with anticipation.

She groaned, rolling her eyes, but I caught the slight twitch of her lips as she fought a smile. She followed me out the door, her hand in mine, and the warmth of her touch eased the tension in my shoulders as I led her up to the roof.

When we got there, she stopped suddenly, inhaling sharply, though I still held her hand. She turned to face me, a look of confusion crossed her face, but I stayed silent.

A path of rose petals and tea light candles led to a single chair. I guided her into it and stepped back, neither of us saying a word.

I was shaking, but I took a deep breath and forced myself to speak. Tears were already streaming down her face, and I knew she understood exactly what was happening.

I cleared my throat, willing myself to say the words I'd been waiting so long to speak. "Fallon, the roof is where I first tried to kiss you, and where we had that huge fight. I thought I was going to lose you, so I took a chance and told you how I felt. The roof was my place, the spot I'd go when I needed space to think and find peace. But since I met you, I don't come up here anymore. I don't have a reason to. You're my safe space. You're my peace."

I was trying so hard to hold it together, but my strength weakened the longer I looked at Fallon. Her eyes were filled with tears and her smile was so bright, we didn't need any of the candles.

I clenched my jaw and tried to keep going. "I've wanted to do this long before I told you I loved you. I think I always knew I didn't want to exist in any universe you weren't a part of. I've never loved anyone the way I love you, Fallon. And if you'll let me, I promise to love you fiercely every single day, no matter what life throws our way. I promise to never stop loving you."

At this point, I couldn't stop the tears, and we were both crying. But she was still smiling, so I had some hope for how this would end. I pulled the little black box from my pocket and got down on one knee.

When I opened the box, she gasped and covered her mouth. I'd snuck around with Drea a few months ago to get this ring.

Our relationship wasn't back to normal by any stretch of the imagination, but I didn't expect it to be. I knew I was going to have to work just as hard to earn back Drea's trust as I had with Fallon, but it was something I was prepared to handle.

Drea was like Fallon's family, and I didn't want to lose either of them. I knew it was going to be an uphill battle, but I was confident we would get there someday.

The ring was a one-carat cushion-cut diamond, and Drea said she would absolutely love it, which I agreed with. It was perfect—as long as she said yes.

"I love you more than I can even put into words. You are my only choice in this world, and I will always choose you over anything and anyone. Will you be my eternal sunshine and marry me, Fallon Rose?"

She uncovered her mouth and stood me up. My heart raced, and I couldn't stop my body from trembling as I waited for her to say something.

It had been a long journey to get here. After our breakup, I had to start over, earn back her trust, and prove myself to her. We'd come so far since that day, and now there was nothing I wanted more than to spend the rest of my life showing Fallon just how much I loved her. I never wanted her to doubt, not for a second, that she was the only thing that truly mattered to me.

I could have lived my life without ever knowing her, but it would've always felt like something was missing from my soul. I couldn't imagine another day in this world without Fallon in it, without my better half.

She smiled sweetly, pulling me close as she whispered, "Tell me not to."

Bonus Content

If you made it this far, congratulations! Here is a sneak peek at book two. Let's see if you can guess who said this...

"Oh, for fucks sake, where is my dildo?" I was trying to be as quiet as I could so I didn't wake up... Carla... Kylie... Kameron? Whoever.

I wouldn't see her again, so I didn't make it a point to get her name last night when I was taking off her underwear with my teeth.

The curvy blonde stirred on the bed while I frantically, albeit quietly, searched for my favorite pussy pleasuring pal. It was my favorite color, neon green, double sided, and it vibrated; a triple thrusting threat.

When I found it under my clothes, I snuck out of her room and changed quickly as I walked toward the front door, hoping I wasn't forgetting anything.

I finally stumbled through my door just after six in the morning, thankful it was Sunday so I had all day to recharge before work the next day.

Not thirty seconds after I had settled into bed and closed my eyes, my phone rang. Ignoring it, I snuggled further back into my bed, waiting for the room to become silent again. After five minutes passed, it rang again and I picked up the infernal phone, desperately trying not to hurl it at the wall. Who the fuck calls at this ungodly hour on a Sunday?!

"Hello," I said with bitterness coating my tone.

Have any guesses? Let me know and be on the look out for book two of the Sapphic in Seattle series coming soon!

Acknowledgments

Thank you to my wife for inspiring quite a few things in this book and for being my hype woman through it all. I love you 3,000.

Thank you to all my amazing readers for helping me along this journey.

Thank you to Melissa for talking me out of my spirals and not letting me become a dumpster fire! And thank you for your invaluable contributions.

Thank you to Cat for bringing this book to life with the cover. I am obsessed with it, and I cannot thank you enough!

Thank you to my work ladies for supporting this freaky journey.

Thank you to Teresa for all of your editing magic, and for the rooftop scene... you know what you did! But seriously, I feel like this book wouldn't be what it is without your help! You have put up with so much of my nonsense, and I can't tell you enough how grateful I am to have met you!

And finally, thank you to Abby. If it wasn't for your weird-ass dating story, this book would've never been born.

About the Author

Elee Rose is a lover of all things smutty and sappy, which inspired her to start writing her own stories.

A hopeless romantic at heart, she writes the kind of books that make her swoon, sweat, and maybe even sob.

Happily married, Elee often draws inspiration from her own life, and you'll rarely find her without her wife. When she's not writing about love, she's reading about it or living it.

Stay Connected!

Follow Elee Rose for updates, sneak peeks, and more behind-the-scenes content.

Instagram: @authoreleerose
Facebook: Author Elee Rose
E-mail: eleeroseauthor@gmail.com

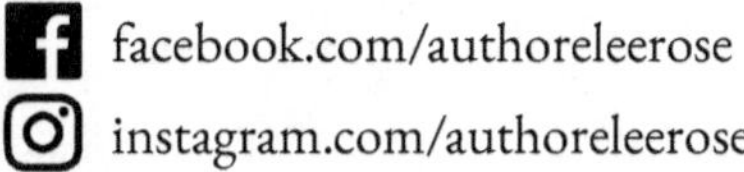
facebook.com/authoreleerose
instagram.com/authoreleerose